"How many of those drinks have you had?" he asked, hearing her moan as she slipped her head back beneath his chin.

"Three, I think," she said. He was barely able to make out her words as he felt her mouth now moving against his neck. What was she doing?

"How about we get you home?" He tried to push her away. She pushed herself closer.

"I don't want to go home unless it's with you."

He chuckled. "You don't mean that. You've just had a little too much to drink." And as tempting as she was, as her small, firm body pressed into his, he didn't do women who were anywhere near drunk—too many potential dangerous side effects. She seemed just a little tipsy but one never knew for sure what people could do under the influence.

He looked around the room for a spot to take her to sit, maybe to find her a ride, so she could get home, but apparently she had a different plan in mind. It was approaching midnight and someone had started the downward count signally the end of the year. Others joined in and he could hear her begin to softly count, her mouth now next to his ear. She'd only stopped kissing his neck a minute ago. When they reached the part about the Happy New year, she turned his head with her hand and captured his lips with her own.

She opened over him, her tongue moving in, aggressive in its desire to taste and tangle with his, and because it was the New Year and she was very tempting, he kissed her back.

❧

STEADY

RUTHIE ROBINSON

Genesis Press, Inc.

INDIGO LOVE SPECTRUM

An imprint of Genesis Press, Inc.
Publishing Company

Genesis Press, Inc.
P.O. Box 101
Columbus, MS 39703

Copyright © 2011 Ruthie Robinson

ISBN: 13 DIGIT : 978-1-58571-393-6
ISBN: 10 DIGIT : 1-58571-393-7
Manufactured in the United States of America

First Edition

Visit us at www.genesis-press.com
or call at 1-888-Indigo-1-4-0

ACKNOWLEDGMENTS

To my family and friends, thanks for your support.

PROLOGUE

Hampton Heights was an average-sized city in the southern part of the grand state of Texas, nestled into the part of the state known for the beauty of its hills and lakes, hot summers, mild winters, and neighborhood gardens. Billboards all over the city proclaim its famous slogan: *Gardening in your 'hood, where the food is always fresh, always good.*

To say people in this city took gardening and all things green seriously was an understatement. The city had been trying for the last fifteen years to remake itself into the neighborhood-garden capital of the world in order to change the long-term eating habits of its populace. The city had grown tired of being known for having the heaviest population in the country, the most poundage per square yard. The citizens of Hampton Heights wanted to live differently; it had become their quest.

By providing tax incentives, supplementing homeowner association dues, and scraping together federal monies from agricultural grants, the city's leaders were able to provide concrete financial assistance to its residents to help make its mission a reality. Over the last ten years, Hampton Heights had slowly but surely attained its goal, now boasting twenty-four out of twenty-five neighborhoods with gardens and, more importantly, a healthier population.

Hampton Heights was equally famous for its annual gardening competition. The competition had begun as another way to motivate its residents to garden. A substantial cut in property taxes—a 50 percent one-year reduction—went to the winning neighborhood, an incentive that proved hard for the city's residents to resist. Like its grander city gardening plan, this idea also surpassed participation expectations; twenty-three out of twenty-four neighborhood gardens participated in the competition.

So no more 'Heavyweight Capital of the U.S.' for Hampton Heights. It was now known as a green city, where the people were friendly and the produce locally grown, which meant grown a few blocks away from your home in your neighborhood by everyday people. Working in and receiving food from the neighborhood gardens had become woven into the fabric of the lives of people in this town, as routine as going to work or taking the kids to school.

So in the city where neighborhood gardening was king, the winner of its annual garden competition was considered queen.

CHAPTER 1

December 31

Katrina slid into the backseat of a beautiful canary yellow Camry belonging to Amber, who was behind the wheel busily buckling her seat belt. The last of the trio, Claudia, popped into the front passenger seat, perfumed to the max, making breathing difficult. They were ready—finally—and headed to *the party*, the New Year's party to end all parties, and this year's most difficult party to get an invitation to. Amber was Katrina's co-worker; Claudia, Amber's wealthy mate. It had been through Claudia's connections, a friend of a friend of a friend, that they'd managed to wrangle this coveted invitation.

Katrina hadn't planned to attend. Parties were so not her *thing*. But Amber had hounded her until she'd given in. "And don't come dressed like a church lady or my mother," she'd added. That meant shopping for Katrina, whose wardrobe consisted of sweats and XL T-shirts for working in her yard, or slacks and shirts for work. The night of the party Amber and Claudia had arrived at her doorstep earlier than expected and had taken her over—applying her makeup and switching her usual glasses for contacts. They'd given her a complete makeover, taking a picture at the end to make sure she wouldn't forget what she could be.

Katrina had stood in front of her mirror, trying to find herself behind her new front. What had she been thinking? Choosing this scrap of a dress, her shoulders, legs, and thighs bare? She'd been thinking of Will, that's what. And those thoughts had propelled her to choose something that would make him sit up and take notice. Sitting here now, she'd never felt more naked. She looked down at herself once more, acknowledging that she looked great, way different in that vampy, slightly skanky way. Here she was, a piece of white fabric wrapped tightly over her breasts, stopping just below her . . .

"You're not changing," Amber said to Katrina's reflection in the mirror, perhaps having seen something in Katrina's eyes. "It's too late, anyway, so let's go!" she added, grabbing Katrina's hand and pulling her to the door.

Katrina hoped Will would be there, at least—maybe seeing her in her near-naked state would make him *see* her, for once, instead of giving her his usual skim-over followed by a friendly wave. It had bothered her that she'd wanted him to notice her, that she was standing here changing herself so that he would.

Will Nakane was her neighbor and the object of a major crush. She'd watched him since he'd moved in fourteen months ago, watched as he'd pulled the for-sale sign from his lot, and she fell instantly in lust—the unrequited kind, of course; no other kind would do. It was a crush she'd yet to shake.

She'd watched as he built his new and now-famous environmentally friendly home. Watched and monitored his life, taking in his many outside activities, from cycling—which she believed was his favorite—to kayaking, motorcycling, and fishing . . . and the matching women that accompanied those activities, all of which she catalogued.

Hell, who knew if he would even be here tonight. A good chance, though; a party of this magnitude usually drew all the area singles. And if she didn't run into Will, maybe she might meet someone else, someone to replace the crush she had on her neighbor.

She sat in the backseat, now feeling anxious, rethinking for the umpteenth time her decision to come. She usually gave parties a wide berth—all that small-talking, schmoozing, and flirting seemed more like work than fun to her. She leaned forward and looked out the window as they approached the house where the party was being held. Impressive. Old World elegance, living large at its finest, and, if the cars snaking their way along this road were any indication, packed with people—a New Year's Eve party for the ages. She sighed, finally relinquishing her hope that they would get lost, experience engine failure, or have a flat tire. No such luck. The only upside to the night's adventure was that she'd come with friends. Amber and Claudia had been her friends going on three years.

Amber pulled her car into the wide circular drive located in the front of the house, which was filled with double-parked, wall-to-wall cars, mostly expensive ones mixed in with a few hoopties.

"There's another place in the back for parking," Katrina said. "I've been here before on a gardening tour."

Amber made a rude noise. "Hey, can I help it that I like gardens?" she asked.

Amber pointed the car toward the back of the house, where a makeshift parking lot had been set up to handle overflow; judging by the size of the overflow, there were an obscene number of people inside. Amber squeezed her car into a space between a truck and an Escalade and they all disembarked, deciding to go through the back door instead of walking back around to the front, hoping for a quick entrance. It was more than a little cold out, and Katrina had left her coat in the car. She'd worn a little sweater—arm candy only—resting just below her breasts with one lone button at the neck.

To keep her mind off the cold, Katrina took the opportunity to look over the grounds. She learned from an earlier garden tour that this home, inherited and built on twenty acres of land, belonged to the younger son. Outside of the city proper, but not quite in the country, the property boasted magnificent manicured gardens. They walked past the stables, continuing past the pool house with the glass-enclosed, where clumps of people were dancing, drinks in their hands, talking, laughing, apparently having a grand time. The more adventurous had shed their clothes and were now skinny dipping, causing Katrina's eyebrows to lift.

Music, some rap song, pounded from the speakers. The words were unintelligible—probably about pimps and hoes. It seemed to her that it was always about pimps and hoes, with the occasional bitches thrown in for added effect. They continued onward, Claudia and Amber in front, holding hands, doing their couple thing, Katrina trailing behind. They passed the tennis courts, which had been turned into a makeshift dance floor, her eyes searching beyond them for the entrance to the more formal gardens. She loved those gardens. As they made their way to the house, rap gave way to R&B, now Maxwell smooth.

Good Lord, where did all these people come from, Katrina wondered; this town wasn't that big. She watched people dancing on the deck, the dance-floor crowd moving en mass, resembling a swarm of bees on the attack. People dressed to impress, women with dresses that rivaled hers in shortness and tight fit mixed in with the jeans-and-T-shirt crowd. She walked up the steps leading to the back deck, looking over the men and women here—all types, all colors.

She squeezed her way through the back door. "Excuse me," she said, breathing a relieved sigh when she entered the house and stepped into a room big enough to hold a hundred people. There were fewer people in here, most with some kind of yellow-and-pink swirly drink in their hands; a few were dancing in place to the sounds coming from outside. Waiters stood at the ready with more trays of those cute drinks.

Not knowing what to do with herself, she stopped and seized a drink from a passing waiter—her own pink and yellow concoction. Not too bad; pretty tasty, actually, she thought, taking a sip. "Ohmigod!" she thought seconds later as the drink worked itself into her veins. That was some kick! She wasn't driving; non-drinking Amber was their designated driver.

Now what to do with herself, she wondered, her eyes roaming around the room, taking in all the beautiful women and equally remarkable-looking men. She spotted a chair in a corner, way in the back, with only a small number of people in its vicinity. Great, she thought, heading in its direction, only to pull up short as she reached the chair. Someone had beaten her to it—a man, pulling a laughing woman down to his lap.

"Okay, now what?" she whispered to herself, her eyes moving around the room, searching and landing on Will, and not just any Will. It was *her* Will, her neighbor, her jones, who stood off to the side of the room, talking to a gorgeous model type—always his preference.

She spotted a plant a few feet away and stepped closer to it, out of the way, to watch him, a favorite pastime of hers. He was smooth, her Will, agile and elegant, decked out in a dark suit, untucked white dress shirt underneath; all casual class. He stood tall, a little under six feet, with a cyclist's physique, all lean muscle. Katrina loved, loved, *loved,* lean muscle. She knew his body, had seen it on too many occasions as she'd watched him. She'd watched him come and go during the construction of his home, cycling on his bike—always cycling on that bike, clad in that body-conscious cycling gear.

He was a third-generation Japanese-American, his face striking in its male beauty. She surveyed it now, watching him talk, his lips small but slightly full. They made their home on a face sculpted with high and pronounced cheekbones and dark almond-shaped eyes. Oh, and don't forget his hair, her absolute favorite attribute—

thick and short, but not buzz-cut short. It was standing at attention on his head, shiny and inky jet black.

He was also driven, her Will, with enough energy to power a small city. She knew that, too, as he was always doing something. She'd gotten worn out from just watching him from the safety of her front yard. Now he stood laughing at something his companion had said.

She watched until he and the woman walked away, leaving her standing alone by a plant, the ultimate wall-flower. Still feeling more than a little out of place, she walked back the way she'd come in, squeezing her way back outside, taking in the bodies moving en mass again, hurrying back down the steps. God, these shoes, she thought, walking to the entrance to the gardens.

She entered the main gate: it was quiet, though cold. Her time here would be limited, a minute or two, or else she'd be the one to freeze to death; this cute sweater wasn't a match against much of anything. She walked around the gardens for a while, taking in the green of the grass shimmering under the lights that marked her path. Rye grass—or *Lolium spp*, its more formal name—had been over-seeded to provide green during the winter months. Then there were the many evergreen shrubs and hedges, geometric in shape, that ran throughout the gardens. Someone in charge here had a sense of humor, she thought, taking in some of the hedges that had been shaped into things that were emblematic of the holiday season—a Christmas tree, round ornaments, a wreath.

"You're not lost, are you?" a male voice asked from behind her, startling her. He'd been stealthy in his

7

approach. She turned and looked into the eyes of her daydream, Will Nakane, in the flesh.

"Thank you, God," she whispered under her breath.

"Sorry, I didn't mean to scare you. You're not lost, are you?" he asked again.

"Nope, not lost, just getting some air."

"I know how you feel. Needed some air myself," he said, smiling at her, his eyes roaming over her, their movement tracked by hers. He merely smiled back at being caught, as if looking over women's bodies was his right.

"You're cold," he said, noticing her arms wrapped around her body. Her sweater was pretty, but not much protection against the cold; nor was the small dress that barely covered her body.

"Take my jacket," he offered.

"No, I couldn't," she said, stepping back, hands outstretched to stop him. He'd already shifted out of his suit jacket, switching the drink he held from one hand to the other as he did so, and handed the jacket to her.

"Yes, you could," he said, smiling, watching her stare at his jacket with longing.

"Okay, I could," she said, laughing, accepting it. "I won't be here much longer, anyway."

"Had to take a break?" he asked.

"Yes, I'm not much of a partier."

"Me, either. I went to school with tonight's host, Gerald—G for short. I'm Will Nakane," he said, extending his hand.

"I know who you are. I actually live a couple of doors down from you," she said, putting her hand in his.

"No way. I would have remembered you," he said, smiling, taking another sip from his glass as he studied her face, trying to place her.

"Two doors down from Oscar and Lola's," she replied, watching him try to hide his shock as he choked on the swallow of drink he'd just taken into his mouth. She laughed.

"It's okay; I don't usually look like this," she said, patting him on the back as he started to cough. "I'm Katrina Jones."

"I've seen you. The woman who loves to garden. I guess that explains why you're standing here now," he said between coughs.

"Yes, I do," she said, pausing, looking around, and spotting a bench. "You want to sit for a while?" she asked, hoping to prolong her time with him.

"Sure," he said, clearing his throat. He followed her over to the bench and waited for her to sit. He sat next to her, stretched his legs out in front of him, and leaned back into the bench, taking another sip of his drink.

"So," she said, fishing around for a topic, looking over at him, relaxed, his eyes moving around the gardens. "Did you know that these gardens were part of a larger plantation back in the early 1800s, and that your friend G's family was the original owners?" she asked.

"No, I didn't know that," he said, looking at her with surprise.

"The gardens here are influenced by the Europeans, who were initially influenced by the Italians, known for their very formal gardens: clipped plants and parterres, geometric and very symmetric," she said.

"So, you're a historian *and* a gardener," he said, still looking at her.

"I like both subjects," she said, quiet for a second. "Did you know that a few of the slaves, one in particular, named Samuel, worked closely with your friend's ancestors in the formal gardens here and also worked in the major kitchen gardens, which were located toward the back of the property? He was sort of like a head gardener," she said, smiling. "Some slaves were known to have small plots of land called slave gardens, to grow small amounts of potatoes, peas, that type of thing, using the money to buy things for their families."

"You're *really* into gardening," he said, giving her his full smile, his eyes roaming over her, laughter present in them.

"Sorry, yes, although sometimes I can get carried away with it," she said, looking away, now self-conscious.

"No problem. I have an appreciation for them both, so thanks for the mini-lesson." She shook her head, looking away again. It was quiet for a while between them.

"So how long have you lived in the neighborhood?" he asked.

"Three years. I finished building my home about a month before Lola and Oscar built theirs," she said. He nodded, taking a drink again, emptying his glass in one swoop. She watched that, too.

"It's a nice neighborhood, at least from what I've been able to see in the limited time I've lived there."

"Well, you do travel a lot," she said matter-of-factly. His head whipped around to face hers, his smile falling away, scrutiny in his eyes now as he re-evaluated her.

"I'm not a stalker or anything, if that's what you're thinking. You don't have to worry about that. Just keeping track of the neighborhood comings and goings, is all."

"I didn't think you were, or at least I would hope not. And, yes, you're right, I do travel a lot, for business mostly, some pleasure. I like to keep busy," he said, turning to look out into the gardens.

"I know," she said.

"You seem to know a lot about me," he said, turning to look at her again, speculation in his gaze.

"I know a lot about most of my neighbors," she answered, watching as the speculation cleared, but only just a little. "I'm a one-woman neighborhood watch system." She hoped the humor made her seem less odd. "So where does all this traveling take you?"

"Nowhere in particular."

"Right. Come on, you can tell me." He was silent for a second, watching her again, measuring.

"Well, mostly I travel for work. Most of my trips take me overseas—Japan, Singapore, mostly Asian countries, with some Europe thrown in there now and again. I like the travel, living in other cities, exploring them, discovering the people and their culture, their customs."

"How do you explore and discover?" she asked.

He looked her over again, measuring once more. "Sometimes I'll explore on foot or, if the roads are good and if the traffic is not too intrusive, by bike. I guess you already know that I'm gone for weeks at a time," he said, watching her nod in affirmation. "Work provides an inexpensive way for me to see the world, which I enjoy tremendously."

"I've seen you on a motorcycle and with kayaks on your jeep. Do those go with you when you travel?"

"You really *don't* miss much, do you," he said, leaning forward, laughing fully now, his elbows on his knees, the empty glass twirling in his hands.

"Nope, all that time in the yard," she said again, her chuckle joining his. He turned his head to her.

"I mostly ride the motorcycle in the city, the kayaks I take out with G around here or to the Gulf. Sometimes we'll take an occasional trip together to other parts of the country," he said. "It's harder now that we both work and are no longer students."

"You're active," she said, more statement than question.

"Yes."

She looked over at him from beneath her lashes. The wind was blowing through his hair, and his eyes were moving around the gardens again.

"Well, I'd better get inside. Let me give you back your jacket," she said, standing up and handing it to him. "Thanks for letting me use it." She decided she'd taken enough of his time; desperate woman in love was not the impression she wanted to leave.

"No problem, and you're welcome. It was nice meeting a new neighbor and talking to you," he said, standing up along with her.

"You, too. See you around," she said, turning and walking away. He resumed his seat, his eyes following her, assessing her as she walked away. She was much shorter than her heels made her out to be; she was almost his height tonight. Who knew his neighbor was pretty; she wasn't gorgeous, but pretty in that girl-next-door kind of way. She had smooth, dark-brown skin that filled in that small, barely-there white dress very nicely, and she was way interested in him. That he'd garnered almost immediately.

Still, she was attractive—slender, with shapely, beautiful legs, and a thick head of coal-black hair. She had nice brown eyes, with long, thick black eyelashes, and her lips were full and covered with something really glossy.

Her appearance tonight was so different from the way he usually saw her, no wonder he hadn't recognized her. He'd only seen her dressed in work clothes that could easily belong to a field hand, and she was missing her nerdy glasses. He would have sworn before meeting her tonight that she wasn't attractive at all. Who knew? It wasn't a surprise to have found her out here, now that he knew she was his gardening neighbor.

He looked around G's gardens; they were indeed beautiful, he thought, his mind returning to Katrina and her mini-history lesson. He'd known G and his family from his college days and they'd remained in touch with each other, making time to take trips together. They had always shared the same passion for adventure, to pit themselves against the external, sometimes extreme, elements. He'd come tonight for G. People assumed he loved to party, that he was happiest in a crowd, but that was a misconception. He preferred his solitude. Most people also would be surprised to know that he usually gave parties a wide berth. They were so not his *thing*, all that standing around talking seemed like a waste of time when one could be outside, under the clear sky, away from the noise and demands of work, city, and life. The sooner he mingled, the sooner the New Year arrived, the sooner he could leave.

An hour later Katrina sat in the back of a room taking in all the beautiful people dancing and talking. She was feeling more than a little buzzed; two more of those pink-and-yellow thingies had gone a long way toward making her more relaxed. She wasn't used to drinking, but those pretty cocktails had been great. The world had become a beautiful, glittery place where anything was possible. She had taken off her shoes and pulled her feet up into the chair, tucking them underneath her body, and sat back to watch. It was a little less crowded in this room, which was a study or perhaps a small library.

The people in here were into all sorts of things. Take that couple over there; they really needed to get a room. Nothing like watching other people make out to get one's juices flowing, but, as always, there wasn't anyone to take advantage of hers.

Or maybe not, she thought, seeing Will enter with two other males. She'd bet good money Will would know what to do with her juices; a germ of an idea took root in her muddled head, now awash with too much alcohol, a flammable fuel for her ardor for one Will Nakane. She recalled watching many a woman on many a morning leave his home, all smiles, clinging tightly to him as he said goodbye. She could do clingy.

Katrina watched as he walked into the room, one of three, all handsome, all sure of themselves and their looks. All dressed in suits, all but Will holding one of those drinks. She watched them talk amongst themselves for a while, watched Will laugh at something someone said, stealing her breath and making her insides all gooey. She watched as one woman, and then another, joined them, each leaving with one of the males until only Will remained, leaning against the wall, alone.

"Okay, get your butt in gear," Katrina's inner drill instructor snapped. "It's your turn. Hurry, before someone else takes him." She bent over, slipped her feet into her shoes, and stood, taking a moment to get her bearings.

Whoa, horsey, who is making the floor move? She stood still a second until it stopped and then proceeded to walk over to Will, not stopping until she stood in front of him. He was magnificent in that intense way of his, like he could handle whatever task was handed to him coolly and give it all back solved.

His eyebrows lifted in surprise. "Katrina," he said, smiling. "You've had some more of those drinks," he said, laughter in his eyes. He'd spotted her sitting in the chair when he'd entered, watching him and confirming his earlier assessment of her interest in him. He hadn't come with anyone, unlike his two buddies, who had disappeared with their dates, and he hadn't planned on leaving with anyone, either.

He'd watched Katrina make her way over to him, swaying a little on her feet, and he had to fight back his laughter. Too many drinks, he imagined, although he wouldn't have pegged her as the drinking type—she seemed way too serious.

She stopped in front of him now, stepping in close and moving her arms slowly around his neck, pushing her face into the curve of it, swaying a little more. "No more talking," she said.

Okay, he thought, *not so shy or quiet after all.* He smiled again as his hand went around her back to help steady her. He pulled back, looking down into her eyes.

"What are you doing?" he quietly asked, smiling softly, humor in his eyes.

"Keeping you company. I saw all of your friends leave, desert you for those women, and I thought you might be lonely. We couldn't have that, could we?" she said, drawing out each word as if speaking had become a difficult task.

It had taken three of those drinks to get her to the point where she was willing to ask for what she'd been wanting from him for a long time. She felt bold, sexy, and invincible, like all the other women she had seen with him. Her newfound alcohol-induced courage had found a friend in her longstanding desire to be near him. She was feeling quite proud of herself for taking the bull by the horns, so to speak.

She pushed herself closer, if that were possible, feeling the hard strength of him as she lowered her face back into the crook of his neck again. He smelled delicious and felt incredible, all hard male. She hadn't been close to one of those in a long, long time. She moaned, softly but discernibly, breathing in the cool, clean scent of Will.

"How many of those drinks have you had?" he asked, hearing her moan as she slipped her head back underneath his chin.

"Three, I think," she said. He was barely able to make out her words as he felt her mouth now moving against his neck. What was she doing?

"How about we get you home," he said, trying to pull back away from her. She pushed herself closer.

"I don't want to go home, unless it's with you," she said. He chuckled.

"You don't mean that; you've just had a little too much to drink," he said. And as tempting as she was, he didn't do women who were anywhere near drunk—too many potentially dangerous side effects. She seemed just a little tipsy, but one never knew for sure what people could do under the influence.

He looked around the room for a spot to take her to sit, maybe find her ride so she could get home, but she apparently had a different plan in mind. It was approaching the midnight hour, and someone had started the downward count signaling the end of this year. He could hear her begin to count softly, her mouth now next to his ear. She'd only stopped kissing his neck a minute ago. When they reached the part about the

Happy New Year, she turned his head with her hand and captured his lips with hers.

She opened her mouth over his, her tongue moving in, aggressive in its desire to taste and tangle with his; because it was the New Year, and she was very tempting, he kissed her back, sweeping his tongue into her mouth, taking over. She moaned, her arms tightening around his neck, pushing herself in closer.

And, because she felt so right in his arms, he gave into another need, moving his hands lower, pulling her hips in closer, moving her in a slow barely detectable grind, but one she felt down to her toes.

She wanted this to go on forever, but he pulled back and looked at her with a strange expression on his face.

"Let's get you home," he said. *Hell, yes,* she thought, *now you're talking.*

"Let's get us home; your place or mine?" she asked. He shook his head, laughing a little.

"I said, let's get *you* home," he said, reaching behind his neck to secure and remove her hands from him.

"Let's get us home," she repeated.

He laughed again, turning her, positioning her in front of him, preparing to propel her forward and out the door. Before he could move, she pushed back into him, her butt aligning against the part of him that was ready and willing to take her up on her offer. It had come to life after that kiss. She moved her hips slowly in a circular motion against him, her hands moving up and clasping his neck again. He let her move against him just for a second, giving in to her seductive pull

before reaching for her arms and pushing them down to
her side.

"Let's go, Katrina," he said softly into her ear, a little
breathless. Potent, she was turning out to be.

"My place it is," she said, walking out the door, if perhaps more crookedly than she was aware. He held on to
her waist, continuing to guide her as she walked.

"Did you come here alone?" he asked.

"Nope, came with Claudia and Amber," she said.

"What do they look like?" he asked, stopping to look
around. Big mistake. She turned, her arms around his
waist this time, and resumed kissing his neck.

"Katrina, who did you come with again?" he asked,
again keeping his focus on finding her ride.

"I came with friends. Where's my phone? I'll text
them," she said, moving her arms away and reaching for
her purse.

"Okay," he said, watching her fumble for a while
before deciding that, in the interest of time, he'd better
send the text. "Let me," he said, taking her phone from
her hand. Great, it was the same brand as his.

"Who should I text?" he asked.

"Amber," she told him. He found Amber's name and
typed in "looking for u, need 2 go."

"ICU" was the immediate response, and Will looked
around, searching. He watched a woman walk toward
them, obviously surprised to see Katrina nibbling his
neck. She picked up her pace, hurrying over to them.

"Katrina, I believe your friend is here to take you
home," Will said.

"You're taking me home," Katrina responded.

"No, I'm not," he said softly, which was followed by her arms becoming vice-like in their grip around his waist.

"So . . ." said her friend. "You are . . . ?"

"Will," he answered.

"Will, huh? I'm Amber," she said, her eyes narrowing, recognition dawning in them. But he couldn't recall having ever met her.

"Well, Amber, I think Katrina has had a little too much to drink. Maybe she needs to go home," he said.

Katrina turned her face around, her arms still locked around him. "Will is taking me home. It's okay, he lives a couple of doors down from me. I know him and he knows me, don't you, Will?" she said, giving him an exaggerated wink. "It's not an imposition, is it, Will?" she asked, looking up at him, earnest, sexy and funny, which was an irresistible combination for him, at least tonight.

He laughed. Fine. He'd wanted to leave, anyway. "Sure, I'll take her home," he said to Amber.

"Kay," Amber replied, watching him closely, her gaze penetrating and scrutinizing. Turning his attention back to Katrina, he said, "Okay, let's get you to the door. Did you bring a coat?" he asked.

"No coat with me," she said, turning back into his body. "I've got this pretty sweater, though," she said, looking down at herself. It was plenty warm enough for her next to his body. He took off his jacket and placed it around her shoulders again. He then walked them through the throng and out the front door. She was glue, stuck to his body, her hands gripping his waist. Once they'd reached his jeep, he leaned her against its side while he opened the door.

"You're really pretty, did you know that? Especially in your cycling outfit," she said, looking at him, running her hand down the side of his face, desire on full display in her eyes. He opened the door, slipped her onto the seat, and reached for her seat belt. He didn't have anything to say to that.

She leaned forward and captured his lips again, surprising him. He pulled back, watching her through hooded eyes. He buckled her in. "And you taste good, too," she added, falling back against the seat. He ran his fingers through his hair, taking a deep breath before walking to the other side of his jeep and getting in. He looked over at her and saw that her dress had crept up. He reached over and secured the tails of his coat together, providing cover for her legs. He started the jeep and pulled away.

After a few minutes, he glanced over at her; her head was leaning against the door, eyes closed. This could not be the same neighbor he had seen as uninteresting because he'd only seen her working in her yard. Always working in that yard. He knew few women—no, make that *any* women—who spent as much time in the yard as she did. She was so young; she couldn't be much younger than his twenty-seven years, he thought, looking over at her again. Her eyes were still closed. Until now, he'd kind of felt a little sorry for her life.

He drove most of the way home with her quiet; maybe she'd fallen asleep. He peeked over at her to find eyes staring back at him. He smiled.

His smile was slow in forming. A lot went into that smile of his—sex, confidence, intensity, all the ingredients that gave it so much power. "You're a sight to behold," she said, serious now, her hand reaching over to trace his eyebrow, skimming his face lightly before moving downward to brush over his cheek.

He smiled fully, finding humor in her. Her thumb brushed the small brackets on his face, a set on each side of his mouth, like he smiled and laughed often. He turned his eyes back to the road, and she moved her hands up and through his smooth, silky hair.

Twenty minutes later, he arrived at her home and pulled into the drive. He opened the door, got out, and walked around to her side.

"Where is the key to your door?" he asked. She reached into her bra, fished around for a while as he watched, spellbound, and then leaned forward and pulled out a key. She handed it over to him.

"Do you need me to help you walk in?" he asked, the key warm in his palm.

"Yes," she said. She was much calmer now, no longer in her earlier attack mode. He put his arm around her waist and walked with her to the door, then unlocked it and walked her in.

"Where is your bedroom?" he asked, looking around her home, taking in the spotless neatness of it. No clutter; a woman after his own heart.

"To the left," she said, and he walked her to it. He walked her over to her bed and pulled back her covers.

"Okay," he said, removing his jacket from her shoulders and laying it on the bed, deciding to skip the sweater. He was about to remove his arm from her waist and help her into bed, but she was quick, putting her arms around his neck and falling back onto the bed, pulling him with her to land partly on top as she found his mouth again.

He reached for her arms to pull them away from him, but her mouth felt soft, welcoming, and warm on his, and her body warm, soft, and pliant beneath him. *Okay, I'll leave in a minute,* he told himself. He pushed her further upward on the bed so that she was completely underneath him, her body aligned with his, and he kissed her as he'd wanted to from the beginning—open, aggressive, taking over her mouth. She didn't need much coaxing. She opened wider for him, her hand going behind his head to hold him in place as he paid homage to her mouth.

Her dress had worked its way upward, allowing him to fit snugly into the junction of her thighs. His hands were at the sides of her hips, his thumbs circling her skin, loving the feel of it before he gripped her hips, tilted them upwards toward him, and pushed inward—he couldn't seem to help himself. She pushed back and moaned, her hands moving toward his waist, frantic, demanding, trying to work themselves between their bodies, finding and unzipping his pants, working her hand inside. He caught her hand, but not before it ran over the full length of him. They both groaned at the contact, and he knew he'd better stop. He did, albeit reluctantly, pulling back and looking down at her, breathing hard.

"I'd better go," he said, looking into her hungry eyes.

"No, stay," she whispered, lifting her upper body to meet his again, her hands moving to his neck to pull him back to her.

"If I don't leave now, I won't," he said, pushing himself up off the bed. His body was screaming its displeasure at having to stop.

He lifted his jacket, which had fallen to the floor, and put it on. He ran his hands through his hair and down over his face, taking a deep breath. He picked up her purse, setting it on the nightstand, and stood for a second, hands running through his hair again, an internal struggle taking place within him. He sighed.

"I'll lock your door and drop the key in your mailbox, okay?" he said, standing beside her bed and looking down at her. She turned over onto her side, moving her head up and down, acknowledging his comment. Her lips were full from his kisses, her hair had come undone and now lay spread out over the bed. Her smooth dark-chocolate skin was a stark contrast to the white of her dress, to the white of her sheets, her white barely there panties. It was an invitation he would have willingly accepted under other circumstances, but he didn't think it wise to pursue her. She was so not his type, and, as tempting as she was tonight, it would only be a one-night thing and she lived too close to him for that.

"Better take these off," he said, slipping her shoes from her feet, placing them on the floor. He turned and walked toward the door, stopping at the door, turning back to see her lying in the same position, soft brown eyes staring back at him.

"Good night, Katrina," he said.

"Good night, Will," she said softly, watching him leave.

Katrina didn't feel so well, her head hurt something fierce, and her mouth felt like sandpaper. She looked over at the nightstand, reading the time and groaning. It was nearly eleven o'clock, the late morning light falling in through the windows. She pulled back the covers. She was still in her clothes from the night before. What had gotten into her? Oh, she knew—too many of those yellow-and-pink drinks.

Will had delivered her home, she remembered that; remembered her behavior, too. Oh, God, where had that come from? What did he think of her now? A part of her answered *who cares?* The least he could have done was sleep with her and really given her a reason to regret last night.

No, he had to be the good guy. She pulled the cover back over her head. Can't hide in here forever, she thought a few minutes later. She threw the covers off again, got up, her head reminding her of its critical condition. Thank God it was Sunday and she had the day to recuperate. She needed a shower first, then food. Before that, she needed to text Amber.

She grabbed her purse off the nightstand and found her phone. Of course, a text from Amber was already waiting for her.

"If I don't hear from you before noon, I'm calling the police," it read. She smiled. Amber knew of her crush on Will; most of her closest friends did. She texted, "Head banging, shower, food, talk 2 U ltr." Katrina slowly sat up on the side of her bed. First shower, and then food.

CHAPTER 2

January 2

The following Monday morning found Katrina hunched over her phone, trying to decipher a message left by one of her customers, no longer surprised by the odd times they'd call asking for money. Amber entered the cubicle and walked over to stand next to her, placing her hip on Katrina's desk. Katrina pushed the play button on her telephone and turned the volume up as far as it could go.

"Listen to this. It's one of my clients; he called last night," she said, looking up at Amber. "I can't quite make out what he's saying. I think, above the static, you can hear what sounds like traffic in the background, like maybe he was standing near a road or highway. See if you can understand him," she said, watching Amber's face twist in confusion as she listened.

"You've got some crazy customers, but I believe, besides the gibberish, he wants his check. 'I need my check' were his exact words. Who was that, anyway?" she asked.

"Winston Hardwick the Third, son of the famous Hardwicks, the very prominent family from Houston. Winston lives here."

"Why is he your customer? Doesn't he belong with a city officer?" Amber asked.

"He has problems with drinking and mental illness. After a long internal struggle, his mother finally gave up hope of helping him, so she set up a trust for him with access to funds so he could eat and have a place to live. Sometimes he's pulled himself back from the edge, sought help, and lived well for a time, only to stumble again. It was better for the family this way. It keeps him at arm's length, fed and sheltered but with no more surprise visits to their home in the middle of the night asking for money, unclean, drunk, or off his meds," Katrina said, pulling up his account information on the computer.

Amber was right. Most of the larger family personal trusts accounts were managed by the larger city offices in the cities where those clients lived. Her customers were small potatoes as far as trusts went, and small potatoes were accounts valued at $3 million or less. She and Amber worked as trust officers, employees of the Western Bank and Trust Company, in the more ambitious sounding Client Trust Department.

Most officers in her division carried a load ranging in size from 250 to 400 accounts. With about 350, Katrina was on the high end.

Katrina's eyes were glued to her computer where Winston's account information had been made available online, technology aiding her in the management of her account load.

"He gets a bi-monthly distribution, and, believe it or not, he's able to get by, to manage, but sometimes he needs more. I'll move some money to his checking account. I'll do it this morning," she said, returning her attention to Amber. "Thanks for listening to my customer."

"No problem. Want to go for coffee?"

"Sure, let me grab some money. My treat for your translation," Katrina said.

"That'll work," Amber said, walking out of Katrina's cubicle.

She and Amber often went for coffee at the local coffee shop across the street from the bank. Lights Out Coffee it was called, a small regional chain owned by an ex-boxer and his daughter.

"I'm ready," Amber said, and they both walked out of the building. Almost immediately Amber started in on her.

"So, tell me about Will. Finally, huh?" she said, not waiting for Katrina's response. "Now aren't you glad you dressed up. Woo, I can't tell you how shocked I was to see you, Katrina of all work and no play, kissing a man. Girl, I didn't even know you even knew what kissing was. And you got him to take you home. Okay, give it up."

"Give what up?" Katrina asked.

"You are not going to make me beg you for details, are you? Really?"

"Nothing to detail; I drank too much, he took me home. I was all over him; he wasn't all over me." She paused, remembering. "Well, he was once, maybe for a second, but he didn't stay the night and he didn't take me up on my offer. Let's see, oh, and a hangover the next day with nothing to show for it. Is that detailed enough for you?"

"Sorry, but it's his loss, although I must say that when you finally picked one, you picked a nice one; a beautiful smile and a body to match. Hey, you didn't tell me he was Asian," Amber said, stopping so they could cross the street.

"Why, what difference would that make?" she asked, walking to the door of the coffee shop.

"I don't know. It just surprised me, that's all. I didn't know you were interested in other races."

"I'm not interested in other races. Just Will," she said.

"Well, anyway, sorry it didn't work out the way you wanted. Are you going to try again with him?" she asked.

"Nope, it was embarrassing enough having him turn me down the first time. I mean, if me served up on a bed all liquored up and loose wasn't enticing enough, I don't know what else to do. Anyway, you do know that only 11 percent of men consider finding a life-long partner their top priority," Katrina said, opening the door, waiting for Amber to enter.

Amber paused in the doorway and looked at her, shaking her head. "So it's back to that again. You are something else, you know that, don't you? You don't have to quit after your attempt just because you tried something and it didn't work out as you planned. Don't go back to your old ways. I was so proud to see you all over him, drunk or not. Don't stop. Now if we could find you a new target while keeping you from drinking," she said, walking through the coffee shop door.

"I wasn't drunk, just tipsy," Katrina responded, following her in.

"Sure you were," Amber said over her shoulder.

Katrina entered the doors of the garden center later that week. She was there to attend the monthly meeting of the citywide gardening board; she'd been a member for the last five years. The board met the third Wednesday of every month, east of town, in the oldest of the founding neighborhood gardens.

"Hey, Gloria," she called out, speaking to the secretary of the garden board. She was hired help, unlike the rest of them, who were volunteers.

"Hello, Katrina, how are you?" she answered, stuffing something in a bag, her purse already on her shoulder. She was apparently leaving for the day.

"Is everyone here?" Katrina asked, not breaking her stride.

"Yes, the usual suspects and one mighty fine surprise," she answered, causing Katrina to pause.

"What?"

"Not going to tell you; you need to see for yourself. Like a Christmas gift, part of the good feeling comes from taking in what you've gotten after you've had the pleasure of unwrapping it."

Only mildly curious, Katrina said, "Okay," and started down the hall leading to the conference room where the committee usually met.

Entering the room, head down, she spotted an empty chair next to Sonja, a representative from one of the predominantly Hispanic parts of town. Six women and three men comprised the nine-member board, which included their leader and board chairman John, whose voice she was now hearing. She walked over, dropped her purse on the floor, pulled out her notebook, and sat down. She wasn't as late as she'd thought; the meeting hadn't even started. All that worry for nothing. She took a breath and looked around. Yep, everyone was here, all right. Suddenly her eyes stopped and the breath left her body as she comprehended Gloria's cryptic message.

Will Nakane, her neighbor, sat looking good—nothing new in that—in a chair next to John. Will was turned sideways away from her as he sat listening to John. He smiled at something John said, and Katrina had to sit back in her chair at the power of that smile.

"I know, right?" Sonja whispered into Katrina's ear. Apparently she approved of Will, too, if her eyes roaming over him was any indication. They were glued to him as if he was manna from heaven sent by the gods for female consumption.

"He is something else," Sonja added, rubbing her hands together. "I don't ask for much in this life, but I would take one of him, any time, any place," she said, grinning at Katrina.

"Board members, before I call this meeting to order, I would like you to meet a new resident of our city. I am happy and proud to announce that he has built a home in my neighborhood, Shining Creek, and not just any home. His home will be featured in the Sunday addition of the Hampton Heights newspaper because it is one of the few homes in our city built from the bottom up to be green. I've asked Will Nakane to stop by to talk a little about his home and to answer questions that are related to green building. Will and I have discussed the city's commitment to living green and green gardening, and I thought he would be helpful in suggesting ways we can improve our efforts in our home spaces. I had to twist his arm a little to get him to attend, so please give him a warm welcome," he said, smiling at Will again, plainly awed.

John was something else, Katrina thought, the epitome of the master gardener and lover of all things green. A scattering of applause greeted Will as he sat forward and smiled, his eyes moving around the table. All the women sat up straighter, Katrina included, before she caught herself and sat back, not wanting to join in the fawning over him. Besides, she was all about the hiding. She hadn't expected to see him so soon afterward; had actually been avoiding him, choosing to work in her back yard instead of the front. Lastly, she preferred to conduct her ogling incognito, usually from the safety of her front porch.

"As I've told John, I'm by no means an expert on green living. My travels via work and hobbies have taken me to many beautiful places around the world. It's the exposure to those places that fostered this desire to do my share, to live greener. So, as part of that effort, I decided to build a more environmentally friendly home," Will said with a self-deprecating smile, pulling in Katrina and every other woman present.

"I'm not much of a lecturer, so how about I field questions from you instead," he said.

"What makes a green home green?" This from Cheryl, another single woman on the committee, who, unlike Katrina, favored clothing that accentuated her assets. She leaned forward to give Will the optimal view of her two double D's. He didn't take the bait, and Katrina found herself more impressed. Hard to miss those two; hell, she'd even glanced at them a time or two, more than a little envious. Don't hate the playa, Katrina, respect the game, she reminded herself.

"Good question," Will said, leaning back, all relaxed and casual.

"A green home can be green in the way you go about building it, green because of the materials you select and use to build with, green in the way in which it uses energy, heating and cooling, and, finally, it can be green in the way in which you dispose of the waste that comes from building it," he said, looking back at Cheryl before his eyes roamed around the room to touch each of them. "From the beginning, I worked with a green architect who listed the alternatives for me, starting with something as simple as the size of my home and where it sits on the property to take advantage of the sun and wind to its best advantage." His eyes traveled over Katrina; did his mouth twitch a little before he continued?

"Building green can be expensive at the front end, so my first decisions were also based on affordability," he said.

Katrina was tuned in, like every other woman at the table, watching him, letting his deep voice wash over her. His hands were on the table, moving independently of him, long, slim, masculine hands drumming some internal tune on the table while he talked. She loved those hands, remembering the feel of them on her body the other night.

It was quiet in the room now. He'd answered the question and sat waiting for the next one, pulling her attention back from its wanderings.

"We can take one more question," John said. "We still have a board meeting scheduled tonight. I promise to invite Will back some other time," he said.

Mr. Sanchez lifted his hand. "Do any of these green things we do make any real difference? Aren't they just small potatoes, this use of green light bulbs, hybrid and electric cars? Aren't they too small to have any impact, at least not in any meaningful way?" he asked.

"Good question," Will said, looking directly at Mr. Sanchez. "I don't think we should abandon our individual efforts to live greener. But, yes, I do see your point and agree individual efforts are not enough. It is equally, if not more, important that we push our legislators both on a national and international level for a carbon-cap bill. We must also seek alternative energy sources that don't pollute our skies. So, yes, we need larger-scale actions to get this problem under control. I would also encourage you to continue in your individual efforts to make a difference. Thank you for your questions and your kind reception."

"No, thank you, Will. I wish we had time to take a few more," John said, standing up and clapping Will on the back before looking around the room. "Why don't we take a minute to stretch our legs? Will is available for a few minutes to talk, or, for those of you with additional questions, he has made his e-mail address available for further communication. Let's be back to start our board meeting in ten," he said.

The board members applauded and some stood and walked around the table to Will. Sonja hit Katrina in the side with her elbow, leaning over to whisper into her ear.

"You think he'd be interested in helping me make my home greener?" she said with a shark-like smile on her face. She stood and walked toward Will while Katrina continued replaying Will's words in her mind. She appreciated his passion for the environment, and not just because she agreed with him. She appreciated passion; his passion in particular was always welcome. But not today. Today she hoped he'd leave without saying anything to her. Maybe now was the perfect time for a bathroom break, before the meeting started, before he saw her. And not those bathrooms located just outside the hall, either. She would head toward the ones located in the back of the building. Great idea. Those were so much cleaner, she thought. *You're such a coward,* her inner voice taunted. It loved to chide. Okay, so she didn't want to face him after her failed attempt at seduction. Her confidence had been bruised, and more than just a little; it was a normal reaction, not cowardly at all. She walked out, eyes averted, hoping he hadn't seen her.

Will finished talking with Sonja, noting Katrina's exit from the room. He'd recognized her. It was easy now that he knew what to look for. She was back in her normal, nondescript clothing, glasses covering her eyes, shy and oddball personality back in place. He wasn't surprised by that; she'd probably only approached him because she'd been under the influence. He wanted to say hello before he left, anyway, to make sure she'd found her key. He was on his way out the door to see if he could find her when John appeared at his shoulder.

"Thank you again, Will, for stopping by," he said.

"Sure, no problem."

"I'd like to stop by this week to take a look at your famous home, if you have the time."

"Sure, I make a point of getting home early on Friday evening. Would that work?"

"Yes, perfect. Thank you again, Will," John said, walking away.

"Sure, no problem," Will said, stepping into the hall and searching for his neighbor.

Okay, that should do it, Katrina said to herself. Her hands were some kind of clean now, seeing as she'd washed them three times. Cleanliness was next to Godliness, she'd heard somewhere, reaching into her purse to find her lotion and slowly applying it to her hands. She looked at her watch. Yep, Will should be long gone by now. She'd waited an extra five minutes beyond the meeting's start time, just to be sure.

She opened the door and looked both ways. No one there. So far, so good, she said to herself as she walked back down the hallway leading toward the conference room. Her footsteps faltered as she took in Will, leaning against the wall a little way down from the door to the conference room.

She inwardly sighed, her hands twitching at the picture of him. She sighed again. He could have had sex with her that night; would that have killed him? He turned to her and remained there, watching her walk to him, a smile on his face.

"So, we meet again," he said, standing up straight, his smile widening, showing off perfect white teeth. He secured her hand in his strong grip. "I didn't want to leave without saying hello. I haven't seen you around much lately. I assume you found your key," he said, watching her.

"Yep, sure did. Thank you," she said, her eyes skimming across his face before moving away to a spot just above his right shoulder.

"You're welcome. I can tell that you've recovered," he said, beckoning her eyes back to his face. She wished she'd worn something nicer, something other than her usual jeans, extra-large T-shirt, and baseball cap.

"Yep," she said, looking into his eyes.

"That was some New Year's Eve party. Did you enjoy yourself?" he asked.

"Hey, congratulations on your home," she blurted out, a blatant attempt to change the subject.

"Thank you," he said, slightly taken aback by the turn in the conversation.

"Oh, look at the time. I'd better get back in there. You'll excuse me, won't you? I'm late enough as it is," she said, pulling her hand from his and walking quickly away.

"Sure," he said, his voice trailing away, watching her disappear into the room, inwardly smiling. She was not so bold today.

He'd seen embarrassment and discomfort in her eyes just then, and he hadn't seen her out working in her yard anymore, not as he was used to. He'd given some thought to going over to check on her, but decided against it. She liked him, very much it seemed, and he now knew how much. He liked her, too, in a mostly friendly way. Okay, it was not all friendly; there was a little sexual interest mingled in there, but not enough to act on. She had been funny and interesting that night and different from what he'd originally thought her to be. He headed toward the front of the building, realizing that he'd been standing there lost in his thoughts. He walked out the main door and headed to his jeep pulling his keys from his pocket, recalling Katrina's earlier behavior. So she was going to try and avoid him, to pretend that night hadn't happened. He understood the merits of her plan, and he should allow her to implement it, but for some reason he didn't want to.

Thank God for Fridays, Katrina thought later on that week as she made the left turn on to her street, passing Will's home. He and John were standing in front, John with his hand around Will's shoulder as if he was Will's father. What that was about, she wondered, pulling into her drive. She parked and sat for a minute, contemplating her mail. The mailboxes for her street sat directly across from her home. She thought she could scoot across the street and pick up her mail undetected by Will. By all appearances, he and John were deep in conversation, their heads together, Will listening, John talking— nothing new there. She got out of her car and turned to walk across the street.

"Katrina," John shouted just before she took her first step into the street. She looked up and saw him and Will walking toward her. Groaning under her breath, she walked toward them, deciding to meet them halfway.

"Katrina, I was just discussing the city's annual gardening competition with Will."

"Oh," she said, glancing at Will, who looked smoking hot, as usual. But he had a new look on his face now, one that said he was up to no good.

"Hi, Katrina," he said, as if they were old friends from around the way.

"Hi," she responded, not sure what to make of him now, and turned her eyes toward John. She was sticking with her original course, though, and pretending that night had never happened.

"I stopped by to take a look at Will's incredible home and was surprised to find that he has also designed and landscaped an equally impressive backyard. It is remarkable the continuity between his home and the land surrounding it," John said.

Incredible, huh, Katrina said to herself, lifting her eyebrows at all the praise and pushing her glasses, which had a habit of slipping, back up her nose. "That's nice," she said blandly, looking at Will, who was grinning and waggling his eyebrows at her. She turned away before he could see her smile.

"I was just telling Will about you and your gardening abilities, although the two of you have very different styles," John said, looking between them. "You should come and take a look at Will's home and garden."

"Right now?" she asked, looking around somewhat frantically for a way to escape. It was all Will could do to keep from laughing outright.

"Oh, no, I couldn't. I wouldn't want to impose, plus I just got home from work," she said, making herself yawn and covering her mouth. "Long week, you know," she added.

"It wouldn't be any imposition," Will said, that big-ass grin still firmly in place on his face.

"Maybe later. I'll stop by soon, I promise."

"Sure you will," he said, causing her to look back sharply at him. "Stop by anytime. You know where I live. Come see how pretty I am in my natural setting," he said.

She made a face at him, remembering her words from the night of the party. How sweet of him to hand them back to her, and in front of John, too. She gave him one of her sharpest glares, along with a sugary smile for John's benefit. He laughed. John looked from one to the other, unsure what to make of them. Katrina started walking backwards.

"I'll see you later, John. Nice seeing you again, Will," she said, backing up and turning toward her home, feet moving her away quickly.

The night of the party notwithstanding, Will's initial assessment of her had been plain and boring. The first time he'd seen her in her yard, she had a bag of something or other slung over her shoulder, looking like a farmer. Her appearance today had not changed that opinion; she was garbed today in plain brown trousers and matching plain top, hair in a ponytail and those nerd glasses back on the bridge of her nose. Brown was not a friend to her skin, and of all of her physical attributes he'd seen the night of the party, her skin had become his favorite. It was a strong, smooth Kahlua, warmth on a cold night. Apparently, New Year's Eve had made more of an impression on him than he'd thought.

He'd watched her pull up a few minutes ago in her little electric car, watched as she looking around, calculating whether she could try and sneak by them. So when John called her over, he'd decided to mess with her a little, ruffle her, finding that he didn't want her to avoid him. It was easy and so much fun—a twisted benefit for him, he knew—but sometimes twisted worked for him. Most women didn't ignore him, especially ones that liked him as much as he knew she did. What was the big deal, anyway? There was nothing to be ashamed of, no need to hide.

"So, Will," John said, pulling him from his musings, "I would like you to give some thought to leading the gardening competition this year."

"Who, me? I don't think so," he said.

"Do you know anything about the city's annual competition?" John asked, walking back toward his home.

"Not much, just that it requires a year-long commitment, which I can't see making. I just don't have the time for that," he said.

"Hear me out before you turn me down. Our city is the neighborhood garden capital of the country. It's an effort we gave birth to and encouraged, and, as part of that commitment, we host a citywide competition in two areas, vegetables and flowers. The neighborhoods can enter in either the vegetable or flower categories, separately or in both. We usually enter in both categories, with different leads for each section. The city considers all the entries before inviting the top five designs in each category to participate in the final. You will have nine months from the selection of the final five to complete your garden," he said, his arm wrapping around Will's shoulder.

"Some years the city has provided a theme. I believe one year it was gardens with water conservation features. Anyway, all of the entries tailor their gardens around that theme. I have a hunch that this year's theme will be a perfect fit with you as lead, duplicating your beautiful backyard garden on a much larger scale."

"I don't know, John. That sounds like a huge commitment, and I travel quite a bit. I'd have to check my long-range calendar before I could even consider it."

"Sure, sure," John said, continuing his explanation of the competition. He was in full-out persuasion mode, walking with Will back to his home. He stood outside talking about the competition for another hour before leaving. It was dark when he left.

Katrina knew how long it had taken because she'd stood at her window watching and wondering what was up with Will. Since when had they become friends? *Well, you did have him in your bed not too long ago,* her inner voice reminded her. She'd get her mail in the morning. John worked her nerves with his gardening quest, and that was saying something, because she, too, loved all things plants, and Will, well, because she was still avoiding him.

The next morning Katrina walked across the street to pick up her mail. Just as she'd opened her box she looked up to find Will pulling up alongside the curb in his jeep, bike secured to the back of it. He hopped out and walked over. *Why me*, she thought. The other night notwithstanding, she really was okay with the loving him from afar bit.

"And yet again we meet," he said, reaching into his box, which was located next to hers, and looking over at her. "I think you've been avoiding me, Katrina, and here I'd gotten used to seeing you in your yard," he said, grinning as he took in her less-than-glamorous attire.

"Nope," was all she could find to say. He was now in his full-on cycling gear, and her mind split between listening to him and trying to take him all in. She scooted closer to him and took a deep breath, inhaling the cool, clean scent of him. She remembered that scent from the other night, and moved over just a little more to take in another lungful.

"Katrina, what are you doing?" he asked, curious as he watched her body shift toward him. She was short, reaching to the top of his chest without her heels, and the brim of her cap obstructed his view of her face, so he couldn't see what she was doing exactly; he could only hear breathing.

"Me? Nothing. Just taking in the beautiful morning air," she said, stepping back and looking up into his eyes. "I see you're going for a ride this morning," she said, changing the subject.

"Yep, I have this restless streak that needs feeding," he said, looking down at her, amusement again in his eyes.

"Oh," she said, returning his gaze. She could be food, yeah, that could work for her, she thought.

"Not that kind of feeding," he said, apparently reading her mind or what was reflected in her eyes. "But who knows, maybe now that you're in your right mind and not under the influence, I might give it some consideration." He gave her a cheeky grin as he unlocked his box, cocky and confident, and pulled the mail from it, some spilling onto the ground.

"You don't check your mail often, huh?" she said, trying to change the subject again. "Not as often as I should, apparently," he said, bending down to pick up some of his mail that had fallen.

"Do you need some help?" she asked.

"Like the other night kind of help?" he asked, turning the conversation back around again, just to shake her. She was such an easy mark.

"All right. Enough. What's with you bringing that up all the time? You turned me down. Even my jumbled head remembers that. I'm sure that night was of no consequence to you, anyway. It's not your first time bringing a woman home, I know. I've seen you in action," she said.

"Oh, I forgot. Katrina, the one-woman neighborhood watch program," he said, shutting her up. He shrugged. "I don't know why, except it's kind of fun, watching you try to avoid me, trying to pretend nothing happened. It brings out the demon in me. I've told you before, it's nothing to be ashamed of. I've had too much to drink before. It's not a big deal. Plus, it was fun, putting you to bed," he said, moving his eyebrows up and down.

"See what I mean? Let's forget it. Thanks for bringing me home. Is that what you want? Okay, I won't pretend anymore that it didn't happen and you can move on," she said, looking into his eyes. He placed his stack of mail under one arm and locked his mailbox door with the other. "I'll think about it," he said, tugging at the bill of her cap. He chuckled as he walked back to his jeep.

She watched him leave, her hands twitching at the sight of a firm and fine ass over well-toned thighs. She still hadn't gotten past that night, how he'd felt next to her. She wished she could have persuaded him to do more. She sighed as his jeep started up and he waved a final time to her before turning and driving away.

She was too easy, he thought, chuckling, gazing at her through his rearview mirror; she was uncomfortable, but still interested. Her eyes had told him that. *No, Will,* he reminded himself again, *too close to home.* She was out of the ordinary and that's what had caused this new fascination and interest in her. Or that was at least the way he had chosen to explain it to himself.

Later on that evening, Katrina sat perched, as was her custom, on the top back step of her deck, her cell phone in hand, waiting for a call, *The Call.* In the next five minutes, this year's gardening competition's theme would be announced. Katrina checked her watch. Gloria, her friend on the inside, always passed on the news to her as soon as it became available. Her cell rang. Answering on the first ring, she said, "Hey."

"A World of Gardens," Gloria said, skipping right to the reason for the call.

"A World of Gardens?" Katrina repeated, puzzled, moving her hand to her forehead. "What does that mean?" she asked.

"It means the gardens in the competition this year will reflect gardening styles found in other countries. It's our little city's attempt to go global. As if producing our own vegetables wasn't a big enough task, and going green

47

wasn't an even larger additional burden, the city would like to add a little international flavor to the growing list of its attributes," Gloria said.

"Okay. That so works for what I have in mind," Katrina said.

"I'm sure, Katrina. You're always cooking something up in that mind of yours. Good luck, although I shouldn't wish you any. You've won the last three years; the rest of us would like a chance."

"Thanks, I'll need it. Last year's win was only by five points, and that was closer than it's ever been. I hope I'm not losing my edge," Katrina said.

"We'll see. I've got to go; I've got other garden junkies to call with the news. See you soon," Gloria said, and hung up.

"A World of Gardening," Katrina said out loud, looking over her backyard. She'd designed her space to reflect what she'd hoped one would find in a typical English cottage garden. She loved the abundance of color, the fullness, warmth, variety, and energy she'd found in those gardens.

She had taken only one trip in her lifetime so far, and it had been to England to visit the Queen—not really, just to stand outside the gate of Buckingham Palace to watch the changing of the guards. She and her parents had toured London and the surrounding countryside and she'd fallen in love with the flowers and gardens she'd seen there. Back home she'd tried to replicate those gardens with varying degrees of success. What she wouldn't give for a wetter climate and less heat.

The competition this year would finally offer her a chance to design something she had so much passion for. She could hardly wait to get started.

A week later, Katrina went to the garden center to talk with two of her mentors, Sandy and Mrs. Washington, both residents of her neighborhood and members of its gardening committee. She had dropped by to run her initial plans by them, having immediately started work on her design for this year's competition after her conversation with Gloria. The women had been good and dear friends of Katrina's mother.

Most neighborhoods were managed by some small governing organization that was responsible for all of its garden-related business. Some were more effective and better organized than others. Shining Creek's board was very organized and productive. Katrina had never sat on the actual committee, and as long as she was the leader, she wouldn't. Her sitting on the committee would be a conflict of interest, as the board selected the leader each year.

Sandy and Mrs. Washington had helped her the last three years, offering helpful hints and critiquing her designs. She entered the gardening center. Gloria was at her usual post by the door. Today the room was filled with visitors, most here to pick up information regarding the history of gardening in this city. There was ample information here, both for the novice and the master gardener.

"Hey, Gloria, thanks for the call the other day," Katrina said.

"Don't mention it. If you're looking for Sandy and Mrs. Washington, they are already in the library, waiting for you."

"Thanks," she said, smiling but not breaking stride as she walked down the hallway. The library was the last door at the end of the hall, and was not a library per se as much as a small room filled with gardening books, and a small table that could seat four, if you didn't mind being close to your neighbor. She heard voices as she approached. "I'm not going to be the one to tell her," was the last thing she heard before entering the room.

"Good morning, ladies," she said, smiling brightly. She paused in the doorway, feeling like an interloper interrupting an intense conversation. "Sorry to interrupt. Do you want me to come back, give you a few minutes?" she asked.

"No," they said in unison. Both looked very uncomfortable for some reason.

"You sure?" she asked.

"No, now is a good time. We weren't talking abut anything important, just sharing gossip," Mrs. Washington said. Mrs. Washington was African-American, her hair permed and curled, always dressed like every day was a trip to church. Sandy was red-haired and small next to Mrs. Washington's larger frame.

"Okay, well, I've gotten a head start on the designs for the garden competition this year. I made some preliminary sketches that I would like you to look at and give me your honest and constructive feedback on."

Katrina put her designs down on the table, took a seat, and began talking in earnest.

"This is my idea for my entry this year. The design you see here is based on an English cottage-style garden, where you'd find a mixture of shrubs, annuals, and perennials native to Texas, a merging of the English style with Texas plants. It would be a replication of what's in my backyard, but on a much larger scale, as you can see from my first drawing," she said, pointing at the table.

Katrina spent the next thirty minutes with them discussing her ideas and plans. She was so engrossed in her work that she didn't pick up on the furtive glances between the two women or on their lack of enthusiasm for her designs.

"Well, you've certainly put a lot of work into this," Sandy said.

"And you are ahead of schedule this year, too," Mrs. Washington added.

"Well, once the city announced the theme, I knew that finally my time had arrived. Don't get me wrong; I've enjoyed all the past themes. I mean, there is fun in transforming any outdoor space, but this year's theme works so well with my love of English cottage gardens. Getting the chance to design a larger one would be a dream come true," she said, pausing, catching herself before she got started again. "Sorry, I can get way carried away, but you two know that already," she said, grinning sheepishly.

"Well, we really appreciate the hard work and dedication you've given to gardening in this city, and to our neighborhood in particular. Always remember that," Mrs. Washington said, placing her hand over Katrina's as it rested on the table.

"Okay, sure," she said, wondering about that last comment. "Thanks for your time. I didn't mean to hold you two hostage so long," she added, standing up and gathering her designs. "Goodbye."

Standing inside the foyer of Will's home, John said, "Thank you again for taking this on, Will. I can't tell you how impressed the committee was with your backyard and your abilities. We are so excited to have you as leader this year," he said, holding out his hand to shake Will's for the third time.

"You're welcome. I'm looking forward to the challenge," Will said.

"I didn't mention this at the beginning, as I didn't want it to influence your decision, but I think we should be prepared for a not-so-favorable reaction from Katrina, your neighbor," he said.

"Oh?"

"Not surprising, as she has been the leader for the past four years, three of which she's won. The first year is difficult for everyone," he said, by way of explaining Katrina's first year loss. "Katrina is a very valued member of the city's gardening community, very good at what she does, and, as such, it might be a little hard for her to accept your selection; not you specifically, but someone other than she," he said, seeing the concern on Will's face.

"Oh, don't worry; it'll all work out. Here I am, as usual, borrowing trouble. Really, don't worry, she'll be fine. The committee would like her to work as your assistant this year. And I must say, you'd be hard pressed to find a more knowledgeable person as an assistant."

"I don't have to lead this year. I am flattered by this opportunity, but it's not set in stone for me," he said.

John cut him off. "No, no, it will work out. Katrina always does what is best for our neighborhood," he said, his expression somewhat pained and at odds with this statement.

"Are you sure?" Will asked, taking in John's expression.

"Yes, sometimes life can be difficult," he said, as if shoring up his internal resolve. "Thank you again, Will. You'll be hearing from the committee soon. Hopefully Katrina will be the one calling you, and all my worries will have been for naught. You two will meet, work out all the details and deadlines, and everything will be fine," he said.

Will opened the door for John and followed him out.

"You sure?" Will asked.

"Absolutely."

When Katrina saw John standing outside Will's home again, she thought, okay, really, what's up with those two?

She'd gone from seeing Will from afar to always running into him, and it had left her in a state of confusion. She didn't know what to make of this friendliness, this teasing; what to make of *him*, what to do. Was he interested in her now? She didn't think so; she was still the same old Katrina. With the exception of that night, she wasn't anywhere near the level of sophistication he seemed to require of his women. She was more than okay with distance; preferred it, actually. There was safety in distance. This new playful, friendly Will she didn't know what to do with.

Shining Creek's vegetable and flower gardens sat on five acres of land encompassing the neighborhood park, about four blocks over from Katrina's street. She was headed to it now, pleased to have gotten home early enough from work. She found working at the gardens a great way to decompress and lose the stresses of her day. Working with her trust customers at the bank left her emotionally exhausted more days than not. She had come home from work today, changed into her usual garden-work attire, pulled on her baseball cap, stuck her work gloves into her pocket, and walked out her front door. Now it seemed she would have to pass them.

"Katrina," John called out, waving her over as she approached Will's home. She paused, sighed, pulled her cap down to meet her glasses, rearranged her face to what she hoped would pass for pleasant, pushed her glasses up, and turned in the direction of John and Will, walking midway up the sidewalk.

"Hello, Katrina," Will said, glancing over her as she approached, a head-to-toe once-over. He was subtle, smooth about it. She admired his skill.

"Hi John, Will," she said.

"I was telling Will that you held the record for the most wins in the gardening competition in the city. We were discussing this year's competition. Did I tell you about Will's backyard?"

"Yes," she said, starting to get a funny feeling in the pit of her stomach.

"Did I tell you that he has designed a beautiful Japanese garden?"

"No, you didn't," she said, looking down at her watch. *Enough already with singing his praises.*

"Look at the time. I'd better get going if I'm going to get any work in before it gets dark," she said, starting to walk away. "See you around, Will, John."

"Katrina, wait, I'll walk over with you. I need to discuss the upcoming competition with you. Will and I were finished here," John said.

"Okay."

"Thanks for seeing me again, Will."

"No problem. See ya around, Katrina," Will said, watching her.

She waited for John to reach her and they started walking, making a right turn on to the main thorough-fare that would lead them to the gardens.

John was a pleasant enough guy and in charge of all things gardening in this neighborhood. He and Katrina had bumped heads before over previous competition designs, but he was totally committed to their neighborhood and she respected him for that.

"I've been meaning to talk to you about the next competition. I'm sure you've heard the city has selected this year's theme."

"Yes, A World of Gardens," Katrina confirmed. "I can't begin to tell you how energized I am by this year's theme. You'll be happy to know that I've already drawn up the preliminary designs using an English cottage garden theme. You'll also be happy to know that I should have them completed by the end of this week and ready for review by the committee. I've also been giving some consideration to the budget and the planting schedule."

"About that, Katrina," he said, stopping, as they had reached the entrance to the garden. "The garden committee met, and we've decided to go in a different direction this year. We won last year, but the margin between first and second was closer than the committee is comfortable with. So we have asked someone new to lead this year."

"Oh?" she said. And there went the wind in her sails.

"I wanted to let you know firsthand who we've selected."

"Okay," she said, trying to wrap her mind around the fact that she'd been replaced. She'd never considered it happening, not really.

John paused, and then plunged ahead. "We've asked Will Nakane, your neighbor, to head the flower garden portion of the competition."

"Will?" she asked, dumbfounded. Her Will? Traveling the globe Will, never at home or off to one adventure after another Will. Never worked at the gardens Will—surely not that Will. "Will? Are you sure?"

"Yes, I'm sure. The committee is sure. I've told you about his backyard garden. It is impressive, and he designed and landscaped it alone. It would be so appropriate for this year's theme, and it is really exceptional, Katrina. Did you ever go by to see it?" he asked her.

She shook her head.

"You should see it as soon as you can." His face took on a rapt expression as he looked out into space, apparently remembering Will's garden. "It's beautiful, serene, calming, extraordinary, really. He's combined so many aspects of the Japanese gardening styles."

"Yes, I'm sure it's all that and more," she said curtly, taking a deep breath. "Has Will done anything remotely on the scale of the city competition before?" she asked, cutting into John's moment of rapture.

"I believe he has some gardening experience. I'm not sure if it's on this scale."

"I see. And you're okay with that, the committee is okay with that?" she asked, trying to remain calm. "I mean, I don't need to remind you of my first attempt," she said.

"No, you don't, and yes, the committee is okay with that."

"Okay, so you're telling me that we are going to turn a major project over to someone who can design a great backyard, who will probably lose his first time out, just as I did, just as most people do, and the committee is okay with this?"

"Yes, but we've come up with an outstanding alternative. A surefire way of ensuring Will's success," John said, taking a deep breath. "The committee thought, had hoped, that you would be available to help him this year, to act as his assistant, show him the ropes, so to speak."

"You want me to show him how to win?" she asked incredulously, her face reflecting her horror at the suggestion. "And to be his assistant? Me?"

"Not an assistant, at least not in the way you mean. Not in the traditional sense, of course not. You're too knowledgeable to be anyone's assistant. We had hoped that you would help him sort it all out, act as an advisor of sorts. You could probably enter this contest in your sleep," he said, opting to go the flattery route in the face of Katrina's rising anger.

"John, I have to say, I don't feel this is fair. Not at all. I've worked with the committee going on four years now, and every design—and I do mean *every* design—I've submitted has been questioned or altered. It seems like I have to prove myself every year, even with the wins. Now along comes someone new, and he is given this chance with no prior experience. That's so not fair, and you know it," she spat out, fully angry now. "Here I am with four years of hard-earned competition experience and a master gardener training certification, and finally the city has introduced a theme that is appropriate for my ideal design and you give it away without even giving me a chance. And not to someone with more experience, but to the new, unproven guy."

John sighed. "We discussed at the time why the committee felt modifications were necessary, Katrina."

"That's not even what this is about," she said, her hands going to her hips. "I want to discuss it with the committee members, face to face, to state my case. I shouldn't even have to make a case; my record should speak for itself. But apparently, winning is not what is required to keep your job around here," she said, taking a deep breath. "I know that others deserve a chance to lead. I get that, but this year in particular is important to me."

John raised his hands as if to deter further comments. Katrina kept talking.

"I know you and I have bumped heads before, and that you don't care for my gardening style. I know I wasn't always conservation-minded enough, but I've worked hard to change. You cannot give this to Will, not this year. This year was going to be my year," she said quietly.

John sighed. He'd known that there was not going to be a good time for this, no matter who was chosen.

"The committee has made its decision. I had hoped that you would put your disappointment behind you and work toward what is in the best interest of the neighborhood. I know you love this community that your parents helped to build, and I know you well enough to know that you'll do what's best."

"Nope, not buying it this year. I always do what is best for this community, and that won't change. But I'm asking you all to let me have this year. It's important to me," she said.

"I'm sorry, Katrina."

"I want to talk to the committee. I want to present my design," she said.

"It won't change the decision. It wasn't just me who wanted Will to lead this year. All of the committee members voted for him, so talking to them won't change things."

"I want to talk to them, anyway. And after all I've done for this neighborhood, I deserve at least a chance to explain my design before you turn it down."

John stood silent for a few minutes, looking into Katrina's set face. "If I call a meeting for next weekend, give you a chance to present your design before the committee, will that satisfy you?" he asked.

"Yes."

"Afterward you will accept the wishes of the committee? Do I have your word?" he asked.

"Yes," she said, suddenly fighting back tears.

"I'll send you an e-mail with the meeting time and place. I'll see you then," he said.

"Fine!" she said, turning to walk into the garden entrance, anger in every step she took. She needed something physical to do, something to beat up, so she headed back to the compost pile, stopping by the tool and equipment shed to pick up a pitchfork first. She weakly smiled at her neighbors, at least the ones she could see through her red haze of anger. Gone was her desire to be close to Will. It was replaced by annoyance and anger. She stopped in front of the compost pile, where the soil needed to be turned often—fork in, anger out.

CHAPTER 3

Katrina didn't sleep well that night. She tossed and turned, angry. That's what you get for working hard for other people. Nothing. They pull the rug from underneath you when you least expect it. The next morning, she got up early and drove over to Abernathy and Co., the largest locally-owned landscape and gardening store in Hampton Heights. It sat on about ten acres of land purchased a long time ago, a partnership between two single men without families, who'd survived the Vietnam War and had the scars to prove it.

About an acre held the store and the main plant, tree, and shrub sections. Near the middle of the land, with its own separate entrance, one could find any and all types of soil, compost, manure, and sand, along with rocks, bricks, and stones. If you needed anything plant-related for any size project, chances were you'd find it at Abernathy and Co. At the very back of the property, the owners' home stood next to three industrial-sized greenhouses.

Katrina entered the main store and spotted Charles Abernathy, one of the owners, behind the register ringing up purchases for a customer. She walked over to him. "Hey, Uncle C," she said, leaning in to give him a kiss.

"Hello, Kat. How's my favorite goddaughter doing today?" he asked.

"I'm your only goddaughter. Where's Colburn?" she asked, looking around for her other godfather. Henry Colburn was the Co. of Abernathy and Co. and the opposite in appearance and temperament from his partner. African-American, short, stocky, and sturdy— the three S's, Katrina often called Colburn. He and Charles were partners, both in business and in life, had been partners at a time when it wasn't a safe thing to be.

Charles was the easygoing one of the two, Caucasian, tall and whippet thin, friendly to Colburn's intolerance for bullshit.

She knew they both loved her, had performed their own godfather ceremony after her adoption. Colburn and Charles had both served in the Vietnam War— Charles with her adopted father—and the three men had forged a bond that hadn't been broken. They were in their late sixties, but you couldn't tell it by the amount of work they did at the store each day.

They were, as her adoptive parents had been, avid gardeners. Her gardening education growing up had been supplemented by them. She was twenty-one when her parents were tragically killed in a car accident and she had been taken firmly under her godfathers' wings. They'd helped her settle her parents' estate, sell their home, and build a new one. They attended her graduation from college and looked on as she began working at the bank. They had always been there for her; without them, she would have been lost. She tried to stop by at least once a week, more when her day job was easy. She walked over and took a seat on the stool that sat next to the register, preparing to bring Charles up to date with the happenings of her life as he rang up customers.

"Why the long face?" Charles asked.

"You are not going to believe this, C, but my neighborhood committee has chosen someone else to lead the gardening competition this year."

"Who?"

"My neighbor, Will Nakane. You know, the one who built that eco-friendly home on my street. I know I've told you about him. Well, he apparently has a green thumb as well as a green home. He is being asked to lead this year, and, get this, all because he's built himself one heck of a backyard. Can you believe that? Apparently it's one wonderful, stupendous backyard. Did you hear me say backyard?" she asked sarcastically.

"Backyard," Charles repeated.

"Backyard," repeated the customer, a little old lady standing at the counter. Katrina smiled at that, letting go of some of her anger just that quick.

"That's not the worst of it. The worst part is that they want me to be an assistant to him to help him work through the process."

"Is that so?" Charles said, handing a bag to the customer. Charles knew all of this, of course, he had listened to John one day last week when he'd stopped by the store. The avid gardening community was very small and knew each other very well.

"Is that the guy you have a crush on, the one you talk about all the time?"

"I do not talk about him all the time," she said, C's comment bringing her up short. "Do I?" she asked, looking intently at him. "Do I?" Had she?

"Yep, you do. 'His home is interesting, Uncle C'. They are doing this. They are building that," Charles said, mimicking her voice, and even the movement of her head. "You've provided me and Colburn with a running commentary cataloging the complete details of the building of his home. When that was done, you moved on to describing his comings and goings. I know who he is, the Japanese kid, right?" he asked.

"Right," she said, mortified that she'd been so transparent. She hadn't realized she'd talked that much about him.

"Okay, be honest with me, C. Does it seem fair to you that he's being asked to lead? I mean, one Japanese garden in the backyard and the competition is his for the taking," she said, returning to her main beef.

"You do know, Kat, that you can't lead every year. It seems fair that someone else should have a chance to lead for a change. You've been in charge for the past, what, four years?"

"Not really. They've never given me full control, not like they're going to give Will."

"So his design won't require the neighborhood committee's approval?" Charles asked.

"Yes, I guess so."

"Well then, they could reject portions of his design as well, couldn't they?" he asked, smiling at the next customer in line.

"Yes, but I bet they won't. Everyone loves Will, the golden boy, his fantastic home, now fantastic backyard, fantastic women, and fantastic body." She stopped, catching herself, but not before she heard C's bark of laughter.

"Yes, your crush is still with us," he said, still laughing. "Have you voiced your concerns to John and the committee?" he asked.

"Yes, I've demanded a meeting with the committee. I will argue my side next Saturday morning. I want this year, C. Any suggestions as to what I should say?"

"No, I bet you've got it covered," he said.

∞

Will answered his cell on the first ring. Twelve o'clock and he was in between meetings.

"Hello, Will, this is John. I hope I'm not interrupting your day. Can you talk for a second?" he asked.

"Sure, I've got a second, but not much more. It's been a bitch of a day," he said somewhat distractedly. He needed to get ready for a meeting in thirty minutes and wondered if he had time to grab something quick for lunch.

"It's about the competition. My premonition concerning Katrina has come true. She has asked the committee to reconsider your selection as leader," John said, rushing on. "She doesn't have anything against you personally, but she wants to make sure the committee has heard her ideas and seen her design before the decision is final. Normally we wouldn't have this extra meeting, but she has done quite a bit for the neighborhood so we need to at least give the appearance of hearing her out."

"Okay," Will said, looking down at his watch, starting to gather up what he needed for his next meeting. So Katrina was taking exception to his leading. He guessed he wasn't surprised by it; she loved her plants and twigs. Nope, no surprise there.

"I would like for you to attend. You don't have to, but it would be nice for the committee to see you, and if they have any questions you would be available to answer them."

"John, I really don't have to do this. It certainly wasn't something I sought. You asked me. I certainly don't mind if Katrina heads up this year."

"No, the committee has made its selection, and we want you to lead this year. We also believe that, with Katrina's assistance, we could win, and not by some small margin as we did last year."

"When is the meeting?" Will asked.

"Saturday morning, nine o'clock," John said, rushing on. "I know it's short notice, but we would like to resolve the issue sooner rather than later."

"Okay, I'll see what I can do. I've got to go."

"Sure. Thanks," John said as Will disconnected. He would be missing lunch again, and he was hungry, he thought, heading toward his next meeting.

⁕

The following Saturday morning, Katrina walked over to John's home, the regular meeting place of the neighborhood committee. Made up of only four people—Sandy, Mrs. Washington, Stan, and John—it was much smaller than the larger city one to which she belonged.

The meeting was starting in about ten minutes. She'd debated her arrival time endlessly—should she get there early to talk to some of the board members before her presentation or arrive on time? On time won out; she opted to stay home, using the extra time to try and settle her nerves. She was never nervous; the garden was her home away from home, where she felt the most comfortable.

Cowgirl up, Katrina, she told herself, grabbing the bag that held her designs and the extra copies she'd made for the committee members and headed out the door. John lived to the left of her at the end of the street where it rounded into a cul de sac. Katrina rang the doorbell and waited.

"Hi, Katrina," John said, opening the door. "Glad you could make it," he added, giving her a smile as if she had not been the one responsible for them meeting again today.

She walked through a small foyer that opened up into a large living room where all of the members sat awaiting her arrival, looking up at her with various expressions on their faces. There was annoyance on Stan's face, patience on Sandy's, love and encouragement on Mrs. Washington's, and John, well, she knew how he felt.

And then there was Will—she hadn't expected him—his face unreadable before he looked at her and smiled. It was a small one, not the teasing one she'd gotten used to; this version was empathetic and encouraging. She was too angry today to be encouraged. What was he doing here? He shouldn't be here, she thought, not returning his smile. The members were either on John's couch or in the surrounding chairs. She stood in front of the group.

"Hello," she said, smiling, hoping to camouflage her nerves. A chorus of greetings came back to her.

"Well, let's get started," John said, taking a seat between Will and Sandy and extending his hand outward to indicate that Katrina should start. She opened her bag and pulled out her designs.

"Okay, first let me say thank you for holding this special meeting and giving me this opportunity to present my ideas for the competition," she said. She then passed out copies of her design to everyone, including Will, who looked at her again, eyes still unreadable. He'd dropped his smile.

"So I'm sure everyone knows the theme for this year is 'A World of Gardens'," she began, looking around the room. "I've given you a copy of what I feel is the winning design. One I believe captures this year's theme perfectly. I think it's our best chance of winning. It reflects a gardening style that has been around forever, at least since late nineteenth century England, modified a bit to include the use of Texas native plants," she said, pausing, taking in the five bowed heads reviewing her design.

"As you can see, I listed the items and steps that are needed to transform our existing garden to meet my design." She looked around again and heads were still bent over her plans. Encouraged, she continued. "As you know, I've led the past four years, and during that time I have incorporated some of the English gardening styles into our existing garden already in subtle ways. See the sweep of the beds in the right section of the garden. Those would only need to be extended a little, providing us with a cost savings," she said.

"We aren't worried about cost, Katrina, you know that," Stan said, turning to look at Will. "The neighborhood sets aside money every year, and if we make the final five, the city kicks in a stipend."

Katrina's lips stretched thinly at Stan's comment, which had been directed to Will as if his leadership was a foregone conclusion.

"I know, I just thought it would be an additional selling point in light of last year's runner-up and their endless resources," she said, rebutting Stan's comment before turning her attention back to her audience. All were still looking at her design except Will, who was looking off into space, face still unreadable. "I've always loved the color, the beauty that this particular gardening style showcases," she continued.

"Katrina, let me just cut to the chase, as I haven't got all day. The committee had already decided on Will's Japanese garden design, which we've all seen. It's fresh, innovative, I'd even call it art. It would be a welcome addition to the other similar, homogenous styles that already exist in this city. So if this is all you have to show us, then I, for one, am ready to vote. Again," Stan said, looking up at her, annoyance on his face.

Ouch, Will thought, feeling sorry for Katrina. He'd arrived early and had taken the pulse of the room before she'd gotten there. It hadn't looked good for her, and he'd known before she began her presentation that it wouldn't matter what design she introduced, this committee would not be receptive. He felt bad watching her try to make her case, standing in her brown outfit again, hair pulled back, glasses in place. Her case had fallen on deaf ears, except for Mrs. Washington, who had defended Katrina earlier, much like a mother bear defending her cub. But she was outnumbered by the other committee members, and she voted for his designs despite her defense of Katrina.

"So this was a waste of time for you and for me. Your minds were made up long before I arrived, is that it? Is that what you're telling me?" Katrina said, folding her arms across her chest, her professional demeanor giving way quickly to anger.

"Why don't you step outside and get some air, Katrina, while we talk?" Mrs. Washington said softly. Katrina took a deep breath and looked over at Will. "I stay if he stays," she said, continuing to stare directly at him. *So much for her interest in me*, he thought.

"No problem. I don't mind," he said, standing up. Katrina turned and walked out the door, Will at her heels. She walked fast, her steps sharp, short, and purposeful. Will, smooth and easy, followed behind her. They walked out the front door and he watched while she stalked back and forth in front of the door. Will pushed his hands into his pockets, leaning against the wall next to the front door and watched her. She repeated this process for about three minutes before turning to him.

"Why are you here?" she said, eyes hard and unfriendly. Just as he'd predicted, the I-want-you-in-my-pants Katrina had disappeared. She'd stopped the stalking, at least. He removed his hands from his pockets slowly and crossed his arms at his chest.

"I was invited."

"You shouldn't be here."

"John invited me, anyway. It seems without your approval."

"That's not what I meant. You shouldn't be in this competition. What do you know about gardening?"

"I know some things. Even you might be surprised," he responded evenly. He knew she was angry and he understood why, so he was willing to give her some room to take some of that anger out on him, but just a little.

Who was he to stand there, calm and cool? He, who didn't deserve or earn this opportunity, Katrina thought. But stand there he did, continuing to watch her, arms crossed at his chest, watching her the same way he did New Year's night. It was exasperating.

"So you've designed the great backyard," she said, pronouncing *backyard* as if it was something the cat had dragged in.

"It's not that great, but yes, I designed and landscaped it," he said.

"Well, even if I could get behind the idea of a Japanese garden being acceptable, there is the small issue of scale. And not knocking your *backyard*, but backyards are what I would consider small scale," she said, sticking out her chin as if she was spoiling for a fight.

"Katrina, I know you are angry," he said.

"Why would I be angry?" she interrupted, lifting her hands. "You've been asked to lead a competition that you probably aren't even qualified for. Nothing to be angry about there. Oh, and I don't think you can win, did I tell you that?" She was desperate to elicit some other response from him besides cool, but he remained silent, annoying her even further. "And why is that, Katrina?" she said, talking to herself as he didn't seem inclined to take her bait.

She seemed to be on a roll, so he just continued to watch.

"Well, reason number one is that it's a Japanese garden. Nothing special about that, is there? Two, you've only worked on a small scale, one backyard to be exact," she said, ticking the reasons off on her hand as she talked. "Isn't that correct?" she asked.

"This is your story," he said, calmly.

"And if those reasons aren't enough, there's the issue of your availability and commitment. You would have to be willing to commit to a year, to being here working. The competition can't work around or come second to bike road trips, jeep rides to Kalamazoo, or hiking the Amazon, or whatever it is you do in your spare time."

He gave a short laugh at that.

"It's not funny. But back to that garden of yours. The final limitation, and it's a major one, I think, is that I don't see the committee getting hyped about or being impressed with a *Japanese garden*," she said, irritated that she couldn't pierce his cloak of calm. Or maybe she had; he dropped his arms and straightened, looking down into her face now.

"And why is that?" he said, all traces of patience gone.

"It's my experience from having worked with them, that's all," she said, looking up into his eyes.

"You're a sore loser, Katrina, and a bit of a snob when it comes to gardening," he said calmly. His voice had dropped in volume, though. Katrina stepped closer to him, close enough to see the hairs on his chin, a day's growth.

"Bet you don't have the nerve to say that to me again," she said, too angry now to appreciate being this close to him again. If she wasn't so mad, she would have been turning cartwheels over his body's proximity to hers, maybe even trying to test his interest in her again.

John opened the door and looked at them standing inches apart, shock and surprise registering on his face. "The committee is ready for you. You can come in now," he said, standing back to let them enter. Katrina turned abruptly and entered. Will followed, and John closed the door behind him.

Mrs. Washington sat up. Will guessed she'd been designated the spokesperson, and she was a good choice, he thought, as he watched Katrina resume her place standing in front of the committee. He remained standing off to the side.

"Katrina," Mrs. Washington said, "the committee would like to first say thank you for all of your hard work and dedication to this neighborhood, past and present. I'm not sure we've told you that as often as we should have. To most of us, you've been like a daughter. We knew your parents and watched you grow up trailing along behind them in all things gardening. After their deaths, we've watched you grow into a lovely woman and exceptional gardener. This year, we have decided to go in a different direction, and I'm sorry to say that your presentation today did not sway us from that decision." Will could tell she was trying to be gentle with Katrina, who stood there listening, her face blank.

"This was nothing personal against you or your abilities. It was a decision to give someone else a chance as well as move in another direction. We would very much like for you to seriously consider working with Will. Your talents and knowledge of the competition and the overall process would be so invaluable to him."

Katrina shook her head.

"I'm asking you, Katrina, as a personal and dear friend of your mother's, to please think about it," Mrs. Washington said.

"Thank you all for listening," Katrina said abruptly, walking over to the table and collecting her designs. She stuffed them into her bag and slung the bag over her shoulder. "Good luck, Will. I'll see myself out," she said, turning and walking toward the front door with John trailing behind her.

It was quiet in the room after her departure. "I wish that had gone better," Mrs. Washington said.

"There wasn't ever going to be an easy way to do that; we all knew it," John said.

"You all baby her too much as it is," Stan said, standing up to leave. "It should have been done last year, especially after we came so close to losing. I'll see you all at the next meeting. No need to see me out, John. Goodbye everyone. Good luck, Will. I look forward to seeing your designs."

Turning to Will, John said, "Don't let this put a damper on your selection. It really wasn't anything personal against Katrina. Most of us have known her since she was adopted. Her parents were excellent gardeners, one of the founding families in our neighborhood. I believe Katrina somehow thinks it's her responsibility to maintain their mantle, or to win the competition as proof of her place as their daughter. This isn't the first time we've wanted to change leaders, but we have been reluctant to for this very reason."

They all sat silently for a minute or two. Sandy stood up to leave and Will joined her, saying their goodbyes and walking to the door. Once outside, Sandy turned to him and said, "Really, congratulations on your selection. It's an honor, and Katrina will come around; she just needs some time."

Will walked home, passing by Katrina's. He didn't quite know what to think or to make of her now. She'd gone from major interest in him to major anger in the span of two weeks. He felt bad that she'd been hurt, and he knew hurt when he saw it. You couldn't fake the expressions she'd worn earlier. This was a very different Katrina from the night of the party or the one he'd seen working in her yard.

She'd lost her parents, adoptive ones at that. He wondered what happened to her birth parents. He was more than a little captivated by the fire he'd seen in her today as she argued with him, the same fire mixed with desire that had been on display New Year's Eve. It was so at odds with Katrina, the shy farmhand.

He didn't need this fuss, and he hoped he hadn't gotten in over his head accepting this job. Katrina was correct—his work *was* demanding. He was responsible globally for ensuring customer satisfaction with his company's product. It was the reason behind his travel, usually for weeks at a time. So he really didn't have time for any gardening competition. He could send others in his place, and sometimes did, but he liked the travel. As he had told her that night in the gardens, he placed a premium on his free time. He loved to be outdoors doing something other than work, something physical, something that pushed him beyond the daily grind, to quiet the restlessness he often felt.

He learned gardening at an early age at the feet of his grandfather in San Francisco. Nature had calmed and soothed him almost from the beginning. He entered his house, found his keys, and walked to his garage, where he hopped into his jeep and backed out. He needed a little space so he started driving with no particular destination in mind, but he realized a little later that for the last fifteen minutes he'd been driving in the direction of his sister's home. He had three sisters, and the oldest had moved here five years ago. The other two were married and lived in San Francisco with his mother and grandfather. He was the baby and the only male.

He turned on to her street, her home three houses from the corner, a fairly large home in a beautiful gated neighborhood, as befitting a part-time ophthalmologist and her doctor husband. His sister had married well, if outside her race, and had produced three kids of mixed heritage. They were beautiful children: one boy, thirteen, and two girls, ages ten and five.

He pulled up into the drive. The garage door was open, and two cars were inside; his sister and brother-in-law were both home. He had to park close to the edge of the drive to avoid the portable soccer goals and hockey sticks that lay on the ground.

He parked and walked into the garage, knocking on the door. He heard his name and turned to look over his shoulder. It was his nephew.

"Hey, Uncle Will," Dennis Jr. said. He was tall for his age; that definitely came from his father's gene pool. Will was the only height exception in their family.

"Hey, Dennis," he answered. "What's up?"

"Nothing, dude. This is my buddy, Trevor," he said, pointing to a tow-headed kid, also tall, following behind him. They both walked up to him, skateboards in their hands. Will stepped back, allowing his nephew to pass.

Dennis Jr. opened the door and entered, Trevor trailing, Will bringing up the rear.

"Mom, Uncle Will is here," Dennis screamed at the top of his lungs as he went into the kitchen and grabbed two sports drinks out of the fridge. He handed one to Trevor and said, "Come up when you get done talking to Mom. I'll beat Trevor first in Halo, and by the time you're done, I'll be ready to whoop your aspirin, too," he said, grinning wickedly at Will.

"Watch your mouth," Will said, smiling back at him as he started up the stairs, Trevor following.

"Hi, Will. This is a surprise," his sister said, entering the kitchen. "What brings you by?"

"Just in the neighborhood and thought I'd stop by."

"Okay. Want something to drink? Dennis is out back working in the yard," she said, walking to the refrigerator, grabbing a soda, and handing it over to him.

"Thanks."

"You okay?" Jennifer asked. When work at the store had demanded a lot of her mother and grandfather's time, she'd managed her younger siblings. Since she'd helped with the rearing of her sisters and brother, she could tell when they were bothered by something.

"Nothing much. I was asked to be the lead of the garden competition for our neighborhood."

"You?" Jennifer asked, surprised.

"Yes, me, and don't act so surprised. You've seen my backyard. Some of my neighbors were impressed with it, too," he said, watching her take a seat in one of the chairs next to the kitchen bar area. He stood with his back to her sink, drinking his soda. "They felt my design fit this year's theme, 'A World of Gardens'." He smiled and added, "You should be proud of your little brother."

"That's great! I am. So what's the problem?"

"It's no problem, really. I was selected to lead over a woman who is having a hard time accepting the decision. She's led for the past four years, three of which she's won. They would like her to work with me, assist me, but I don't think she's going to agree. Apparently, she knows all there is to know about gardening and this competition and she can't fathom why I was selected," he said, pausing for a second. "I knew gardening was a big deal, I just didn't know it was such a big deal."

"Where have you been? Oh, I know, off traipsing across the globe on one trip after another. But, yes, gardening in this city is a huge deal," she said.

"I get that now," he said, finishing off the last of his soda. "I was going to tell the committee no initially, but I didn't, and, well, after I agreed to accept the lead, I sat down and started to design my entry and I actually started to get excited about it. To accept an opportunity and challenge to create a new space and a chance to showcase another style of gardening to the city held a huge appeal. You know how it can be. Other cultures are displayed and appreciated, ours not so much, or not as much as I'd like. It seemed that if you weren't black or Hispanic, mostly black in this country, you were the invisible minority."

He had grown up fighting against being invisible or something more than the smart Asian. He'd had friends who were Asian, but he'd also opted to hang out with people of other races; the world seemed to be moving in that direction. But sometimes it was tough fitting into all worlds, and he wondered sometimes if it was worth the effort.

"I don't see the problem," she said.

"There's not one, really, besides me feeling a little sorry for her. She likes me, underneath all her anger." Will told his sister about Katrina at the party, consciously omitting the bedroom scene. "I think gardening is all she has, and I found out today she lost her adoptive parents. I'm not sure when, but I know that's hard."

"Interesting," Jennifer said, watching him.

"What?" he said, looking up and catching that look in her eye. "Don't start. I just feel bad for her is all," he said, putting his hands up to ward off her comments.

"What does she look like? Oh, no, let me guess," Jennifer said, smiling as if she had his number. "Let's see, she's tall, willowy, or athletic. She's not merely pretty, she must be closer to gorgeous. Oh, yes, you like them with long hair, mustn't forget that," Jennifer said, tilting her head to the side, her finger softly bumping against her forehead, striking a thinking man's pose. "Let's see, moving past the outside attributes, they must also be commitment-phobic, ambitious, attached to you, but not too dependent on you; you don't do cloying. Isn't that your usual type?"

He laughed, taken aback by her callous description of his dating preferences. "That's a little harsh, don't you think? And, no, Katrina is not my usual, but as I've told you, I'm not interested in her in that way. Let's see, she's short and pretty in a sisterly kind of way," he said, stopping to laugh at his sister's frown at his comment. *And sometimes not so sisterly,* he thought, remembering her the night of the party.

"But you're right, she is not my type, no. She favors large clothing, and I can't tell what she looks like under there. Hair stuck in a ponytail mostly, nerd glasses, contacts the night of the party. Let's see, she's African-American, and she has a temper," he said, smiling a little at the image of Katrina squaring off with him earlier that morning.

"Nope, that's not your usual type, that's for sure," Jennifer said, looking at him speculatively. "So what happens next?"

"Don't know. I guess Katrina was supposed to help with that, but since she's said no, I don't know what happens. Can you imagine someone turning down working with me?" he asked playfully.

"There's the Will I know and love. You had me worried there for a second, acting the concerned one."

He laughed. "Where's that husband of yours? You're terrible for my ego," he said, changing the subject.

"He's in the backyard. He could use some help, and I need to pick up a kid from softball practice," she said, getting up from the table to give him a kiss on his cheek. She had to tiptoe to do it, but it worked. She'd done that to him and his two other sisters forever, taking care of them while their mother and grandfather worked. She had been a good mom then, too, Will thought.

He threw his soda can in the recycle bin and headed out the back door in search of his brother-in-law, Dennis Sr. His favorite part of his sister's home was their backyard. It was designed with children in mind. The deck ran the full length of the back of their home. On the deck were tables, the biggest one designed to seat about twelve. He'd attended many birthday parties and other holiday celebrations out here. There were two couches with end tables and ottoman, a comfy living space outside, shaded by a large canopy extending from the roof of the house. Two steps below the deck stood the pool, the old-fashioned rectangular kind, volleyball net across the middle of it. The rest of the yard consisted of flower beds, with a playscape area for the kids. Oh, to be a child of parents with money.

Dennis was digging up one of the flower beds. Will started over toward him.

"What are you working on now?" he asked.

Dennis turned at the sound of his voice. "Your sister wants to plant something here. I just provide the brawn and she provides the brains," he said, stopping and watching Will as he walked over to him. "Good to see you. Did you see your sister?"

"Yes, she went to pick up Monica from softball practice," Will said, looking around at the tools spread out before him on the ground. "Let me help," he said, picking up a shovel.

"I'm never, ever going to turn down help," Dennis replied.

Will and Dennis talked and worked, more like Dennis listening while Will talked about the contest and

RUTHIE ROBINSON

Katrina, about being maybe just a little, more than a little, interested in her. He liked her body for sure, and had been involved in a little internal struggle over wanting to sleep with her. His body was still complaining about the loss. He talked about the temper she'd shown earlier, making her even more interesting, and that he felt bad for her. He'd lost his dad when was very young, too.

They cleaned out the two main beds per Jennifer's request, and, since Will was here and in a working mood, Dennis used him. After the beds were done, he and Will added compost to the remaining ones. Dennis inwardly thanked this Katrina person who'd given Will this burst of energy; they'd completed his list of 'honey-dos'. Jennifer would be pleased. Dennis preferred her pleased.

It was starting to get dark when Dennis and Will called it quits. Will helped gather up the tools and put them back in the garage.

"Come over anytime; there is always something here that needs doing," Jennifer said, walking out to meet them. Will smiled.

"Dinner's ready. You're welcome to stay," Jennifer said.

"No, I'd better get home, but thanks for the offer," he said. "Tell your son I'll kill him in the video games the next time I stop by."

"Thanks for the help," Dennis said again, walking over to stand next to his wife, putting his arm around her waist.

"Sure, no problem." Will walked toward his jeep, hopped in, and pulled out, waving a final time at his sister and brother-in-law, pushing Katrina and the earlier conflict to the back of his mind. Hopefully, it would work itself out.

After Katrina left the meeting, she spent the day holed up in her home, licking her wounds, feeling sorry for herself. She replayed her argument with Will; well, *she'd* argued. He, to his credit, hadn't taken her bait. She felt a twinge of guilt. It wasn't his fault he was selected. He must think her a loony tune. One minute she was practically begging him for sex and the next she was angry over a gardening competition, of all things.

Seems Sandy and Mrs. Washington had known he'd been selected. That's what those glances between them were about the other day when she showed them her designs. Shouldn't they have told her? She acknowledged to herself that it probably wouldn't have made a bit of difference, anyway; she was hell-bent on being the lead. Always.

Their rejection still hurt. There was no way she'd work with Will. He could figure it out for himself, just as she had. One part of her thought that, anyway; the other part was crying over not being able to spend time around him. All that potential time, poured down the drain. It was still pleading its case for her to work with him; maybe her wish to touch his body again would come true. *Please, please, please let it come true.*

Let the precious committee help him if he needed it. She couldn't believe he called her a gardening snob. Still, she felt a little twinge of guilt that perhaps not helping him wasn't the right course of action, that she should just get over herself and help, that somehow her parents would have been disappointed in her today. Since when did this competition start being about her, anyway? She ignored that line of thought, choosing to feel sorry for herself instead.

She'd worked hard for this neighborhood, and it was apparently not enough. Was she ever enough? Could she ever have life work for her benefit, and longer than the eleven years she'd been lucky to have her parents before their death? She'd never met her birth parents; she had been an orphan for as far back as she could remember.

The bright spot in her life had started with her adoption at age ten. She stood up from her couch, tired of her thoughts, kicked off her flip-flops, removed her hair from its pony tail, and pulled her shirt over her head, leaving her in a sports bra and sweat bottoms. She walked over to the counter and poured herself a glass of water, taking it with her to look out the windows over her garden, which was illuminated by solar-powered lighting.

She loved working in her garden and the neighborhood gardens; well, any garden for that matter. It was one of her fondest memories of time spent with her adoptive parents. They'd plunged her knee-deep in dirt as soon as she came to live with them. She, who had given up hope of having a mother or father, took to dirt like a duck to water.

Her parents were an older couple, in their early fifties, when they'd seen Katrina on a TV show—some station asking people to adopt foster kids. Because they'd hadn't had any of their own, they'd picked her, ten-year-old, rag-tag Katrina of the big nerdy glasses, thick unruly hair, and chip the size of Texas on her shoulder, and they tried to make up for her years without parents.

They taught her everything they knew about gardening, and, like a flower, her heart had opened and blossomed. At their death, an accident that she didn't like to think about, she'd taken the proceeds left to her from their life insurance, retirement, and savings and used a large portion of it as a down payment on her home in their old neighborhood. She'd sold the original home, couldn't bear living in it without them; it was too big, anyway. She had a smaller home built for her. The rest of the money she'd put away, learning to live on just her salary. She knew the value of money, having gone without it most of her life.

She missed her parents and the unconditional love they'd shown her, loved that they'd been able to see the scared, lonely little girl underneath her barbed walls and thorny defenses. She loved her parents tremendously and missed them fiercely, and learned early that life was tenuous and filled with risk. One had to be careful.

CHAPTER 4

Monday morning at work, Katrina washed her hands and went in search of her favorite mug, the one she regularly used to make tea. She and Amber were taking a morning break. Katrina added hot water from the dispenser and a tea bag, orange spice. She purchased a package monthly and hid them in the back of the cabinet behind the paper towels. She added two packets of sweeteners and joined Amber at the table.

"So what's the latest on your neighborhood's competition? Looking to win again?" she asked. Katrina brought her up to date on the committee's selection of Will.

"What are you going to do?" Amber asked.

"I don't know."

"I tell you what I'd do if I had half your talent. I'd quit this job, one that you only endure, and start my own landscaping business. How many times have I told you that you should turn your passion for gardening into a business? I don't know anyone who loves it as much as you do."

"Don't start with that again," she said, giving Amber the evil eye. "Did you know that 95 percent of small businesses fail within the first five years? People mistake a hobby for a business. Just because you love to cook doesn't make you a restaurant owner," she said.

"Oh, Katrina, you make my head hurt sometimes," Amber said, putting her fingers against her temples and rubbing them. "I know you love what you do with flowers and gardening. I know you do. And you already have an in with your godfathers; they would help you. I bet they would provide funding if you were to ask."

"They have done enough for me."

"Fine, but you should give some serious thought to doing your own thing. And speaking of doing your own thing, Claudia and I are having some folks over. You remember I told you that we'd hooked up with an entrepreneurship group we found through the chamber of commerce? Every member has to host a party, and it's our turn this month. You have to come."

"Why do I have to come?" Katrina asked.

"Just come, see if you're interested. You may catch a good vibe and decide to quit this job the next day and start your own business."

Katrina blew out a breath. "I doubt that. This isn't you and Claudia's attempt to set me up again, is it?" she said, squinting at Amber, not putting anything past them.

"Will you come?" Amber said, smiling but not answering the question, a detail not lost on Katrina.

"When is it?"

"A week from Sunday, 7 p.m., and once you commit you can't back out, either. I know you."

"Okay, I'll come, but you had better not have an ulterior motive."

"Who, me?" Amber said, smiling. "I'd better get back to my desk. I'm behind schedule."

Katrina raised her eyebrows.

"I know, right. I'm never behind. But don't worry, it won't be for long," she said, walking out the door.

What Katrina hadn't shared with Amber was that she had given serious thought to starting her own business, doing her own thing, had even considered switching her major to agricultural economics, especially after she'd started in the master gardener's training program. It was so much fun, didn't seem like work, really. Practicality won out; she'd decided to stick with her business degree instead, her parents' recommendation. After their deaths, she'd felt like she should honor their wishes. They'd taken a big risk on her.

Amber was into baking—pies, cakes, any type of dessert. And she was also big into entrepreneurship; hence her desire to push Katrina. She'd launched her own website a few months ago and had successfully begun taking orders. She joined this network of other small-business owners in the city, and was always after Katrina to make her hobby work for her. But Amber had financial support from Claudia, her Mommy Warbucks. Katrina just had Katrina.

And anyway, what was wrong with having a job you could tolerate, okay, endure, and a hobby that you loved?

"What a mess," she thought, looking inside the pantry at Charles and Colburn's home. She was here to cook dinner for them. She stopped by the grocery after work, picking up a few things. She'd known not to expect much from their refrigerator. With Charles at least, there was an outside chance that he might have cooked something healthy. Not so with Colburn; he could eat off of that little truck that came around selling tacos every day and not miss a beat.

"What are you cooking?" Colburn asked, peering over her shoulder at the chicken breasts that lay on the counter. "You're going to fry those up, Katrina girl?" he asked.

"No, I'm putting them on the grill."

"Grill, huh?" he said, giving her a noncommittal response. "I can't remember the last time I had some good old-fashioned fried chicken," he said, going for the pitiful look.

Katrina rolled her eyes and opened the refrigerator door, pointing to the bucket of KFC on the top shelf. "It must have been this week. Not so long ago, it appears," she said, closing the door.

Colburn smiled. "Can't get anything past you, Katrina girl," he said, walking away.

"You really need to watch your diet, Colburn. Did you know that a heart attack occurs about every twenty seconds with a heart attack death about every minute?"

"Don't start. I've got one more job to do. How long before dinner?" he asked.

"Give me thirty," she said.

She was in the process of slicing vegetables when Charles walked in. "Thanks for dinner," he said, taking a seat at the table to watch her, stretching out his long legs.

"Long day?" she asked.

"Not too bad," Charles said, stretching his arms over his head. "Pass me a cold one, Kat, would you?"

She grabbed a beer from the refrigerator, searched around in a drawer for the bottle opener, removed the cap and handed it to him.

"Thank you," he said taking a long swallow. "So you couldn't convince the committee this year."

"You heard that, huh?" she said.

"Yep, gardening news is big news around here. The unseating of a legend is what it's being called. You had to know it would happen at some point."

"I know," she said, continuing to slice vegetables.

"So are you going to help him?"

"Don't think so," she responded, turning on the grill. It was quiet while she seasoned the chicken and vegetables.

"Come on, Kat. I thought you said he was attractive. There's something in that," he said, trying for humor, to make her smile at least. He knew what losing had meant to her.

"He's not interested in my type, so what would be the point?"

"I don't need to remind you how difficult it was to lead without prior knowledge. You do remember your first year?" he asked, looking at her and putting on his cloak of the parent about to deliver a lecture to a recalcitrant child. "And remember, you had us to help, too, and it was still extremely difficult for you." She didn't respond. "It wasn't his fault he was selected," he added.

She sighed. "I know, C, I know what you're saying is right, and maybe I will, but give me a little time. I know, I know, I hear you coming through loud and clear. Okay?" she said, looking at him. He gave a small shake of his head.

"So how is work, your customers still making you crazy?" he asked, changing the subject. She was grateful. Her loss still smarted. She smiled and brought him up to date on some of the more interesting customers she'd dealt with this week. Colburn joined them ten minutes later and they ate dinner together in their regular way, talking and harassing each other, followed by coffee to go along with the dessert Katrina had purchased.

She left later, leaving them to their cigars on the front porch, having enjoyed the evening with them. She always did. They loved her and she took comfort in that knowledge. She didn't even want to consider them not being in her life. They were all the family she had.

Will walked out of his home mid-morning, headed to the gardens on a beautiful Saturday to look around. This would be his first trip there. He probably should have taken a tour before agreeing to lead the competition, but he'd been sure he would be up to the task. Very few things got in his way for long. After giving his consent to lead he'd started to pay attention to the gardens in the city, particularly this one.

There always seemed to be people here at all the times of the day, especially children. He could vaguely recall his

RUTHIE ROBINSON

real estate saleswoman mentioning a playscape and park area for the neighborhood children, but kids had been the furthest thing from his mind at the time he'd been in the market for a home.

He looked up ahead as he turned the corner and spotted his neighbor. Of course, she was dressed in sweatpants, flannel shirt flapping in the breeze behind her. But it was her pony tail sticking out of the back of her cap that had given her away. He hadn't had a chance to talk to her since the committee meeting last weekend.

"Katrina," he called out. She kept walking, but he bet she heard him. He watched as her steps picked up a little in speed. "Katrina," he called again. She still didn't turn around. Okay, she was going to be difficult, he thought, jogging lightly to catch up to her.

Katrina had stepped off the sidewalk, pretending to look over some of the flowers that were blooming on the fence in front of the entrance to the garden, hoping Will would run past her. Of course he didn't. He stopped, coming over to stand by her side.

"I guess you didn't hear me calling your name?" he said, not even breathing hard, the dirty dog. Did nothing come hard for him?

"Guess not," she said, turning to face him, her eyes coolly regarding him now.

"Heading to the gardens?" he asked, and looked her over as she shrugged.

"Yep," she said.

"Mind if I walk the rest of the way with you?"

93

"What, the last *twenty feet*?" she asked, looking toward the entrance. "I don't care," she said, shrugging.

"So, how have you been? I haven't seen you around lately."

"Been busy."

"Busy at work?" he asked. He didn't know where or if she worked. He'd assumed so.

"Yep."

"Not going to be helpful, are you? You could give me something other than those one- or two-word answers," he said, smiling, hoping that would help.

"I could."

"Look, Katrina, I'm sorry for the way things turned out. It was not my intention to usurp your place as leader of the competition. They came to me, and if it's any consolation, I think the committee was going to select someone new this year anyway, even if it hadn't been me," he said. Ignoring her grunt of a response, he plowed ahead. "If you're not busy, this is my first trip here. You could show me around, give me the tour. After all, you are at the top of the gardening food chain, or at least that's what I've been told," he said, trotting out his sexiest smile.

"Your first trip here, huh?" she responded, disdain clear in her voice.

"Yes, oh leader of the gardening world, my first trip here, but don't hold it against me. Give me a tour. You know, help me, give me the experienced gardening professional's perspective," he said, bending at the waist, teasing her.

"Why would I do that?" she said, walking away.

"Because you want what's best for the neighborhood, even if the committee has made a mistake in choosing me," he said, picking up his pace and turning to face her, walking backwards so he could see her face. "Come on, Katrina, give me a tour . . . please?" he cajoled, smiling playfully, his eyes twinkling. Dangerous, this one was, she thought as she flashed back to them on her bed, with him pushing into her, making her all gooey inside.

Sensing her resistance fading, he intensified his pleas. "Come on, Katrina, you used to like me, remember? Used to think I was pretty, tasted good, too. Hell, I'll even wear my cycling gear if that will help," he said, repeating her words to him the night of the party, turning on his full arsenal of charm, puzzled that it mattered to him.

"So it's back to bringing that up again," she said.

"I learned a lot about you."

"Okay. Fine. One tour. Come on," she said, walking away.

He followed, pleased with the outcome, with having her here. *Slow down, dude*, he said to himself, turning his attention to the beautifully designed wrought-iron gate and fence that ran in both directions away from the large arched entrance to the gardens.

"We've just entered the main gate to the overall garden," she said, stopping and letting Will look around. "The land for the gardens was set aside by the original developers when they purchased the land from the city for subdivision development."

They took a few steps down the main path that separated the garden into two large halves. The right half, the more developed side, contained large flower beds filled with native plants, shrubs, flowers, and trees, and a white medium-sized pavilion was set in the middle of a large expanse of grass.

"For weddings," she said, answering his unasked question. "Shining Creek's gardens sit on about five and a half acres, one of the largest gardens in the city. One acre holds the flower portion, another two contain the vegetable section, and the remainder is for our new composting business, which is small scale for now. We are trying both the old-school system and vermin-composting. So far, we've managed to produce enough to supply the neighborhood and local businesses only. But we're hoping to grow that area of the gardens. What you see now is the flower section, to your right and left. This is the part you'll be redesigning."

"With your help, maybe?" he said.

She made a face. "Don't push your luck. I only agreed to give you a tour. The vegetable section sits in the back behind the flowers, behind our composting area and greenhouses. You can't see it from here, but there's a fence separating the flower section from the vegetables," she said, pointing to an area off in the distance. The area she pointed to was covered in vines—Carolina jasmine mixed in with English ivy. Will recognized the plants.

He turned to look over the other half of the garden, the more unused section. It was similar in style to the right half and not completely undeveloped; the play area was there. The left side had the highest point of the garden and was a perfect spot for the waterfall feature Will wanted to include in his design. It could start here, the beginning of a stream that would wind itself throughout the garden.

Toward the back, near the children's play area, surrounded by several enormous old oak trees, was an area filled with swings, a sand pit, and a few rocking horses. Here the flower beds weren't as deep, allowing space for the many chairs and loungers placed beneath the trees or inserted between medium-sized shrubberies. People were sitting and reading on benches and loungers; a mom with a child appeared to be sleeping in a very large hammock under one of the trees. Very nice, Will thought.

"I like this area; did you design it?" he asked.

"Yes. It was last year's winner, the first year we've ever had anyone nipping at our heels. This new neighborhood is gunning for us; lots of money behind them, too. Anyway, last year's theme was Family Living Outside."

"It's very thoughtful," he said.

"Thanks," she responded, smiling a little. Looking over the garden, Will was quiet. He always liked a challenge, and making changes to this one would be a big one, as well as a whole busload of hard work. They reached the end of the flower section and walked through an opening.

"About two years ago we started a rainwater collection and irrigation system. Are you familiar with those?" she asked, pointing to two large rain barrels placed side by side.

"Yes. Expensive," he noted.

"Donated," she explained. "In this part of Texas, it's feast or famine with the rain. These bad boys hold up to about 3,500 gallons and fill up five to six times a year," she added. She started walking again.

"Behind them are our greenhouses. Most of our perennials, annuals, and vegetables come from seedlings. We hope to start producing our own Shining Creek salad mix. Long way off, though," she said, walking over to the greenhouses and pointing in. "This is the short tour, you'll have to roam around on your own," she said, pointing to the other side. "That's our worm casting factory, or what we hope will grow into one. And last in this area is our old-school composting part," she said, stopping at huge piles of compost, piles of sand, and another pile of what looked like evergreen mulch.

"So on to the vegetable section," he said.

"Sure," she said. Walking back through the composting section, they entered the gate leading to the vegetable area. Totally different from the flower section, here about fifteen rows of plants stood in raised beds. Four or five people were working here bent over plants, some further back digging in the dirt, some with wheelbarrows, others picking vegetables from the plants. Will's eyes traveled over all of it, stopping at what must be the garden's farmers market over in the corner, covered by a small tent to provide shade. Katrina walked toward it, talking still.

"Most of your neighbors volunteer to work in either one of the two gardens. There is always plenty of work to do. A committee of volunteers work alongside a master gardener who oversees the planting and work schedules."

"You're a master gardener, the youngest in the state, right?" Will asked.

"Yes," she answered, impressed and surprised that he'd known. "I am one, along with John and Mrs. Washington."

"I do my homework."

"So I see. Anyway, as a neighbor, whether you worked in the Shining Creek garden or not, the vegetables are available to you, usually free or at a very minimum charge, just enough to cover seed cost. On the weekend, we, like most of the other neighborhoods in the city, run a small farmers market for people who live in other parts of the city and are looking for a specific item. Our gardens also provide fresh vegetables to some of the local restaurants.

"This is where I was headed before you stopped me. I'm scheduled to work here this morning," she said, stopping at a table with vegetables in round bins ready for purchase.

"Hey, Paige," she said to the bored-looking teenager behind the table.

"Hey, Katrina, can I go now?" she asked, her eyes on Will. She suddenly didn't seem so bored anymore.

"Will, this is Paige. Paige, Will," Katrina said.

"Hello," he said, eliciting a smile and a blush from the teenager.

"I'm ready to take over if you need to go," Katrina said.

STEADY

"Sure, see you next time," she said, taking a final peek at Will before leaving.

"So, Katrina, would we, if you were to agree to work with me, that is, be the only people working on the transformation?" he asked. "This is a whole lot of garden for two people to change."

"No, the whole neighborhood joins in. Lower taxes will bring out the volunteer in anyone, and of course you'll always have the diehards who love to garden," she said, moving the small tubs filled with onions, turnips, squash, and kale around the table. Flats of winter flowers sat along the ground—snapdragons, ornamental kale, and pansies.

"Like you?"

"Yes, like me. We usually have more than enough people to help; some even look forward to helping every year. Most of the major physical work is done from September through February. The city's rule is that work cannot commence before that time; only planning and ordering plants and equipment in preparation for the larger renovations that usually occur during the time-frame I just mentioned. We will have volunteers working both Saturdays and Sundays to complete the major work. Plus we use the students from the local high school," she said, pointing to a clump of high schoolers. Will noticed that more goofing off than work seemed to be going on.

"Buckling down in those months means less work in the spring. The volunteers provide the muscle; you provide the design and leadership."

"So do you think you might be willing to work with me?" he said, smiling again.

She shrugged, captivated by his smile, by him, all over again. What a beautiful smile; his eyes were bright, his hair standing up on end, taking her back to the night. Her body responded accordingly.

"So that's not a no, is it?" he asked, smiling again, noting the change in her, recognizing desire when he saw it.

Shrugging, she said, "It's a maybe." She smiled back at him, her anger long gone. He was hard to resist.

He dropped his smile, serious now, a little intense even. "Seriously, give it some thought. I've heard nothing but good things about your abilities, and, as confident as I am in mine, it would be nice to have your help, especially since it will be the first time for me."

"Thank you. And I'll think about it," she said, pausing and looking down at her hand. "I know it wasn't your fault that I wasn't selected. I know that," she added, now looking down at her feet. She took a deep breath, her eyes returning to his. "And I owe you an apology for my behavior toward you the other day, for trying to pick a fight with you during the meeting. I was angry; I don't usually get that angry."

"I understand, and your apology is not necessary. Okay then, I'll let you get to work. Thanks for the tour," he said, aware now of the few customers standing in front of Katrina's table patiently waiting for assistance. He had been solely focused on her.

"See you later," he said.

She just smiled, turning her attention to her customers.

Going back the way he had entered, Will looked back over the vegetable section a final time. His eyes moved back to her, watching her as she stood smiling, talking to another woman.

She'd done a great job creating the family living space, and even though it wasn't his style, he could appreciate the hard work, creative ability, and dedication that had gone into it.

Katrina walked home from the gardens, having spent the day there. She had been restless and antsy after giving Will a tour that morning. It had been his first time at the garden, and she shook her head at that again, the anger, the utter unfairness of it all still fresh. She'd worked at the small market until around three before heading to the back of the gardens and plunging headlong into cleaning out the equipment shed, rationalizing that it needed to be done. Someone needed to assess the condition of the equipment in light of the upcoming competition, so it was a good use of her excess energy. The equipment needed to be in working order before the competition got underway. She worked in the shed until well after dark, finally checking her watch and deciding it was time to go. She walked through the gardens, heading home, her thoughts returning to the subject of Will.

So was she going to help him? Hell, yes, if it meant she would get to be up close and personal with him again. It seemed that, along with his other qualities, he was actually a nice guy. So much for holding out. He was one fine man, and here she was cleaning out a shed, wanting to make sure things were as they should be. Not just any fine man. For some reason, it was just Will that *affected* her so, and she didn't even know him that well. What if she really got to know him? What then? She'd wanted to be up close to him ever since he'd moved in, and he was truly something up close and personal. She remembered him covering her on her bed and later standing in front of her while they argued outside John's home.

She reached to the top of his chest, and she'd taken in the new growth on his chin, eyes hooded, looking down at her through those jet-black lashes. He'd been sexy to the nth degree. And after being with him today, it seemed her anger at losing the competition was apparently no match for her body's desire to be near him. Was there anything sexier than a man who was comfortable with himself, smart and in control? Why pass up an opportunity like this one?

This was a job for Lola, her best girlfriend and neighbor. Lola and her husband, Oscar, had moved in a month after Katrina had built her home, a time when she was still suffering the immediate pain of her parents' accident. Lola and the godfathers had helped see her through it. She walked home, passing by Will's house, then the Sheppards', before reaching Lola's. Lola had been away the last few weeks, helping her younger sister with the birth of her baby, leaving Katrina to figure things out for herself; that was never a good idea.

She and Lola had been friends from the first day they'd met. Lola and Oscar had purchased the lot and built themselves a home next to hers. It was preordained, Lola liked to say. Two sisters torn apart at birth, at long last reunited. Lola and Oscar had one child, three-year-old Sydney.

Lola was as different from Katrina as one could be. Lola was tall to Katrina's short five-foot frame, white to Katrina's dark-chocolate skin, round to Katrina's slim build, plus Lola had that don't-mess-with-me-or-I'll-kick-your-ass attitude while Katrina tended to go along to get along—all bark, small amount of bite. She reached Lola's front door and knocked. Lola opened the door about a minute later.

"Katrina, hey girl, what's up? I was just reading a story to Sydney. Come on back," she said, stepping away from the door to let her in and then closing it. She reached around and gave Katrina a hug. "I've missed you," she said.

"Me, too," Katrina said, holding on a little longer. Lola pulled back, searching her face.

"Wait, let me put Sydney to bed, and you can bring me up to date," Lola said. Lola led the way down the hall to her daughter's room. Katrina followed, entering a room that was a profusion of pink.

"Hey, Auntie Katrina," came a voice from the bed, surrounded by pink netting, where Sydney lay waiting for the completion of her story.

"Hey, sweetie."

"My mom's reading me a story," she said. Lola was as close as Katrina would get to a sister, so Syd was as close as she had gotten to a niece.

"I'll just be a second," Lola said as Katrina took a seat on the end of Syd's bed. She started reading and Katrina could tell from the million times she'd read it before that it was almost over. She joined in. She knew this book by heart, as she'd read it when she'd babysat for Lola and Oscar. It was one of her favorites, *Green Eggs and Ham* by Dr. Seuss. She picked up the story's final refrain, adding her voice to Lola's and Syd's. "*Say, I will eat them ANY-WHERE! I Do so like green eggs and ham, Thank you! Thank you! Sam-I-Am.*" They finished in unison, shouting out the last lines, all laughing together at the end.

Katrina bent to kiss Sydney goodnight and went in to the hall, sliding down the wall to sit on the floor, waiting for Lola to finish. About five minutes later Lola joined her, and they both now sat on the floor, their backs resting against the wall.

"What's up, girlfriend?" she asked, looking over at Katrina.

"You won't believe what I've been through," Katrina said. "But first, how is your sister?"

"Fine. New mothers are something else. A new baby girl, eight pounds, twenty-one inches long, and you'd would think she was the only woman who has ever given birth to a child. It was good to get away, though, see my family. My parents, of course, loved up on Syd, and Oscar missed me something *fierce*, and that's always a good thing," she said, smiling.

"I missed you, too," Katrina said. Lola reached over and grabbed her hand.

"So tell me what's going on. What's this I hear about you not leading the competition this year? Is that correct?" she asked, concern on her face.

"Yes, you've heard right. It seems our neighbor, Will, in addition to building green, has designed a beautiful Japanese garden in his backyard," she said, bringing Lola up to date—from the night where she had placed herself out there to her most recent meeting with Will at the gardens this morning.

"Girl, that'll teach me to leave you alone," Lola said, squeezing Katrina's hand, knowing how much the competition meant to her, and how much Will did, too.

"So are you going to help him? I know you want to. You've talked about that man since he moved in. Of course, you're going to work with him," she said, looking over at Katrina. "And after the party, he's probably been up at night trying to figure out how to get next to you. This is maybe your chance to take your crush to the next level. This is perfect, better than you could have wished for. See? Lemonade from lemons," she said. "May I suggest that you lose your usual clothing preferences, Katrina, now more than ever."

"Did you know that men on average would like to have eighteen sex partners, and women are happy with about four or five in a lifetime?" Katrina said, looking at Lola. "And, nope, I am what I am, no changing."

"But you could be so much more," Lola said.

"I'm good. I'm not his type, anyway. Don't fool yourself, Lola girl, as much as I'm excited about the prospect of being around him, I'm not delusional. I'm nowhere near the type of woman he prefers. I've seen his revolving door of arm candy, remember? He turned me down too, don't forget that. I might have been born at night, but not last night," she added, smiling.

Lola sighed, knowing this path was useless with Katrina. She knew, in her own way, Katrina was testing, always testing, to make sure people wanted her for her, something from her pre-adoption days; it was innate and unshakable. "So back to my original question. Are you going to work with him?" Lola asked.

"Hell, yes!" Katrina said, making Lola laugh. "But I'm not going to divulge that just yet. Let's make him and that committee sweat a little longer," she added, joining in with Lola's laughter.

CHAPTER 5

February

Katrina stood next to her neighbor's front porch looking at the not-so-small Mountain Laurel tree that she needed to replant per the instructions of said neighbor, Ms. Stone, who was also an old friend of her mother's. Her mother, Ms. Stone, and Mrs. Washington had been supreme gardening buddies; Katrina secretly called them 'the three amigos'. They'd met most Friday evenings during her childhood for a little wine and gardening. Although it seemed more like wine and gossip to Katrina, but she was 'but a child,' as Ms. Stone so often reminded her, even now at the ripe old age of twenty-five.

The movement of the tree was part of a much larger plan to re-landscape Ms. Stone's front yard. She had hired some local workers to build her a flower bed made of some specially colored brick from this shop that charged her way too much. She and Katrina were currently re-designing the flower bed, or more like Katrina was re-designing it. The plans were spread out on Ms. Stone's kitchen table. Katrina had brought them over earlier for her review, which meant more mark-ups and redos for Katrina. Since the death of her mother, Ms. Stone required Katrina's attendance every so often, her method of checking to make sure she was okay and on the right path.

Praise God from whom all blessings flow, Katrina thought. The ducks were finally getting the old heave-ho. Yes! Ms. Stone was going to get rid of those two clay ducks that stood near her front flower bed. She had dressed them religiously, coordinating their outfits with the holiday season. It was odd seeing ducks in small Santa suits. Katrina stood now divesting them of the yellow rain slickers they'd worn in deference to the showers that had lingered off and on in the city for two weeks. The showers had finally moved out, leaving behind clear and sunny skies.

Ms. Stone stood at her shoulder, monitoring everything, making sure her babies weren't hurt—translated for Katrina, that meant scratched, chipped, or, heaven help her hide, broken.

"Have you given any thought to starting your own business, dear? You're exceptional at gardening. You should charge for your services," she said to Katrina as she peered over her shoulder. "Oh, not me, of course. I'm a senior citizen, and entitled to all kinds of discounts," she added, holding out her hand for Katrina to pass the newly stripped duck to her. "The days of women not being able to start their own companies are long past."

"I know, and I've given that idea serious thought. I worry, though. I've been told that the landscaping businesses can be so volatile. Statistics show that it fluctuates with changes in the economy, which hasn't been that good of late."

Ms. Stone looked at her, concern mixed with steel in her eyes. "Nothing beats a failure but a try, Katrina," she said. "You're no spring chicken; you can't afford to wait too long to start."

Katrina just shook her head at that, making a face. She wasn't that old. Did she look old? "I know, and I promise to give it some thought." Apparently satisfied, Ms. Stone moved on to a new topic.

"I've heard that the new kid, you know, the one that just built that odd house down the street from you, is heading up the competition this year. Is that true, dear?" she asked.

"Yes, it is," Katrina responded.

"Is he any good? I don't want the taxes in our neighborhood to increase. My taxes are fixed, of course, I'm a senior citizen, but we must be mindful of others who have gotten used to the lower rate."

"I'm sure the committee wouldn't have chosen him if he wasn't good. I know for a fact that the committee members have seen his work. They were impressed with what they saw, although I haven't seen it myself," she said, passing the other duck over to Ms. Stone.

"Does he have any idea of the amount of work that goes into the competition?" she asked.

"Don't know. I sure hope so."

"You know, these young people think they know everything nowadays. They don't think experience is necessary anymore to do anything," she added, like she and Katrina were the same age. Mrs. Stone was pushing her early seventies.

"I know," she said, going along with the conversation, having found it was easier that way. She used to argue, and tried talking back one time, when she'd been younger. That hadn't gone well. At all. She hadn't tried that again. Live and let live was her motto for today. She looked around the yard, taking in what was left to do before she could finish and head over to the godfathers. She had promised them dinner.

Later that evening, after she got back from the godfathers', she dropped her purse and keys onto her kitchen counter and went out to her deck, taking a seat at her favorite spot on the top step, relaxing. Her mind went back to something Mrs. Stone had said earlier. She still hadn't seen Will's backyard. Between her behavior at the party and her losing the competition to him, she couldn't bring herself to go over and ask him for a tour. There was more to that sore-loser comment than she cared to admit. She'd gone out her front door twice with the intention of walking over to his home and knocking. "Show me the great backyard, Will," she practiced saying, but she never made it past her yard.

You could go look now; he's not home. Where had that thought come from? She knew he wasn't home, or at least his home was dark when she'd driven by earlier. He usually worked late on the weekdays, and who knew where he was on the weekends. Knowing him, he was probably off somewhere playing with one of his girls, cycling, or maybe both. She'd seen them riding with him sometimes.

See, Katrina, all that monitoring of him is paying benefits, and not so stalker-like after all, she told herself. *You could go check again, make sure he hasn't returned, and then go take a look at his yard, see for yourself.* Maybe she should, just to see for herself without him around to make her nervous. The more she thought about it, the better the idea seemed.

She really did need to find out what she was working with, right? After all, her name and reputation would be attached to this project. She should check him out before she officially committed. It was the smart thing to do. She stood up, her feet taking her into the backyard, around and out the side gate and over to Lola's front door. She looked over at Will's place again; it was still dark. She hoped that meant it was the dark associated with him not being home, not the dark associated with sleep. He couldn't be asleep; it was too early for Will the adventurer. She knocked on Lola's door and stood there until it opened.

"Hey, Oscar, is Lola home?" she asked, peering over his shoulder.

"Hey, Katrina," he said, giving her a smile. "Lola!" he hollered.

"What?" Lola said, walking toward the door. Oscar stepped aside so Lola could see Katrina. He then left them alone.

"Hey, Katrina, what's up?" Lola asked as Katrina opened the door and walked in.

"Nothing much," she said, grabbing Lola's hand and walking past her, dragging Lola along behind her. She walked them straight to Lola's back door and out, continuing to pull Lola behind her. Once outside, Katrina turned to face her.

"I was thinking that this would be the perfect time to tour Will's backyard; you know, to take a look around. I just checked his home and he's not there."

"So, out of the blue, you've decided that now would be a great time to sneak into his backyard," she said, shaking her head in wonder. "Girl, you're crazy. It's those fertilizer fumes. I've told you time and time again to lay off them, but do you listen?" She placed her hand on Katrina's forehead. "You don't feel warm," she said. Katrina swatted her hand away.

"I'm not kidding. I need to see his backyard. He has agreed to lead the competition, and I'm going to agree to work with him. It's imperative that I see what his abilities are, and what better way than by getting a good look for myself, especially when he's not around," she said, walking toward Lola's back fence.

"So now it's *imperative*," Lola said.

"You don't have to come; I just need you to play lookout," Katrina said.

"Look, Katrina, this is trespassing; you *are* aware of that little fact?"

"How is this trespassing, Lola? I am in your yard all the time, and some of the other neighbors' yards all the time. Most times, I don't have their permission. They know me."

"Whatever you need to tell yourself to sleep at night," Lola said, hands going to her hips.

"Hey, he is my neighbor, right? He and I will be working together, and I bet he would understand why I would need to check his yard out. He would consider it doing my homework, research. He's a big-time businessman; he would understand that logic, right?"

"You could ask him, Katrina; I'm sure he wouldn't mind."

"Why wait? Who knows when he'll be home, anyway. And what's that expression you always use? Oh, I know, there is no time like the present."

Lola didn't immediately answer, which was a sign that she was giving in.

"Come on, Lola, you don't have to come in; just tell me when he gets home. Use your cell, send me a text, and I'll leave."

"Katrina, if it isn't trespassing, then why do you need a lookout?"

"He works so hard; I wouldn't want to interrupt his evening, give him a scare, so I just want to be gone by the time he gets back."

"You are something else. I've told you that more than once, but you're my girl. So hurry your ass up," she said, walking back to the front of her home.

"Don't forget to text me. One word, 'him', and I'll leave. I promise. Thank you, oh, great one, Super BFF, always got my back, my one and only," Katrina said, reciting a steady stream of praises to Lola's back.

"Shut up," Lola said. Katrina giggled. She knew she could count on Lola. She walked through the back gate and out into the greenbelt. It was quiet. It was always quiet except for the occasional coyotes crying or an owl hooting and crickets chirping. The homes on this side of the street backed up to a greenbelt. No homes were built across from her or her neighbors' backyards—protection for St. Paul the Salamander and his habitat, which was in the creek that ran behind their homes. So no building permitted around him.

Most of her neighbors had some kind of lighting to illuminate their yards after dark, but it wasn't completely dark yet and wouldn't be for twenty to thirty minutes. She passed by the Sheppards' home next to Lola's before coming to a stop in front of Will's back fence. Of course, his gate wasn't the usual run-of-the-mill fence; it stood about ten feet high, and was made with a nice wood design. You could count on him to be different, she thought, checking the gate's latch; it opened, and she pushed the gate open a little and stepped inside, looking around. "Wow," she whispered under her breath. "This is more than just a garden; this is art." She wondered if that made him an artist. God, she hoped not; this was hard enough to swallow.

His yard was huge, his house smaller than some of the others on her street. She'd guess it was because it was eco-friendly and all; small home, small footprint. She stood facing the back of his home gazing at what looked like floor-to-ceiling windows running the length of it. An overhang extended from the roof, for cover or shade, she imagined. He could probably see his complete backyard from anywhere in his home.

To the left of his home, taking up almost half of his yard, was a beautiful light-grey gravel bed, raised, with large boulders placed strategically throughout, some leaning on their sides, others standing three feet in height; some were in groupings, and a few stood alone, like rocks in water. The gravel had been raked into some type of design. She walked closer to get a better look; yep, it had been raked, all right, the design resembling ocean waves, swooping and curving. How had he managed to make those? Had to have had a special rake of some kind.

Shrubbery ran along the fence line, relatively new and small in size, but once it reached its full height, it would completely cover the fence. Katrina knew that species of shrubbery grew tall. It would feel like living in his own private world, his own personal enclosed oasis. Looking over to the right back corner of his yard, she found a waterfall, a couple of feet in height, beautiful in its design. A huge flat stone served as the lip, sending water spilling onto the rocks below and then running into a small pond at the bottom that was filled with fish. Gold and orange koi looked up at her as she gazed down at her reflection in the pond. How had he managed to make all of these features feel and look as if they belonged here and had been here for ages? He hadn't lived here that long, yet these features felt like a natural part of the land-scape.

Next to the small pond and closer to his home stood what looked to be some kind of outdoor living room. It was completely enclosed, with two doors leading to it, like saloon doors of old, but Japanese in design. The doors were open, beckoning her. She walked through them to find walls made of smooth brown wooded planks. The room was about the size of her bathroom, and covered with a ceiling made of the same wood planks. Two small lanterns hung from overhead, giving the space a warm glow. A large wooded seat was attached to the lower back wall, protruding outward, large enough to seat two or three people. Katrina felt a little wet and looked upward to see mists of water coming from tiny spouts attached to a cord running along the ceiling. This feature had to come in handy on one of their hotter-than-hell summer days.

She looked up again, staring at the lanterns that hung suspended from the ceiling, taking in the chimes that hung from the top alongside the lanterns. She touched one and was rewarded with a low chime. She liked this space, really liked this space, and contemplated how she might recreate something similar in her backyard. She turned around and walked out.

The patio outside near what she assumed was the back door was covered in a beautiful stone and was smooth to her touch. She stood with her back to his home and looked at his garden again, her position closer to how he viewed it from inside. There were lanterns and solar lights at various points of the garden, following a small path throughout the whole of it; a few lanterns hung from decorative poles, too. She now understood the reason for John's push for him to lead, why the committee had been so impressed. So was she, finally understanding how it had excited them.

She jumped as her cell vibrated in her pocket and scooted back in the direction she'd come just as the lights came on in his home and the man himself stepped into his living room. Shoot, she thought, Lola was going to get her caught. She slipped out his back gate, hoping he hadn't seen her, but not waiting around to find out. She walked quickly back over to Lola's.

"You should have texted me sooner; I almost got caught," she said as soon as Lola came into view.

"Sorry, my cell's battery was low; I had to find Oscar's. But I thought you said he wouldn't mind you being back there?" Lola said.

"No grief, Lola," she said, holding up her hand up. "I had enough of a shock seeing the lights come on in his home."

"Well, what did you think?"

"Think about what?"

"His backyard. You know, the reason for this clandestine trip."

"Oh, it was beautiful, and you can't know how much I hate telling you that," she said. "Anyway, thank you for being my lookout," she said, walking out of Lola's back gate and back over to her home, quiet now, her mind still in Will's backyard.

He had an eye, that was for sure. Okay, so he could design a backyard, okay, a beautiful backyard, but could he duplicate it on a much larger scale? Within a budget, with volunteers, sticking to a schedule? She still had her doubts that he really understood what he was getting himself into, beautiful backyard or not.

Will was tired, ready to crash on his couch. He and G had spent the day fishing after a long week at work. He walked into his home and turned on the lights, and his eye caught movement in his backyard. He turned to see the back gate closing. Was that Katrina? He'd seen someone dart out his back gate, and it looked liked her, her signature hat, ponytail protruding from the back of it, giving her away. He walked out the back door and looked around. No sign of her now. What would she be doing in his backyard, he wondered. Who knew with Katrina? She was turning out to be nothing if not interesting.

March

The first Saturday morning in March found Katrina standing over two cubic yards of dirt. Some of the best dirt and compost mix you could get your hands on had just been delivered to her home. She planned to spend the weekend spreading it over her lawn. She could have used some help here, kicked herself for not taking her godfathers up on their offer to send someone over to help her. Nope, she could do all things by herself.

She regarded the pile of dirt again. Well it wouldn't move itself.

"Hey, Katrina, I didn't know it was your birthday." Tom the retiree was standing there in his usual retiree dress: a white T-shirt pulled tightly over his round belly and tucked neatly into shorts that were shorter than they should have been. Black knee high socks and white tennis shoes completed the ensemble.

"Morning, Tom. It's not my birthday," she responded, looking confused.

"You're courting then?"

"Courting as in dating?" she asked, tilting her head. "Nope, there's no courting going on over here."

"I thought one of your beaus gave that pile of dirt to you as a gift. You know gifts are the way to a woman's heart, and who loves dirt more than you," he said, smiling as if he knew Katrina inside and out.

"Ha, ha, very funny," she said, smiling back at him. "How's Billie?"

"Fine. She's enjoying the life of a retiree, trying not to let her lazy husband bother her too much. We're expecting the grandkids in the next week or two. Maybe you've got room for me at your house while they're here," he said, laughing heartily at his own humor. "Speaking of dirt, sorry to hear that you're not going to lead us to victory this year."

"No, not this year. Will, your new neighbor, is leading this year," she said.

"The guy who built the green home?" he asked.

"Yes, him."

"Ump," was Tom's response. "Well, I know you're anxious to stick it to your pile of dirt there, so I won't delay you further. Goodbye now," he said, walking away.

Katrina stuck her shovel into the pile and dumped a load into her wheelbarrow, then repeated the step; shovel in, dirt out, again and again. The one upside to this type of work was that she could skip her run on the treadmill. This would be her workout for the day, maybe even the next couple of days. Once the wheelbarrow was full, she pushed it over to a spot in her yard and dumped the contents. She'd spread it later. The goal for today and probably tomorrow would be to reduce and divide the major dirt pile.

She walked the wheelbarrow over to the dirt pile, stuck her earplugs in her ears, turned on her mp3 player and began again. Shovel in, dirt out, shovel in, dirt out; her movements in time to the latest Beyoncé tune that played in her ears.

You're the man, she told herself a few hours later, internally patting herself on her back for what she'd accomplished so far. She was one-fourth of the way done and she was also very hungry. Removing her earphones, she plopped down on the ground for a second to catch her breath and replenish the water she'd lost; unfortunately, she could sweat with the best of the pigs. Where was that water bottle, anyway?

She was feeling lazy, didn't want to stand up again to search for it, so she turned over on to her hands and knees—thank God for knee pads, she thought—and climbed up on all fours and crawled around the dirt pile in search of water. Ah, there it was, behind her pile. Wasn't that always the way things worked? When you need something it was furthest away from you.

While she was bent over, she took in a big whiff of her dirt. Tom was right; was there anything more fragrant than the smell of good soil mixed in with a little manure? She put her face close to her pile and took another deep breath. She would always love this smell, the smell of outdoors, the smell associated with her parents. She took another whiff, closing her eyes, remembering times spent in the backyard growing up. For some people, home was food; fried chicken and gravy, mashed potatoes and biscuits. For her, it had been spending time working with her parents in the garden, helping out, learning from them. She took another sniff and froze.

There was someone behind her now, she could hear the sound of feet, maybe even suppressed laughter. She dropped her head and looked past her stomach, in between her legs, to find a bicycle with two legs standing behind her. Yep, there was someone standing there, all right. She lifted her head and inwardly groaned, imagining what she must look like to the untrained eye. What the hell. She turned and looked into the eyes and full smile that belonged to Will. Why him and why now, she thought.

"Hey, Katrina, what *are* you doing?" he asked, lips tightly pressed together, as if he was trying not to laugh.

"Uh, nothing much. I was searching for my water bottle," she said, pulling it over to show him as she pushed herself up to her knees, looking back over her shoulder at him.

"It looked like you were sniffing that dirt pile," he said, fighting to keep a straight face.

"I do not smell dirt," she responded, pushing herself into a standing position and turning to face him fully. Bad idea, as she felt an immediate rush of warmth enter her abdomen and move to her lower body at the sight of him in his cycling gear, all long and lean. Way past angry with him, her body had returned to its normal reaction to seeing him this way. Like Frodo and his Orc sword, her body turned the color warm whenever he got close, and it didn't help that he was dressed in her favorite articles of clothing, sky blue in color this time.

She looked at him, her eyes moving to his chest, clad in that tight cycling shirt, remembering how it had felt next to hers as he lay over her and kissed her like nobody's business. Her eyes moved down to take in his waist; her hands had been around that waist, which was flat, hard, and with definition for days. Her hands starting to twitch, her eyes trailing lower, moving downward to...

He cleared his throat and she froze, her eyes moving up to find his. His eyes gleamed with unshed tears. She must look some kind of funny.

"I was on my way out and saw you bent over here. I just wanted to make sure you were okay," he said.

"Yeah, sure, I'm okay. Thanks for stopping by to check," she added, looking anywhere but at him.

"No problem. Take care," he said, turning to leave, waving a final time as he pedaled away.

What a fine ass, she thought, watching as he stood up, pushing hard on the pedals to get his bike moving, the muscles of his ass moving hard, too, making her hand twitch again. She wouldn't last long as his assistant if she couldn't get a handle on her hormones. At the very least, she needed to learn to not be so obvious.

Will chuckled as he pedaled away from Katrina's. Five minutes ago he'd pulled out from his driveway, planning to go in the opposite direction from her home, but he'd seen her on all fours over a huge pile of dirt, her butt in the air. It was a sight that had been too good to pass up, so he turned and cycled over to her yard.

He found her decked out in baggy overalls, her baseball cap fixed firmly to her head, thick, long ponytail sticking out of the back, and those glasses . . . she'd resembled a nerdy *farmhand*. He watched, perversely fascinated, as she'd pressed her nose close to the dirt pile, taking in a large sniff. Her eyes were closed in the throes of pleasure at the aroma, and she looked nearly orgasmic. He'd seen that expression before, the night of the party, at her home, he on top . . . Okay, enough, he told himself. That image of her, and the others he'd accumulated of her since, were becoming hard to forget.

Managing to stifle his laughter, he started pedaling again, heading out of their subdivision. What a riot she was turning out to be; cute and compelling in a way he couldn't explain . . . or maybe he could, but wasn't ready to.

A little before dusk, a tired Katrina walked over to Lola's for a beer, having called it quits for the day; it was getting too dark to work, anyway. A beer would be her reward for a day spent playing in the dirt. She needed a shower, but she needed a beer more, and Lola and Oscar always had cold ones.

Katrina walked over to Lola's front door, pushing the doorbell while pulling off her work gloves. She waited and then waited some more. What could be taking so long, she wondered, moving her hand to the knob to test it; maybe it was unlocked. It opened before she could touch it.

"What took you so long?" Katrina asked, walking past Lola and heading to her kitchen.

She opened the kitchen door, the old-fashioned swinging kind, just as Lola said to her back, "Katrina, wait, we have . . . company."

Katrina's eyes skimmed her neighbor Will as she walked into the kitchen, turning back to Lola.

"You have company," Katrina said, her voice all accusation.

"Yes, nothing gets past you," Lola said sarcastically.

Katrina looked over at the kitchen table again where Will sat, a beer on the table in front of him, a cocky grin on his face. Why him and why now? This was the second time that day! He gave her a smile, a quick flash of perfect white teeth, laughter from this morning's encounter still present in the eyes shining back at her.

"Well, if it isn't the neighborhood heiress of horticulture," he said, smiling. "I see you've made a dent in your pile of dirt," he said, giving her another smile before giving into his laughter.

"Yes, I did," she said.

"Will and Oscar are just getting back from a motorcycle ride," Lola said, explaining while looking at Katrina.

"Oh, where's Oscar?" Katrina asked.

"Checking on Sydney. I'll go see what's taking him so long," she said, turning before Katrina could form a response.

Katrina stood there, just inside the doorway, just looking at him as his laughter died down. Catching herself staring, she walked over to the refrigerator, conscious now of her movements, her clothes, her hair, and her glasses. She opened the door and grabbed a beer, then closed the door and found the opener on the counter. She popped the top and turned to face Will. He was giving her the once-over, and she'd caught him. He didn't even flinch at being caught. He never did; he simply smiled again, his eyes still laughing.

She'd give anything to know what he was thinking . . . or maybe not, considering how she looked right now.

"You weren't in my backyard the other day, by any chance?" he asked.

"Me? No. But you're right, I do need to get by to see your yard. See what all the fuss is about," she said, looking him in the eye, hoping to bluff her way through.

"Still thinking about working with me?" he asked, stretching out long legs, clad in jeans now, in front of him. "So what's the holdup?" he asked, not waiting for her answer. "You might be surprised at how capable I am."

She shrugged with feigned nonchalance. "I don't recall ever saying you weren't capable. Your backyard is a testament to your ability to landscape, or at least that's what I've heard. So I can assume that you're capable at a certain level, anyway," she said.

"But not at your level," he said.

"Not many people your age are. I just think this is larger than you think," she said.

"Considering how we are around the same age, that's funny. Don't worry about me. I can handle whatever you can handle," he said, all seriousness, as if her remark was a personal affront to his masculinity.

"You think so?" she said, a look of steely determination in her eyes. For some reason today it was a sexy look for her, even in her too-big clothing. He was letting this gardening stuff get the best of him if a short girl with nerdy glasses and clothes covered in dirt was becoming somehow sexy to him.

"I do, but you don't," he retorted.

"You could prove yourself," she said.

He sat back in the chair, his arms folded in front of his chest, T-shirt snug over that chest.

"Prove myself," he echoed, his eyelids lowered as he gazed back at her through hooded eyes, assessing her. She loved that look on him, saw it too many times to count in her dreams as she replayed her memories of the night at her home when he had gazed down into her eyes before giving her the kiss that had knocked her socks off.

"How would you propose I do that?" he asked slowly, almost as if she'd asked him to strip naked in front of her.

"I don't know, maybe spend the day working as *my* assistant at the gardens, Mr. 'I've Only Been There One Day.' "

"Sore loser," he said, smiling.

"Not even," she replied.

"Okay, then, little girlie, when?" he said, standing and walking over to her, all sexual confidence, stopping in front of her as she leaned against the counter. She wasn't intimidated; okay, she was, but she hoped it didn't show. She stood up, her whole five-foot self, looking up into eyes that regarded her with interest. Get out of here, she told herself at that thought. Not the way she looked—hell, *smelled*—today.

"Sure you have time? I wouldn't want to interfere with your outside activities, take you away from your female friends," she said. *Where had* that *come from?*

"Female friends, huh?" he said, looking down at her as if she was a small mouse underneath his paw. "Careful, your green color is showing. As I recall, you wanted to be one of those female friends. But I won't bring that up again." He pausing, looking at her, speculation in his eyes. "So, getting back to your dare, say when and I'll be there," he said, standing close to her.

"Next Saturday, 6 a.m. Meet me at the entrance to the gardens."

"What do I get if I satisfy . . . if I meet with your approval?" he asked.

"You get me as your assistant. No back talk, no extra lip, no questioning," she promised.

"Could be worth it," he said, backing away as the door to the kitchen swung open.

Lola and Oscar entered the kitchen before she could say anything further. Oscar, beer in hand, walked over to the table.

"You okay, Will, do you need another beer?" he asked.

"No, I'm fine," Will answered, walking back to his chair.

"So, what were you and Katrina talking about?" Lola asked, looking over at Katrina, her eyebrows lifted, a question in her eyes.

"Nothing," Katrina said, looking away.

Oscar sat next to Will and Lola took the seat opposite Oscar. Katrina remained standing, leaning with her back to the sink.

"Before you arrived, Katrina, Will was describing one of his favorite cycling trips. Where did you go again?" Lola asked.

"I'm sure Katrina doesn't want to hear about me," he said.

"Sure I do," Katrina said quickly and stopped as his eyes swung over to hers, laughter in them again.

"Okay then, just remember you asked once boredom sets in," he said, looking at her, his eyes then gliding away. "Anyway, I was telling Lola about my first cycling experience in Japan. I figured I needed a guide; I was new to the country, didn't want to break any laws that I wasn't aware existed. So after I finished work in Tokyo, I took some vacation time, two weeks, and signed up with a tour that started in Tokyo, first riding through bike paths and some of the back streets of the city."

"Exploring and discovering," Katrina said, remembering his explanation of his travels from her first conversation with him that night at the party. He smiled.

"Exactly," he said, his smile growing. "Exploring and discovering. So from there, we cycled around the countryside, circumventing Mt. Fuji, and over into the northern Japanese Alps. I totally loved it. I've gone back several times since that initial trip."

Katrina watched him as he talked. She didn't think she could ever get enough of watching him. What she wouldn't give for him to have finished what started at New Year's, a desire that grew stronger the more time she'd spent with him.

"Have you ever cycled, Katrina?" he asked, pulling her thoughts away from her study of him. She was starting to do that a lot more lately, watching him, he thought, like he'd make a nice-sized meal. Maybe she had always watched him and he'd really been oblivious. He hadn't begun to notice until he'd left her stretched out on her bed.

"Me? Nope. I'm a feet-planted-on-the-earth kind of girl."

"You should try it, it's both relaxing and challenging."

"I want my relaxing to be strictly relaxing. I read somewhere that it was harmful to your health to mix the two," she said.

"Is that so?" he said, laughing.

"Yes, sir. I wouldn't lie about something that serious."

"There are some beautiful places on this Earth, Katrina. You've never wanted to see, know what's outside of here?"

"Nope, here works fine for me," she said. Sorry, but she was a homebody. Hell, it had taken her forever to get a home, and with the exception of that one trip overseas, the source of her love for all things English, she stayed close to it.

She listened as Lola and Oscar peppered him with more travel-related questions. She wished otherwise, but knew he wouldn't be interested in her, not outside of a little bit of interest in sex. She tried not to lie to herself much. His travel was another thing that separated his type from hers. She watched him continue to talk, answering Lola and Oscar's questions. She could watch him endlessly, but had had enough for tonight; she was sleepy and starting to smell herself, and she still had that pile of dirt waiting for her in the morning.

"I'd better get going," she said, pushing herself away from the counter, rinsing her beer bottle out, and dropping it in the recycle bin.

Will sat back in his chair, his eyes following her as she left, Lola trailing behind.

"What?" he said into Oscar's questioning eyes. Oscar just smiled.

She was amusing, he'd give her that, and she *had* been in his backyard. The eyes don't lie, and hers had said yes; funny, her trying to bluff her way around his questions. He didn't understand why she dressed the way she did.

He'd only known women who accentuated their assets, not hid them.

With the door closed, she was now out of his sight. He continued to ponder her. If she would just lose the nerdy black-rimmed glasses permanently and let her hair down out of that perpetual ponytail . . . he wanted to see more of her skin. He'd fallen in love with her skin, a rich, dark, sinfully creamy chocolate.

On the surface, outside of that one night, Katrina mostly reminded him of his sisters—reliable, consistent, hardworking women, maybe even a little on the lackluster side. Courtesy of the gardening competition, he was beginning to see the side she'd kept hidden. Or, he thought, maybe she hadn't been hiding at all. She'd just finally gotten his attention.

Sunday morning had arrived faster than Katrina would have liked. Her muscles hurt, but as she regarded her pile for the second day, she knew that she was almost done. She pulled on her work gloves. A small pile of dirt remained; she could finish its distribution by lunch and spend the afternoon and evening spreading it over her lawn with her rake. *You can do this, Katrina*, she thought, giving herself another let's-get-moving pep talk.

She popped her earphones in got to work. She had been working for about an hour when she looked up and saw Will walking down the sidewalk. He turned in at her yard, walked up to her, and stopped, watching her. He wore jeans that hung low on his hips, a T-shirt that was tight across his chest, and flip-flops on his feet. He walked over to stand in front of her and reached down and pulled the earplugs from her ears. She was frozen; she didn't seem to be able to do much more than stare when she was around him these days.

"Can I help?" he asked, reaching for her shovel.

Not if you want me to finish, she thought. "Sure, if you want to. It's boring work, though. You sure you don't mind?" she asked.

"No, I don't mind," he said.

"What, no hills to climb or rivers to cross?" she asked.

"Nope, not today. What else do you have to do here?" he asked, looking around at the small piles on her grass. "Do you have to spread those piles you've made?" he asked before she could answer his first question.

"Yes."

"Do you want the rest of this dirt there?" he asked, pointing to the other part of the yard, which was devoid of small piles.

"Yes," she said.

"Why don't you start distributing the piles while I finish up here?" he said, reaching for the shovel and kicking off his flip-flops, leaving his feet bare. Nice feet, she thought, staring at them. Now that he'd started to be around her more, up close even, she found that she liked looking at him more and more.

"Katrina," he said, watching her face until her eyes returned to his. "You have to stop doing that, you're giving me a complex."

"Stop doing what?"

"Staring at me," he said, with a smile that professed his confidence in his looks and charm. What does one say to that? She hadn't realized that she had been that obvious.

"I'm just surprised to see you here, that's all."

"Whatever," he said, brushing aside her reply. "Give me the shovel," he said, reaching to take it from her. He effortlessly pushed it into the pile. She picked up the rake she'd pulled from the garage yesterday and headed toward one of her small piles. She began spreading it, but her eyes returned to him. She watched his arms lift the shovel, muscles playing beneath his skin, and watched his chest move as he scooped dirt and deposited it into the wheelbarrow. She watched his ass as he turned and pushed the loaded wheelbarrow away from her, giving her his back. He emptied the contents and started back over to the pile.

"You're watching again."

"Am not," she said, feeling like a five-year-old, making him laugh.

"Are too." And they both laughed.

They worked through the morning, skipping lunch, not wanting to stop when only a small amount remained. Will had spread most of the dirt over her yard, then took her rake from her hands to finish her area. She went inside to get him a bottle of water, surprised to see him putting the tools onto her front porch when she returned.

"You're done," he said matter-of-factly, placing the last of her tools at her feet.

"Thank you," she said, handing him a cold bottle of water.

"Thank you," he said, removing the top from the bottle and taking a huge drink. Almost half of his water was gone when he stopped. "I'd better get home; work comes early in the morning and I have my own chores to do. See you next Saturday, bright and early," he said, taking another swallow of water, handing the now-empty bottle back to her. "Don't be late," he added, tugging at the brim of her cap, his knuckle moving down to rap on one of the lenses of her glasses.

"I'll be there; you just take care of yourself," she said as he turned and left, giving her a final wave as he walked past her home. Of course, her eyes tracked him to his door. She couldn't touch, but last time she'd checked, looking was still free.

Later that evening, after a much-needed shower, Katrina was preparing for the much-dreaded evening she'd agreed to spend at Amber and Claudia's entrepreneurship meeting. Nope, no way she could get out of attending, but she had given a lot of thought to calling and cancelling. She would have, could have, told them she was too tired from all that yard work, but she decided against that as that was her normal operating procedure. She also didn't want any grief from Amber at work.

She put the finishing touches to her hair. She hadn't done much to it really, just twisted it into a bun instead of her usual ponytail. She fished around in a drawer for a pair of her old glasses. Yes, the red ones would do; they were way outdated, the prescription a little off, but just the right touch to give her the stumbling, bumbling look. They would work nicely when added to tonight's outfit, a dress-to-not-impress look always necessary to waylay any plans made by Amber and Claudia to play match-maker. It was her ace in the hole should the get-together be more of a fix-her-up than an entrepreneurship meeting.

She found her plainest black slacks and a plain black blouse tied at the neck in a bow, something that could be found in one's granny's closet. Black flats and stud ear-rings completed the look. She was ready. Nothing she wore would show off her assets, and that was the way she wanted it. The best defense was always a good offense.

Amber and Claudia didn't live that far away, so she pulled up to their home in less than fifteen minutes. Medium-sized and quaint, the house was in one of the older neighborhoods in the city. The gardens here were small, reflecting the neighborhood's aging population. She volunteered here once last year; others did, too, filling in, helping out with gardens in places where the population was in flux. She got out of her car and walked to the door, looking around. Their home was nicely kept, with maintenance-free evergreen shrubs the plant of choice. Amber and Claudia were not yard people.

Claudia opened the door, well dressed and beautifully coiffed as always. Claudia was also African-American, shorter than Amber, but not as short as Katrina. Long curly hair framed a heart-shaped face. Claudia gave Katrina's outfit the once-over and smiled.

"Katrina, Katrina, you are something else," she said, shaking her head from side to side; she knew Katrina's game. "Come on in."

There looked to be about fifteen to twenty people present, standing around and talking in small groups. Amber walked over to her, a cup of what looked like punch in her hand.

"Katrina, you've surprised me; I didn't think you would show. I expected you to call me sometime today with some reason or other for not attending tonight," she said, trying not to show her disapproval of Katrina's clothing choices.

"Nope, here I am, just as I said I would be."

"Well, then, let me introduce you around. There are a few people here I'd like you to meet," she said, grabbing Katrina's hand and pulling her toward a tall, handsome African-American man holding a cup and standing next to a table lined with finger foods and red punch in a bowl. A shorter Hispanic man standing next to him was filling his glass with a drink.

"Darius Williams," Amber said to her, looking her in the eye, and then turning to face the two men. "This is the person I was telling you about, the one who can do wonders with plants. Katrina, meet Darius and Javier." Darius put down his cup to shake Katrina's hand.

"Katrina, Darius owns two restaurants in town, and we've eaten at both, The Vegetable Garden and the Vegetable Pot."

"Yes, I have, and the food is great," Katrina said.

"And this is Javier," Amber said.

"Hello," he said.

"Hi, Darius, hi, Javier," Katrina said. The introductions confirmed Katrina's suspicion that this had been Amber's true purpose all along, and so now she needed to implement the second part of her plan. Amber had turned to speak to a woman who'd walked up to her.

"Hello," Darius said. "Amber tells me you are quite the gardener."

"Yep, I do like to garden." Keep answers simple; don't follow up a question with a question. She turned her head and looked around the room, deploying another tactic in her arsenal—indifference.

"So Amber tells me you work with her at the bank?" This from Darius again.

"Yes, we work in the same division."

"How do you like it?" he asked.

"It's okay. Gardening is what I love, though."

"Oh, really?" he said.

Here goes nothing, Katrina thought. "Yes, I love flowers. The lantana plant is especially my favorite. Its more formal name is the *Lantana horrida*, which is the name for the native Texas lantana. I also like the *Lycoris radiate*, that's the formal name for the lily. It grows as an annual and you can set it out early without having to worry about frost, plus it comes in several varieties: Celebrity Carnival, Salsa, Porter, and my favorites, Brandywine and Whopper."

Katrina continued to talk about flowers for another five minutes, not letting either of them get a word in edgewise. At the four-minute mark, she inwardly smiled. There it was, that glazed-over expression in their eyes. She internally patted herself on the back. She loved it when a plan came together. Stopping to take a breath, Katrina watched Darius and Javier furtively looking around the room, seeking an escape.

"You know, I need to find the restroom," she said, helping them out. They looked relieved. She had to bite her tongue to keep from laughing out loud. Amber walked over to them.

"Is Katrina playing a game with you? She does that at times. Talks incessantly about her gardening; it's a ruse to make you think she's boring," said Amber, cutting her eyes at Katrina. Darius looked at her through new eyes and smiled.

Javier still wanted out. "There's Mike," he said. "I've been meaning to talk to him about our next meeting. It was nice meeting you, Katrina," he said before moving quickly away.

Thank God, she thought she heard him say as he walked away.

"So you were playing us?" Darius asked, starting to laugh. Katrina was trying to hold back her grin, her eyes bright from suppressed laughter.

"She can be crafty, our Katrina," Amber said.

"Is that so?" Darius remarked.

"Yes, it is," she said, looking sharply at Katrina. "Now cut it out." She walked away, leaving the two of them alone.

"Cut what out?" Katrina asked to her back, still pretending innocence.

"So, trying to scare us away?" he asked.

"Be honest, it was working before Amber said something," she said, grinning.

"Yes, it was," he said, and laughed with her. Maybe she could like this one, and what wasn't to like—tall, slim, milk chocolate-brown skin, owned his own profitable business. But of course, Will popped into her head.

She remained at the meeting for another hour, spent mostly talking to Darius about gardening, his businesses, and the possibility of hers. After she finished talking with Darius, Amber came back for her, taking her around, introducing her to others in their group. All were nice and encouraging, singing the praises of owning their own businesses and giving advice. She added it all to her store of information. An hour later she was headed for the door when Darius intercepted her.

"Leaving?" he asked.

"Yes, work tomorrow," she said.

"Well, it was a pleasure meeting you," he said smiling and starting to laugh again, remembering her earlier stunt.

"The same," she said, and meant it. And then she, too, laughed.

"May I call you sometime?" he asked, watching indecision flicker on her face. She had been funny, a little on the smart-mouthed side, but he liked women who challenged him and he'd enjoyed talking to her. "Come on," he said, seeing her resistance. "My tomatoes might get sick, and my doctor doesn't make house calls," he said, winking at her.

"That was so weak," she said, laughing, "but okay." She took a business card from her purse and scribbled her cell number on the back.

"Take care, Katrina. It was nice meeting you," he said.

"You too," she said, walking away.

Amber walked over to him and they both watched her leave.

"Told you she was nice," she said.

"Yes, you were right, but don't start again with the match-making, I'm nowhere near ready," he said.

CHAPTER 6

Friday evening. It was dark out save for the lighting in Will's backyard. He held a hose turned to the hard-stream setting and was cleaning some of the algae that had formed on the top rocks of his pond. Mindless work, really, but relaxing. He had just finished fishing out the leaves from his pond, trying to avoid the koi, glad for a break. Work seemed to be in overdrive, this being the first free night he'd had all week; he was home early, too. It was a sad state of events when 8 p.m. was considered early. He looked up when he heard the back door to his home slide open and watched Josey step out, clad in jeans that had to have been spray-painted on. She walked toward him, a grin on her face and plenty of female swagger in her step. She was tall like him and had passed up striking, probably at age ten, moving on to dazzling, with her long brown hair, and golden tan. She exuded vitality.

"I don't know why you insist on playing the field worker. There are plenty of people one can pay to do this for you," she said, coming to stand behind him, putting her hands around his waist, resting her chin on his shoulder, and turning to kiss his neck.

"It's relaxing," he said.

"I can come up with other things that are far more relaxing than this," she said, moving her hand upward, following the contours of his chest, and continuing to kiss him. He turned off the water, letting the hose fall to the ground, and turned to her, his hands going around her waist, pulling her in close, searching for her lips.

"Glad you invited me over?" she asked between kisses.

"Yes," he said against her lips.

"You're going to love me then," she said, pulling back and smiling. "I brought dinner."

He didn't answer, just smiled against her lips, resuming his onslaught of her mouth, finding her tongue and playing with it a while before guiding her back through his gardens. He pulled back and smiled. "How about we eat later? I'm a different kind of hungry," he said, turning and pulling her behind him into his home.

His cell alarm was going off; he'd set it for 5:30, plenty of time for him to shower and eat before he was due at the gardens. Time to meet his maker, or close to it. He was tired and hadn't factored in Josey, or a difficult and long week, when he had signed up for this. Josey was still sleeping, her long hair spilling over her shoulders and across the pillow. Josey had most of what he preferred in a woman—athletic, adventurous, independent, and fun, but, more importantly, she wasn't interested in being committed. A woman after his own heart. If he ever considered permanence, she would make a fine candidate. For some reason, Katrina wearing her *Gardeners do it in*

the dirt shirt popped into his mind. He shook his head to clear it.

He sat up and moved his legs to the floor, the movement waking Josey.

"You're not leaving already?" she asked, pushing hair away from her eyes.

"Yep, I've got to work at the gardens this morning, part of that gardening competition I told you about."

"Yuck, dirt and bugs. Why would you want to put yourself through that?"

"I like it," he responded. "Go back to sleep. I'll call you later."

"Okay, but let me give you something first," she said, sitting up and scooting out of the bed, walking over to stand in front of him, beautiful in her nakedness. "I need something to sustain me while you're gone. Who knows when I'll see you or when you'll call me again," she said, pushing him back down to lie on the bed and then straddling his body. His eyes went to the clock on his nightstand; he had time, but he'd have to keep it short, maybe forgo breakfast. He extended his arm, trying to reach his nightstand for a condom.

"Don't worry, I've got you covered," she said, stretching her arm out, pulling one from the partly open drawer, tearing it open with her teeth, and then placing it on him.

"Much better," she said, lifting her body and settling down on his, slowly taking him into her. She leaned forward and groaned, her mouth trailing kisses over his body, taking the scenic route over stomach, chest, and neck before arriving at his mouth. Finding his lips, she settled hers on top. She moaned at the upward movement of his hips, reminding her to move. She kissed him, seeking his tongue as she started to move. His hands reached for her hips, helping her as she moved up and down. He assisted, lifting her and then pushing her hips firmly downward, slowly, letting her find her rhythm, watching the expression on her face change as she got lost in the sensation of having him in her.

He gave her a few minutes on her own before taking over, increasing the pace, watching and then feeling her reach her climax, pulling him along. He came quietly, a sharp intake of air the only sound he made. He let her lie there for a few minutes, both catching their breath, relaxed and ready to start the day . . . he was, anyway; she still lay languid across his chest.

"I got to go, don't want to be late," he said.

"Explain to me again why you're doing this?"

He lifted her off him. "I want to." He gave her a kiss before getting up and going to the bathroom. He had to move a little faster now. No way was he going to be late, but he smiled a little at the thought of what Katrina would say if he was.

About ten minutes later, Josey said, "Don't forget to call me."

"I won't," he said over his shoulder as he hurried to the kitchen and grabbed a cup of coffee, preprogrammed, before walking through the front door and out to his jeep. It was quiet out. He appreciated the early morning; it was free of sound, free of movement. The only part of him that he kept to himself was his interest in horticulture, not a topic he brought up much with his boys. G knew, but it was one of the few things about himself he didn't share openly.

He had to trust that the other person would treat that part of himself, the part he most valued, with care. It wasn't just the subject that he didn't share, but more what it did for him. Its influence was both calming and centering for him, and had been for as far back as he could remember.

Josey and others spent time at his home often and they all had admired his backyard, but it wasn't of interest to them, not really; he'd yet to meet one who was truly interested in that part of him. Most weren't even aware that he'd done the design and actual landscaping. They'd been more interested in other aspects of his life, ones they considered more fun, more interesting, and more lucrative. He never considered that he'd find someone who shared his love for gardening, his need for it. Yep, that was something he'd continue to keep way down low.

"So what do you think of my idea?" Katrina asked.

"It should work," Thomas said, winking. "Just remind me never to get on your bad side."

"He's not on my bad side. I just want to show him the level of work required for the competition."

"Sure, Katrina," he said skeptically, stopping and turning around.

"What?"

"We aren't to give him any equipment that would make his job easier. If we do give him anything, it has to be the old, slightly broken stuff. That is more than measuring his work ethic," Thomas said.

"Okay, maybe it is, but so what?"

"I'm just saying," he replied, raising his hands in surrender.

"I know, I know," she said, quiet now, looking over at him. "Still going to help me?"

"Yes, I am, but only because I like you," he said, smiling at her.

"I'll bring him over to you when he gets here and I'll pick him up before lunch," she said to Thomas's retreating back. He lifted a hand in acknowledgment as he walked away.

It was bright and early Saturday morning, and Katrina hadn't slept much the night before. She had been too excited on a variety of levels. As always, the possibility of spending time with Will was appealing. He would be hers for the day; not quite in the way she would have wanted, but she would take what she could get. Thomas was the main overseer of the garden, so Katrina had arrived early to discuss her plans for Will. She'd known Thomas since she'd come to live in her new home. As a seventeen-year-old, he had been her first major crush.

She wanted to make sure Will's assignments were tough enough for her to get a good measure of the man. How else would she determine what he was made of? Of course they would be difficult, as difficult as she could find. And she could find difficult.

They had agreed to assign him the mulch detail first, followed by a little wood chopping after lunch.

The city, like all others in the state, collected Christmas trees and delivered them to the neighborhood gardens. Most of Shining Creek's neighbors dropped theirs off themselves, and volunteers helped to shred them for use as mulch and for the compost bin. Most of the trees had been shredded already and were in a pile in the back of the gardens for residents who wanted to pick them up for use in their homes. Elderly neighbors who required assistance to maintain their yards could have their mulch delivered to their home by a volunteer, and lucky Will would be that volunteer this morning. That meant taking a shovel and loading up the truck with mulch.

They had equipment that would reduce the time and labor, but he wasn't going to use it. Will was in shape with all that cycling; he shouldn't mind the old-fashioned way, she thought, grinning. And she'd picked out a special wheelbarrow for him to use; so what if the front wheel was a little wonky?

Will would then deliver the mulch to three of their elderly neighbors and would place it as instructed. That should keep him occupied until noon.

After lunch, she would bring him back over to Thomas to help chop wood and shred brush. The trees and brush wood came from areas where land was being cleared and included trees that were cleared from power lines. These were all delivered to their garden.

The garden owned both large and small chainsaws for that purpose, but she wasn't going to tell him that. *Let's see how Mr. Leader of the Competition figures that out.*

And then, if Will was still around, Thomas would send him over to help her in the compost area. The compost pile always needed turning, and her worms needed feeding. And if there was any daylight left, she planned to have him deliver compost, by wheelbarrow, to the different beds in the vegetable sections.

The garden owned two bobcats, both large and small, and if his assigned tasks proved too much work for Will, she planned to bring them out. Until then, the old-fashioned way was going to be it. It was getting close to six and time for her to head to the front gate to meet him. She smiled. This was going to be so much fun.

There he was, just as he said he would be, leaning against the main gate, his back to her. He was clad in jeans, his flannel shirt open, some thin-looking shirt on underneath, baseball cap turned backward, work gloves in his pocket, work boots on his feet. So he'd worn the appropriate gear, at least. She walked up and tapped him on his shoulder. He turned, all smooth. Did nothing rattle him, she wondered? He gave her a smile, those brackets in place next to his mouth, eyes twinkling.

"You're here," she said.

"As I said I would be."

"Ready to get started?"

"Yep."

"Follow me, then," she said, turning and walking away. "I've assigned you to work with Thomas. He's been working in the gardens almost as long as I have and he is charge of the volunteers."

Watching her, he had to bite back his desire to laugh out loud. He didn't know what she'd assigned to him, but he knew it would be hard, probably cutting individual blades of grass with scissors. She was so transparent; but if it would get her to work with him, he'd do it. For some reason, he *wanted* her to work with him.

They walked over to an area surrounding big piles of what looked liked mulch and she introduced him to Thomas. Thomas was African-American; think Coffey, but not the drink, more like the big guy from the movie *The Green Mile*. Intimidating didn't begin to describe him. He walked over to Katrina, his expression blank. So Katrina had enlisted help, Will thought, glancing at her standing next to him. Seeing her small frame next to Thomas's tall, muscular one, reaching to the top of his waist, one could easily mistake her for his child.

"Thomas, this is Will. He is the leader for the flower portion competition of our neighborhood this year. He lives a couple of doors down from me. He is new to the neighborhood and to the garden, so you may need to explain how things work around here."

"Sure, no problem."

"Hey, Will," Thomas said, stretching out his ham-sized hand, which Will took.

"Hey, Thomas," he replied.

"I'll come back for you at lunch, okay?" Katrina said.

"I'll be here," Will said, grinning at her, conveying a message with his eyes: *I know what you're up to.*

She grinned back. "Don't work too hard," she said.

Just as he thought, her plan was to be difficult. Thomas assigned him the task of loading, delivering, and laying mulch at three homes. He was to use the truck that belonged to the garden; a donation, he was told. He was also given a beat up-old wheelbarrow, the front tire a little flat. Katrina's doing, he imagined.

The detail took him all morning. The first home went relatively fast, as it just needed mulch around the trees and the front flower beds. The second home had belonged to Ms. Stone, who was beyond persnickety about her yard. She'd been in his ear the whole time. He laughed about it now, at how she was standing by the curb waiting for him when he pulled up, decked out in what must have been the latest in horticulture wear in the 1950s: pants tucked into rubber boots, a pink twin sweater set, a safari hat on her head, and gloves on her hands. To what purpose he had yet to figure out, because all she did was talk.

"It's about time you got here," she said upon his arrival, giving him the once-over. "You're that new kid with the odd home that snuck into the garden competition, stealing it from under Katrina's nose this year, I hear."

Yep, that would be me, he thought. He hadn't anything to say to that, so he just asked her where she'd like her mulch. She spent the entire time giving him her thoughts on the competition and on Katrina. If he was so smart, she said, he would have gotten Katrina to help him. He had to agree with her there.

The last home delivery hadn't been easier, but at least it had been quiet. After Ms. Stone, his ears had needed the rest. He pulled the truck into the back entrance to the garden and parked.

He spotted Katrina walking over to him, an insulated container in her hand. Lunch, he hoped, but who knew with Katrina? It could easily be a thin gruel and a crust of bread. He got out of the truck and walked toward her. He'd removed his outerwear, leaving him in that thin form-fitting shirt, which fit like a second skin. She walked halfway and stood waiting until he reached her. He lifted his baseball cap, and his hair was now plastered to his head. It was so unfair that he should look this good after a hard morning's work. He looked her over, taking in her outfit in the light. Those overalls again. He smiled and winked at her.

He was going to be the death of her; after all she'd given him, he still was smiling, his eyes roaming downward, stopping at the lunchbox he saw in her hands. His smile widened.

"I hope that's lunch, 'cause I'm starving," he said, reaching for the bag and pulling it from her hand. "Let's see what you've packed for me," he said, unzipping it and looking inside. She had packed herself a lunch and added enough for him, too.

"It's just a couple of sandwiches, some chips, and fruit I brought with me from home. I packed enough for two," she said, reaching for the bag, which he smoothly moved out of her reach.

"So where do you want to sit? I assume you've been waiting for me, to eat with me," he said, smiling.

"I hadn't planned on eating with you."

"Sure, you didn't," he said smoothly, walking away from her.

"Wait, where are you going?" she said, jogging to catch up to him.

"I'm going to find the family section, near the playscape area, the one you designed last year. I like it," he said when she caught up to him. "And maybe if you're nice to me I'll even let you lie down with me in that big hammock in the front. You've been wanting to do that for a while. It'll be my treat for making my job today so easy." He smiled at her.

She was quiet. They walked to the front where the flower section was located. Katrina waved to a lot of her neighbors and spoke to more than a few children along the way.

"You know a lot of your neighbors," he said.

"You would, too, if you wanted to. If you stayed put long enough to meet them," she said, stopping next to a small, kid-size picnic table.

"Is this okay?"

"Yes."

They both sat down on the tabletop. Katrina took the bag from his hands, pulling out and handing over a sandwich, chips, apple, and a bottle of water.

"Thanks," he said, taking a bite of his sandwich. "So tell me, why all this gardening?" he asked in between bites.

"I'm sure you know by now that I was adopted by two of the original founders of the gardens here. I came to live with them when I was ten. They introduced me to dirt, and we've been pals ever since," she said. He smiled at that. "How about you? You don't seem the gardening type."

"Why is that?"

"I don't know. I see you a lot, and you seem to be busy doing all kinds of adventurous stuff. You seem too busy to settle down long enough to garden."

"I don't know, I lost my dad when I was really young, too. I don't really have any memories of him. My grandfather came to live with us, helping my mother in our family store, which was started by my mother and father before he died. Anyway, my grandfather built a small garden out back and I found myself there a lot, restless from having to work in the store.

"He put me to work growing small vegetables and weeding, and he began to introduce me to the history of Japanese gardening. The notion that it was a sanctuary, a respite from the world, held an appeal, even as a kid. More so as I grew older and needed a break from being successful and smart. It's a lot of work," he said, smiling again.

"You're so full of it," she said, watching him smile. "I don't even try." He looked at her in question. "Try to fit in. I used to, but it's too much trouble. So how much do you know about composting?" she asked, changing the subject.

"A little. Why?" he asked.

"That's where you're going to be after lunch—after you finish your wood-chopping detail, that is," she said. He laughed outright, loudly, and it took him a while to stop.

"What's so funny?" she asked.

"You are," he said, getting up from the table. "I'm ready," he said. Apparently, that was to be the extent of his explanation.

She picked up the remains of their lunch before delivering him to Thomas, who stood next to another guy, also African-American, but shorter and thinner.

"Hey, Will. Back, are you?" he said, grinning now.

"So far. I'm still here."

"I am going to put you with Rufus. You guys are clearing out that pile of trees and brush behind you." Taking in the size of that pile, Will inwardly groaned, thinking, *Not just the two of us.*

Thomas must have seen some of that reflected on his face because he smiled and said, "Just do what you can; it's enough for more than a few people. The brush you can shred, using the shredder, and the wood you can saw and then chop into splits. There is a small chainsaw and some goggles in the shed over there," he said, pointing. "You can use it instead of the ax Katrina left for you," he added, getting a laugh from Will. Thomas laughed, too, and walked away.

Will and Rufus started working, Rufus immediately going for the brush job and leaving the tree cutting to Will, who worked alone for a while before Thomas joined him. They worked together through most of the afternoon. During one of their breaks, Will walked over to grab some water and Rufus joined him.

"What were you in for?" Rufus asked.

"In for?" Will responded, not sure of the question.

"You know, you are here working, getting your community service hours in, right? You know, part of your sentencing. What were you arrested for?"

"Umm, interesting question. I was arrested for failure to show proper respect for the leader," he said, causing Rufus to look at him strangely.

"I've never heard of that, but, you know, they're always changing the laws up on a brother," he said, causing Will to laugh.

They worked steadily for another two hours. It was close to 5 when Thomas called it quits.

"Thanks for your help today," he said, extending his hand to shake theirs. "Will, Katrina is waiting for you over in the compost section. You know where that is, right?" he said, teasing Will now.

"Yes," Will said, going in search of Katrina. He found her standing next to the neighborhood compost pile, pitchfork in hand.

"You survived, I see," she said, taking in the undershirt again plastered to his skin, watching as he pulled on his flannel shirt and began buttoning it. His head was bent over his task and she took this time to once again look her fill.

"I am surviving in spite of your best efforts," he said, looking up.

"Hey, that was a normal workday," she said.

"Sure it was," he said, looking down at the fork in her hand. "What are you doing here?" he asked.

"Turning the compost. I was waiting for you to finish with Thomas," she said, handing him her pitchfork.

"Are you just going to do your normal watching of me, or will you be helping this time?" he asked, all cocky.

"I'll help, as I'm sure you're tired," she said, picking up another pitchfork. "Composting is our latest gardening venture, new as of the beginning of last year. We decided to make our own for use here and for those in the neighborhood who need it," she said, folding her arms and resting them on the top of her fork.

"I'm sure you're pleased with that. You can smell as much dirt as you'd like," he said, chuckling.

"Ha, ha. Neighbors contribute their yard waste, vegetable waste, coffee grounds, and grass clippings for those who like the idea of compost without the fuss of composting themselves. We also pick up the coffee grounds from the local coffee shops as well as vegetable waste from neighborhood restaurants."

"Waste taken and used for composting is waste not being sent to landfills," he said. She looked at him with approval. "I have an interest in green; what can I say? You know that from the meeting."

"I know, I just thought it was targeted more toward building."

"It's all connected, Katrina. You know that."

"I know, just didn't think you did," she said.

"So are you pleased with the city's approach to this neighborhood gardening idea? Is it the way to go?" he asked, moving his fork in and out of the pile, turning it over.

"I do. I mean, some consider it a small effort, compared to the large-scale changes needed in the way we grow food in this world, but it's a start, I think. As you said at the meeting, the changes we need should be larger in scale and scope. But we have to start somewhere, and the city's efforts make it easier to live greener."

"You're a teacher?"

"School? Nope, no patience."

"Business owner?"

"Nope, but it's the question people ask me the most."

"Maybe they see something in you."

"Small business can be a big risk. Ninety-five percent fail within the first five years," she said, obviously having given the possibility some thought.

"It's a dangerous business going out your door," he said.

"Bilbo Baggins," she said and smiled.

"I'm a fan," he said.

"So what do you do that makes you travel so?" she asked, back to watching him work, her arms resting on her pitchfork.

"I'm director of what's called Global Production Support—GPS for short. I work with customers on a global basis to improve the performance of the systems we produce and sell."

"Uh-huh," she said, not really understanding his explanation. "So that's the reason for all your travel?" she asked, watching as he steadily worked his way down to the end of the composting area, turning it over with his fork, in his own rhythm now. She picked up her fork and moved closer to him, sticking it back into the ground.

"Yes. We are an original equipment manufacturer for the semiconductor industry.

Sometimes I spend a few weeks working, meeting with customers to discuss product-related technical and performance issues." He straightened and stood, now at the end of the pile.

"Okay," she said, not understanding that, either, but moving on. "You're fast," she said, walking over and taking his fork from him, putting it with hers, and leaning them against a fence post.

"Last thing we need to do today is to add manure to my worms," she said, walking toward the first row of bins.

"We?" he said, following her.

"This area is just starting. Thomas built these bins for me last year," Katrina said, lifting the cover and scooping out a handful of manure, compost, and worms to show him. "Know anything about vermicomposting?" she asked.

"Cultivation of worm castings for use as organic fertilizer? Worms eat, poop, and have sex. Not a bad life," he said, pleased that she seemed surprised that he knew. "I worked at a small community garden during graduate school. They were into vermicomposting, too. They were known for their organic vegetables. I helped, watched, and learned." He took the shovel from her.

"Graduate school?"

"MBA," he said, "Stanford. Where's your manure?" he asked.

"Over here. We get ours from a local farmer. We're still working out the kinks in this whole worm poop process. We have to go take the truck over to his farm and load it up ourselves."

He laughed. "I'm surprised you didn't save that chore for me."

"I wish. Pick-up is during the week or else I would have," she said. He laughed.

"Did you know that there's this one restaurant in India, saw it on internet, that takes all of its vegetable waste and puts it out back, along the fence. Nothing elaborate, just feed for their worms who, as you know, produce great organic fertilizer, which in turn is used in the restaurant's gardens. What a great use of resources."

"Yep," he said, spreading manure into two of the bins.

"We use both the compost from the pile you just turned and my worm fertilizer for the gardens here," she said.

"Your worms?" he said, dumping another shovelful of manure and spreading it over another bin. Katrina stood back and watched as he worked, muscles moving under his shirt, jeans stretched tightly over superb thighs. She sighed, large and loudly, he looked over at her and laughed. Ten minutes later, he was done.

"What next, boss?' he asked.

"That's it for me," she said. "I'm sending you back to Thomas, to help with the end of the day cleaning, making sure the tools are put away. You aren't too tired, are you?" she asked.

"Why would I be tired?" he asked, a hint of sarcasm mixed in with his question.

"You can find Thomas in the back where you met him this morning."

"Are you leaving now?" he asked.

"Nope, come find me when you're done," she said, walking away.

"Sure," he said to her back, laughing inside at her determination to make him work until the bitter end. He found Thomas and helped him haul tools left behind by volunteers, clean out the wheelbarrows, and do general upkeep. It took them about an hour to finish.

"Good luck on the gardening competition. Don't let Katrina push you around too much," Thomas said, laughing.

"She hasn't agreed to help me yet," he said.

"She will. Let me know if I can be of any help," Thomas said, smiling and shaking Will's hand.

"Sure. Thanks," Will said, heading back to the front.

He found Katrina sitting atop the picnic tables near the kids' area watching the children play. He sat down next to her. They sat in silence for a while. It was dark now; the solar lights were on, along with the lights surrounding the kids play area. It was nice out. He breathed deeply and looked over at Katrina, who had just done the same. They laughed.

"You're more knowledgeable than you let me believe," she said.

"You didn't really try to find out how much I knew. You just assumed," he said, bumping his shoulder into hers. "Don't worry, you're not the first. It's hard for women to give me much credit sometimes, the downside to having such a pretty face," he said, making her laugh again. "I like this place," he added, pointing to the playscape. "It feels easy, relaxed, and comfortable, like an old pair of jeans. I like the way you inserted the hammocks, especially hidden among the trees, they make this place feel like part of a whole neighborhood. But also, if you close your eyes, you can pretend that you're in your own backyard and you're all alone and that's so cool," he said, gently bumping her shoulder again.

She turned and looked at him, appreciation in her eyes; not just for his looks, but for understanding what the outdoors meant to her, what she had tried to create.

"Thanks for working today. You didn't have to. It wasn't necessary to have my approval," she said.

"But I wanted it, anyway, and I really would like for you to work with me."

"Why?"

"You get what all this means, the need to take care of what has been given to us," he said, then quiet for a few minutes before adding, "Plus you need me to improve your gardening education. You could learn a lot from me."

"Oh, I could, could I," she said, hitting his knee with hers.

"Yep, you must be open to all things, little one," he said, all fortune cookie-like.

She laughed. "I promise I'll think about it, and today went a long way toward helping," she said, smiling shyly.

"I'll take that as a start," he said, standing up. "I better go. Taking the motorcycles out with Oscar tomorrow, and I need to be alert," he said, standing there watching her.

"Okay, thanks again," she said, watching, but having no idea what he was thinking. He tugged at the brim of her hat before turning and walking away. She followed him with her eyes until he was no longer visible, giving a final sigh for all that he was.

Sunday arrived sunny and clear, but a little cold—a perfect day for a bike ride, the motored kind this time. Oscar stood outside Will's door and rang the bell for the second time. A few minutes later, the door opened. Will was standing there, hair standing in every direction, in need of a shave, and not dressed.

"You still up to riding today? You look a little tired," Oscar said teasingly. He knew about Will working with Katrina yesterday; he heard it from Lola.

Will ran his hand through his hair, turned, and walked away from the door. "I must have overslept," he said, turning and heading into the kitchen for a cup of pre-programmed coffee.

"What time is it, anyway?" he said, grabbing a cup from the cabinet and filling it with coffee.

"Around ten. You want to postpone? Ride another day?"

"Hell, no, just give me ten. I'll meet you outside," he said, taking his cup and walking toward his bathroom.

"Okay, if you're sure. While I'm here, I need to borrow a wrench." Will spun around and headed toward his garage.

"What size?" he asked.

"Half-inch."

Will went over to where his wrenches were and retrieved the one Oscar wanted.

"I don't know how you keep this place so clean and organized. You're a one-man tool supply."

"I'm just anal that way," Will said, going back into his home, now headed for the shower.

"See you in ten," Oscar said, walking out the front door.

"Sure."

Will was tired. Attila the Gardener tried to kill him yesterday; that thought caused him to smile. He'd known she would give him the worst, most difficult assignment, and she had not disappointed. He stepped into the shower, turning the setting to hot. He'd considered himself in excellent shape, and that fitness had saved him from Katrina's work detail. Even so, he was still a little sore.

He had actually enjoyed the work, having missed the level of labor required by community gardens. He'd met people he'd seen around often, but didn't have the chance to meet. They came over and introduced themselves and congratulated him on being selected the leader. For the first time since graduate school, he'd felt a part of something large and meaningful. He was surprised and impressed by the scale and reach of the gardens and Katrina's role in them.

About ten minutes later, Will emerged from his home. Oscar was already on his bike.

"Ready?" he asked.

"Yep."

About two hours later, they were sitting at a picnic table on the inside patio of the best rib place in the state, having worked through a pound of ribs washed down with sodas.

The Big Rib was the name of this particular barbeque pit. It was nestled at the bottom of a hill, surrounded by green fields and a large pond. The Big Rib had been an added treat at the end of their ride through beautiful countryside among the hills of this region. Even in winter, it was still beautiful. They'd stopped for a late lunch.

He and Oscar were now contemplating a bowl of hot peach cobbler. Of course the answer was yes. They flagged the waitress down and ordered. After she'd taken their orders and gone, Oscar spoke.

"So how does it feel to have unseated the legend of the gardening world?" he asked to Will, teasing him.

"I had no idea it would end as it did. I didn't know she wanted it as much as she did, although I'm excited about the opportunity," he said.

"Gardening is huge in this town, and being chosen leader is the dream of most serious gardeners. Katrina has been that leader for us for the last four years. So congratulations," he said.

"Thanks."

The waitress arrived with their dessert.

"That was quick," Will said, thanking her as she placed two bowls of the finest peach cobbler in the state before them, loaded with fresh peaches and juice served piping hot over the state's equally famous homemade vanilla ice cream. Taking a bite, Will took a moment to savor the pleasure he'd always gotten from his first bite of this dessert. Oscar looked at him and grinned; he loved his peach cobbler, too.

"So how did it go yesterday? You survived, I see," Oscar said.

"Not because Katrina didn't try to kill me. But I'd sort of expected it, would have been disappointed if she hadn't."

"Okay," Oscar said, drawing out the word.

"How well do you know her?" Will asked nonchalantly, or so he hoped.

"I've known her a while, although Lola knows her better. They've been friends for a long time. She babysits for our daughter when we go out."

"So what do you think of her?"

"She's good people, dude—steady, committed to the neighborhood, responsible for a lot of what you see at the garden. I for one certainly don't get gardening, not at all. Cutting the grass, edging, and trimming was all I signed up for. I wouldn't want anyone to put me in the same category as those little old ladies in the neighborhood who live for gardening," he said, a big grin spreading across his face.

"*Screw* you," Will said, laughing. "So what do you know about her?" he persisted, willing his face to be neutral. "The only time I've seen her, she's working in the yard."

"What do you want to know?" Oscar asked.

"You ever wonder why she dresses the way she does, does nothing to inspire attention?"

"Maybe she doesn't want attention."

"Right. What woman doesn't want attention?"

"You've just been around all the beautiful ones too long. Not every woman wants the same things. Katrina is different is all, but you would have to look at more than the surface view," Oscar said.

Will barked out a laugh. "That was harsh. Just call me superficial next time, why don't you. Don't hold back," he said, laughing more. Oscar joined in.

"I see your point, and, yes, I do like women to look a certain way. Don't see what's wrong with that. It's not the only characteristic I want, it's not even the first, but by some stroke of luck, those women are attracted to me. What's a guy supposed to do?" he said smugly.

"It's your mug. Some women find that serious, somewhat exotic face appealing."

"Between you knocking my looks and Katrina knocking my backyard and gardening skills, it's a wonder I have any confidence left," he said, laughing. "What else does she do?"

"Why do you care?" Oscar asked, looking at Will more closely.

"We'll be working together. I'm just doing my homework."

"She works for Western Bank and Trust, started right after she finished college."

"Doing what?"

"I don't know, man, something with wills and estates. She's always telling stories about her trust customers."

"Is that so? Any boyfriends?"

"Nope. She's had very few boyfriends, a few now and again, but no one for very long," Oscar said, watching Will. "Are you interested in Katrina?"

"Maybe, and I'm as much surprised by it as you are. She is different from what I'm used to, an anomaly, and that's the pull, I think. I like her, like being around her, in a friend kind of way. She's different," he said, thinking, growing quiet. "Not what I expected at all."

Oscar shrugged. "I wouldn't worry about winning; you can't lose if she's working with you, though. She knows more than one person should about gardening."

"We'll see. Anyway, we'd better head back."

"How does your bike feel?" Oscar asked.

"Great. I love it; just wished I had more time for it."

The waitress came over and handed them each a check. Will picked up both. "Let me get this, for dragging you away from your wife on a Sunday," he said, pulling out his wallet and searching for cash. He paid and they walked out and got on their bikes for the return trip home.

❦

Lola was on the couch, watching some reality show on TV. Not her reality, but hey. She looked up as Oscar entered. "How was the bike ride?" she asked, lifting her face up for a kiss.

"It was cool. We just rode up and back. We stopped for lunch at The Big Rib. We should think about moving out there, purchase some land, learn to farm or raise some cows. It's really beautiful country there."

"No farming for me; I'm strictly a city girl," she said. "How's Will?"

"He's good, the same. Funny, though, he talked mostly about Katrina today."

"Oh, did he now?" Lola perked up, all ears.

"Yep, and that's all I'm going to say on the subject. Next thing I know, you'll be planning the wedding."

"There could be worse things than that, and Katrina could use a little non-gardening-related drama in her life. I can't remember the last man she's gone out with, seriously anyway. She's so serious, more than her age dictates; her childhood and all, I guess. This could be fun to watch," she said, rubbing her hands together.

"Maybe," Oscar said.

Katrina was watering the roses at Abernathy and Co. today, her least favorite and oldest assignment given to her by Colburn. She had been difficult when she'd first come to live with her parents, and Colburn had told her that, seeing how she was the thorniest and most easily offended kid he'd ever run across, her task would be to take care of and water her other brothers and sisters—the roses with their thorns.

Thankfully, her duties had changed over the summers and had expanded after she'd become more comfortable and confident. She'd learned from experience the value of love, water, and sunshine to ailing plants and people.

She was going to be Will's assistant, for sure. She was pleased and impressed by him yesterday. She'd notified John and he'd been as excited as she'd ever seen him. There were benefits here for her, too, she reminded herself. New Years' night seemed so long ago. She'd get to see him up close and personal, maybe even rub up against him, and there was always value in that. She was going to give him and the competition her best effort; she was competitive enough that she wanted her 'hood to be victorious, so of course she'd do what was necessary to win.

"So Colburn has stuck you over here, I see," Charles said, walking toward her.

"Yep, he with his old thorny joke."

"And I hear you are going to help out your neighbor," he said, coming to stand next to her, reaching for a cigarette in his pocket. Katrina made a face.

"Those things are going to kill you, Uncle C," she said. He grunted, his usual response when she commented on his habit.

"You must belong to a really powerful grapevine. How you keep up with all the gardening stuff that goes on in this city is remarkable. I'm really impressed," she said.

He chuckled.

"But to answer your question, yes, I am. He took up a dare I offered and spent most of yesterday at the gardens working under my command," she said, frowning when he lit his cigarette and took a drag.

"Poor fellow," he said. She just laughed.

"You don't know the half of it. But he conducted himself well, worked hard, didn't complain. He knows more than I gave him credit for. Plus, I didn't tell you, but I've seen his yard, and I was truly impressed. It *is* beautiful," she said.

"Good."

"We'll see."

"You know, working with him could have some side benefits you didn't expect. I believe you've said he was handsome? Maybe you could use your wiles on him."

"What wiles?" she asked, and they both laughed.

"I don't need to tell you that Colburn and I are proud of you, and we're here if you need us. Always."

"I know," she said, wrapping her free arm around his waist and resting her head on his shoulder.

CHAPTER 7

Mid-March

Will had one more stop to make. He'd just delivered his design to John's home. This was the first step in the competition—review and approval by the neighborhood's committee. He had dropped his plan off this morning, and had listened to John extol the virtues of having him paired with Katrina. They were destined to win, all the stars had aligned, and so on. He was early, a whole two weeks before the April 1 deadline, leaving the committee with more than enough time to review his plans and leaving him time in which to make any needed changes before submissions were due to the city by May 1. With his schedule, he always built in wiggle room for himself. Who knew when he'd have to leave unexpectedly? John had promised to have the approved design back to him in two weeks, earlier if he could manage it.

He was headed to Katrina's home to give her a copy as well, even though it wasn't necessary. He wanted to demonstrate his commitment and show off a little at being ahead of schedule, proving that it hadn't been a mistake in making him leader. She would eventually need a copy for developing a planting schedule and a budget. And he just wanted to see her; he liked her, enjoyed working with her, felt they'd made progress, that she could be a really good friend. She reminded him of his sisters in some ways; she was funny and easy to talk to, uncomplicated.

He walked up to her door and rang the doorbell once. No answer. He waited a minute and rang it again. Still no answer. He'd turned to walk away when the door opened. He turned around, unconsciously taking a step back. She stood there before him, sweating and pulling a T-shirt over her head. She wore a white sports bra with what looked like matching white underwear, or very, very short shorts. They were so tiny, both pieces a beautiful contrast against her dark skin. Her body was glistening, glowing. Running shoes were on her feet. He must have interrupted her doing some kind of exercise. He'd only seen parts of her that night, or he thought he had, but he would have remembered this. Her hair was back in its usual ponytail, but some of it had come loose, falling against her back and around her face, framing it, and she wasn't wearing glasses today.

He was speechless for about three seconds, his eyes blinking, thinking what a shame it was to cover her body. He must have looked like an idiot standing here, staring at her, but he couldn't seem to get the image of her out of his mind long enough to form a coherent sentence. The reaction to her body was immediate, and he hoped she hadn't noticed.

"Will, is there something you wanted?" she asked, a hint of a smile on her lips.

"Uh . . . uh . . . yes . . . I-I, stopped by to tell you that I have given the plans to John," he said, stammering because he'd been caught off guard. "You know he lives down the street," he said, pointing in the direction of John's house, by now feeling like a complete simpleton. "I also brought over a copy of the plans for you, to, uh, get started on the budget and schedule. The committee may require changes, so keep that in mind," he said, still staring at her.

"I will," she said, fighting to keep from smiling at his stammering, holding out her hand for the designs. His appreciation of her body was evident, and it amused her.

He placed them in her palm but didn't let go, waiting for her attention. She smiled.

"I wanted to tell you that I enjoyed working with you at the gardens the other day, and John told me that you've agreed to work with me. So thanks for that, too."

She really was pretty, and what a smile. When she gave a full one, like now, it was spectacular. He returned it, still a little dazed.

"I'll let you know when I've put together a preliminary schedule and budget for you," she said, moving to close the door.

"Sure," he said, turning to leave.

He heard the door close, and started walking toward his house, the picture of her in white stuck inside his head. It reminded him of that night and prodded him to rethink the rule about not having a sexual relationship with his neighbor. She was an adult. He could talk to her, maybe she'd be up for friends with benefits. Before he knew it, he was back home.

"Will." He saw Oscar standing by his car, clearly working on it. He crossed the Sheppards' yard and went up to him.

"I watched you walk by, called your name twice. Lot on your mind, huh?"

"Sorry, I was thinking about something else. What's up?"

"Nothing, just hanging out, changing the oil in my car," Oscar said.

"Yeah."

"Hey, you okay?" he asked, concern in his gaze.

"Yeah, I just left Katrina's house; dropped off some plans for the competition."

"I heard she's agreed to work with you."

"I can't believe the rumor mill in this neighborhood."

He walked into Oscar's garage and stood against the wall, his mind already back on Katrina.

"Will?" Oscar said, looking at him strangely. "You okay?"

Will shook his head, laughing at himself a little. "Yeah, I'm okay," he said. "So oil change, huh?" He had tuned into Oscar now, having pushed the image of Katrina to the back of his mind.

❧

She parked a little way from the Vegetable Garden, the site of her second date with Darius; actually more like her first real date. She'd met him at a coffee shop, and it hadn't been so bad. She'd enjoyed it, had decided that she liked him—just not the Will kind of like. She was mostly feeling friendship, but she was going to try this dating thing if it killed her. They'd talked and gotten to know each other better over coffee, and it had ended with him asking her out to dinner.

As she walked down the sidewalk, she passed by a small garden next door to the restaurant. She could smell dirt and the scents of herbs in the air, could see plants in rows, neatly marked in this well-lit little garden.

She walked up to the restaurant, which was housed in a mid-sized building with a small wooden sign reading The Vegetable Garden. She reached for the carrot-shaped door knob on the very old heavy wooden door, pulling hard to open it. She had eaten here twice before, and both times she'd found the food exceptional.

The décor mimicked an old tavern, with a huge fireplace flanking the main wall directly across from the entrance. She knew from her earlier visits that the bread was baked over that fireplace, a tribute to days of old, giving off an aroma that made you want to beat your momma. Old chairs, fabric-covered, large, worn and broken in, were positioned around equally worn wooden tables that matched the old wood-covered floors. There was even a scattering of small couches with coffee tables or ottomans in front, all the comforts of home but with a wait staff. A couple was cuddling on the couch, coffee cups in their hands, a plate of cookies on the table in front of them. Lights were turned low, creating a cozy ambiance.

A little boy stood behind the reception stand, barely reaching the top of the podium.

"Welcome to The Vegetable Garden," he said, smiling. "How many are in your party?"

Katrina smiled back. "I am meeting one for dinner, but I haven't seen him yet."

Looking at her with interest, the boy said, "I bet you are here to meet my big brother, Darius? All the girls come here to meet him. He's a very good chef, plus they want a man with means," he added.

"Oh," she said, surprised.

"Here he comes now."

Clad in his chef uniform, Darius was indeed walking toward them.

"Thanks for meeting me for dinner," he said, smiling while reaching for her hands. "I hope you've brought your appetite with you. I hear the chef here is a wonder in the kitchen, known for transforming fruits and vegetables into something you'd kill for."

"I did bring my appetite," she said.

Darius turned to the little boy behind the podium. "Katrina, this is my little brother, Sebastian. He helps out on weekends for a small fee," he said, looking at the boy with pride.

"Sally will take over for you in ten," he told Sebastian. "Mom will be here by then to pick you up."

"Okay," his little brother replied, younger brother idol worship in his eyes.

"Shall we eat?" he said to Katrina, extending his elbow.

"Sure," she said, putting her arm through his. He led her back to a small room he told her was normally used for private dining or parties. It was empty now except for them.

"So when did you know you wanted to be a restaurant owner?" she asked, after she'd taken a seat at the main table.

"I started it about two years ago. Grew up loving to cook, not formally trained, unless you count endless hours with my mother and grandmother. My parents always had a garden. Our neighborhood was one of the last to get on board with the whole gardening thing, so they developed their own backyard garden. I didn't take to gardening all that much, but I have the small one next door. But before you get too impressed, I don't manage it, have nothing to do with it other than providing the land."

"That's okay. It's a gift to cook as well as you do," she said.

"Thanks, and speaking of dinner, may I choose something for you? Surprise you maybe?"

"Sure, surprise away," she said.

"Wine, tea, or would you prefer a soft drink?"

"Tea works," she said.

"Is there anything you don't like, or are allergic to?"

"Nope, I have the constitution of a horse."

"Give me a few seconds and I'll be right back."

"Okay."

He was fine, Katrina thought, watching him leave. She should like him. Looking around the room, she paused to study pictures hanging on the wall. Old black-and-white photos showed African-Americans farming, bent over rows, picking cotton or holding up vegetables in their hands.

"So, you're the citywide winner, what, ten years running?" he said, smiling at her.

She turned at the sound of his voice and thought, *What beautiful teeth you have, they go so well with all that smooth brown skin.*

"No, just three," she said. He pulled out a chair and sat across from her.

"So still getting the push from Amber to start your own business? She swears that you are the best she knows. It was how I met her and Claudia, at a small-business forum." He then talked about getting started with the restaurant and what went into the running of one, pausing when the waiter arrived with their food, placing two plates filled with an eggplant dish before them. Steam and delectable aromas rose from their plates.

"Am I drooling?" she asked. He laughed, pleased that she was pleased. The main dish was followed by a heavenly dessert, fruit cobbler, and coffee.

"Wow!" she said two hours later. "I'm stuffed; the food here is beyond delicious. You've created a wonderful place and food to die for." Placing her napkin on the table, she said, "I had better get going before I grow into this chair." She smiled. "I had a really, really nice time."

"I did, too," he said, standing along with her.

"Thanks again for inviting me."

"Thank you for finally answering my calls, for finally meeting me for coffee, and for finally agreeing to go out with me. You are a hard woman to get to know."

"I know, sorry, it's just me. Old before my time," she said, smiling shyly.

"Well, anyway, I'm glad you made it. Let me walk you out. I'll give you a tour of my garden," he said. "That doesn't sound too cheesy, does it?"

"Nope, and I like cheesy, anyway."

He laughed and followed her out, stopping at the small gardens for a few minutes before walking her to her car. She unlocked it and got in.

"May I call you again?" he asked, holding on to the top of her car door.

"I think so," she said.

"But?" he asked, sensing her hesitation.

"I'm just looking for friendship is all," she said.

"Friendship it is then," he said, smiling back.

"Thanks," she said, starting her car as he pushed her door closed. She backed out and left, looking at him in her rearview mirror, pleased and pleasantly surprised at how the evening had gone. He was almost too good to be true, and had provided a nice respite from her fixation with Will.

The clock on Katrina's computer showed 7:30. Time for her to go home. She gathered up her stack of trust documentation to send back to the vault in some far off corner of the bank, having completed the last of her assigned account reviews for the month. Yay, team. She was required to review each of her accounts every eighteen months, and that usually meant either Saturday morning at the office or toiling after work.

Reviews required perusal of the original will or trust document that had created the account. Distributions from the trust were checked against the language of the actual trust document scanned into the computer file; review was vital. It would be a major breach to have handed over money for ten years for health and maintenance only to find out later that it was only to be used for, say, college tuition, or perhaps was intended for some charity. It had been known to happen. She also needed to review the investments, the oil and gas property or real estate if they were a part of the trust, and to make sure all distribution requests had been documented. This process was time-consuming, and more so for Katrina, due to the size of her account load.

"Girl, what are you doing here?" Amber asked, startling Katrina and scaring her out of her skin.

"What am I doing here? What are *you* doing here? You never work late," Katrina said, her hand at her heart, trying to recover from the scare Amber had given her.

"I know, right? I'm usually so good. I finish well ahead of time, but I've gotten behind. It can happen to the best of us," Amber said, coming to stand inside Katrina's cubicle. "So I heard that you and Darius had hooked up for dinner. He must be really interested in you, wining and dining you at his place of business. That's a good sign." Then, after a pregnant pause, she asked, "So, how did it go?"

"It went okay."

"Just okay?" she asked, walking further into the cubicle and sitting down, clearly in a chatting mood. "So no more Will then, huh?"

"I didn't say that, but Will and I are just friends, anyway, working on the competition together. There is nothing else."

"But that's only because he said no. Are you still interested in him?" she asked.

"Unfortunately, yes, although I don't think anything will come of it," Katrina said, shutting down her computer.

"So that means you're going to see Darius again? You could use him to help you get past Will. You guys have more in common, anyway."

"I don't really like him in that way," Katrina said.

"What's not to like, Katrina? He's handsome, he's a brother, owns two—not one, but two—businesses. What does Will offer that Darius doesn't? You have a lot more in common with Darius, I think. I mean, really, what do you and Will have in common?" Amber asked.

"We have a lot in common," Katrina said, taken aback a little by Amber's bold assertion.

"Like what?"

"Gardening."

"Okay. What else?"

"We're both concerned about the environment."

"I'm throwing that in with the gardening," Amber said, waiting a few seconds. "See, you don't have all that much in common, but I can tell you how you're different. He is Asian, you are African-American, right? He's adventurous and you're content to live every day with plants. He likes to travel, you're a homebody. He likes women who are glamorous in their appearance, and you don't even like to wear clothes that fit."

"We're both American, we have that in common," Katrina said, clearly not intending to give an inch.

"So do the rest of the people in this country."

"Okay, I think being outdoors working with plants speaks to him in the same way it does to me."

"Okay, so you're both plant whisperers, but I also have to remind you that you argue over gardening styles."

"Maybe at first, but I've come to see the beauty in his style even though it's different from my own. We're alike," she said defensively.

"I'm just saying it would seem easier to love someone who is more like you," Amber argued.

"What does 'like you' mean? And you're one to talk. You and Claudia don't have the standard relationship."

"What? Claudia is African-American, right? Her childhood was a lot like mine, same unsympathetic view of our way of life by our parents, same negative responses from people to who we are, same challenges. But we like similar things, same culture, get the same jokes. I just think you should find someone who has the same background as you, and shared goals—like Darius."

"We do not. I grew up in a group home for the parentless. He had two parents who are still around. Someone else does his gardening for him."

"But he has a restaurant that utilizes stuff from the garden," she said, as if that made sense.

"Really, Amber," Katrina said, starting to get a little angry. "Will and I have a similarity of sprit, and that supersedes race and all that other stuff. I think it is race you're getting at, and it's also the reason for this push toward Darius," she added.

"Similarity of spirit? You are the only person I know who says stuff like that. Similarity of spirit," she repeated, shaking her head from side to side. "Are you sure Will feels the same? I just don't think it was similarity of spirit that he turned down on New Year's Eve."

Ouch, Katrina thought to herself. "I'm tired of talking about it, tired of work. I'm going home," she said, putting her desk in order and then reaching for her purse, a little stung by Amber's comments.

Taking the hint, Amber stood up. "I'm sorry, I didn't mean for that last comment to come out that way," she said and sighed. "I just want you to find someone to make you happy."

"I am happy," she said.

"You know what I mean," Amber said.

"Let's just leave it, okay? I understand. But I don't know if I can like Darius just because I should. I wish I could. It would make things so much easier. But I can't. Anyway, I'm tired," she said, standing up and walking to the entrance of her cubicle. "Are you sticking around here, or do you want to walk out together?"

"I'll walk out with you. It's dark out and we have to stick together, look out for each other, right?" she said, apologizing again in her own way.

"I'll meet you at the door then," Katrina said, walking out of her cubicle.

Later on that evening, Katrina sat on her couch flipping through the TV channels, not really seeing the picture. Her mind went back to her conversation with Amber. Granted, Amber had offered some good points, but she could see only friendship with Darius. She didn't like him beyond that. So what if her desire for Will wouldn't lead anywhere? Outside of his teasing, it seemed Will wanted nothing more than friendship with her, excitement over her body notwithstanding—and even that hadn't been inducement enough.

Tired of her thoughts, she went to her kitchen table, where she'd placed the copy of Will's design. Thinking back, she smiled at his reaction to her then. She decided to spend some time on his designs this evening as a way of distancing herself from Amber's comments; a fresh reminder of the futility of her desire for Will.

John had called to inform her that the committee had accepted Will's design as is, and that no changes from him were needed. This of course, rubbed her the wrong way. That had never happened to her, but she was going to move on, the whole water-under-the-bridge thing. She needed to get started on creating a budget and planting schedule and now seemed like a perfect time. And as painful as it was to admit, Will's design was good, very similar to his backyard, but with a few additional features.

Using his plans, she compiled a list of plants they could use to transform the current garden. She knew cost, and what she didn't know she could ask the godfathers, particularly Colburn. It was his area of expertise, plus he loved haggling with sellers; it worked so well with his personality. She'd put all that into a planting schedule and put together a tentative work schedule that the volunteers would need to help them with the changes. She needed to get with Thomas soon.

She was proud of her ability to grow things, to see what could be and put in the work and time to make it happen. She stood up, needing to go outside to breathe. It always helped to center her, to remind her of the good and beauty in the world.

She didn't bother with shoes. She liked the feel of grass on the soles of her feet. She headed out her back door, walking slowly. It was starting to get dark, that time of the evening when it was not so bright and shining, like the lights in a restaurant being dimmed for a quiet dinner. The outside had an ambience, too. The air was cool, and it was quiet. She walked down the deck steps, taking in the colors surrounding her. She thought of Will's garden and the mister in his enclosed courtyard; it beckoned her, gentle and soothing to her soul, along with the chimes and lanterns. She was dressed in a long-sleeve T-shirt and sweats. There was still a little nip in the air, especially at night.

Soon, she had walked out the back fence and into the greenbelt. Why not, she thought. If he wasn't home, he'd never know she had been there. She'd check to see if it was dark in his home first. She walked past Lola and Oscar's house and the Sheppards' place until she reached Will's fence. She stopped, looking for a wide enough space between two fence slats to peep in, trying to determine if anyone was home.

It took her several tries to find a hole in the fence big enough for her to see in. Perfect. It was dark in his home. She opened the gate and walked in slowly, allowing time for any lights to come on inside, alerting her of his presence. All good, all quiet. She tiptoed over to the enclosed courtyard and went in, closing the doors behind her. The misters were working and they went off as if they knew she needed the burst of spray. She sat, stretching her legs out in front of her, and lowered her back until she was lying flat, full length, her hands and arms at her side. She closed her eyes, taking in deep breaths of air, letting go of her worries and doubts for a few minutes. The deep sounds of chimes eased her worries like her mother's hand on her shoulder, telling her that things would be okay.

She probably lay there for about thirty minutes, even dozed off for a while. She was tired. When she opened her eyes, it was dark out. Her watch told her that not only had she slept, but she'd been there close to an hour. She was pushing her luck and needed to get home before he did. She stood up, slowly opening the door and peeking out. Crap, she thought, taking in the inside of his home. All the lights were on. *Shoot, Katrina, what were you thinking? How had this been a good idea?*

Peeking through the door she could see into all of the parts of his home through his bank of windows. The room directly in her line of vision must have been the living room; thankfully, the sofa was free of him. She stepped out, hoping it was safe but remaining cautious. Looking over to the left, she could see into the kitchen and dining area. He wasn't there, either. She stepped away, backing up quietly toward the back gate, keeping an eye on his home; still no sign of him.

She looked to the far right, at what must have been his bedroom. Great, still no sign, but just as that thought flittered through her mind, he stepped out of his bathroom wearing nothing but his birthday suit. And what a suit it was. He had a towel in his hand, and was rubbing it over his hair, facing away from the window. He moved over to his bed, providing her with a view of a beautiful backside. Her breath caught, hands starting in with that damn twitching again. Damn, he was some kind of fine. She'd always known that from seeing him in his cycling suits, but those visions of him in his riding gear were something different and had in no way prepared her for this.

He had an athlete's lean muscle, but she knew that already. Her eyes roamed quickly over him from top to bottom. Why the hell not, she thought. When would she have this opportunity again? She might as well take her time and commit this to memory. Her eyes moved back up, started at the top. His head, wet and shiny from his shower, peeked out from underneath the towel he was using to dry his hair. Her eyes journeyed downward, taking in the muscles of his back, watching them move beneath his skin as he dried his hair. His back narrowed down into a firm and fine ass, which she watched for a second or two, pondering the possibilities and uses for it as she watched the muscles play under its skin. She took a deep breath bracing herself before her eyes trailed lower to beautifully well-developed, well defined legs. Bicycling had really paid off for him. Maybe she should consider it for herself.

Katrina, this is wrong on so many levels, she thought to herself. She needed to leave, because now she was a trespasser *and* a voyeur, or, as the police would call it when they slapped the handcuffs on her wrists before hauling her ass off to jail, *a peeping Tom*. But did she move? Shit, no. She was staying put; if she was going to jail, it would be so worth her while.

She watched him walk from the bed over to a mirror hanging on his wall, still giving her the back view. He was looking at himself in it, had his face tilted up as he leaned into the mirror to look at something on his chin, an up-close perusal. Looked like he'd just shaved, too. His eyes looked up and into hers, slanted eyes over beautiful high sharp cheekbones. Shock registered in them, and he slowly turned to face her, his eyes unreadable now.

Caught, Katrina took a step back. She watched him walk slowly toward the window that separated him from her, while she stood trapped, her eyes locking on his. *Fuck it*, she said to herself. In for a penny, in for a pound; she was not missing this opportunity. Her eyes moved down to study his chest; *better hurry*, her mind said. Hell, no, she thought, taking in hair black and straight laying against skin; not a lot, but enough to make it interesting, enough to run her hands through. It trailed down over a nice slab of abs, trim and way developed, each muscle group outlined in painstaking detail.

Okay, her hands had gone beyond twitching, they were now holding on to each other, trying to contain their desire to reach for him. Her eyes moved lower. Oh, God, his feet had stopped moving, having reached the window, but another part of him had taken the baton and was now rising against his lower stomach. She watched that part of his anatomy grow, fascinated and entranced.

He was leaning forward now, his forearms resting against the window as he continued to watch her watch him. She, who now stood engrossed, following the growth of his body avidly, swallowing, but unable to look away. Finally, after she'd gotten her fill, it seemed like forever, but more like a couple of seconds, her eyes lifted to his, and he smiled back at her. Not a barely there smile, but a full one, a punch to her solar plexus. God, he was beautiful.

She slowly walked backwards to the gate, her eyes locked with his, communicating her approval, pleasure, desire, and embarrassment at being caught. Her back hit the fence and she reached behind her body to open the gate. She stepped through it, finally breaking the stare. She practically flew home, up the steps, and inside, where she flopped down on the couch. She stared into space, her internal eyes locked in on the picture of him naked and now on display for her private viewing pleasure. WOW!

◈

Will was stunned and shaky after Katrina's perusal of his body. He took a deep breath, allowing his body to return to its normal setting. He'd stepped out of the shower, getting ready to meet a friend for dinner—and maybe more—and looked up to find Katrina, of all people, standing in his backyard, watching him with more than casual interest in her eyes; more like he was her last meal before her meeting with the electric chair. But that was nothing new; she'd never hidden her interest in him.

This was something different tonight, and this he would not be leaving alone, not after seeing her standing outside his window with so much need in her eyes. It was the kind of desire that would be a challenge to harness and control, hell, to even hold on to; even so, he was sure he was up to the task.

So no more dithering, debating, or rebuffing, he wanted what she wanted, and the sooner the better. He'd watched her hungrily take her fill, and he'd replaced her standing there in a too-big T-shirt, sweats, and bare feet with the picture of her in her white work-out clothes. His body had responded to those images.

Katrina was turning out to be one complex creature, chock full of contradictions; shy, aggressive, sexy, and as far from sexy as one could get. At this moment, she was also someone he wanted in his bed. He should not have turned her down when she'd first offered; hell, if he'd seen that look in her eyes, he wouldn't have. He was so over being cautious now; he just wanted her dark skin against his, filled with him, holding on and pleading for more. *Then what,* popped into his mind. Then *nothing* was the answer that followed. She was a woman, and, in her not-so-subtle way, she'd just communicated her want, her need. Lucky for her it happened to be what he wanted. Finally. Now.

CHAPTER 8

April

A week later, Katrina sat at Lola's kitchen table, watching her prepare lunch for Sydney. Katrina had brought Lola up to speed with her life, Darius and the date, her subsequent talk with Amber, covering the basics of the Darius-versus-Will debate. She'd just finished providing Lola with her trip over Will's nude body.

"That good, huh?" Lola asked.

"You have no idea. *I* had no idea," Katrina answered, her mood today somber, her mind taking her back to Will's backyard. She stared out into space, remembering again.

"So, he called?" Lola asked.

"The next night."

"What did he say?"

"Did I want to come over?"

"And?"

"I told him no, told him that it had been a long day for me, that I was tired."

"Okay. And he said?"

"Nothing."

"Nothing, huh?"

"I didn't really give him a chance. I changed the subject, started talking about the competition. You know, the expectations, dates, deadlines; covering the steps that would be required of him going forward, just sticking to the competition stuff."

"Why?" Lola asked. Katrina simply shrugged. "Okay. And then what?" Lola asked.

"And then nothing. He was mostly quiet, listening to me."

"I'm hungry, Mommy," Sydney said, coming into the kitchen and plopping down in the seat next to Katrina. "Hi, Auntie Katrina."

"Hey," Katrina said, running her hand over Syd's head.

"Okay, baby, sit. Mommy has your lunch ready," Lola said, standing up, and placing a kiss on her daughter's head. She went over to the microwave, hitting the button to reheat Syd's lunch. Using the remote, she turned the TV on the counter to *Sesame Street*, one of Syd's favorites.

While Lola played mommy, Katrina was thinking yes, Will had called, but there was the part that had gone unsaid. Will's call had been all innuendo, all for moving on the desire that her watching him in the nude had implied. What had she expected from him, really? After all, she'd started this, beginning with her New Year's Eve solicitation and ending with her standing in his backyard with major lust and need in her eyes. So he now wanted some of what he'd seen offered. She'd heard it in his voice. How could he have known that she'd talked herself down from that ledge?

Lola set the plate of food in front of Sydney, whose eyes were now glued to the TV, watching Elmo and India Arie singing the ABCs.

Katrina took a deep breath. "I've been rethinking this whole Will situation, Lola, and I've realized that we wouldn't work," she said.

"Katrina, are you kidding me? Why? You think he's too much for you? Is that it?"

Katrina shook her head.

"Then what?

"Then nothing," she said.

"You saw the man's response to the idea of sex. It happens to men all the time, it's a natural reaction, believe me. Don't let it scare you and don't run from it. It's what you've wanted. You can't call it off, not before you even start," Lola said.

"That's what makes it the perfect time."

"Don't, Katrina."

"What?"

"Don't quit before you start. This is so your pattern," she said, shaking her head in frustration. "This is so you. In like or lust, always from afar, of course, and just when it could be more, you quit. You always say it won't work out." She gave Katrina her best motherly look. "You're scared is what you are."

"Am not," she said.

Lola pursed her lips and gave her a 'don't bullshit me' look. "Sure you are, and I know what you're afraid of."

Katrina rolled her eyes, steeling herself for a lecture.

"You're afraid to take a chance, scared that you'll be hurt, so you just back away, curl up in your shell, like Sydney's turtle," she said.

"Whatever."

"I mean, really, Katrina. Will hasn't done anything besides showing you that he's interested in you sexually, and you're quitting. Sex that you wanted, may I remind you, and not too long ago. Wasn't that what New Year's Eve night was all about?" Lola asked, placing her hands over Sydney's ears as she said the word "sex." No need, as Syd sat with a fish stick suspended in mid-air, eyes glued to the TV as she sang along with the count.

"I've changed my mind is all," Katrina said.

"Katrina," Lola said, disappointment in her voice.

"I'm just saving myself some time here. It wouldn't work out. I'd want more, and I can tell he wouldn't. Plus we both know I'm not his type," she said, giving the reason she'd decided to tell Lola.

Lola shook her head, disappointed in Katrina. "How do you know you'd want more; you have to try it first. He may not be any good, awful even."

"Doubtful."

"Yeah, doubtful," Lola said.

"So, you see. I'd only end up hurt," Katrina said.

"What I see is that this is so classic you," Lola said, looking at her. "How many times have we been here? Remember Stanley?"

"I know, but what kind of name is Stanley?"

Lola shook her head. "Katrina."

"I didn't like him, anyway, too pushy," she said, squeezing her nose in distaste.

Lola rolled her eyes. "Franklin, then?" she asked, eyebrows lifted.

Katrina squeezed her nose harder. "Momma's boy," she said.

"Zach?" Lola asked.

Katrina pretended to gag, moving her hand to cover her mouth.

Lola sighed. "Katrina, don't quit again," she said, sitting back in her chair and looking aggrieved.

"I know you like Will, *really* like Will, leaps above the others," Lola said, now exasperated.

"See, that's what I've been trying to tell you. I would only end up hurt. Better to see me stop now. See, Lola, we're here, you and me," she said, pointing two fingers between her and Lola's eyes. "We are in agreement."

Lola shook her head and laughed. "What do I do with you?"

"I don't know," she answered, tuning in to *Sesame Street* now, where Kermit the frog sat alone, perched on a tree limb, singing mournfully, 'It's not easy being green.'

'I'm feeling you there, Kermit," she whispered, admitting to herself that Lola was right. But seeing Will in the nude was enlightening, her light-bulb moment.

She'd recognized the potential for some major hurt from this one. Nothing small about her desire for Will, and hurt would be the prize at the end of it all because she wanted that man something powerful. Wanted him fiercely, forcefully, and limitlessly, the scariest adverb of them all. She wanted him more than was safe for her sanity and more than he wanted her for sure. And that kind of want scared her shitless. It was way too much.

This man, unlike the others, was one she could truly love, and so far love had not been good to her. For her, love mostly brought loss, and she wasn't up for any more losses. She'd had her fill, thank you very much. She was quitting while she was ahead.

Katrina picked up her cell phone a week later to call Will. She'd put this off long enough. They had exchanged numbers due to the competition, but she hadn't called him. It was back to hiding out again since the backyard scene. The competition, her responsibilities to it and to Will, had her calling.

He was leaving, and he would be gone for a while—overseas, somewhere in Asia—for three weeks. He'd given her a copy of his schedule. The first set of plans was due to the city May 1, and, according to her calculations, Will would be overseas.

She dialed the number and waited. No answer, so she left a message.

"Hey, Will, I've finished the preliminary budget and planting schedule and I was hoping I could drop if off. Maybe you would have a chance to review it while you're gone, maybe on the plane. Also wanted to make sure you're okay with the first deadline. Anyway, call me and I'll drop them by, or if I don't hear from you, I'll leave them on your doorstep," she said, hanging up.

"Will, please, baby. Oh, that's it, harder, yes, more," Charlotte groaned, her head bent over, hair covering her face. She was on her knees in the middle of Will's bed, her arms out-stretched before her, her wrist captured in one of Will's hands in a firm grip, his other hand at her hip, holding her in place as he pushed into her. "Oh, please," she said, her request ending in a groan so loud and so filled with pleasure that Will had to grit his teeth to keep from coming.

He pulled back for a second, centering, and he pushed back into her body, loving the way she felt surrounding him. Perspiration ran down his face, his hair glistening from the effort of fucking her. He pushed in harder, focused solely on moving in and out of her body, sure, strong thrusts, forceful, a little bit punishing in their power. He was attuned to only the movement, the glide in and out of her body.

Her arms gave out and she fell forward. He let go of her wrist then, moving his other hand to the side of her body to lift her hips and hold her still, relentless in his quest to fill her. He felt her climax begin, and, in spite of his best efforts, he came, too, and collapsed on top of her.

He lay there breathing for a second, regaining his breath before separating from her and rolling over onto his back. She rolled onto her stomach. His eyes found hers staring back at him between strands of her hair.

"What got into you?" she asked, giving him a huge smile. "And do you think it could get into you more often?" He gave her a small grin.

He took a deep breath, turning at the sound of his cell phone ringing in the distance; ignoring it, he pondered the answer to her question. Katrina had gotten into him, he thought, but he didn't think telling Charlotte that was a good idea so he remained quiet.

He had wanted Katrina, but since that idea had fallen through, Charlotte was the backup plan; a good one, an energetic one, but still the backup.

This was maddening; the push from Katrina to sleep with him, from New Year's Eve night to her standing in his backyard, and now that he'd finally gotten on board, she was backing off. He didn't know what he'd expected or had hoped would have happened after his slideshow.

He'd called the next evening, raring to go, and had gotten a wall instead of the your-place -or-mine question he'd expected. So what now? What did she want? He didn't do games; this push forward and now pull back was not for him. He wanted to tell her that it didn't need to be complicated. He had what she wanted; hell, what she'd wanted for a while now, and he was so on board with giving it to her. Only now she was giving him this "I'm Not Interested, Let's Keep This Professional" act He hadn't seen her outside, either. At all. Not like before, so it was back to square one. Back to avoiding him.

That wasn't the worst of it; the worst was she was becoming a frequent and annoying intrusion into his thoughts. She'd silently and quietly taken up residence just under the surface of his skin.

Charlotte blew the hair from her face and sat up. "Are you listening to me?" she asked, her body a pleasure to look at.

"Sorry, thinking about my work trip tomorrow."

"Not a good comeback, Will. No woman wants to hear that after what we've just shared," she said.

He smiled, turning to her, leaning over to kiss her mouth in apology.

"That's better, and you can't know how much I'd like some more of this, but I've got to go. Meeting my sister to try on bridesmaid dresses," she said, looking over at him, beautiful body stretched out still, and sighed. "Want me to come back by later?"

"Nope, heading out of town tomorrow; I'll call you when I get back," he said, sitting up, putting his feet on the floor. "I'm going to take a shower. Can you see yourself out?"

"Sure. Try and miss me while you're gone," she said, crawling across the bed to him, pushing her body into his back, wrapping her arms around him.

"Of course," he said, removing her arms, standing up and going into his bathroom.

Charlotte was gone when he emerged, towel wrapped around his waist in deference to the Katrina-in-his-back-yard incident. He went to check his messages and, speak of the devil, it was Katrina wanting to drop off the work she'd completed with his designs. She had called fifteen minutes ago. He picked up his phone and dialed her number; she answered.

"Hello."

"Katrina, I got your message, and I'm home if you haven't dropped off the plans yet. Come over; I needed to ask a favor of you," he said, trying out his own version of her business tone. He could do businesslike, too, he told himself, still smarting from the change in her behavior.

"Sure," she said, once again trying out her new professional voice, dialing back the sex quotient, going for the just-friends thing now; she would have to remind herself of that often. She would have much preferred the dropping-off option; she was nowhere near ready to face Will.

She rang the doorbell and waited, hearing movement inside. The door opened to reveal him in sweats and a plain T-shirt.

Heaven help me, she thought, shaking her hands to quiet them; they were back to that damn twitching. Pulling back from him was going to be harder than she'd thought.

"Come in, we can work in here," he said, pointing to his study, giving her a small smile and stepping back to let her enter. She followed him, taking a seat on the couch, speaking up immediately.

"So I'm returning the plans you gave me. I made a copy for myself, and these are the budgets and planting schedules. Take your time and look them over. Remember, the plans are due to the city May 1. The budget and planting schedules aren't due until July, and that's only if we are one of the five selected. I like to get an early start," she said, handing over the packet of information, which he accepted, placing it on his desk.

He turned and sat on the edge of it, legs extended, arms crossed, looking beyond sexy, and watched her. She had no idea of his thoughts, but her eyes were eating him up. Such a feast. *You are in danger*, she wanted to tell him, her eyes drawn to his body, covered today in clothes, but still naked to her.

He cleared his throat and Katrina's eyes jolted back up to his. Okay, this moving on wasn't going to be easy. She knew it, but hard choices rarely were. What was she saying? Oh, yeah.

"Okay. Have you made arrangements to have them dropped off to the committee May 1, or will you be back in town by then?" she asked.

"No, I won't be back by then. I'm leaving tomorrow, which is why I wanted to see you in person. I was hoping you wouldn't mind turning them in for me."

"No, I don't mind. I've done this for a while, and I'll have an opportunity to check up on some of my friends from the old days," she said.

He continued to watch her. Having nothing further to add she stood, preparing to leave. "Well, okay, I'll see you later. Have a safe trip," she said, turning to walk out of the room.

"Are you in a hurry?" he asked, reaching for her hand, catching her before she walked out. He was suddenly not in any hurry for her to leave now that she was here, his irritation with her behavior falling away. He wanted her to stay, and he was a little bewildered by this need.

"No," she said, shaking her head, not sure what to do now. Startled by the contact, she pulled her hand away. "Why?"

"I had hoped you might want a personal tour of my backyard. You seem to like it so much, I thought you might be interested in the reasoning behind its design," he said, going for humor, back to teasing.

"That's okay."

"No, I would like very much to show it to you. You need to feel at home back there," he said. Watching her face scrunch up, he smiled. "You're welcome back there whenever you want, by the way," he said, again smiling at her facial expressions, embarrassment and interest flickering across her face. "If I have company over, however, you may get more than an eyeful," he said, and laughed out loud at her expression. "How about I leave a white towel on the back fence? If I have someone over, then you'll know to stay away, unless you're really into voyeurism."

"You're so not funny. One time, and you make such a big deal of it," she said, choosing bravado over embarrassment.

"One time?" he asked, looking at her in disbelief.

"Okay, twice. But I must say in my defense that I needed to see the competition."

"I'm not and never will be your competition, Katrina," he said, reaching for her hand again. He walked her through his living room, which sat in the back portion of his home, toward the bank of windows that separated him from the outside. Katrina's head whipped around as she tried to catch glimpses of his eco-friendly home. He stopped at his windows, looking outward.

"It's nice to be able to see outside whenever you want," she said, coming to stand next to him, looking out.

"Yes, it is. Typically, a Japanese home offers some primary viewpoints into the garden from inside, even if it's only into a small courtyard or Zen garden. Japanese gardens are designed to provide a break from the outside world, a respite, a spiritual place, leaving the profane beyond the fencing outside."

She turned to face him, listening.

"In some ways I need a disconnection from the stress of life and work, and this garden supplies that for me. Almost unconsciously, peace and calm seep in," he said, growing quiet, looking out his window. "I also wanted to create a garden that would be in harmony with my home, and I wanted to be able to see the whole of it."

"I certainly understand your feelings. I get that, too, from my garden," she explained, adding, "Although its design is very different from yours."

He held a door open for her and she stepped out onto the patio, he following behind and then moving to stand beside her.

"This is it," he said, looking around. Her eyes wandered over the trees next to his home, reaching to his roof, their trunks clean except for clusters of green on the top branches, as were most of the trees in his yard.

"Japanese gardening isn't a total complete design so much as it is a mix of about five different parts, ideas, or theories, and not all may be found in Japanese gardens at once. Some aspects are uniquely Japanese, others with influences from the Chinese and Korean cultures."

They continued to stand on the patio overlooking his yard as she took in his mini-history lesson.

"My garden, I hope, is Japanese at heart, but mixed in with my own take on gardening and bits and pieces taken from my travels," he said, walking further out into his yard. He pointed to the tall fencing at the back. "I like my privacy, thus the need for above-standard fencing," he said, pointing. "The hedges and shrubs, when fully grown, will hide the fence," he added.

He put his palm outward, reaching for hers again. She looked at it for a second and shook her head. He turned and started walking toward the waterfall and pond, not hurt by that small rejection.

"The lawn before I made changes to it was basically flat, although it had a bit of a slope upward toward that corner," he said, pointing to where the top of the waterfall stood. "I had soil brought in to build the corner up further, to find the rocks to form the waterfall. I spent too many weekends looking for that main rock," he said, laughing at her expression. "I know, one rock, but it needed to be perfect, and it is."

"Yep, it is," she agreed, tracking the flow of water as it fell onto the rocks below and flowed into the pond filled with fish. They walked over to the pond to get a closer look.

"I was hoping to do something similar to the pond feature at the neighborhood gardens." He stood and walked over to the enclosed courtyard, standing outside its doors.

"This is my favorite spot in the whole garden. It's my take on the courtyard style. Usually courtyards are more for viewing from inside the house than for using, but again, I've combined the typical courtyard with my own ideas. I added the mister in deference to the heat. The lanterns and chimes take me to another place, sort of like the hammocks in your design," he said. She nodded in acknowledgment.

"I loved this space for the reasons you just gave," she said, walking over to his side, passing him to open the door and step in. He followed her.

"I love the soft glow that the lanterns create, while the chimes create a rhythm that I listen to. I try to breathe to their sounds. It's a very relaxing, calming exercise," he said, taking a step closer to her, lining up behind her back. She could feel him there.

"I'll have to try that," she said, stepping away.

"You really are welcome to come over anytime. The gate is never locked."

"You sure?" she asked, turning to look into his face. He moved closer to her, in front of her, his eyes matching the want she'd heard in his voice when he'd called.

"Feel free. It would be nice to know that someone is watching over my home," he said, looking over her face, seeing the beauty she tried so hard to hide; the brown eyes, lovely long lashes, and enticing lips.

She turned away, stepping out of the door and back into his garden. "So what about this area?" she asked walking, over to the rock and stone bed.

"My stone garden," he said, pleasure in his voice, walking over to the largest section of his backyard. "I took this trip once to the city of Kyoto, near Osaka and Kobe." Noting her blank look, he chuckled. "Like you,

I'm interested in history, and there's a large number of temples in and around that particular city, most with beautiful gardens surrounding them. I try to incorporate what I like from those places, too, sort of like what you did in your garden with what you saw in England.

"What you see here comes from my take from some of the dry gardens in and around those temples. There's this one, the Ryoan-ji Temple gardens, often referred to as the embodiment of Zen art and perhaps the single greatest masterpiece of Japanese culture. It's a stark assembly of fifteen rocks sitting on a bed of white gravel. No trees, no hills, no ponds, no water features. As far from romantic as you can get. Strangely enough, the absence of all of what could be considered a distraction focuses your mind, or my mine, at least," he said.

She could tell he was back at that garden in his memories.

"There is a plain garden behind the temple that over-looks the rock garden and in it there is a stone washbasin called Tsukubai, which displays a simple yet profound four character inscription. *'I learn only to be contented,'* — a personal goal of mine," he said, chuckling a little at the serious turn the conversation had taken. "I loved that place," he said, surprised that he shared that with her.

Katrina listened, nodding at his comments, aligning this Will with her earlier impressions of him, more than a little surprised by his knowledge and the personal aspects of why he gardened. He was more like her than she'd known, confirming that her intuition to put distance between them had been the correct one. This gardening Will, along with all the others, would be so damaging to her, way more than she could handle.

"Well, I'd better go. I bet you have a thousand things to do before you leave."

"No, I'm fine. It doesn't take me long to pack, and I don't leave until the morning. Sorry, didn't mean to get carried away."

"No, I understand what you feel," she said, looking at him seriously. "It's beautiful here. What you've created is amazing. I love it, as different as it is from mine. I'd better get going, anyway. Let me know if you have any questions when you get back about the budget or planting schedule."

"Sure," he said.

"And thanks for the tour. I'll just see myself out through your back gate," she said, walking around him and out of the courtyard doors and over to his back gate. She unlatched it and after a final wave, left. He turned and followed, stopping as he watched her leave.

May

She left work early Thursday evening to drop off Will's plans to the city. The Garden City committee headquarters was located east of town in one of the older neighborhoods, and it was one of the original founding neighborhood gardens. This was one of her favorite gardens in the city and one of the three original gardens still in existence and still competing. This garden's volunteers were aging hippies. Once they got past the idea of growing marijuana, they became the city's main and first growers of basic herbs, specializing in the hard to find.

Katrina also loved their flower garden, walking through it now on her way to the building where she needed to turn in Will's design. She knew most of the people who worked in it, either through her time spent as a board member or through Abernathy and Co. This garden was unique and popular because it had incorporated five Volkswagen beetles into its design. Herbie's Garden was the name selected for it; a throwback to the old 60s name for the VW Beetle. There were about five of them, painted new and wild colors each year, where they sat among patches of wild flowers that someone took the time to plant to coordinate with the cars' colors. It was an awesome display of creativity combined with nostalgia. The wildflowers had made their appearance in force this spring, due to the bounty of rain they'd gotten during the late fall and early winter this year. The east side was almost always a finalist in the competition.

Katrina opened the door to the main building; one large room was filled to capacity with neighborhood representatives submitting designs for both the flower and vegetable categories. There were two lines, and designs were being accepted by two people sitting at a table at the front of each line. She knew all those sitting behind the flower garden tables; she'd worked with all of them at one time or another. Katrina stood in line, submitted the design, spoke to a few old garden volunteers, and left.

∞◇∞

Will needed a break from people, so he had taken himself to one of his favorite restaurants for yakitori. It was more a hole in the wall, but that worked for him most days. It was called the Captain and run by an ex-Japanese naval officer who retired and opened this place. It was located near his hotel in Tsuchiura, outside Miho, where his company's plant was located. It was quick and convenient after a long day, and it was usually dark when he finished up with work. Not a big place at all, it held about twenty or thirty people comfortably.

He sat drinking a Kirin, his favorite Japanese beer. He had just ordered and was waiting for his food to arrive. He was back to thinking again, aggravatingly enough, about Katrina. He was going to call her in a few minutes, his mind searching for a suitable excuse to call. Checking in to make sure the garden plans were dropped off was the best he could do; lame though it was, but he was going to use it, anyway. He liked talking to her, and he wasn't ready to relinquish the possibility of having her in his bed.

He had a week left to go on his trip, and for the first time ever, he was ready to get home. Restless for home was an unusual feeling for him. He had fallen asleep with the image of her, her skin next to his, fixed in his mind. Thoughts of her filled the moments during the day when he took a mental break from work.

Okay, he would call, reaching for his cell and dialing her number before he could talk himself out of it. He looked at his watch and saw that it was eight in the morning back home. He hadn't changed his watch to Asian time; it was easier for him not to.

❦

Driving to work, Katrina answered her cell. It was Will; this was a surprise.

"Hello," she said.

"Hi, it's Will." Her breath left her body in one sudden whoosh, but she played it off.

"Aren't you in another country?" was all she could think to say. No other words seemed to want to form in her brain.

"Yes, I am. I wanted to make sure you were able to drop off the plans to the city without any problems."

"No, no problems," she said, trying to sound professional.

"I felt a little guilty about leaving it to you."

"No, don't worry about it; It was no trouble," she said, a very professional answer, she told herself, internally patting herself on the back for having the wherewithal to give it.

"How are things going otherwise?" he asked.

"Things are going okay," she said.

He was silent and so was she.

"Well, I better let you go."

"Sure. Thanks for checking."

"No problem. Thanks for helping me," he said, disconnecting the call, disappointed. What had he expected her to say? She was distant again, leaving him wondering what, if anything, he should do about it. Maybe pulling back was for the best. This wouldn't be a long-term thing for him, anyway. Would it?

⌘

"Hello, Mr. Franklin. How are you today?" Katrina said into her telephone. Mr. Franklin was one of her favorite customers. He called on behalf of one of his four boys, all with separate trust funds set up by their great-grandfather to fund their college. The trust allowed a little discretion over non-school items, but it had been established primarily to fund college.

"Hi, Katrina," he said. "I got a little bit of a problem with Andrew."

"Okay," she said, waiting for him to continue.

"Andrew went to a party at someone's house and had too much to drink. The parents of the child having the party weren't home at the time. Andrew left with a friend in a car—he wasn't driving—the other kid was—but both had been drinking.

"They were stopped by the police on the way home, tested, and both were arrested. Andrew started arguing with the officer and was more than a little belligerent, I've been told," he said, blowing out a big breath, before continuing. "We've raised the funds to have him released after I let him sit in there for a while. Anyway, I will need some assistance from the trust to help cover court costs and attorney's fees for this incident. I'm calling to see if the trust can help?"

"I have to check, but I believe it can. I just need to make sure. How is Andrew?" she asked.

"Fine. Frightened, disappointed with himself, as well he should be. I've never had any trouble with any of my boys before this. Andrew is a good kid, but this was a major mistake for him."

"Children," she said, as if she had some of her own. "Let me review your account to make sure that the trust can help with this kind of incident. Could you fax paperwork from the attorney that you've hired over to me and an itemized list of the expenses associated with it?"

"Sure. I'm embarrassed by all this, by having to ask, as is Andrew. It's been a wake-up call for him. He walks a finer line than the others. He is the next to the oldest, and, as difficult as this was, it has been good for him and his younger brothers to witness the consequences of bad choices. I don't have to tell you how much worse it could have been. Just imagine the trouble he'd be in if they'd had an accident or hurt or killed someone. Andrew understands and sees that more clearly than he ever has."

"I understand. Send me the information and I can get started. As with all of the requests, this will have to be reviewed by the committee, but I'll send you an e-mail once I verify that the trust can be used for this purpose."

"I do, and thanks, Katrina. I'll send the paperwork and documentation to you this morning."

"Goodbye, Mr. Franklin," she said, disconnecting the call.

Katrina was summoning the godfathers via the walkie talkies: "Colburn and Uncle C, it's time for dinner," she said, listening to the static for a minute.

"Okay," answered Colburn; "on my way" said C.

She'd stopped by about two hours ago and worked a little in the store in the check-out line before heading back to cook dinner. Baked salmon was on the menu tonight. She had stopped by the grocer's on her way over, knowing she wouldn't find anything in the godfathers' refrigerator that she'd approve of. And she had already girded herself for the moans and groans she expected to hear after the godfathers took a look at what was on the table. But you know what? She was the cook, and they ate more pizza, fried chicken, and burgers than the law allowed.

Colburn strolled in first, his eyes scanning the table. "Lord Almighty, Katrina! When you promised me fish, I thought you meant some good old home-fried catfish, not this pink fish. What kind of fish is pink, anyway," he grumbled as he went over to wash his hands.

"It's salmon, and it's good for you. Remember it has the good fat, helps to increase your good cholesterol. Remember HDL, good cholesterol, LDL, not so good," she said.

"Don't start that again. You and your damn facts," Colburn said, watching C enter the kitchen and walk over to the spot at the sink.

"I only tell you these things because I love you. Would it kill either of you to eat a little healthier?"

"You'll never nab a man by nagging, Katrina," Colburn said, taking a seat at the table.

"You haven't seen nagging, yet. I'll show you nagging," she said, enjoying the push-back she always got from the godfathers.

She was pushy and prickly when she'd first come to live with Wes and Marlene Jones; she tried to show them her worst, hoping it wouldn't be bad enough for them to send her back. They hadn't. Then she moved on to striving for perfection, realizing how lucky she'd gotten with her parents. She became a rule follower, helped out when most kids her age were shooting the shit, stayed close to home to be with them, and almost didn't survive their death.

She sat down between Charles and Colburn and led them in grace. It was quiet for a while as they set about eating the dinner they had complained so much about.

"Good, huh?" she asked.

"Not too bad," said Uncle C, chewing heartily. "So how's it going with the Japanese fellow?"

"It's going good. I've delivered the design to the city committee on his behalf—he's in Japan on business—so all we have to do now is wait."

"So when do we get to meet this new boyfriend of yours?" Colburn asked.

Katrina looked up, her eyes narrowing in on Colburn. "Cut it out, you two. He's not my boyfriend."

"Is that so?" Colburn said, smiling at C.

"What's the smile about?" she asked.

"Nothing, it's just a smile. A man can't smile in his house anymore without being questioned? A man can't have any secrets of his own? That's not right, Katrina," he said, smiling and enjoying, as always, the ribbing he gave her.

"So things are going okay with you working with him?" Charles asked.

"Yep, all's good," she answered. She wasn't going to talk about him anymore, was going to keep it strictly professional and garden-related. It was hard, though. She was still interested in spite of her fears, but couldn't seem to get past them.

She and the godfathers finished dinner and then she cleaned up the kitchen. She kissed them goodbye and left for home, enjoying, as always, her time with them.

First weekend in June

Katrina sat at her home computer checking the website for the list of those selected for the top five. There, listed among the other four, was Shining Creek. Yes! They'd been selected. Her phone rang. She noted from the caller ID that it was John, probably as excited by the results as she was. "Hello."

"Katrina, did you see the results? We made it again!"

"Yes, I just finished checking, and yes, we did."

"This is proof positive that choosing Will for the job was the correct thing to do."

"It would seem so," she said, noncommittal. Being selected in the top five did not a winner make, although she had to admit they were off to a great start.

"Well, you two have to really get moving. Have you gotten the planting schedule and budget worked out? I don't have to remind you that all of it is due to the committee by July 1. Will you be ready?"

"Yes, we're ready. I worked up the preliminaries for both budget and schedule for Will to review before he left for Tokyo."

"Will's in Tokyo? Has he returned?" John asked.

"Think so, I don't know. I'll promise to get with him and make sure we are on schedule, okay?"

"All right. Have you talked to Thomas? You know you and I need to meet with him to make sure that we have enough equipment and volunteers. The major work should begin in September if we're on schedule. You must give the volunteers time to plan it into their schedules."

"I know, John, I've been at this for a while now."

"I know I can always count on you, Katrina. I'm sorry to bother you, but you do know as head of the neighborhood gardening committee, I have to ensure that the winning tradition of Shining Creek continues."

"I know, and it will."

"You're a gem, Katrina. I knew you wouldn't let the neighborhood down. I must tell you that your parents would be really proud of the young lady you've become."

"Thanks, John. I appreciate that and I'll talk to you soon," she said, hanging up.

She sat at her home desk. She hadn't told John that Will had been due back a week ago, not that she was keeping tabs or anything. His house had been dark this week when she'd driven by. Maybe he'd had to stay longer. Good thing she'd given him her plans before he left. He hadn't called since calling to make sure the plans had been dropped off. She had been professional, needing to squash his interest before it made her life miserable. It must have worked. He hadn't called again; why did that make her sad?

They were now heading into the first week of June. She'd give him until the middle of this week before calling.

Bringing her mind back to the business at hand, she needed to check his design one final time to make sure the budget and planting schedule would work. Once they submitted it, there would be no going back. Plus, the city divvied up their monies based on the entrant's projections, and if you were under, you were shit out of luck. So she and Will needed to accomplish two things—one, walk through the site again, reviewing the design; and, two, go to Uncle C's and Colburn's place to shore up Will's plant selections and their pricing. She knew that they had the best prices in town, and she wanted to get the budget nailed down. The city was particular about the pricing when it had to fork over money. John was correct; they needed to get moving. July 1 would be here before they knew it.

Will sat on the patio of his home looking over his backyard, legs stretched out, taking in the calm of the evening and the fresh air. It wasn't quite dark out, and it was pretty cool for June. He had changed into shorts and a T-shirt, his feet bare, which was how he preferred them to be. He tried to calibrate his breathing to the sound of the chimes to release some of the stresses he'd accumulated from his trip and the firestorm at work that followed. He had ended up staying another week. He blew out another breath at that, still tired, still jet-lagged. Returning hadn't been a picnic, either, as he'd been knee-deep in calming down clients. Finally, at the end of today, the end of a long month, things appeared to be looking up. Finally, he'd get to take a breather.

Tomorrow was Saturday and, for once in a long time, it wasn't taken up with work. He owed himself a trip somewhere to pay homage to his freedom, but he also needed to get to work on the gardening stuff. This was the reason his instincts had told him to say no initially.

He'd taken the budget and planting schedule with him on his trip, managing to review both, and was impressed by Katrina's attention to detail. He knew he needed to check in with her, see what was next on the gardening schedule, but her behavior since the backyard incident still bothered him. He'd hoped his desire for the body of one Katrina Jones would have slackened during his break from her. Nope. If anything, he was more interested.

You could go see if she is home now. Where had that thought come from? But it had him standing up, walking to his back gate. He rarely exited from this entrance and hadn't seen much of the greenbelt in a long while.

He passed the Sheppards'. Their backyard was filled to capacity with all things children—swings, toys, goals, swimming pool—enough for their large brood, six boys and one little girl. No way would he ever have seven children. They had that iron fencing, making their yard visible to him.

He walked by Oscar and Lola's yard, arriving at Katrina's. She had the same fencing as the Sheppards, so you could see into it. He proceeded to her gate, opened it, and walked in.

He stood there for a second, looking over her yard. It was his first time seeing it, taking in all her flowers; they were everywhere and in every shade and hue imaginable, filling the huge beds, leaving only a small amount of yard. Along with the flowers were flowering shrubs and rose bushes. It smelled wonderful. He was impressed by the sheer amount of work that was required to maintain this garden.

A very large and very old oak tree stood sentinel in the yard. It could very well be sixty or seventy years old. He appreciated that about this town; they loved their trees and enacted large penalties for chopping them down. You could shoot your neighbor or beat your children as long as you were kind to trees. He appreciated the city's firm desire to protect the earth. Her tree was huge and provided shade for her backyard, making it feel somewhat cooler. To the right, toward the back of her yard, stood a large shed painted in bright yellow, with what looked like butterflies in different colors painted on it. Pots in different sizes sat next to a potting bench near the shed and a small rainwater system.

He continued walking until he reached the steps leading to her deck. As he placed his foot on the first step, her back door opened and out she stepped to greet him.

"Doing a little wandering of your own, I see," she said, walking over to stand at the top of the stairs, looking down at him.

"One good turn deserves another, don't you think?" he said, returning her look. She was predictably dressed in her large T-shirt and shorts, only it didn't matter anymore, because he knew what was underneath, and that was all he saw whenever his eyes landed on her.

She smiled, but not the full, dangerous, promising one that he'd come to love. She wasn't his usual idea of beauty, but she had slowly, insidiously worked at changing his idea of what he wanted.

"How was your trip?" she asked, breaking into his reverie.

"Successful, but never-ending. I had to stay longer than I'd planned. Then work here was crazy, which is why I hadn't come sooner to discuss the competition."

"I figured as much. In case you didn't know, we were one of the five finalists selected. Congratulations, they liked your design."

"Thanks, and we'll see. It's not over yet," he said, looking intently at her.

"Did you have time to look over the budget and schedule?" she asked, uncomfortable with his scrutiny.

"Actually, I did, on the trip home. It all looks great."

"Thanks. Then you know we need to get moving. I was hoping I could drag you to the site to review it against your design. Would some time this week or next weekend work for you? John called, anxious after finding out that we'd been selected. He's going to get in touch with the volunteers. He and I and Thomas are meeting to plan their schedules, to maximize their help. It's full steam ahead now, no going back," she said, in full-on professional mode.

"Okay, this week at work should be easier than last."

"Are you sure you have time for this?" she asked.

"I do. I'll make time. Why don't we meet this Friday night to review the site and then on Saturday morning we can drive over to a local garden center that I like, Abernathy and Co. Have you heard of them?"

"Yes, they're the best in town," she said.

"So it's a date then? Friday night?"

"What?" she said quickly, startled.

"A date, you and me Friday night," he said again, smiling at her startled expression and at the mix of interest and desire he'd seen in her eyes just for a second before she masked it.

"I'm not sure that it would qualify as a date, but I'll meet you," she said, an odd look on her face.

"A date it is; see you Friday night," he said, turning and walking out the way he'd come. What had he been thinking? A date? But after he'd said it, it felt right. He wanted to see her again, and no more of that bullshit professional façade, either. At that moment, he'd instinctively decided that he wasn't going to get pushed back. He was going to follow his initial decision after seeing her in his backyard and push for more.

It had shifted, this need of his, becoming more than a desire for sex, although that held so much appeal. He wanted something different, wanted to know her better, and he suspected she wanted that, too.

Nope, he wasn't ready to quit just yet. She may have tripped him up a little with that new professional demeanor of hers, but he was beginning to see behind the many faces of Katrina; and was that fear he'd seen for a second in her eyes?

CHAPTER 9

Friday night arrived without much fanfare; work had been tolerable today. Katrina drove down her street, passing Will's home. His garage door was open, and he was outside in his driveway talking to Oscar and Lola. Sydney was skipping around the adults. She pulled into her drive and wanted to kick Lola, who was now waving her arms above her head like a crazy person, motioning for her to come over and join them.

Thanks, Lola. Hadn't she recently told Lola that she'd kind of changed her mind about Will? But no, Lola had called her out. After all, what were friends for?

She pulled into her garage, got out, and began walking down the sidewalk toward them. Will watched her, thinking, *This is more like it.* Her attire was much more suited to display her nice slim body. She was dressed for work in a form-fitting black skirt that ended just above her knees, accompanied by a plain black blouse. Medium-sized heels graced her feet, making her taller. Her hair was pulled back into a bun instead of its usual ponytail, and she wore small, dangly earrings. Her glasses were gone; contacts, he guessed. The attire didn't do for him what her white workout clothes or the tiny white dress had done, but it was working its mojo nonetheless.

"Hello, Katrina," Will said, his long muscular body casual in shorts, a polo-style shirt clinging cozily to his upper body.

"Hello, girlfriend," Lola said, grabbing her arm and pulling her in closer to the group.

"Hello, Oscar, Will," Katrina said.

"I was telling Oscar and Lola that we had a date tonight," Will said, smiling, a teasing glint in his eye.

Katrina gave him a you're-not-nearly-as-funny-as-you-think-you-are look and said, "We are going for a tour of the gardens—for the competition."

"That's no fun, is it, Oscar?" Lola said, looking at Katrina's face as it strived for neutrality.

"It's not fun, it's work," Katrina said, looking directly at Will. "I need to change. Give me ten minutes and I'll be right back."

"I'll be here."

"See you guys later," she said, walking away, giving him the back view, slim of hip with a very, very nice ass. His eyes followed her as she walked back to her garage, disappearing inside. It had been quiet during her walk back, and when he looked up, both Lola and Oscar were staring at him with teasing smiles on their faces.

"*What?*" He hadn't bothered to hide his appreciation. "She's a very pretty girl when she's not hiding herself, and I would have to be dead not to notice, especially in that outfit," he said.

"Whatever you say," Oscar said, and he and Lola started laughing. Will joined them.

True to her word, Katrina walked out of her home ten minutes later and headed for his. Lucky for her, the funny crew had dispersed. She walked up to his door and rang the doorbell. She'd changed into her normal at-home attire, ending his chance to see her body. Her copy of his design and her pad and pencil were tucked into her small backpack. He opened his door, giving her a smile.

What was up with him? Seriously, didn't he know she was backing off? She'd been nothing but professional, yet he didn't appear to be taking her hints. He actually seemed to be really interested, his teasing more intense now. Whatever. She was sticking to her new approach toward him, keeping it strictly professional.

"You're on time, just as you promised."

"Yep," she said. "You ready? I thought we could walk over."

"How about we take my bike?" he asked.

"I don't think we can both fit on your bike, unless you have a two-seater."

"No, I meant my motorcycle."

"Oh, no, *I don't think so.* No motorcycles for me, thank you very much," she said, shaking her head. "Did you know that motorcyclists are more likely to die in accidents than those in automobiles? Or that approximately three-quarters of motorcycle accidents involve collisions with another vehicle, which is usually an automobile?" That popped out of her mouth before she caught it.

Blinking in surprise, Will's jaw dropped.

"What?" he said.

"Nothing," she said quickly, her eyes shifting.

"Where did that come from?" he asked, continuing to examine her as if she was a visitor from another planet.

"I try to be aware of the risks associated with stuff is all," she said.

"Oh. Anything else you want to tell me that I should be worried about?" he asked. "Well, most motorcycle accidents occur because they aren't recognized in heavy traffic or at night."

A laugh escaped, and she smiled back at him, finding the humor in it.

"Really?" he said.

"Did you know that in a typical accident, you only have less than two seconds to avoid a collision?"

"No, I didn't know that," he said, watching her intently now. "The more *salient* question is how and why you know this?"

"The web. Downloaded an app on my cell, one that cites facts, and I read," she explained as if it was the most normal thing in the world to do. Noting his baffled expression, she added, "You are the one who should know those facts if you are going to ride."

"Is that so? Is that what you do? Know all the facts before you make a decision to do something?"

"Yes, and don't pretend you don't. You would not have the job you have if you didn't do your homework. It is what most rational thinking people do—plan ahead, control what is within your power. So much in life is not."

"Okay," he said, his laughter fading away. "I am careful in some things, but not in everything. There are some things you can't control, Katrina. Life is weird that way."

"Okay, Mr. Philosopher, how about I walk over and you can ride your motorcycle. The gardens are only ten or fifteen minutes away," she said, starting to get miffed.

"That's okay, I'll walk with you."

"It doesn't matter to me either way," she said, starting to walk away. He reached for her hand, which she not so subtly kept close to her body.

"No, wait. Let me close the garage. I'll be back in two seconds, okay? Don't leave." He walked into his garage and closed it. A few seconds later, he exited his front door, locking it behind him.

"Let's go," he said, joining her on the sidewalk. They walked in silence most of the way. Katrina didn't feel like talking; her mind was occupied combing through their earlier conversation. He'd laughed at her facts. What was so wrong with being cautious in life? She knew the upheaval life could bring. *Come on, Katrina, you had great parents. They were people you could depend on.* That was, of course, true, but they'd died. How about Uncle C and Colburn? Once she came into their lives, they had looked after her, and would continue to do so, she was sure of that.

"You okay?" he asked, breaking into her quiet. She seemed lost in thought now, tense.

"I'm fine," she answered.

They arrived at the gardens five minutes later. He stopped and waited while she pulled out her copy of the design. She was a bottle of surprises, he thought, and wondered again how he could have imagined her boring. She kept so much of herself hidden, and what a hoot she was with all those facts. A regular Jeopardy contestant. He could understand someone Googling information, maybe, but to be able to pull it out like they'd been talking about the weather was something else entirely.

They started their tour at the beginning of the gardens, walking through them, marking the spots within the garden where changes would be made. She verified his plans with what would actually be accomplished here on the ground, checking the design against the planting schedule to make sure they reconciled the plants on the design with the actual site. It took about thirty minutes to walk through everything; she taking notes, following along behind him.

"Well, I guess that's it," he said.

"Let me show you the equipment shed, tools, and pottery sheds," she said, walking out through the flower garden toward the back of the property. "I didn't show you this area. You've seen the small one, the sheds we use near the composting section, but the main ones are located in the back," she said, waving back to people working who'd called out her name as she and Will made their way through the gardens.

They walked about twenty more yards, stopping in front of two sheds. Actually they were more like small buildings than sheds, one larger than the other. Katrina opened the door to the equipment building, the smaller one, which was remarkable with three backhoes and an army of other tools all lined up and neatly arranged.

"Impressive," Will said. She closed the door and walked over to the potting building, which was almost twice the size of the equipment building, and walked in. Counter space ran along the walls of this room, with two huge sinks along the back wall. A massive battle-worn oak table sat in the middle of the building. Pots of every shape and size were tucked under the counters, and tools lined the walls.

"We're fortunate to have gotten equipment over and above most neighborhoods," she said.

"It seems so. Thank you for the added tour," he said, standing in the middle of the room, next to the table.

"You're welcome," she said, looking around, noticing now that they were the only ones here. She turned back to find his eyes locked on her.

"What?" she asked, not knowing what to make of this new Will. There was more than simple teasing in his eyes, making her nervous, fidgety.

"Nothing, I'm just admiring a pretty woman who knows and loves her dirt and who will be working with me, helping me to win a major competition for our 'hood. Thanks again," he said, laughing.

"I know the first time is tough for most gardeners, but I believe you'll be the exception. Again, your backyard is beautiful. And you know more than you let on," she said.

"And I passed that work test. And without the equipment which would have made the job soooo much easier," he said, smiling.

She laughed. "You figured that out."

"Yeah, I did."

"We have a strong tradition of winning in this neighborhood, and I'll do my part to see that it continues," she added.

"For the good of the country, then?" he said, smiling at her, holding out his hand for a fist bump.

"For the good of the country," she said, walking over to meet his fist with her own and smiling back at him.

"Are you ready to go?" she asked.

"Yep," he said, and they left the shed, making their way back to the front of the gardens. She put the designs back into her backpack and they walked home. She listened as he talked more about what he wanted to tackle in September with the volunteers. They arrived back at his home and stopped.

"So we'll meet again in the morning?" he asked.

"Yes. How about I drive? We can leave at eight, if that's not too early for you."

"Nope, that works. I'll knock on your door a little before eight," he said.

"Okay, see you then," she said, walking away.

He let her take about four steps before calling her name. She turned and stopped, looking at him questioningly.

"Good night, Katrina. I had a good time tonight. Thanks for going out with me," he said.

She made a face at him and turned and resumed walking home. She took about two steps before turning back around, slowing down, but continuing to walk backwards.

"You're welcome," she said, giving him a shy smile before turning around once again.

∞

Later on that night, Katrina called Colburn, as he managed most of the plant pricing at Abernathy and Co.

"Hey, Kit Kat, what can I do for you?" he said, using another one of his nicknames for her.

"Nothing. I was just calling to let you know that I am coming over in the morning."

"You wasted a phone call just to tell me that?" he asked in his usual gruff manner.

"No, Will is coming with me."

"Will? Who's Will?" he asked.

"You know, the guy who is leading the competition for my neighborhood this year."

"I remember him, the Japanese kid with the gardens you don't like."

Katrina sighed. "I like them now; remember, we're working together now. I called to tell you that we're stopping by tomorrow and that he'll need some help with pricing," she said.

"Why would you waste your time calling to tell me that? I'll help him; you didn't need to waste a dime calling to tell me that."

Katrina sighed again, loudly. "Colburn. Enough. Just work with him, okay?"

"Why wouldn't I work with him?" he asked, fighting to not allow the smile on his face to show through the phone. He loved teasing his goddaughter.

"Okay, I'll see you and Uncle C tomorrow."

"We'll be here, same as always," he said by way of goodbye, hanging up.

Colburn laughed.

"Who was that?" Charles asked.

"Katrina, calling to inform us that she will be bringing Will by tomorrow."

"Oh," Charles said, smiling. "Well, our little girl is finally bringing someone home to meet the parents. I didn't think this day would come."

Colburn looked over at him and started to laugh, and Charles joined in.

"Well, I am going to give him the once-over, see if he passes muster. If not, I can run him off if need be," Coburn said, laughing, but serious, too.

Ten minutes before eight the next morning, Will stood outside Katrina's door waiting for her to answer. Katrina had hemmed and hawed all morning, dithering, having recently purchased a few shorts and shirts that fit her better. She had a pair of them on now. She had given up her glasses, too, and wore her contacts practically all the time now. She refused to consider what that meant. So should she change or not? Out with the old, in with the new. She had dressed in the new, only to change back into the old, then back in with the new, which was where she was now. The doorbell rang, bringing a halt to all that changing. What happened to not being interested?

She opened the door and stood before Will. She was dressed in jeans shorts, the skinny kind that followed the curve of her body before stopping just above her knee. And, wonders of wonders, she wore a T-shirt that clung tightly to her upper body. Maybe wearing clothes that fit wasn't such a good idea after all. Not being able to see her body had its benefits; lately it had been all he'd thought about. If she kept this up, he would spend all his time just staring at her.

"Hey, you're early. Come in. I need to grab my keys and backpack and we'll be ready to go," she said, pretending not to notice the flash of desire in his eyes. She stood back to let him in, and then leading him through her home, bending over to pick up her keys and backpack from the ottoman along the way.

Her home was spotless, same as the time he'd delivered her home. He followed her, noting the way her bottom moved in those shorts. He had locked in on that part of her anatomy and ran smack into her back when she stopped at her garage door, bringing him in direct contact with the part he'd admired so much. It worked for him, too, an unobtrusive way to cop a feel.

"Sorry, I wasn't watching where I was going," he said. She looked back at him, her eyes squinting in their appraisal of his comment, seeking the truth. She opened the door.

If he had any question before, he knew it now—he was in love. He appreciated the neatness of Katrina's garage, which almost but not quite rivaled his. The walls here held every imaginable gardening tool, organized by type; saws were side by side on the wall from large to small in size, followed by shovels, hoes, forks, and rakes. You name it, he'd bet it was somewhere in this garage. She was a regular home-and-garden store. She probably had something to do with the sheds at the gardens being so well organized. A girl after his own heart.

"I like the way you organize," he said, smiling as she did the same. She backed her little electric car out of the garage and pulled onto the street.

"Abernathy and Co. is not that far from here," she said, looking over at him. "I saw you there once," she added, watching him search his brain for when.

"Me? When?" he asked, surprised and bothered that he hadn't remembered.

"During the holidays; actually, a couple of days after Christmas. You were looking for some tool, I don't remember what," she said.

"I don't remember," he said, looking at her intently.

"It's okay. Sometimes I'm not very noticeable," she said, smiling.

He was quiet, not sure how to respond to that. "You are noticeable when you want to be," he said, pausing. "I remember the night of the party, I noticed. I remember you in your workout attire. Noticed you that day, too, and I remember your expression as you stood in my backyard. Those things I noticed and remember quite vividly."

"Oh." She was now the one speechless. "Anyway," she said, wanting to change the subject, searching her brain for something interesting to talk about and coming up empty.

"So you never met your birth parents or their families?" he asked, watching her drive. She was a careful driver, going the speed limit, stopping at the yellow lights.

She shook her head.

"How about you?" she asked.

"There are four of us; three girls, one boy," he said.

"Where are you from originally?"

"San Francisco. Two of my sisters, my grandfather, and my mother live there now."

"That's only two sisters accounted for," she said.

"My oldest sister lives here in town."

"Where is here?" Katrina asked, pulling into a large parking area and parking near the main gate.

"Willow Mountain," he said, getting out of her car, looking around. He had been impressed with the place on his first visit here and still was. It had a local feel to it.

"It is busy; they do a lot of business," Katrina said, moving around him, following his eyes. They walked through a huge gate painted barnyard red. The gates had been moved and tied back to the fence. Flowers of all sizes, from small planting flats to larger gallon-size pots, sat on tables surrounding them. Directly in front of them was a big building, its color matching the fence.

"As you know, that's where you can purchase gardening tools, fertilizers, and pesticides, although they strongly discourage the use of pesticides," she said, walking in the direction of the store.

"I should have known you'd know your way around this store," he said to her, following her up the steps and into the building, bumping into her back again as she stopped. He followed her eyes downward to where a chicken and her small chicks crossed before them.

"That's Annie and those are her chicks," she said before continuing inside. An older white-haired guy stood next to the counter talking to a customer. Will watched Katrina walk over and stand behind the counter and wait until they were finished with their conversation. The older man turned to Katrina, gave her a huge smile, and said, "If it isn't my favorite goddaughter." Katrina had placed one of her arms around him and gave him a side hug.

"I'm your only goddaughter," she said, reaching up to kiss his cheek. "I have someone I would like you to meet," she said, beckoning Will over. He walked up and shook the man's hand.

"Uncle C, a.k.a. Charles Abernathy, I would like you to meet Will Nakane. He's the one who came up with the design that our neighborhood will be using this year in the competition. We've made the final five, which is why we are here today; we need to nail down the pricing for the plants. I thought Colburn could help with that," she said.

Charles shook Will's hand.

"Glad to meet you, Will. Colburn is around here somewhere," Charles said, and on cue, Colburn entered the store and walked over to give Katrina a hug.

"Hey, Colburn," she said. Will had watched the man's facial expression move from glacial when he'd entered to warm and open when he smiled at Katrina.

"Hello, Katrina."

"Colburn, this is Will, the one who was selected to head the neighborhood competition." Will extended his hand to Colburn, who stood there, interrogating Will with his eyes.

Uggg! Sometimes her godfathers drove her to drink, Katrina thought, giving a huge sigh meant for all the world to hear. Deliver her from men and their rituals. Will stood his ground, and, a minute later, Colburn extended his hand. He had somehow taken Will's measure and was satisfied now.

"We stopped by this morning to nail down the final pricing. I thought you could help," she said.

"Where is your budget?" Colburn asked, continuing to look over Will from head to toe.

"I have it," said Katrina, looking through her backpack and pulling it out. She handed it over to him.

"Katrina, how about you stay here and help your Uncle C with the store and I'll take Will around. You okay with that, Will?" Colburn asked.

"Sure," Will said.

Colburn continued, "We'll meet you back in here when we're done."

"Okay," Katrina said, looking into Will's face for assurance.

Will smiled back at her, laughter in his eyes.

Will and Colburn walked through the door and out into the sunshine. Katrina tracked them with her eyes until they got lost in the center. She turned around to find her Uncle C watching her, a smile on his face.

"This is against my better judgment, but I'll do it anyway. What?" she asked.

"You like him, and more than you let on. I can see it. I know women well enough to know an interested one when I see one," he said, still smiling at her.

"Okay, I am, so what? He only sees me now that he's working with me. He didn't even notice me before."

"Katrina, you've got a chip on your shoulder about some things still. I'm sure you made it easy for him to see you."

"I did," she said, but she'd hadn't, not really, or at least not before the party.

"Hey, Uncle C, people see what they want to see, and you and I both know that they're only interested if it sparkles and shines."

"You could sparkle and shine if you put your mind to it. You are sparkling and shining a little bit today, as a matter of fact. That's not your usual attire."

"So good of you to notice. You know what I mean," she said, although she wasn't going to tell him of her recent shopping trip.

"You have to at some point let go of your grudges and hurts, otherwise, you miss more than you know."

"Maybe," she said, turning back to look in Colburn and Will's direction.

❧

Will and Colburn walked though the garden reviewing the list of plants they would need from

Katrina's itemized list, with Colburn verifying the cost of each. He knew Katrina had been thorough, but Colburn offered some of the items to them at a discount.

"What's the point of having a godchild if you can't spoil or help her?" he said to Will.

"I hadn't known she was your goddaughter until now. She hadn't mentioned it to me," Will responded.

"She can be independent that way," Colburn said. He and Will stood next to a strand of Japanese maples, the ones on his list that turned a beautiful magenta color in the winter. Colburn pulled a tag over, making sure the price was what he'd marked it to be.

"How long have you been her godfathers?" Will asked.

"We knew her adoptive dad first; served with him. He and Marlene were her adoptive parents, and were two of the most loving parents you could ask for. Katrina had been in a group home and came to live with Wes and Marlene when she was ten. Charles did a couple of tours of duty with Wes, and, after the war ended, we all settled down here.

"When they adopted Katrina, we became her godfathers and love her like she is our own. Wes and Marlene were gardening people. Has Katrina told you anything about herself?" Colburn asked, stopping and watching Will. He knew Katrina liked this young man and she probably wouldn't believe that interest was returned. It was hard for her to believe that people wanted her, one of the legacies of her fractured childhood. She hadn't escaped from that past yet; maybe she never would.

"A little, not much. I think it's safe to say that she was extremely disappointed when I took the offer to lead the competition."

Colburn laughed. "She considers herself supreme in her knowledge of gardening, and Charles and I have continued to encourage her love for plants." Colburn paused, then said, "She doesn't remember her birth parents. Marlene and Wes were older when they decided to adopt. Said they saw her on TV and knew she belonged with them."

"What happened to them?" Will asked.

"Killed in a car accident. Katrina was in college at the time. Took it hard, they were all that had been good in her life. And although it took her a while to pull it together, she did. Grew into a very strong, kind woman, one any man would be happy to have," he said, stopping and waiting until he had Will's attention.

"She can be prickly, skittish, and hard to get to know, but she's a softy at heart. She looks after Charles and me like we were the kids and not the other way around," he said.

Will listened. *Marriage? Slow down, dude,* he thought, still taking in the information and aligning it with what he'd seen of Katrina. He and Colburn walked back to the main building. They entered, his eyes searching for Katrina, who stood near the register talking to a customer. She finished and walked over to him.

"You and Colburn done?" she asked, a smile on her lips. She had really great lips. She'd stopped talking, her face turning cautious as she watched desire move into his eyes.

"We are," he said.

"Well then, guess we'd better leave. Let me get my stuff and then we can go," she said, leaving quickly, feeling that fear again and going into evasion mode. He'd identified it now, the same expression he'd seen in her eyes in her backyard. He got it now. He frightened her in some way. He smiled a little at the idea. He walked over to where Charles and Colburn stood.

"Thank you for your help this morning," he said, extending his hand first to Colburn and then to Charles.

"Come by anytime," they said, shaking his hand. Katrina turned and watched them. She could tell the godfathers liked Will. She knew Colburn enough to know he didn't give anyone the time of day if there was something about the person he didn't like. Uncle C was always friendly, even if he wanted you to drop dead. She walked over to join them, placing a kiss on their cheeks before leaving. She and Will walked back to her car, quiet on the short trip home. She pulled up to his house.

"So I'll take the changes we've made and update the budget and schedule. I'll have them ready to drop off by the deadline. Are you going to be around to do the honors?" she asked.

"Yes, I'll deliver them this time," he said, watching her for a second. "Thanks, Katrina, for all your help so far," he said, serious now.

"Sure, don't mention it. I'll see you later," she said, her professional front up again.

He slid out of her car, watching until she pulled into her garage before turning and entering his home. After today, she'd become so much clearer to him. Fear, he'd bet, played a large part in her decisions, her behavior, maybe even explaining why she dressed the way she did. And wasn't that interesting?

⋘⋙

Tonight would be her third date with Darius. He was a nice guy, handsome, and gainfully employed. All sound potential husband attributes; nevertheless, she wasn't interested in anything beyond friendship. She was still hung up on Will, and getting to know him, being close to him through the competition, only heightened her awareness of him.

She'd invited Darius over to dinner for a heart-to-heart; no use in wasting his time and hers. She sat on the couch waiting for him to arrive, wishing it could be some other fellow. Her choice, right? She'd been the one that stopped this time.

Her doorbell rang and she went to answer it.

"Hi, Darius."

He had a pie dish in his hand. "Dessert," he said, handing it over to her. It was still warm.

"Hey, glad you could make it. Any trouble finding the place?" she asked.

"None," he said, entering her home.

"What's this?" she asked, tilting her head toward the dish she now held in her hands.

"Blueberry cobbler, made by yours truly."

"I'm in for a treat then," she said, walking over to place it on her bar. "Maybe we should eat this instead of the dinner I cooked," she said and he laughed. Katrina had prepared dinner earlier, the only one of her mother's recipes she'd mastered after countless hours spent in the kitchen trying to learn.

"Red or white wine?" she asked, picking up a bottle of each.

"What are you serving?" he asked.

"Turkey and dressing," she said, watching his eyes lift in surprise.

"Bringing out the big guns?" he said, laughing at her dinner choice. "In that case I guess I'll have white." She handed the bottle and a bottle opener to him, and he opened the wine and passed it back to her.

"Follow me," she said, leading him to the table, which was set with her formal china. It had belonged to her mother.

"So, Thanksgiving in June," he said, his eyebrows lifting as he took a seat, teasing her as he took in the turkey, dressing, and sides.

"Don't knock it until you've tried it, and giving thanks shouldn't be limited to once a year," she said, watching the amused expression settle on his face. "My mother loved holidays, loved cooking, which I hate. But she'd drag me in there in spite of my loud protestations. I helped during the holidays, learning how to cook the dishes that she so loved. The rest of the year, I ruthlessly avoided all things culinary," she said, smiling at Darius. "Trust me. This is as good as it gets in the cooking department with me. My culinary skills are way limited. It was either this or pancakes and eggs."

She served dinner and they both laughed when Darius went back for seconds. They talked over dinner about the competition and life at his restaurants. After dinner he helped with the dishes, increasing his estimation in Katrina's eyes. They moved to the living room, finding a seat on Katrina's couch. She'd placed dessert and coffee on a tray on the ottoman before them and they sat back, talking, laughing, and enjoying the evening.

"I need to tell you something," Darius said, growing serious. They were now done with dessert and sat drinking coffee. Katrina had kicked off her shoes, pulled her feet onto her couch, and sat Indian-style facing him.

"Okay," she said, grabbing her coffee cup and leaning back into her couch, curious.

"A year ago, I broke off an engagement to be married," he told her.

"Oh," she said.

"I wasn't always the entrepreneur you see before you now. I was trained to be a lawyer, had worked for a very expensive law firm for about three years. I was on the fast track," he said, smiling, sliding out of his shoes and putting his feet on her table.

"Watch the feet," she said, laughing when he stopped midway. "Just kidding. Really, make yourself comfortable."

"You weren't always in the feeding people business?" she asked, smiling wickedly, reminding him of his place in the conversation.

"Right. I met my fiancée while I worked with the law firm at some fancy meet and greet. Match made in heaven, or at least I thought so. I had the fancy apartment and fancy car, all the trappings of that life, which she liked; so did I, for that matter.

"You've met my baby brother, but I had one older brother, who volunteered to serve his country in Iraq. He died. We are, were, close," he said, sitting quietly for a while. "His death sent me into a tailspin. He was the one who pushed me, looked out for me. I was devastated and angry for a while. What is it about losing someone you love that brings clarity to one's life," he said, feeling Katrina's hand slide over to cover his. Loss was something she knew very well.

"It led to me getting fired from my job. I probably could have gone back, but by then I didn't want to. I realized that the law was just okay, but it hadn't been my first career choice, just a less risky one that was approved of by my parents. Owning a restaurant had been a distant dream of mine. So I didn't go back, and of course, I had to scale back my lifestyle. Going on your own isn't for the faint of heart," he said, taking her hand in his and squeezing it. "So there went the fancy home, the fancy car, and, unfortunately, the fancy fiancée." He smiled, but she could see the hurt that lurked in his eyes. Hurt was something she knew very well, too.

"I'm sorry," she said.

"Don't be. We gave it our best shot. She tried sticking through my career change, I'll give her that," he said. "I'm telling you this to say that I loved her very much, and I've not quite put it behind me. As crazy as it sounds, if she were to walk through that door again, I can't say with any certainty that I wouldn't take her back."

Katrina sat quietly, watching him.

"And here I was all set to dump you," she said, smiling. He laughed.

"I met you at the party and I liked you, thought you were funny in your attempts to get rid of me and the other guy. I thought you could be the one to help me put her behind me. I haven't. I like you and I don't want to lead you to believe that I'm available. I'm not," he said.

"Thanks for telling me," she said. "Seriously, I understand, believe me." She ended up telling him about her crush on her neighbor. He listened attentively, not commenting until she was done.

"I hope you don't take this the wrong way, but you aren't the easiest woman to get to know. You are aware of that, right?"

"Yeah, I know. I get that a lot. I can be difficult," she said with a small smile.

"It's more than being difficult. It's as if you want the world to see your worst, and I've got to say, that's not the ideal method for attracting a mate," he said, looking intently at her, serious now. She shook her head, looking off into space.

"I know," she said turning back to him. "It's my way, though, and as crazy as that sounds, I need to operate that way. It's my way of making sure that the person wants me for me. I mean if someone wants to stick around after seeing the worst, then he really loves me, right? They're in for the long haul."

"I guess that's one way to look at it," he said, her hand still resting in his.

"Before I was adopted, I lived in a large group home for orphans. That's my word for what I was. Anyway, they'd have these sessions the agency would sponsor for prospective parents. They would stop by, kind of like an open house, to see the kids that were available for adoption. I hadn't become as beautiful as I am now," she said with a smile, "but I learned early that people only wanted the beautiful ones, the easy ones. So a lot of me wants to test you, and those around me, to make sure it is really me you want, the part that's not so pretty.

"I need for people to want the woman in the big clothes, the yard worker, more than I need them to love the pretty one. Do you understand?" she asked, looking at him. "I probably go overboard in that, maybe I'm a little too proactive in testing that."

"I see."

"So I've followed my usual approach with Will, hiding, thinking I liked him, wanting him to notice me. I know, so third grade, but it's me. Funny, he did notice me," she said, and explained New Year's Eve night and the events that followed to Darius. "Know what's funny?" she asked, not waiting for an answer. "Now that I know he's interested, I'm not so sure anymore. We were becoming friends, and I don't want to ruin that."

"Maybe you're afraid?" he said.

"Maybe."

"What would you be afraid of?" he asked.

"That we could ruin a friendship, that living around him would be uncomfortable if it doesn't work out, that I could love him a whole bunch and he wouldn't love me back. Every orphan's worst nightmare," she said softly, looking down at their clasped hands.

"Maybe you should give him a try. He may surprise you," he said, squeezing her hand again.

"Why risk it?" she said.

"What's life without a risk or two?" he said, smiling. "Think about it, anyway."

"We'll see. Enough about me," she said, trying to pull her hand from his. He wouldn't let it go, looking into her eyes.

"I would really like for us to continue to be friends, Katrina."

"I'd like that, too," she said, and smiled, she squeezing his hand this time.

CHAPTER 10

July

Will stood outside Katrina's door hoping that when she opened it he could convince her to take a ride with him. This was his most recent attempt to breach the formidable façade of Katrina Jones. Today was July 1, and the finalists' designs were due to the committee. He needed to drop off his design, along with Katrina's budget and planting schedule, and he hoped she would accept his invitation. He was running out of ideas.

She was still being professional and distant, now more so than ever since their "date" and trip to her godfathers'. He'd taken pains to run into her several times since then; he was always on the lookout for her, catching up to her in her yard, at the mailboxes, leaving for work. She always seemed distant, and clearly had retreated back into her shell. So it was back to square one, hoping she'd accept his invitation, banking on surprise working in his favor. Plus, this was something related to the competition, and, after all, she'd agreed to help.

Nine o'clock on a Saturday morning. Who could it be, Katrina thought, walking over to her front door in response to the ringing doorbell. Not Lola, she didn't usually knock, and the back door was her preference, anyway.

Katrina opened it cautiously to find Will standing before her. He was fine, as always, shades covering his eyes, black, shiny hair standing on end, beautiful smile on scrumptious lips, those shorts loose on hips that she knew by heart; she would put good money on her ability to pick them out of a line-up.

Breathe, Katrina, she told herself, forcing her eyes to his. "Hi, Will. This is a surprise," she said, her heart beating something crazy in her chest at the shock of his sudden appearance on her doorstep. "Were we supposed to meet?" she asked, frowning in confusion.

"No, I stopped by hoping you weren't too busy to ride over with me to drop off the schedules, budget, and final design to the city committee. That is where I need to go to turn them in, right?" he asked pointing to an address on one of the sheets. "I just wanted to make sure. I thought with your guidance I wouldn't get lost and have you or the committee angry with me," he said, laying it on thick, watching all kinds of expressions pass over her face. "Don't feel pressured to go," he added. "It was a spur of the moment decision to ask you. You can tell me no." He smiled winsomely. It was silent for a minute.

"I'll go," she said reluctantly. "Let me grab my bag and I'll meet you outside."

"Great," he said.

She closed the door and stood for a second, processing this change in her plans. What plans? She didn't really have any plans. *He's not asking for your hand in marriage, Katrina, just go. You've done nothing but think of him, anyway, and you* are *the assistant. You promised to help him. Take a deep breath and find your purse.*

She did and walked out the door, locking it behind her. Thankfully she'd gotten up early, showered, and dressed for the day in shorts and a T-shirt, all-purpose sandals on her feet, her hair in its usual ponytail. She walked out her door and around to the passenger side of Will's jeep, which was missing its top today.

"Ready?" he asked.

"Yes," she said, getting in and reaching for her seat belt. He backed out and they drove off at full speed, music blaring. She hung on as they drove across town in record time. He pulled into the parking lot, parked, and looked over to find Katrina's eyes on him.

"What?" he asked.

"I'm not saying you were driving too fast or anything, but you do know that speed reduces the amount of time a person needs to avoid a crash, increases the likelihood that you'll have an accident, and makes it more severe once it happens?" she said. He looked at her for a second, really fighting back his need to laugh out loud.

"Thank you," he said, his reply choked.

"Don't laugh," she said, fighting against her need to join in his laughter.

She led the way to the front door of the center. Will would have whiplash if he kept it up, she thought as she watched him try to take in the gardens as they walked to the door.

He was surprised and impressed with the sight of those Volkswagen Beetles and the flowers that surrounded them. The wildflowers from the spring had given way to the native annual plants, but the display was still awe-inspiring.

"You haven't seen these gardens before?" she asked.

"No. I mean, I've been here before," he said, "I was here for that meeting, after New Year's. Remember? I didn't pay much attention, apparently."

"It was January, so there probably wasn't much to see; just the bare Beetles. Let's drop those off first," she said, looking down at the plans in his hand, "and then I'll give you the fifty-cent tour—if you want one, that is."

"Of course. I love your tours," he answered. They walked into the building and located the flower/ornamental gardens table. It was in the same position as it had been when Katrina had dropped off the first set of plans in May. He followed, handing them to the woman sitting behind the table, accepting a time stamped receipt as proof of delivery.

They walked out into the sunshine, she acting as tour guide, showing him the herb garden along with the Volkswagen Beetles.

"I'm really impressed by your knowledge of these gardens and their history," he said to her as they were heading back to his jeep. "I was impressed the night at G's party, and by your yard, and that was before I knew the full scope of your knowledge."

"Thanks. I'm surprised you've lived here for as long as you have and have not seen them. I know now that you like gardens, too. I guess your traveling bug supersedes your gardening bug," she said, smiling, looking around her. "Have you seen any of the other city's gardens?"

"Nope, I have just now seen this one, and, of course, our neighborhood's."

"Would you like to see some of the others? There is one close by. I could show you around more, if you wanted to?" she said, forgetting her decision to keep it professional.

"Great idea," he said, watching uncertainty again flicker across her face. "I have time if you do," he said quickly, before she could backpedal.

"Okay," she said, getting into the jeep again.

"Directions?" he asked as he started it up.

"Let's head to the west side. We are fairly close to it. Go back to the highway and take the Ninth Street exit, and then go two blocks west. A large portion of the African-American community resides on this side of town, or they used to. The city is slowly losing its defined neighborhoods; people are moving everywhere nowadays. This is where I go when I'm on the lookout for old-school vegetables," she said, joining him in his jeep. Will pulled onto the main highway, following Katrina's directions.

"Have you seen every garden?" he asked.

"Yes," she said sheepishly. "I'm weird and nosy, and I wanted to see all the competition and each neighborhood's take on gardening. It could be a small anthropological study. The flower and vegetable gardens in the neighborhoods around the city are reflections of their inhabitants. The vegetables and fruits were planted to be used in the favorite dishes of each of the people of that area, so they're a reflection of each ethnic group and the foods each neighborhood values."

She sat silently for a few minutes, watching him. "You're a really fast driver," she said, noting the speed with which they were moving.

"Fast? I should take you for a ride on my bike to show you fast."

"No thanks," she said, looking over at him, admiring his shiny black hair. He had on his shades, hiding his eyes, but she saw confidence radiating from every pore of his body.

"What, no facts or statistics for me?" he asked, smiling.

"I'm fresh out," she said.

"Seriously, I'm aware of most of the statistics associated with my hobbies, but if you listed all the reasons for not trying something, you'd never do it, and how boring would that be?" he countered.

Not knowing how to respond, she said nothing. He followed her directions and they soon pulled up to a vegetable garden enclosed by an iron fence surrounding the entire garden and taking up a city block of this neighborhood. Directly behind it, about half the size of the garden, was a neighborhood park and flower garden. It wasn't as large as he'd expected. It was a Saturday, so it was more crowded than usual, but Will had been able to find a spot along the street and parked. They both got out, moving toward the entrance.

"The flower portion is smaller than I expected, at least compared to the other two gardens I've seen so far."

"When this garden was founded it was larger, but the neighborhood changed. People here have fewer resources, so the flowers gave way to more food growth, especially during that tough recession a couple of years back," she said.

They walked over to the entrance, where two older African-American women sat behind a long table filled with vegetables and fruits. Katrina groaned out loud, and Will turned to her.

"Are you okay?" he asked.

"Yes, but here sit two of the busiest busybodies you are ever likely to meet," she said, cutting her words short as they reached the table.

"Well, if it isn't Katrina," one of the ladies purred when she and Will reached the table.

"Hello, Mrs. Jenkins and Mrs. Smith," she said. They both smiled at her. Mrs. Jenkins was dressed in a bright orange shirt with matching scarf tied around her hair. Mrs. Smith was dressed in calm yellow. She'd worn her hair in braids that fell to her shoulders for as long as Katrina had known her.

"And who is this good-looking fellow you have with you?" Mrs. Smith asked.

"This is Will Nakane. He was selected to head the flower competition for our neighborhood this year," Katrina said.

"Well, well, you must be really good to have beat out our Katrina," Mrs. Smith said. "Nice to meet you," she said, holding out her hand.

Will extended his hand to shake hers, but she said, "Baby, a lady's hand is not for shaking; plant your lips on the back of it."

Katrina rolled her eyes. Mrs. Smith and Mrs. Jenkins were known to be OC's, original cougars, who ate young men for sport.

"Nice meeting you both," Will said, planting a soft kiss on the back of Mrs. Smith's hand. He reached for Mrs. Jenkins's hand, which was also extended for a kiss, and he obliged. "The committee only gave me this opportunity because they knew Katrina would be around to make sure I stayed on course," he said, his smile never wavering, his eyes intense, putting his sex appeal on full display.

"Well, well, he's a cute one, Katrina," Mrs. Jenkins said, her eyes assessing him, her eyebrows lifting, her smile sly. "Are we going to keep this one?"

"He's a friend," Katrina responded. "And one who I'd promised a tour, so if you ladies will excuse us . . ."

"Why, sure we will, sugar. You come back now, Will," they said, their smiles suggesting they could eat Will up in one big bite.

"I'm a cute one, huh," he said to Katrina, as soon as they were out of the ladies' hearing range. She didn't bother to respond.

"This section of the garden is famous for what I like to call old-school vegetables—any and all types of greens, mustards, collards, turnips, kale—usually available in the fall. This time of the year, it's beautiful cucumbers, tomatoes, okra, and peas," she said, starting to fall into her role as tour guide.

"Katrina."

She turned her head at the sound of her name. It was Darius, who was carrying a huge bag stuffed to the brim with vegetables. He walked toward them. Will stopped and stood watching them. Who was this guy? He watched him walk up to Katrina and reach for her hands, which she gave over without much thought.

"Will, I'd like for you to meet a friend of mine. Darius Williams," she said, smiling at Darius.

"Hello," Will said to Darius, continuing to watch Katrina, taking in her welcome. He was more than a little disconcerted by her reaction and the interest displayed on her face. Who was this guy who still held Katrina's hands in his?

"Darius is owner and sometimes chef for two small restaurants in town, The Vegetable Garden and The Vegetable Pot. Have you heard of them?" she asked, finally turning her head toward Will.

"Yes," Will responded. He had eaten there and the food had been very good, but he didn't feel like sharing that piece of information right now.

"I was giving a tour of this particular garden to Will," she said. "He's never been here."

"Not everyone is into gardening as much as we are, Katrina," Darius said. The proprietary way he spoke to Katrina had Will's hair standing on end.

"Well, I better let you two get back to your tour. I'll talk to you soon, Katrina," Darius said, bending over and kissing Katrina lightly on the mouth.

Will watched their exchange in silence, annoyed with himself for the feelings of jealousy that had crept up. He didn't have any claim on her.

Darius walked away, laughing hysterically inside. He'd known who Will was from his conversation with Katrina, and he'd decided to do a little acting, blowing up his relationship with her, wanting to gauge the man's reaction, wanting to determine if Katrina meant anything to him. It had worked perfectly, too, along with being huge fun. He should have been sympathetic; after all, he'd been there before. Woman troubles were painful. He should be ashamed of himself, and he would be later; for now he was enjoying it. He hoped it worked out for Katrina, that Will would be the one for her. Love, when it worked, was something powerful.

Katrina and Will continued their tour, with Will now only half listening. He was a little disturbed, internally arguing with himself about his lack of claim on Katrina. Maybe he'd gotten it wrong. Maybe it wasn't fear, or at least not fear of him. Could she be involved with someone else? The idea left him feeling strange. His mind kept reviewing the scene he had just witnessed. She walked him through the gardens, continuing the tour, but he heard not a word.

"Of course all of the gardens grew staples, like lettuce, broccoli, and beans, but some neighborhoods were better at growing some kinds of vegetables than others," she rambled on, noticing Will's blank expression. "Most all of them have a farmers market; nothing big, usually mom and pop in scale, all open on Saturday, all cheap. The amount of fresh fruits and vegetables available in the city at minimum cost is amazing."

She stopped, betting he hadn't heard a word she'd said. He looked a thousand miles away.

"So how long have you known Darius?" he asked.

"For a while. Remember my friend Amber from the party?" He nodded. "She introduced us."

"Are you dating him? Not that it's any of my business," he said, looking away.

"No, Darius is still in love with his ex-fiancée," Katrina said.

"Is that so," he said, his eyes finding hers. Was that relief she saw? It was quick, his eyes unreadable now.

"Are you hungry?" he asked.

"A little."

"Can you hang with me a little longer? There is a place I'd like to take you to see, and I promise I'll feed you."

"Okay," she said, not ready to go home, not anywhere near wanting to end her time with him, forgetting that professional manner stuff. She was going to enjoy her time with him. She could think and worry later.

Will felt the same; he wasn't ready to take her home. He'd been surprised at seeing another man, a prospect he'd not contemplated. The experience left him a little unsettled. What an ass he was to have never considered that she might be interested in someone other than him. He was quiet for a while. Did she have her versions of Josey and Charlotte? He hoped not.

"Where are we going?" she asked once they'd gotten back into his jeep.

"I'd like you to meet my sister, if you don't mind. We can stop by the gardens in her neighborhood, since you've seen them all. You can give me another tour. We can get something to eat afterwards at their home, if you don't mind."

"No, I don't mind. Are you sure she doesn't mind? Bringing random people over without calling?"

"I go over all the time without calling, and I would hardly call you random. But for your benefit, I'll give her a call to let her know we're coming," he said, pulling out his cell.

Dennis Jr. answered.

"Hey, dude, put your mom or dad on the phone," Will said.

"Here's Dad," he said, handing the telephone to his father. "It's Will."

"Will," Dennis Sr. said, taking the phone from his son.

"Hey, Dennis. I wanted to let you know that I was on my way over."

"Okay, but that's a first," he said.

"I know, but I'm bringing a friend with me. She is helping me with the garden competition for our neighborhood. We were going to stop by the neighborhood garden in your area before stopping by the house."

"Okay, I'll tell Jennifer and see you in a few," Dennis said.

"Thanks." Will hung up and looked over at Katrina. "See? It's okay."

❧

Dennis hung up the phone and leaned back against the sink.

"Who was that?" Jennifer asked, walking into the kitchen. Jennifer was as short as her husband was tall, black-haired to his blond. He placed his arm around her waist, lifting her up onto her toes, and bent over to kiss her lips.

"That was your brother," he said, looking down at her.

"What did he want?"

"Well, he was letting us know that he was on his way over here with the woman who is helping him with the competition. The assistant, I guess. They are going to stop at the neighborhood gardens first," Dennis said. "Strange, huh?"

"Strange because he's never brought a woman by? Strange because he's never called before stopping by? Or is it strange because he's going to look at our neighborhood gardens? Which strange are you referring to?" They both laughed at that.

"Want some pizza for lunch?" she asked.

"Sure. You're going to turn this into a fact-finding mission, aren't you?" he asked.

"Why not?" she responded. He kissed her on the top of her head. No reason he could see not to.

❧

Will's sister lived in one of the more upscale parts of town, a gated community filled with families with dads who worked enough for their wives to stay at home if they wanted to. Will turned into the Willow Mountain subdivision, stopped at the gate, punched in a code, waited for the gates to open, and drove in. He looked over at her and asked, "Where are the gardens?"

"Follow this road until it ends," Katrina said. "There is a small neighborhood community center where their pool, park, and gardens are." He followed the road until it dead-ended into a large parking lot and found a spot close to the small brick building.

"We're here?" he asked, parking the jeep in front of a small brick building he assumed was the community center. There were older people milling about outside and kids running around. He got out of the jeep, and so did Katrina. She walked around the front of it to meet him.

"Inside the building is a meeting place for the neighborhood use. I think for games and small neighborhood social events," she said.

"Again, I'm amazed by how much you know about this city," he said, taking her hand tentatively in his. She looked over at him, shy now for some reason, but she didn't pull back.

"Come on, let me give you a tour," she said, turning and walking down one of the side paths that led away from the building. The beds were filled with ivy, packed and overflowing. They walked under huge trees that provided a lot of shade for the pool and the large children's playscape.

"This is beautiful," he said, looking around at the tall trees and green foliage everywhere. Katrina was leading him through the flower part of the gardens, although it was mostly green. "This neighborhood always gives us a run for our money. They are always one of the five finalists. They have decided to take a different approach with their gardens, mimicking more the gardens of a Central Park or Hyde Park in England. I should move here; they'd appreciate my gardening style," Katrina said.

"Ready for lunch?" he asked after they were done.

"Yes."

"Knowing my sister like I do, she has cooked something or ordered pizza for us."

They walked back to the front of the gardens and hopped back into the jeep. It was a typical Saturday at his sister's home with kids playing in the front yard as they drove up. Dennis and his buddy were in the middle of the street, hockey sticks in hand, skates on their feet. They moved a goal aside as they recognized Will's jeep and he pulled into the driveway of their home. They watched as Will and Katrina got out.

"Hey, Uncle Will," Dennis Jr. said, pausing a moment in the game to move his goal back into place.

"Hey, Dennis," Will replied, and walked over to the front door. He knocked and opened the door. "Jennifer, we're here!" he said.

Katrina trailed behind him, taking in his sister's home. It was as large as she'd expected it to be, but it had a homey, lived-in feel to it. Soccer balls, maybe five of them, sat in the entry, next to a nice expensive bench.

They walked into the main room, where the ceilings were tall, giving the room an open feeling.

There were signs that kids lived here: tennis shoes were stuck in the spindles of the stairway leading up to the second floor, and pictures of their family sat on the side tables next to the couch. Katrina stopped and watched as Will's sister entered. She was a small woman, an inch taller than Katrina's five-foot frame, followed by a tall man who must have been about six feet and blond.

That was an interesting mix, she thought, watching as Will hugged his sister.

"Jennifer," Will said, "I'd like you to meet Katrina. She is the poor woman the committee has assigned to work with me, guiding me in the competition for this year."

"Hello, Katrina, nice to meet you," Jennifer said, walking to stand in front of Katrina and extending her hand. Katrina shook it.

"Will never brings any of his friends over. I was beginning to suspect that he didn't have any," Jennifer said. Katrina smiled.

"This is my husband, Dennis." Dennis gave her a nod of his head and a smile.

"We also have three kids," she said. "The boy outside is our oldest child, Dennis Jr. We also have two girls, ages ten and five."

"I've set up some drinks and ordered some food for us out back. Let's go have a seat," she said and headed to the back door.

They all followed Jennifer out onto the deck. Katrina fell in love with it immediately. It was a great outdoor living space, and one she could tell was used by their family. Will and Dennis had taken a seat in the chairs that sat in a grouping around a mid-size coffee table. A pitcher of lemonade was sweating on the table, and Dennis began pouring for them. Katrina sat on the couch and Jennifer joined her there.

"So I hear Will took you to see our neighborhood gardens?" she asked.

"More like she took me. I believe she has seen all of the gardens in this city. Isn't that correct?" he said, looking at her.

"Yes," she said. "I'm working with Will on the gardening competition, and I'm interested in what other like-minded people create."

"I bet. I share your love for gardening, too, except I don't have as much time as I'd like. I work part-time and with the kids, I don't have time for much else."

"Don't feel sorry for her. She uses me like a dog, making me work in the yard," said Dennis.

"He enjoys it. Don't pay any attention to him," Jennifer said.

"You have a beautiful yard and home," Katrina said.

"Thank you," Jennifer said, smiling at her. Dennis Jr., walked out on the deck, pizza boxes in hand.

"Mom, the pizza guys are here," he said, walking over to place the boxes on the sideboard they had set near the largest of the tables. It was made of teak, one of her favorite woods, and worn with age, matching all of the outside furniture.

Jennifer stood up and said, "I made a salad. Let me go inside and get the plates."

Katrina stood. "I'd like to help you," she said, following Jennifer back into the house.

Dennis and Will watched them as they walked into the kitchen. They could see them through the windows that looked out onto the deck. Jennifer was pointing to the cupboards and Katrina seemed to be following her instructions.

"She's pretty," Dennis said, watching them through the kitchen window.

"Who knew?" Will said. "If it hadn't been for seeing her at that party, I probably wouldn't have ever noticed."

"What do you mean?" Dennis asked.

"The Katrina you see now is usually covered up in large shirts and baseball caps and working in her yard. She's lived near me for about a year and I didn't know. What does that say about me?"

"You don't expect me to answer that, do you?" Dennis said, laughing. "So she decided to help you with the competition, I see."

"Yes, but not without me proving myself." He told Dennis about working for her that day. Dennis laughed and watched Will.

"She's different from what you're used to?"

"You don't know the half of it, but yes, she is," he said, not elaborating, just watching her through the window as she helped his sister.

A few minutes later, Jennifer and Katrina exited the kitchen with plates, forks, and salad fixings. Jennifer and

Katrina set the table, and the men took their places. Dennis Jr. and a couple of his buddies joined them, as well as their oldest daughter, who brought a friend with her. The youngest was over at a friend's home.

They talked, all of them, kids mixing it up with their parents and their Uncle Will. Katrina watched, taking in the camaraderie, the humor, the jokes, and the happiness and love that this family showed each other. She missed her parents, missed having someone to whom she belonged. She wanted this, a desire she'd kept deep down and folded away after her parents' death, not wanting to go through that again.

She'd wished for this kind of love. She watched Will interact, giving as good as he got from his nieces and nephews. *Be careful, Katrina,* she said to herself. She might be willing to put aside her fears for this one, or to try at least. The kids and their friends ate through most of the pizza, and they remained outside talking for a while with their parents.

Will looked down at his watch. It was getting late. He'd spent the day with her and he'd enjoyed it immensely. He watched her as she watched his family, smiling. She was a pretty girl, and he liked what he was getting to know of her. However, it was time to call it a day. He looked over at her, and her eyes found his. He smiled and so did she, a quiet, small, almost indiscernible shot to his heart.

"Jennifer and Dennis, thank you for the lunch. I'd better get Katrina home; I've hijacked enough of her day," he said, looking over at her again and smiling.

"Katrina, you are welcome back anytime. The next time you visit our gardens, stop by, okay," Jennifer said, standing next to her husband at the door.

"I will. Thank you for lunch," she said.

"See you guys later," Will said, leading Katrina out and back to his jeep. They were quiet on the ride back.

"Thanks for the day. I had a good time," he said, reaching Katrina's home.

"Me, too," she said, getting out of his jeep.

"I'm out of town for a bit, but I will call you or stop by after I get back."

"Okay, sure. Take care," she said, getting out and walking to her door.

He watched until she was in her home. Then he backed out and drove home. Today had been great, and one small step for mankind. He smiled.

August

It was her phone again, another incoming text from Will.

"You busy?" she read.

"No," she responded. He was still out of town. He'd been calling her and texting her with regularity now. It had been a little over two weeks since she'd toured the gardens with him and met his sister. He called her or sent her a text just about every day. It had started out with just checking on the garden plans, but that had morphed into asking questions about her day and her job, until now he knew the names of her craziest customers.

He'd subtly pulled from her information about her life and the godfathers while he talked of his trips, his family, the places and sites he'd taken in. So much for putting him behind her. Her cell rang a few minutes later. He wasn't going to leave her alone, it seemed.

"How are you?" he asked.

"Good. You?"

"I'm okay, just taking a break. Thought I'd call to check to see how your day was, see if all was well in the land of the gardens," he said, a smile in his voice.

"Nothing new here," she said, and it was quiet for a second between them. "So how is your trip? Work keeping you busy?"

"Not too much," he said. "How about you? How was work?"

"Mrs. Stevenson called today," she said.

"What did she need this time?" he asked and sat back in his chair, so many miles away, and listened as she brought him up to date on the antics of her trust customers, the things going on in her life, with the godfathers, and their neighborhood. He was slowly making headway, or so he hoped. He hoped he was coming to mean to her what she'd come to mean to him.

CHAPTER 11

September

Will walked to the neighborhood garden the first weekend in September, which was the official mandated start time for the competition to ensure as much as possible fair play among the final five. Volunteer numbers were also checked to make sure no one team had an advantage over the other.

Today they would begin the major restructuring of the garden to accommodate his design. Six-thirty in the morning was early, but it wasn't too early for him. He usually left home around this time, sometimes earlier, for work or to cycle.

He'd met with Katrina, Thomas, and the committee members first in a small meeting last night and later on with the volunteers to discuss the upcoming work assignments. Captain Katrina had a list of all the volunteers, along with their work assignment for the next three months. She was all business, telling them that she would be monitoring and reassessing the plan against what they had accomplished at the end of each week and would change course if things were moving ahead of or behind schedule.

She answered any and all questions, introduced him around as the leader and somehow getting him and the other volunteers excited about this competition and the huge boatload of work that would be required of them.

Katrina had also explained last night that the backhoes would be mainly used to dig the major pond, the streams, and the waterfall. Will didn't have much experience in that area, so she'd given that assignment to others. He had been assigned, along with John and John's nephew, to digging the area that would hold the Zen garden. September, as Katrina had told them last night, would be the month of the diggers; it was her feeble attempt at humor.

He walked into the gardens to find her standing to the left of him, near where the new pond would be. She had his design in her hand and was staring at a spot in front of her. She was dressed ready to work in baggy shorts and a long T-shirt. Her hair was in one braid, with a hot pink bandanna tied around the front of her head, work boots and thick socks on her feet. He'd missed her on his last trip, but was content to talk to her on the phone. His decision to pursue her slowly had been a wise one.

He walked over, coming to stand behind her; he stood a little closer than was required, but he needed to satisfy his desire to be close to her. He used every opportunity he had at his disposal to touch her, and it was mutual—or it seemed mutual to him—although neither of them spoke about it. He'd bet good money that she probably would deny it, even at gunpoint.

"Here I was patting myself on the back for getting here early. I should have known you would beat me here," he said, looking over her shoulder at the plans.

"I wanted to make sure everything was ready, plus I needed to unlock the equipment and potting buildings. Most of the volunteers have been working here since the garden's inception, so I try to be as prepared as I can. I would hate to waste their time," she said, looking over her shoulder at his face; she'd missed seeing him.

"So do you have everything ready? Can I help?"

"No, I'm okay. You are digging for the stone garden today, correct?" she said, folding her plans and reaching toward the ground for her backpack.

"Yes, sir," he said, giving her a salute, which she missed as she bent over, allowing Will to admire her form, or at least what he could see of it in those shorts.

"Where will you be working?" he asked, looking into her face as she stood up and turned to face him.

"Mostly supervising, making sure we stay on track. I will be tagging the plants that need to be moved, and just filling in where needed," she said.

"You're good at this. Thank you. I can see what John meant by your ability, and I'm glad you're on our side," he said, smiling.

"Thank you," she said, her eyes moving away.

"When are the volunteers due to arrive?" he asked.

"Eight."

"I'll go and pull some of the supplies from the equipment building," he said, turning from her and walking away.

"There is food in the potting shed if you're hungry," she called out, watching him leave.

So far, so good, he thought, walking away from her. He was still in that pushing-her-for more mode, whether she acknowledged it or not. The calls and texts he'd sent, he'd initiated, going alone for a while until finally she started to return the favor, now calling and texting him unsolicited.

They were becoming friends. He knew the other would require time and more than a little finesse to make friends with her fears. He absolutely believed that the slow, cautious route was the best course. He was willing to be patient in his pursuit of her. No sudden moves; just keeping it nice and easy.

Once the others arrived, Will didn't see much of Katrina for the rest of the morning. He'd been working with John and John's nephew. John hadn't been much help, unless you called talking his ear off help. The nephew, Mark, was a big help, though. A sophomore in high school, he didn't talk much, just worked. Will had told both the nephew and John where to start digging and how deep it needed to be, and the nephew had put his earphones on and got to work. John, on the other hand, put his mouth in gear and had not slowed down since. Good Lord, that man could talk. He bet Katrina had sent him to work with him deliberately. He would not have been surprised.

It was now ten and he and Mark were a fourth of the way done with the digging for the stone garden, which was going to be much larger than the ten-by-ten-feet one at his house. If they could get that finished by day's end he would be extremely pleased. Tomorrow would be reserved for more digging, and hopefully they'd finish this detail. If he could get rid of John, he would be ecstatic.

"Hey, John," he said, interrupting John in the middle of his discussion about water conservation. "I'm going to take a break and go find Katrina to see how we're progressing."

John nodded.

"Sure, sure, go ahead. We made great strides this morning, didn't we?"

"Sure did, John," he said. *What's this* we *shit*, he wondered as he walked toward Mark, who was working steadily. Will tapped him on the shoulder.

"I'm going to take a break. Why don't you do the same? I'll be back in about fifteen minutes or so," he said, removing his gloves.

"Okay," Mark said, dropping his shovel. He was gone in sixty seconds. Will looked around for Katrina. He didn't see her, so he took off, headed who knew where, just looking around as he walked. He recognized many people from the neighborhood who smiled and spoke to him. Another byproduct of the competition was that it'd helped him meet and become acquainted with his neighbors. He spotted Oscar and Katrina digging holes for the new trees. He walked over to them.

After she'd gotten the volunteers lined up with their assignments, Katrina received unexpected help with the plant tagging and finished up faster than she expected. She found Oscar and roped him into helping them get a start on digging tree holes for the Japanese maple trees that Will wanted to add. They'd gotten started about an hour ago. Lola had come over with Oscar this morning, but, as Katrina had expected, she mostly sat on the bench, providing humorous commentary. If they were nice to her, she brought over some water for them to drink. Lola disabused them of any notion that she'd help.

"Lola, do I need to get you a shovel?" Katrina asked her.

"My momma didn't spend thirty hours in labor to have her daughter play the role of the field hand," she said, her hands at her hips. "You've got the best of us beat by a mile, anyway, Katrina."

Katrina gave her the middle finger salute and Lola laughed. Syd ran around playing with the children of the other volunteers over at the playscape area, occasionally coming back for something to drink or eat.

Katrina watched Will walking toward them out of the corner of her eye. She'd watched him off and on all morning. He and John's nephew had worked really hard. She intentionally had given him John, but made up for it by giving him Mark. John was one talking man, and since he loved Will so much, she let him love Will up today.

"Hey, Oscar and Katrina," Will said in greeting. Looking over at Lola, he said, "Working hard, Lola?"

"You bet your sweet buns I am, Will. Thank you for asking. You appreciate the little gift Katrina gave you this morning?" Lola continued, smiling like a Cheshire cat. Will smiled back, the full-toothed one that Katrina liked so well, as he looked over at her.

"Thanks, Katrina," he said.

"Hey, I gave you Mark, who can work enough for two people."

"He has to, because his uncle hasn't met a word he doesn't like," Lola added.

"The two of you got a lot accomplished this morning," Katrina said, stopping, resting her hands on top of her shovel, looking directly at Will. "You guys might be finished tomorrow."

"Yes."

"Well, you have the volunteers until five. Not all of them will be here tomorrow—church and all—but the guys working the backhoes will be here. You'll need to see how much is left to do tomorrow evening, and how many people you'll need to finish the major digging and replanting, if any, next weekend."

"Thank you again, Captain Katrina," he said.

"Just doing my job," she said.

"And you do it so well," he said, bending at the waist for her.

"Oscar and Lola, thanks for helping. I'd better get something to drink and then get back to work. I hear the woman in charge of the volunteers can be really tough," he said, smiling as he turned and walked away.

"Why, Katrina, I do believe our Will more than likes you. Don't you think so, Oscar?" Lola asked.

"I am not a part of that discussion and don't intend to be," Oscar responded.

"Ah, Oscar, you're no fun."

Katrina looked over her shoulder, but Will was nowhere to be found. She went back to work.

September 24

Tomorrow would be the anniversary of her parents' death. She picked up the phone and called her Uncle C. It was late, but he'd be up; he was the night owl to Colburn's early bird.

"Hey, it's my goddaughter calling. I was sitting here thinking about you. You all right?" he asked.

"You know me around this time. You would think by now it wouldn't hurt so much, but it still does," she said, trying not to cry.

"I understand. They were two very special people who loved you very much. I miss them, too." He could hear her tears. "You know what, Kat? They would want you to move on, not to forget them but to try and find happiness; maybe find a husband, start a family, or start your own business. You haven't said much about any of those things since they died, and you used to talk about wanting those things when they were here. It makes this life easier to take, having someone around to love."

"Things are different now, and I have you and Colburn. That's enough, isn't it?"

"Only you can answer that, Katrina. I just know that it helps me to have Colburn here. Don't know what I'd do without him, even as gruff as he can be. He and I want that for you," he said quietly.

"I know," she said.

September 25

"Western Bank and Trust. Katrina Jones speaking," she said into the phone.

"Katrina, it's me, Aubrey."

"Hi, Aubrey. How are you?"

"Fine, but I need some money. I need to find me another apartment," she explained, rushing the words out.

"Oh? What happened to the one you've been living in?" Katrina asked.

"It's Darnell," Aubrey said. Katrina inwardly groaned. Darnell was Aubrey's latest boyfriend, and trouble as far as Katrina thought.

"What's up?" Katrina asked.

"Nothing, but Darnell brought this girl home about a week ago; says she's his buddy's sister and doesn't have a place to live. He says there is nothing between them, but I saw them in our room when I got home from work last night. I need to leave."

Katrina was so not feeling this today. Aubrey was one of her more challenging customers, twenty-one going on fifteen, and sexually abused as a child. She had sued her abuser, a wealthy family member, resulting in the creation of a grantor trust for Aubrey. She had family, but they were useless, taking money from her, leeches on a good day.

"I can't stay here with them," Aubrey declared.

"Have you spoken to Darnell about it?" Katrina asked, now in her counselor mode.

"I tried, but he got mad and left with her," she answered.

Katrina blew out a breath quietly, not sure what to do. She'd taken so many trips down this road with Aubrey, gone through too many boyfriends, homes, and animals, but she wasn't feeling it today.

"Are you still working?" Katrina asked.

"Yes."

"So what do you want to do?"

"I want her to leave," she responded.

"How should we go about that?" Katrina asked.

"Would you talk to Darnell for me? He likes you, thinks you're smart. He'd listen to you."

Katrina had met Darnell a couple of times and had thought at first that maybe he would be good for Aubrey. He'd seemed somewhat stable, more on the ball than some of the others.

"I'll call you again when he gets home. She goes to work at three, so she won't be around. Try talking to him, please?" she pleaded.

"Sure," Katrina heard herself promising. "I'll be here until five; call me before then, or it'll have to keep until Monday. Okay?"

"Thanks, Katrina," Aubrey said and hung up.

Of all her trust customers, talking to Aubrey left her feeling the most impotent. Aubrey had graduated from high school, but barely. Her skills were limited. She worked at a pizza place when she worked. She'd gone through two homes already, and the trust was not ever going to purchase another one. She'd left her prior homes damaged and unclean, and the cost of preparing them for sale had been ridiculous. She usually had animals, her true friends, she called them, living with her, and when she moved out of her last house, she left the animals there alone. Katrina had to dole out money for fines to prevent her from going to jail for animal abandonment.

She was responsible for Aubrey's actions, financially at least; the trust was ineffective at changing Aubrey or her choices. The sad part of it all was that Aubrey was a very thoughtful and sensitive girl.

Katrina buried her head in work, hoping to get through the day and go home; she wasn't up for much talking today. Two more difficult calls had come in—one from a woman accusing the trust of not helping her son meet his medical expenses. The mother had faxed over page after page of documentation that Katrina would have to sort through. Another customer was unhappy with the state of his investments. *Aren't we all,* she thought. She was past ready to go home; it was close to 5:30 now, and way past time to jet.

Katrina sat back, pulling her legs into her body as she fell back against the cushions of her couch, tired from work and emotionally exhausted. Four years ago today she had lost two people who'd meant the world to her, who'd loved her, who'd changed the course of her life. Looking back at that first year after their deaths, she hadn't been sure she'd make it. Thank God for the godfathers and Lola. She was grateful to and for them. She knew her parents would be proud of her; they were then, told her so often. Would they be happy with her life now? Was she happy with her life now? Was working for the bank and gardening really all she wanted out of it?

She used to want more, in that window between being an orphan and her parents' death. Maybe C was right. Perhaps it was time to venture outside of her comfort zone. She could pursue her old dream of starting her own landscaping business, for starters. She had enough money saved to cover her for a while; more if she sold her home. The fact that she was sincerely considering it was in itself a promising sign. Oh, to move beyond hurt and to try again.

She stood up and walked out her back door, heading over to Will's garden, her new place of refuge, her garden away from gardening. She'd spent gobs of time over there while he traveled, her little secret.

She hoped he wasn't home, but didn't really care tonight; she just wanted the solace that she found there in his yard, in his space, in the dark. She opened the gate and walked in, thankful for the lanterns to mark her way. There was a small light on a side table in the main room of his home, but she didn't see him. Quietly, she made her way to her favorite spot, her secret chamber. She took a seat, finding as always the wood smooth and cool beneath her legs as she settled back, her back against the wall.

The chimes above her head played a quiet melody in the stillness of the night, blending in with the symphony of sounds that played outside. It was peaceful here. She started to cry then, giving in to the emotion that this day always brought for her. She always gave herself a time limit to cry; just for a moment. *No wallowing, Katrina.*

She cried for the unfairness of life sometimes, for herself and for people like Aubrey, who life had left wounded and on the sidelines. She cried for her inability to make it better, cried because sometimes life was difficult and that was just the way it was. She leaned back and let her tears flow.

She hadn't been there long, but a small sound caught her attention and she opened her eyes, wiping them with her hands. Will stood just outside the doors, watching her. How long had he been there? He was dressed in a T-shirt and warm-up bottoms, his feet bare.

"How long have you been here?" she asked, wiping her eyes again with her hands, standing up.

"Long enough," he said quietly, watching her, his expression unreadable.

"I'm sorry for sneaking in. Today was long and complicated. I hope you don't mind; I needed quiet."

"No, I don't mind. You're always welcome. Did it help?"

"Yeah," she said, looking into his eyes, finding them still undecipherable.

"Do you want to talk about it?" he asked.

"No, I'd just start crying again."

"Okay."

"I'd better go, I've borrowed your garden enough for one day," she said, standing up and trying to smile.

As she started to leave, his arm stuck out and wrapped around her waist. She stopped and looked up at him, taking in his eyes again, and this time she saw compassion and concern in them. He pulled her to him, wrapping both arms securely around her waist, pulling her close to his chest, one hand moving to the back of her head, holding her against him. Her arms moved and secured themselves around his waist and she let herself lie against his chest.

It felt right being here; it was calming to be supported by someone for a while. He stood with her in his arms, not seeming to be in any hurry to let her go. She started to cry again, and he continued to hold her. How long they stood there like that she didn't know, but eventually she pulled back and looked up into his face, watching it move lower until his lips captured hers in a soft and tender kiss.

She kissed him back, taking her time with it. She softly explored his mouth, opening hers wider for him, moving her tongue in search of his. His breathing changed and his hands moved from her waist to cup her butt, lifting her, pulling her closer to his body. She moved her arms up to surround his neck and held on for dear life, losing herself in his mouth, his strength.

She felt movement. He was taking her somewhere. She just held on as he walked the few steps back to the seat, not breaking his kiss. He turned them and sat, pulling her to rest onto his lap, and continued his quiet offensive. One of his hands moved, trailing along her hip, making its way underneath her T-shirt.

She jumped a little at the touch of his hand at her waist and followed the smooth movement as it worked its way up to capture her breast, gently rolling her nipple between his thumb and forefinger. She moaned into his mouth and held on as he turned her body, trailing his hand slowly up her thigh. She moaned as he reached the juncture of her thighs. He went still for a second, giving her time to recognize his intentions.

She held her breath, removing her mouth from his, placing her face in between his shoulder and chin as his hand found her spot and those wicked fingers began to play with her.

"I . . . Will . . . wait . . . oh, don't stop," she pleaded. Before she was ready, she came, quick and strong. She gripped his shoulders, pushing her face into his neck as he held her, allowing pleasure to work through her system, pulling another moan from her and leaving a calm in its wake.

She turned her body into his, pushing herself against him, her mouth now seeking his again. He felt so good. Her lips locked on to his, and she moaned at how good his mouth felt. She moaned again and kissed him harder. She moved her hands underneath his shirt to feel his hard stomach before they traveled lower.

She moved her body so that she straddled him now, legs on each side of his, resting on her knees. Her mouth moved deliberately over his. Her hands moved to the top of his sweats and rested there for a second, giving him time to recognize her intentions. She moved them slowly, first one and then the other, underneath his sweats, moaning again into his mouth at the strength she found there. Her body went lax as she wrapped her hands around the part of him she'd admired from the backyard.

She just held him for a second, and then her hands began to move, starting at the tip, before both sliding slowly downward—she didn't want to waste this chance—and then up again. He moaned. She could come to love that sound. Her mouth continued to feast on his as her hands loved him, moving up and down. God, he felt good, so smooth and strong; she adored the feel of him, so much better than any dream.

"Katrina," he said, pulling his mouth away from hers, his breathing ragged and harsh.

No, don't do that, she thought and went back in search of his lips. Ah, there they were. She'd found them and kissed him again, his tongue no match for hers.

"Katrina," he said after a minute. "You have to stop."

Up and down her hands moved, picking up speed. He moaned low in his throat and Katrina pulled back, wanting to watch him. His hand joined hers, she thought at first to stop her. But maybe not . . .

"Katrina, you, have, to . . . ahh," he said, his hand now gripping hers tightly. He began to help her move up and down. He fell back against the wall, his eyes closed. His face was slightly damp, making his hair cling to his face. He was so very sexy, and she watched him as his climax built.

He blew out a breath, a quiet hiss, pulling her hands from inside his sweats quickly to place them on top, pushing down hard as he came. He moaned, so low she barely heard it. She watched as his climax showed on his face, looking like pain, his face twisting a little, his back lifting a little from the wall.

She went in search of his mouth again, still holding on to him, her hand still trapped under his. She felt small final shudders run through him before she pulled back. She watched as his chest slowed down and his breathing returned to normal. Her hands were still trapped in his. He was still for a time before he released them from his death grip. She pulled them back and stood up. He gave a big sigh and his eyes popped open to stare into hers, scary in their intensity.

"I didn't expect that," he said.

"Me neither," she said.

She sat down next to him, looking over at him as he sat, staring ahead into space. After a time, he asked, "You okay?"

"Yes, you?"

He laughed quietly. "Yes, very much so."

"This is the anniversary of my parents' death, and, as much as I try, I'm never prepared for it when it comes," she said.

"I see."

"I get scared a little without them here. I was used to being on my own, before them and the godfathers. I'd learned how to deal with that. They came along and showed me something different and I thought, okay, I can work with this, but then I lost them, too. It was hard getting started again, and this day reminds me of that," she said, looking over at him, watching him shake his head in acknowledgment.

"Well, I've taken enough of your time. I'd better get home," she said, standing. "Thanks for letting me use your space here," she said, that comment inadequate to describe what had just happened between them.

"See you later," she said, walking out through the doors and then through the back gate. He remained seated, letting her go, leaving him with an indelible mark on his heart.

"Uncle C, Colburn," Katrina called out in greeting the next morning as she entered their home. It was early, before six in the morning, and usually they could still be found at home, drinking their morning coffee and eating whatever one of them could scrounge up. She hadn't gotten much sleep last night.

After leaving Will of the talented fingers and enigmatic expression behind, she hadn't known what to do with what had just happened. She needed time to replay and process, replay and process, her mind twisted, no idea what she wanted to do next. Her body wouldn't settle down or lie still, either, so she quit trying at about 4 a.m., deciding she needed some godfather time.

"Colburn," she called out, hearing sounds coming from the kitchen. She walked through the living room and into the kitchen to find Uncle C pouring coffee into two mugs while the television sat on the counter, blaring out the morning news.

"Hey, Uncle C," she said. He turned at the sound of his name, giving her a smile, welcome and love in his eyes. She almost started crying again.

"Well, how is my favorite goddaughter this morning?" he said, his smile growing in size.

She so needed this. "I'm your only goddaughter," she shot back, thinking she would never ever grow tired of hearing his affirmation of her place in their lives.

"You're up early," he said, standing next to the coffeemaker at the counter near the sink.

"I couldn't sleep, thought I'd come over to help around here," she said.

"That boyfriend of yours giving you trouble?" he asked, taking a sip of his coffee, his eyes roaming her face.

She walked over and opened the cabinet, took out a mug, and walked to stand next to him. He reached for the pot and poured some into her cup. She turned and opened the refrigerator, searching for the creamer that she purchased and kept in stock here to cut the mud that passed for coffee in this house. The godfathers would never dream of drinking anything that wasn't absolutely black in color.

"No boyfriend, just wanted to see you and Colburn," she said.

"Yesterday pass okay for you?" he asked, taking a sip of his coffee. She turned her eyes to him.

"Yes," she said, leaning her head onto his chest.

"It'll be okay, Kat," he said, his arm going over her shoulder.

"I know," she said, lifting her head. "You guys had breakfast yet?" she asked, stepping away.

"Nope, but feel free to cook," C said, and she laughed.

She sat her coffee down and pulled out the ingredients for breakfast. She put a couple of slices of bread into their toaster. "Do you two want bacon this morning?" she asked.

"Of course we do. And not that turkey bacon stuff," Colburn said, walking into the kitchen and kissing her cheek.

Katrina walked over to the refrigerator, grabbing turkey bacon and eggs, ignoring Colburn, and placing them on the counter. She found the skillet and arranged the bacon in it. She put six eggs in a bowl and began to scramble them. Colburn and C took their coffee and sat at the table, watching her and exchanging looks.

"So how is that boyfriend of yours?" Colburn asked.

"He's not my boyfriend, but if you're referring to Will, he's fine. We have done quite a bit of work on the garden. I'm impressed with him; he works really hard, and is more knowledgeable than I had given him credit for," she said.

"Katrina's boyfriend is a hard worker," Charles said.

"He seemed pretty tough to me. He didn't let you intimidate him or push him out of the competition," Colburn said. She opened another cabinet and took out plates and silverware and set the table. She walked back to the stove and picked up a fork.

"You two must think me tougher than I am; trust me, I'm not that tough," she said as she removed the bacon from the stove and cooked the eggs.

Colburn and Charles sat at the table, waiting for her to finish. She removed the last of the toast, placed it on a plate next to the bacon, and put it on the table. She stirred the eggs once, then scooped them into a bowl, and put them on the table. She led the way with grace; she kept it short and sweet so she didn't lose her audience.

"You know, I've been thinking," she said.

"That could be trouble," Colburn said, interrupting and giving her a wink.

"I've been giving some thought to a career change. I could start out small, maybe take on some small land-scaping jobs. I've done it for free in the past. Maybe after the competition I could take on small paying jobs build up a business the way you two have. You've always encouraged me to start getting paid for what I do. I'm sure you'll be happy that I'm finally coming around," she finished, finally looking at them.

Two serious faces studied her.

"You were right the other day, C. I used to want more for my life. I think it's about time I started owning it more. I didn't use all the money after Mom and Dad died; I put most of it in savings. That could be my seed money, plus I could sell my home and take an apartment until I get it going.

"I have enough to live on for a while until I can find another job. I mean, I like my job, it's okay, but I think I would like to try something different, try going out on a limb, test myself," she said. She watched as Colburn looked at Charles, and then turned back to her.

"Katrina," C said, "we promised your parents to always look after you if something happened to them, and we have. Colburn and I have thought about this long and hard. We don't have any heirs by blood, and as you are our only heir, we are giving you the business. We made the changes to our wills about two years ago. We were waiting for the right time to tell you. This seems like it to me."

"That's right, you can quit any time you wish, start a business, fail, start another one. Or you can come and work here with us. I know you can't tell it by looking at us, but we are getting old. Can't get around like we used to," Charles continued.

"Speak for yourself. We had even thought one day of starting a landscaping branch of the business, but with what we have here, we didn't have the time. You could start it for us. You would be good at it, too. Look what you've done to the competition each year, and we would be here to guide you," Colburn said.

"I don't know what to say," she said, her eyes moving between them, tearing up.

"You've got gardening in your blood, just like your family, and we are your family. Until we're gone, we will always be here to look after you," Charles said, watching her tears fall in earnest now.

"Hey there, don't cry. You know I dislike crying women," Colburn said, reaching over and taking her hand in his, his actions belying his words.

"Thank you," she said, smiling through her tears. "I'm too old for anyone to look after."

"No, you are not, and that's the end of that," Colburn said. She left the table for a minute to compose herself and splashed some water on her face. They finished breakfast when she returned without further comment on that subject.

The godfathers knew she needed time to process their suggestion. They hoped she would agree. They ate breakfast discussing the business and the upcoming garden competition. After breakfast they left to start working, and she stayed behind to clean up the kitchen.

They really loved her, and sometimes, even with the adoption, it was hard for her to understand unconditional love. That was why she pushed back so, testing others so much. Why she hid herself, too. Up until she was ten, love had never been unconditional, and that had been the hardest part for her to overcome. Most times she didn't feel she'd ever learn to accept love, to believe in it. She knew it intellectually, had seen it from her parents, but for some reason it had not sunk into her soul. It had always been easier to wait for the other shoe to drop than to trust that people would be there for her and wouldn't desert her.

What a gracious gift the godfathers had given her, even if she didn't take them up on it. They'd shown her what she meant to them. It was a gift beyond measure. She stood at the sink, her tears finding their familiar route down her face, and she gave herself over to the comfort of having someone love her as much as her parents had.

She spent the remainder of the day working at Abernathy and Co. There was always more than enough work to go around. She started out back, running the backhoe, loading up dirt and compost into trucks, large and small. A customer would pull up along a road, park, and hand over their slip, which listed the type of dirt or fertilizer or compost they wanted. She'd take her backhoe and scoop the correct amount and drop it into their trucks.

While she worked, her thoughts turned to Will. She didn't know what to do about him, especially in light of yesterday. He was silently and patiently working at overcoming her defenses, not pushing but not allowing her to run, either. He never said a word to her about it, but he called and sought her out constantly now. He was someone she could talk with. She liked him very much. Liked his energy, the way he took on challenges. They'd become friends. She'd shared more about herself with him, more than she'd ever shared with a potential romantic interest. Could this be more for her?

She hadn't had much luck with guys, but it was mostly her own fault because of her ingrained defensiveness. So should she or shouldn't she try with Will?

She later helped customers in the shop, sitting next to her Uncle C, a perfect ending to a perfect day. The ability to do something she loved every day appealed to her strongly, so she promised herself she would start making plans to take her life in a new direction.

CHAPTER 12

October

The first Saturday in October found Katrina back at the garden bright and early, standing in the potting shed over the main table. The volunteers were scheduled to arrive at nine today, and she stopped by the local taco stand and picked up a bucket filled to the brim with tacos, a few juices, and some coffee. She was not above bribery, especially as the weeks of work had worn on. She swiped some fruit from the vegetable stand and added it to the array of other food items. She surveyed her buffet, pleased with the bounty.

She wanted to make sure everything was in order, always cognizant of her volunteers' time; just 'cause it was free didn't mean they could waste it. Arriving before Will wasn't easy. He was always around, always early, had taken this competition business seriously. Her focus tended to slip away when he presented himself in front of her.

She'd kept her mind from replaying too much of what had transpired between them. It had the power to push her over to his door, begging for more, and she wasn't sure that's where she needed to be. However, her doubts were slowly disappearing. Will the consistent was wreaking havoc on her fears, pushing them aside. He'd become a good friend. She spent an inordinate amount of her time thinking about him. She was coming to believe that he would be worth it.

Since the food was ready, she found her backpack and dug through it for a copy of the plans. She took them with her and walked out toward the flower section. It was always good to check up, make sure they stayed on schedule. She was pleased with the progress they'd made; they were well on schedule. She hoped to have all of the water features up and running by month's end. Next month was the restructuring of the pavilion to Will's Eastern theme, and they needed to enclose his stone garden.

She would order the rocks for the garden this week for delivery next Saturday. She saw some of the volunteers enter and she smiled and waved to them as she reached the main gate. They were headed to the back for food. She walked over to stand in the middle of the path leading into the gardens, looking over the two main trees that they would have to prune, as well as the multitude of shrubs tucked into beds that awaited pruning. There was always something that needed doing, but she was pleased with their progress.

Second weekend

Will entered the garden, looking around for Katrina. Today was rock-delivery day. It was a sad state of events that that had become exciting to him. The past month had been grueling work at the gardens, with Katrina turning into the taskmaster from hell. He thought he could give orders, but he'd had no idea. He knew now what the others had learned long ago: beware of Katrina when she approached you with a wide smile and wrapped her arms around you. It always meant more work. The funny thing was that she asked in a way that sounded reasonable at the time but made you kick yourself as soon as she walked away for agreeing.

She had given up the professional routine, traded it in finally for friendship. One small step for man, one giant leap for mankind, he thought. He had no idea that he could be this patient. Hell, he'd never had to be, not with women, at least. This was a new experience for him, and he'd lost the desire for someone else a while ago; he wanted no substitutes. Wow, that was a powerful admission, but he was long past going back.

Seeing her crying that night had affected him. She had an effect on him and had changed something internally in him that had been slowly changing, anyway. He wanted to know her, maybe even for keeps. His Katrina had been good at hiding, putting up roadblocks. Not so much anymore; she was sending signals his way, or maybe it was wishful thinking on his part, his time away from sex making him delusional. He smiled at that.

Thankfully, the digging was done; next came getting the ponds, waterfalls and streams built, lined, filled with water, and up and running. Speak of the devil, there she stood in the middle of the path, dressed in a large sweat-shirt and jeans, work boots on her feet. When and how had a woman dressed in work clothes become such a turn on? He watched her for a second as she looked at something on her copy of the plans. He walked up behind her, waiting until she felt him at her back and turned around.

"I knew you would be here early," he said, watching the surprise and pleasure at seeing him reflected on her face. It did wonders for his confidence.

"Yep, wanted to make sure we were organized and ready for the volunteers this morning."

"Are we?"

"Yes, we are."

"Again, you're very good at this," he said, looking down into her eyes.

"Thank you again," she said, smiling back. Before she could finish getting the words out, he bent his head and captured her lips with his. He moved his hands to her waist to hold her still, giving her a quick but thorough kiss.

Judging by her sudden gasp, he had surprised her; since she didn't try to leave, he went back for more. Taking her lips again, her lips parted, her tongue seeking his this time. He pulled her closer, wanting more, but determined to be careful with her still, in spite of his need.

She pulled back, breathing hard, a startled expression on her face.

"Good morning, Will," John said as he entered their area, coming from behind him. "Oh, good morning,

Katrina. I didn't see you standing there. I'm headed for the coffee. Katrina, do you have a moment to give me an update on our progress?"

"Sure," she said, stepping back and walking away from Will, glad for the escape.

The next morning Katrina left home and headed to the garden again. She looked around her street, taking in the leaves that had fallen off their branches and wondering where the fall had gone. Between work at her full-time job, working at the gardens, and exploring preliminary ideas for her own business, she'd barely had time to make her weekly trip to the godfathers. No longer able to see them on the weekends, she started stopping at lunch or after work during the week.

This was the last weekend of major physical labor. They were ahead of schedule, so she pushed on ahead to start giving the trees their new, bonsai-shaped haircuts. She was surprised by how much she liked the new look. With most of the major work completed on their section, many of their volunteers had to been reassigned to the vegetable section. Today she would be planting bamboo plants in an area next to the waterfall.

She passed by Lola's home, then the Sheppards', noting the sports equipment that littered their front porch. Seven children—no way, Jose, she thought. She came upon Will's home and glanced over. He was standing in his garage, next to his jeep, loading something into it. It looked liked tools to her. He glanced up, saw her approach, and gave her a big smile.

She loved that smile; it was friendly, open, and promised fun, all of which she'd come to associate with him. He seemed to have moved up his game, letting her know that he wanted more; why the hell not change her game, too?

She walked over and stood just outside his garage. "What do you have there?" she asked, looking into his back seat.

"A statue of Buddha that was given to me by a friend of my sister's," he said, pointing at it sitting alone on the backseat, locked in, somewhat comically, with a seat belt. He looked thoughtful sitting there in the backseat. "The friend was looking to get rid of it, so I picked it up from him last week for the garden. Is that where you're headed?"

"Yep," she said.

"Want to ride over with me?" he asked.

"Yep," she said, smiling back at him. This was what she wanted. Him.

"Hop in," he said, walking around to open the door for her. "I've got one more load and then we'll be good to go," he said, walking away from her and back into the garage.

She sat there watching him. He was looking good, as usual, in jeans and a T-shirt, his baseball cap turned backward on his head, his smile accentuating his sharp cheekbones and those beautiful eyes. She still put herself to sleep nightly watching her favorite nude video of him, feeling her mouth on his, his hands moving between her legs.

"Whoo," she whispered to herself, fanning her face. *Slow down, Katrina.* She watched as he walked back out, put the last load into his jeep, and got in. He looked over at her and smiled again. She did the same. He started his jeep and pulled out of his drive.

She didn't see him again until later that afternoon. She spent the morning moving native plants from one area to another. She went to the planting shed to retrieve the twenty or so one-gallon bamboo plants that had been delivered earlier in the week. She found a two-tiered cart and began placing them on it. She'd have to make two trips. She had put the last of the first batch on the bottom tier when Will walked in.

"You need some help?" he asked, looking at her cart and over to the table where the remaining plants stood.

"You could grab the other cart, and we can make one trip. Do you have something else you're working on?" she asked, trying to remember what he'd been assigned.

"I've completed my task for the day. Did anyone tell you that you were a tough boss?"

"Yes, and no," she said, smiling.

"Where's the other cart?" he asked, looking around for it. She pointed to the corner closet and followed him, admiring him as he walked over to retrieve it. She helped him load the remaining plants and they set off, making their way to the waterfall area. It was working beautifully.

"I really like your designs," she said.

"Thank you," he said. He followed her lead as she set the plants on the ground in the spots where they would be planted. Will picked up her shovel that she'd placed there earlier and pushed it into the ground.

"Let me dig and you plant," he said.

"Because I've already dug about ten holes today, I'll let you," she said.

Will dug a hole and she following behind, removing the plants from their container and setting them into the ground, filling in the hole with dirt. Three down, eighteen to go.

"So how's work?" she asked. "How are you taking not traveling?"

"It's not as bad as I thought it would be, this staying put business," he said, smiling at her. "There is this assistant, this task-master from hell," he said, moving over to the next hole, "that makes sticking around not so bad."

"Task-master from hell?" she said, sticking plant number five into the ground. "I'm not that bad."

"No, you're not that bad. I've actually come to enjoy working here with the competition and with you," he said, moving on, finding his hole digging rhythm.

"Same here," she said.

"Speaking of out-of-town trips, I've got to fly out tomorrow morning, unexpectedly. Couldn't be helped."

"It's okay. We're at a good place," she said. They continued talking, moving on to the godfathers and her work, old familiar territory, until all the plants had been placed into the ground.

"I just need to water them, and then I'm done for the day," she said, walking to a spot in the garden where the hoses were kept.

"We can take it easy for a while, coast a little, since the bulk of the major changes have been implemented. So, as timing goes, this is a good time for a trip," she said, pulling the water hose from its hiding place in the ground and turning it on, moving it to soak the bamboo plants.

"I'll spend the next weeks reviewing our original planting schedule to make sure we haven't missed anything," she said. He watched her until she was done with the watering and then took the hose from her hand, putting it away. They began picking up tools, placing them on the carts and hauling them back to the equipment building. Will entered first and Katrina followed, bringing in the last of the load.

"That's it," she said, handing the last tool to him. He grabbed it from her hand and put it alongside the others. She turned to leave, but he pushed the door closed, locking them inside. She turned to look at him.

"What—" His lips found hers, cutting her off. She may have been surprised, but it quickly gave way to need. *Hell yes*, she thought. She opened her mouth and he wrapped his tongue around hers.

She stood on her tiptoes for better access. He helped, lifting her, wrapping her legs around his waist. He pushed her back into the door with his body, holding her in place while his hands went in search of her breasts, working themselves under her shirt. He applied pressure, dragging a moan from her, before releasing one and moving his free hand downward, seeking out the zipper to her shorts.

His hips began to circle hers, pushing himself into her firmly, and she moaned loud enough to wake the dead. Will pulled back enough to try and remove her shorts, pulling them down. One leg got caught on her boot.

"Skip it," she said, her breathing choppy as he placed her legs around his back, pushing into the junction of her thighs. They moaned again and Will stopped, looking around for a place other than the back of the door. He spotted a chair and set Katrina aside, pulling up short, staring at her standing before him partly naked, shorts bunched at the bottom of her right foot, hair escaping her ponytail, her mouth swollen from his kisses.

He moved back to her and kissed her hard on the mouth, and then retrieved the chair and pushed it against the door. They didn't need any uninvited guests. He sat down, but not before he'd unzipped his pants.

Katrina walked over to stand in front of him, dragging her shorts along with her, laughing at how ridiculous she looked. He looked up at the sound of her laugh, his eyes roaming over her again, and she watched as a sexy, slow grin formed on his face.

"Tell me you have a condom," she whispered, bending over to touch his lips with hers. He nodded, his lips going back to hers as she straddled his lap, his hand moving to pull out his wallet. He pulled back from her, trying to open it. Katrina pulled it from his hand. "I'll find it," she said.

And she did. He watched her, so ready; he had been since he'd stood nude before her. She handed him the condom, which he quickly put on. She lifted herself and slowly slid down him. Their heads fell forward to rest against each other, both appreciating the feel of him in her. He scooted forward in the chair, pulling her legs up and wrapping them around his waist.

He moved her up and down slowly, watching the pleasure on her face. He controlled the pace, entering her, moving her up and down. She was impatient, pushing against his hands, wanting her legs free. He obliged her and she took over. Up and down she moved, his back leaning against his chair as he enjoyed the ride. Her head rolled forward to fall on his shoulder.

"Fuck me," she thought, and he must have read her mind because he proceeded to do just that, holding her hips still, sliding his further off the chair and thrusting hard in and out of her body.

Oh God, she was coming, and coming hard; they came together, his hands on her hips, holding her tightly to him.

Shoot, that was some kind of good, just as she knew it would be, and why the possibility of being with him had scared her so.

His eyes locked on hers, staring intently at her, scaring her a little with their intensity. He lifted her off him, setting her down on her feet, and stood up.

"You okay?" he said a few seconds later, his pants zipped, clothes back in place, while she stood trying to regroup. He bent to help her dress, zipping her shorts.

"Is someone in there?" someone called from outside.

"John," she whispered to Will and he smiled a little.

"Timing is everything," he said, and they laughed, looking around the room and at each other, making sure they were zipped, clothes in place, and that there was nothing to give them away.

"Katrina?" John said as she opened the door. John stepped back, startled, a strange look passing over his face at finding Will with her.

"Well, hello, Will," he said.

"Hi, John," Will said.

"I'm not interrupting anything, am I?" he said, glancing between them. "I was surprised to find the door locked."

"No, Katrina and I were just leaving," Will said, his expression normal, as if he'd hadn't just made love to her a few minutes ago.

"Katrina, do you have a moment?" John asked.

"Sure," she said. "I'll see you later, Will."

"Yes, you will," he said, smiling and heading back into the garden.

❦

It was beautiful this time of the morning. The sun was just starting to break over the city. It was cool and Will felt alone, or as close as he could get to it, living in the city. He'd gotten up early this morning, had left Katrina in her bed and gone home and showered. He needed this ride before the roads became too crowded with vehicles and other cyclists. Cars didn't much care for bikes, and Lance Armstrong couldn't change that fact, although they were a little more tolerant nowadays. Until you got in the way, that is. He was careful. He needed a break from work, the gardens, and, after yesterday, last night, and this morning, from Katrina. He needed some alone time with his thoughts.

He loved this part of Texas; it had enough hills to challenge even the most experienced rider. He had ridden his bike in some of the most beautiful places around the world, but they couldn't compare to the Texas hill country, at least for him.

Amazing was the only word he'd found to describe the night he spent with her. He still couldn't believe the person he knew now was the same woman he rarely noticed ten months earlier.

He was leaving for Taiwan later this morning. He had to soothe a customer, and most didn't take soothing from anyone other than the top of the food chain, which, in this case, happened to be him. It may even take an additional week, but he sure hoped not. But when he returned, Katrina would be all his.

She'd been well worth the time it took to figure her out, and he was there now, finally understanding the conundrum that was Katrina. Even at the party he'd been attracted to the outside. He had no idea of all that she was, and she definitely wasn't boring. Maybe more like steady. That was a better description for her personality, and it had become his internal nickname for her. Steady in the care she gave to her godfathers. Steady in the care she gave to her friends, her community. Steady in the things that surrounded her and mattered to her.

Katrina walked into her home, grabbed a bottle of water, and walked out back and over to Lola's. Will had left yesterday.

He had come over to say goodbye; she hadn't known he had gone, having slept like the dead that morning. Awakened by the buzz of her doorbell, she was surprised to find him standing outside her door, shiny and clean. He kissed her, said he'd call as soon as he could, hopped in his jeep, and drove away, taking his energy with him. God, she'd like to have half of his energy; he had to have a plug-in somewhere.

The lights were still on at Lola's, so Katrina walked over and knocked at the door, but not too loudly as it was probably past Syd's bedtime. Lola opened it.

"Hey, girl, what's up?"

"Nothing much," she said, stepping inside. "What are you doing? Where are Oscar and Syd?"

"Oscar is watching some game, who knows and who cares, the games are all the same and nothing I'm interested in. Syd's asleep. I'm glad you stopped by. I talked Oscar into having a Halloween party this year. One for Sydney, and then later on that night one for the adults after the kids have gone to a sleepover hosted by another parent. Halloween, fortunately, has landed on a Friday this year, so why the hell not," Lola said.

"Works for me," she said, slumping down on the couch.

"What's up with you?" Lola asked, taking a seat next to Katrina.

"Nothing much."

"Right. Don't make me have to beat you."

Katrina told her about Will, bringing her up to date on all that had transpired between them, but leaving out the graphic details. As soon as she finished, Lola bounded up from the couch and started dancing around the room, a one-woman conga line, hands in the air, pulling out every dance step she'd ever seen or done, all the while chanting, "Go, Katrina, go, Katrina, it's your birthday, it's your birthday, go, Katrina, go, Katrina, it's your birthday" over and over for a full minute before she gave out and fell back on the couch next to Katrina. She looked over at Katrina and they both started laughing.

"He's gone overseas. Two weeks," Katrina said after they caught their breath and calmed down.

"Bummer."

"Yep, bummer. Can I help with the party?" Katrina said, changing the subject. She should have known better.

"I'm so proud, so happy for you. Oh, Katrina, who knew, huh? A nice guy for my Katrina. Finally. Yes!" Lola said, all gooey-eyed now.

"Cut it out," Katrina said, tossing a small pillow at Lola.

"So you're all lovesick 'cause he's gone. Isn't that cute. When is he due back?"

"Halloween."

"That's great. Perfect timing. Oh, girl, we need to find you a costume that will knock him out of his shoes, make him want to stay put from now on. This will be fun," Lola said, getting into the spirit. "You're coming with me when I take Sydney to get her costume, and we're going to find something really sexy for you. I've got something in mind. No field hands or farmers, either," Lola said.

Katrina rolled her eyes. Seeking to change the subject, she told Lola about the progress she was making on her business plans.

Friday, October 31

Friday morning, Asian time, found Will sitting in the Chiang Kai-shek airport waiting to board the first leg of his flight back to the States. He was way past anxious to get home. He should arrive Friday early evening, more than enough time to make it to Lola's party. What happened to his spirit of adventure? He had adventure in mind, all right, couldn't wait to get home to start it.

They'd talked nightly, and in between texted like crazy. He'd gone to sleep hard as a rock for the last two weeks. That had to have a negative impact on a man's thinking. He looked around, pushing his mind to something other than his *Steady*.

❀

Katrina sat on the couch, dressed in her Playboy bunny costume. For once, she was okay with her outfit. She wanted to look sexy tonight. She missed Will. All her past fears over what could go wrong didn't stand a chance against the need that rode low in her belly whenever her thoughts turned to him. He'd sent her a text from the plane and then called her telling her that he would be late; he had to make a last-minute stop at work.

She pulled out all the stops, including taking the time to curl her hair, and that was a major feat. She had really thick, long hair, and it required time, which is why she wore it pulled back most days. She looked good enough to eat, if she said so herself; some of the men thought so, too, by the glances she'd received this evening.

She stood up and walked to the kitchen to refill her glass of wine. This was her second, but she was careful; she wanted to be awake for her upcoming reunion with Will. She stood at the counter, looking over the selection of wines, and smelled the cool, crisp scent that was Will's before she felt his hands settle at her waist as he stepped in close to her, his front touching her back.

"Hey," he whispered in her ear.

"Back at you," she said, not moving, relishing the feel of his body touching hers. She leaned back a little and his hands moved to surround her waist fully, pulling her tighter to him. His mouth descended and found her neck, kissing her there. She moved her hair to the side and tilted her neck to give him better access. He kissed her there and his mouth roamed upward to her chin. He turned her around to face him. She watched his eyes as his lips made their descent to hers.

She stood, lips parted, waiting for him. He kissed her, tentative, moving softly before moving in and seeking her tongue. He kissed her again and again and pulled her tighter to him. They continued like this, exploring each other, not in any hurry, just getting reacquainted. He'd missed her more than he'd expected. She was almost his height in those shoes, so he only needed to lift her a little to align their bodies. They tuned out the world around them and almost forgot they were in Lola's kitchen.

He pulled back. "Come with me."

"Kay," she answered, not really in the talking mood, her head still swimming from his kiss. Will took her hand, and she walked next to him as they made their way to the front door. They ran into Lola standing next to it, talking to another couple.

"Good night, Lola. Tell Oscar hello. Thanks for the invitation," he said, opening the door for Katrina to pass through. Katrina turned and gave Lola a smile, which Lola returned, throwing in a wink for good measure.

Her hand remained in his as he entered his home, locked the door, and walked them into the bedroom. It was dark except for a wall sconce in the hallway leading to his bedroom. He hadn't taken the time to turn on lights when he had gotten home. He hadn't taken the time to change, either, just walked over to Oscar's in his jeans and T-shirt.

The lanterns outside provided a small golden glow inside his bedroom. He let go of her hand, moving his bag out of the middle of the floor where he'd dropped it. He turned and watched her as she walked to him, coming to stand in front of him. She turned to give him her back and lifted her hair, moving his hand to the zipper of her costume. He lowered it for her and watched her as she turned, slowly removing it. He watched as it slid to the floor, leaving white barely there underwear attached to slim chocolate curves. He stood there, immobile, his face drinking her in.

"Don't lose the ears or the heels," he said, and she laughed.

She walked over to stand before him, confident and sexy, his complex Katrina. He stood rooted to the spot, watching and waiting. She reached him and took the bottom of his T-shirt in her hand, lifting and pulling it over his head. Her hands then moved to the button of his jeans. She opened and unzipped them, pushing them down his legs.

He was so beautiful, just like she'd remembered. He stood before her in thigh-length form-fitting briefs. She reached to touch him, starting with the hair on his chest, running her hand down to her favorite aspect of him. She'd seen it every night for the last few months in her dreams, and now she stroked it from top to bottom and back again. She moaned as she heard his sharp intake of air. She gripped him firmly, turned, and began walking backward to his bed, towing him along, before turning him and pushing him to lie back on the bed.

He was accommodating, taking pleasure in her control. He watched, spellbound, as she kicked off her shoes, her hands moving behind her back to remove her bra and slip her panties off. He leaned up on his elbows to watch, not wanting to miss a thing. She walked toward him, nude except for the bunny ears, hands now at the waistband of his briefs. He lifted his hips to help. She'd crawled up his body to settle on him near the spot that stood at attention, watching and waiting for her. She rubbed her hand along his length again, up and back, up and back.

"I really like doing that," she said.

"Feel free to do that anytime you want," he replied.

"Okay, I will," she said, looking into his eyes, and rubbed him again, causing his breath to catch once more.

She smiled, and the promise he saw in them was his undoing. He pulled her downward and his mouth found hers, his tongue working its way in. She opened her lips and he moaned at the rightness of his mouth on hers, smooth, warm, so wet.

"Condom?" she whispered against his mouth. It took him a second to register her request, but he pointed to the side table of his bed and watched as she crawled toward the nightstand to retrieve not one, but a handful. He swallowed hard and watched, transfixed, as she settled her body back on his, opened a package, and slowly placed one on him.

Who was this Katrina, he wondered. Tonight, as she'd been before, she was sure and sexy, beyond anything his imagination could have conjured up, blowing him away with her beauty, assertiveness, and confidence.

He caught his breath as she settled on him and he heard her groan. She felt *so good*. Then she started to move, and, holy God, she was breathtaking, smooth, and sensuous. He let her set the pace, slowly moving up and down. His hands roamed over her body, traveling over her breasts before settling at her hips, giving her free rein for a while. Then he started to help her move, speeding her along, pushing her for more.

He lost his thoughts and just felt, felt how right she felt here with him, surrounding him. He pushed and pulled her, feeling her start to come; he couldn't stop his own climax. One of his hands moved up under her hair to cup the back of her neck as she moved above him, pulling her down so that he could feel her lips against him as he came hard. He held her, one hand at her hip to lock her in place, the other at her neck, holding her in place, taking into his mouth her moans of pleasure.

He lay there with her on his chest, again amazed at how good they were together. Of all the things he'd thought of her, this uninhibited, take-control response had surprised him the most. He took her head in his hands, moving the hair that surrounded her face, and kissed her again and again, loving the wetness and smoothness of her mouth. She wasn't what he'd expected; from the beginning, she'd taken him by surprise.

Taking a break from her mouth, he lay his head back on the bed. That was so not steady, he thought, or maybe he said it out loud.

"What did you say?" she asked, leaning her head back a little to get a better look at him.

"Did I say that out loud?" he asked, giving her a small smile and looking up at her through satisfied and hooded eyes, his hair standing on end. She'd like to take credit for that, but it was always that way. She ran her hand through it.

"What's not steady?" she asked.

"You're not steady," he said, pointing his finger at her and smiling as he lifted her off of him. He stood up and walked toward his bathroom. He was only there for a few seconds.

"I'm not steady? What does that mean?" she asked, following him with her eyes as he moved back to bed. He laid down like before and pulled her to sit on him again, just where she belonged.

"You have to promise me that you won't get mad," he said, still smiling.

"Maybe," she said, watching him.

He waited.

"Okay, I promise," she said.

"When I first saw you, you were always out in your yard, working, always dressed in those huge, too-big garments. I wondered what woman that young spends all her time in her garden?" He waited a beat and said, "A boring one was the only answer I could come up with."

She tried to pinch him, but he grabbed her hands, smiling as he pulled her down to him, grabbing her bottom lip with his teeth, moving his tongue in between her lips. She pulled back.

"What was I saying?" he asked, pretending to search through his mind.

"Boring," she answered.

"Oh, yeah, well, after getting to know you more, watching you work with the volunteers, seeing you with your godfathers, I changed the word from boring to steady. It became my private nickname for you."

"Steady, as in man's best friend kind of steady?" she asked.

"No, that's more loyal, and you are that, too, but steady as in always, and I do mean *always*, doing the right thing. You're always working hard and you're always there for your friends, your godfathers, and your trust customers, even though it's hard for you. That kind of steady," he said, pulling her in close for another kiss, separating her lips again with his tongue. She was addictive.

"Okay," she said when he let go of her mouth.

"But I've got to tell you that in this, in the way you make love to me, full out . . ." he said, and then paused to put on another condom.

"This Katrina . . ." he said, settling her over him, pushing her slowly down to take him into her body again, ". . . is so not steady."

CHAPTER 13

Katrina woke up early the next morning and looked at Will asleep beside her. He was spread-eagle, face down, his head facing her. He looked so beautiful. Her thoughts traveled back to last night. That had been so much fun, but more intense toward the end than she was comfortable with. Unexpectedly, her inner voice issued a warning: *Be careful.* She ignored it and sat up. No movement, not a peep from Will.

She stood up and moved quietly around the room, gathering her clothes. She quickly dressed, using Will's T-shirt to cover her costume, and quietly backed from the room. He was dead to the world, jet lag, she'd bet, the same jet lag that had him wide awake at three in the morning, reaching for her. That man was something else, smooth, lean, and intense, staring into her eyes as he moved in and out of her body. She didn't want to leave without letting him know she was gone, but she didn't want to wake him, either.

She stepped into the hall leading to the living room and continued to the kitchen, where she found a note pad and pencil. *Hey, Will. Thank you for a wonderful evening. I went home. You can come over if you want to. Come through the backyard. I'll unlock the door.* She signed it *Steady* and smiled at his nickname for her. She went back to his room and placed the note on the pillow next to him, giving in to the need to look at him again. She stood there a minute longer and then tiptoed out.

She quietly and quickly walked through his backyard and through the gate, down the greenbelt, and into her yard. She entered her home and went to take a shower. After she was done, she located a pair of old pajama bottoms and a T-shirt and went in search of tea.

Will opened his eyes, immediately spotting the empty space next to him, thinking it would have been nice to start the morning as it had ended last night. He lifted his head and saw a note in the space where Katrina's head had been. He reached for it, smiling at her use of his nickname for her. He turned over onto his back and looked up at the ceiling. Steady hadn't been steady. He smiled at that thought, and at all the other images from last night running through his mind.

He had about had a heart attack when he saw her in Lola and Oscar's kitchen, standing at the sink dressed in her Playboy bunny outfit. Thinking of her comment about the rabbit being the nemesis of the gardener, he laughed. He wanted to see her this morning, but he would shower first.

Dressed in a pair of jeans and a long-sleeve T-shirt, tennis shoes on his feet, he walked out the back door and down the greenbelt to her home. He entered and looked around the yard, his eyes sweeping from left to right and landing in the middle as his eyes found hers. She was seated in the middle of her steps, a cup of something in her hand. She'd been watching him silently. Without saying a word, he walked up the steps, stopping just below her, staring into her eyes all the while.

He leaned forward, not breaking eye contact. Her upper body moved back to lower itself on the steps above her, her eyes following his lips as he moved in to kiss her softly. Her body lifted to his; she couldn't seem to get enough, even after last night. He placed his arm on the rails of the steps for balance as he continued to kiss her mouth, intertwining her tongue with his. Her arms slid to the bottom of his T-shirt and moved under it, touching him, loving the feel of him. He placed his arms around her and she wrapped her legs around his back as he lifted her and walked up the steps leading into her home. She reached behind her and opened the back door, and he walked them over to her couch and sat, placing her feet on the floor in front of him.

She removed her clothes, pajama bottoms first, until she stood nude before him. He pulled her to him, his head leaning into her stomach, holding her still. He lifted his head and looked up into her eyes. She placed her hands around his neck and bent to meet his lips, softly and reverently kissing him. He slid his hips outward on the couch, unzipped his jeans and pushed them past his hips, stopping to dig a condom out of his wallet. Putting it on, he turned her so that her back was to his chest.

He lifted her to sit on him and they groaned together as she took him into her body. He leaned back and pulled her with him, one hand on her breast, the other around her waist as he started to lift and then lower her. He closed his eyes, reveling in the feel of her wrapped around him, astonished still at how she managed to take control of him with such quiet authority.

She continued, stopping when she felt he was close, to start over again. He couldn't hold back much longer. His hand found the place where their bodies met to help speed her along. He came then, a quiet gasp the only sound he made; she moaned quietly as she came, too. He held on to her as if his life depended on it, more than a little stunned at the direction his life was taking.

End of December

"We better get going," Katrina said to a half-asleep Will, standing next to his side of the bed and running her hand through his hair as he lay sleeping. This was the second time she had come in to wake him. He grabbed her hand, pulling her down to lie next to him.

"What time is it?" he asked, closing his eyes again. "Give me thirty more minutes," he mumbled, pulling her in closer and locking her in tightly to his side with his arm.

"Nope, you made me promise to not listen to your pleas for more sleep this morning. Remember, you wanted to show me some bridge you've found for the gardens, and then we have to go over to the godfathers to help out," she said, watching him closely, his head still resting on the pillow. She ran her hands though his short crop of hair again, loving the way it stood up.

Today they were going to help the godfathers at the garden center with the Christmas rush after Will showed her this wonderful bridge he'd found. They were at his home. She had brought some clothes over last night and had already showered and dressed. She was hungry, and as soon as she could get him going, she was off to find some food.

"Come on, Will. Let's go."

"Okay," he mumbled into his pillow, but then he rolled over until he was on top of her. He kissed her and then just as quickly rolled off, sitting up on the side of his bed, running his hand over his face and through his hair before standing. She sat on the bed and watched him as he walked toward the bathroom, admiring the body that she couldn't seem to get enough of. He turned around and gave her a smile, the one that she liked so much, moving his black eyebrows up and down, teasing her. He knew she was watching. She always watched.

A few minutes later she went to the kitchen and stood in front of Will's refrigerator; nothing much there except the yogurt she had brought over earlier in the week. She'd gone down this empty refrigerator path before. She grabbed a banana from his fruit bowl, found a bowl, and added her banana and yogurt to it. She found a spoon, hopped onto the counter, and ate. She couldn't believe she was here sometimes, approaching two months with him. This was all so new to her.

She'd dated before, but it had never led to this; there was sex, maybe, but not this need to be around each other constantly, this wondering what he was doing when she wasn't there and hurrying to get through whatever she was doing so she could get wherever he was.

He walked into the kitchen, dressed in jeans and a long-sleeved T-shirt, grabbed a banana, peeled it, and walked over to stand in between her legs. He pushed into her lower body with his, touching her while he dunked his banana into her yogurt and took a bite. He chewed for a minute, and, before taking another bite, asked, "Ready?"

"Almost," she said.

"I'll meet you in the garage."

"Kay," she said, watching him as he walked away.

She finished eating, placed the bowl in the sink, grabbed her backpack, and followed him out the door. She'd taken about four steps into the garage before she pulled up short. He was standing next to his motorcycle, one helmet on his head and another one in his hand. She shook her head and started to walk backward. He placed the helmet he'd held for her on the ground and, taking his off, walked toward her.

"Come on, Katrina. Try it. I'll be careful and I'll go really slow. I promise," he said, his face a study in contrast; his shining eyes were earnest and pleading, at war with his sexy, slightly cocky smile, the one she could never seem to resist.

"Don't be scared; I'll be careful with you," he said, losing the smile, serious now. She wasn't sure he was just talking about the bike ride. He reached for her hand and slowly pulled her to the bike. He kissed her lips, smiled again, and quickly slid the helmet on her head before she could speak. He replaced his own and sat on the bike, waiting. She got on behind him, and he started the engine. It was quieter than she had thought. She moved her hands to circle his waist. He grabbed them and pulled them so that her hold on him was tight. He backed out, lowered his garage door, and took off. She held on, eyes closed, head resting on his back.

They rode for about twenty minutes before she opened her eyes. He was up in front of an old beat-up barn with old stuff on the ground all around it. A middle-aged African-American woman was sitting in a chair by a tree. Will pulled in and stopped. Katrina climbed off first, followed by Will. Both took off their helmets. He looked at her and smiled and then grabbed her hand and led her towards the woman, who was now headed toward them.

"Hello, Will," she said, smiling, her eyes drinking him in.

I'm feeling you there, sister, Katrina thought.

"I see you came back," she said.

"Yes," he said with a big smile and then introduced Katrina.

The woman's name was Sallie. They followed her to the back of her property, and Katrina thought most of the stuff she saw looked like junk; hell, the bridge looked a little like junk, too. She could see some potential, though. This could work, she thought.

He thanked Sallie for holding it for him, paid her, and told her he would pick it up next weekend.

He and Katrina left as unceremoniously as they had arrived. She opened her eyes and looked around at the traffic and the life around her as she rode behind Will. This wasn't as bad as she thought. She was still a little nervous, but it had turned out to be fun. Who knew? She smiled to herself. She wasn't going to tell Will; he was too sure of himself already as far as she was concerned.

January

Somehow, over the following weeks, Katrina found herself, after much prodding from Will, attempting her first long bike trip—the cycling kind. He'd already talked her into shorter rides with him around the neighborhood. But today they'd awakened earlier than usual and he was taking her for her first bike ride that would last longer than an hour. He was decked out in his usual Lance wear—just with longer pants in deference to the weather—and he'd picked out an outfit for her. She'd spent last night trying it on, wiggling into it, only to be interrupted by Will after seeing her in it proved more than he could take. So they'd spent time in bed helping her out of it.

Truth be told, she didn't think she'd be at this riding stuff long. Will had warned her that he'd be introducing her to new and different things, and, true to his word, he had, pulling her from her yard work for just a little while. It wasn't going anywhere, anyway, so she let herself be coaxed away, trying things she didn't normally do.

She was once again preparing to try something new. She was in shape; she ran regularly on her treadmill, plus gardening, for her at least, was tough stuff. She hoped it was enough to keep up with him. She'd looked up some facts on the internet regarding bike safety, starting to enjoy his reaction to her facts and statistics. He found it amusing, and she liked it very much when he laughed at her jokes.

"Ready?" That one-word question had become his standard question for her, as if she would ever be ready for all the new things he'd planned for her. If she were honest with herself, she would think they were fun, too. Work had been less pressing, less tiring, and less inter-esting now that he was here.

"Did you know that statistics on bike injuries are under-reported? The police don't even bother writing up a report if the cyclist or bicycle isn't seriously injured."

"Is that so?" he asked, smiling. As if on cue, he asked again, "Ready?"

"Ready as I'm going to be, but if I run out of steam, I don't want to hear any comments from you," she said, going for firm and serious. He just smiled, swinging his leg to straddle his bike, looking over at her as she stood there straddling his other one.

"Don't worry, Steady, let's go. I've got you," he said, smiling, and rolled outward, she trying to catch him.

❧

Will parked in his garage and let the door down. It was dark; the return flight always put him back into town late. He was a little tired from this trip, a short one out to California to check in with the head cheese, but he still wanted to see Katrina. He missed her; he also loved her, and had been saying that in his mind, adjusting to it, trying to figure out where to go from here.

He dropped his bag near the door leading from the garage into the kitchen. He needed to get his mail; had promised himself he wouldn't let it pile up again. He hadn't called Katrina from the airport for fear of waking her. He looked around his home and decided to walk out back and over to her house. If she was up, he'd go in; if not, he would return to his home and call her in the morning.

He walked out the back gate and down the greenbelt and breathed a sigh of relief when he saw lights on at her house. They'd exchanged keys, so he could let himself in. He entered her backyard and saw her sitting in what seemed like her favorite place in the yard, her deck's top step.

"I hoped you be up," he said, walking up and sitting on the step just below her. She opened her legs and pulled him back to rest between them, his head near her waist.

"Couldn't sleep," she said. "Scary, but I've gotten used to having you near."

"Why is that scary?' he asked.

"You may not always be here," she said.

"What if I were?"

"What if you were what?"

He looked at her. "You know what I mean."

"I don't know," she said. "Let's talk about something else."

Not wanting to push, he changed the subject. "You've never told me about your backyard. Why the design?"

"I like large and bountiful, large groups of color, the more variety the better," she said. "I love the English gardens, as you know, even though I know they aren't at all suited to our climate. It's a lot like how I felt pre-adoption, not suited, so I found a way to make it work, adding natives when I can. I also have a fondness for native roses; they are some tough customers, don't need much to survive, just sun, rain, and air."

"Well, you created a beautiful place here," he said, taking her hands and holding them in front of him.

"Thanks. It does for me here," she said, pointing at her heart, "what yours does for you. It's a simple pleasure, and it's beautiful. In the spring when it's still cool and the jasmine and honeysuckle are blooming, it smells like heaven and looks like it, too. It's God's gift to me."

"To you personally, huh?" he said, smiling, his head bent back, looking up into her face.

"Yep. How was your trip?" she asked, bending over to kiss him on his mouth and then running her fingers through his hair.

"It's work," he said.

"Are you tired?" she asked.

"Not too tired. Why?" he asked, pushing himself up to his feet and then turning and pulling her up, too.

"Just wondering," she said, leaning in to touch his lips with hers.

He smiled and lifted her up. She swung her legs around his waist and he walked them up the steps and into her home. Will walked straight to her bedroom, depositing her on her bed. She wiggled out of her sweats and underwear, tugged her T-shirt over her head, and released her hair from its ponytail. Sitting on her bed Indian style, she watched Will undress.

"I'm glad you made it back safely, although I know that flying is one of the safest forms of travel."

"Is that so?" he asked, unzipping his jeans and pulling his T-shirt over his head.

"Yes, that is so."

"You and your facts are really growing on me," he said.

"Is that so?" she said, mimicking him, watching as he lowered his jeans; God, she loved his body. He shed his shorts and walked toward her.

"Yes. Who knew that stats could be sexy," he said, pushing her backward on the bed, untangling her legs, and moving his body to cover hers and then flipping over so she was on top.

"Miss me?" he asked, pulling her head down for a kiss.

"Missed parts of you," she said.

"Parts, huh? Which ones and how much?" he asked, moving his hands to her breasts, tugging at their tips, smiling at her intake of air. He pulled her down for another kiss, continuing to rub and play with her breasts.

Katrina moaned loudly into his mouth, feeling his smile against her lips.

When she could catch her breath, she said, "Did you know that, at age seventy, 73 percent of men are still potent?"

"Really? Interesting," he said, lifting her up and impaling her on him in one smooth movement. He didn't move then, just lay there with her surrounding him, loving the feel of her body wrapped around his. He'd really missed her.

"And did you know that the man is the most likely partner to be tied up during sex?"

He lifted her and slowly lowered her to him, pulling another moan from her.

"Do you want to be tied up, Katrina?"

"No more talking," she said, moaning at the pleasure she felt. He laughed. "You're so weird," she panted.

He lifted her and pulled her down again, harder this time; then reversed their positions and commenced a demonstration of just how weird he could be. She loved it, if the volume of her moans was any indication.

∞

The next morning Will was at her back door, about to make the trek back to his home.

"Before I forget, Katrina, my company is having a mandatory shutdown during the week of spring break. I know it may be late notice, but would you like to spend the week with me?"

"What's a mandatory shutdown, and what does 'spend the week with me' mean?"

"We are shutting down the whole company for a forced vacation; it's a cost-saving measure. I've got a small, and I do mean small, condo down south, near the Gulf. I go sometimes to fish, kayak, or whatever."

"A girl pad, huh?"

"Nope. You would be the only girl I've ever taken. Do you want to come or not?"

"Can I check at work? See if I can take the time?

"Is that a yes? You'd like to go?"

"Yes, I'd like to go."

"I'll stop by later; will you be here?"

"Yes."

She'd been surprised and happy to see him walk into her backyard last night. The last few months spent with him had been great—work seemed less stressful, the flowers bloomed more brightly, and she had even pushed her plans to start her business to the back burner. She was both happier and more afraid than she had been in a long time.

She liked him a lot; hell, she loved him, if she were honest with herself. Where to go with that, she wasn't sure. Did she want more? And what did he want? Her old doom and gloom, her fears of this not working out, were quietly making a comeback.

CHAPTER 14

February

"Okay, girl, we need to start from scratch," Lola said, rummaging through Katrina's drawers and closet. Katrina had told Lola about her upcoming trip with Will—that was about thirty minutes ago, and, of course, Lola had taken over, dragging Katrina's home to plow through her clothes.

"Girl, you've got enough pants to dress an entire army. Where do you buy these clothes, anyway?" Lola asked, looking through Katrina's pants and shirts, all of which were either black or brown or some other dark color.

"They aren't that bad for work. I've got other stuff I just bought last fall," she said, showing off the shorts and shirts that actually fit.

"Right, you're going to wear the same outfit every day? Didn't think so," she said, answering her own question. "Does your work have something against you wearing color?" she asked, moving from Katrina's closet to her drawers. "Girl, even your underwear is basic, like you grew up as an orphan and your clothes were rationed to you."

"You forget, I did," Katrina said.

"Girl, you know what I mean," Lola responded, not missing a beat. She held up a pair of Katrina's white brief-style panties in her hand, shaking her head. "I didn't know they were still making these," she said, throwing them over her shoulder. "Okay, we need to go shopping, and I don't want to hear the word no. I know you have money, so save the lip. Give me a pen and some paper. I'm going to make a list."

Knowing it was useless to argue with Lola when she was in her I'm-now-in-charge mood, Katrina left the bedroom, returning a few seconds later with notepad and pen in hand.

"We need everything. Cute underwear, small, boy-cut only, they'll work on your figure, and cute bras, not the ones we've worn since World War II. One skimpy bathing suit, but no cover ups. You can borrow your boyfriend's T-shirt." She said this with a goofy grin. "You know, like in high school. You'll need a pair of flip-flops and shorts and tops that fit, plus one pair of jeans. That should do it."

"That's not very much," Katrina said, looking over Lola's list.

"If things work out as they are supposed to, girl, you won't need much. Now what are we doing with that hair of yours?" Lola asked.

"What about it?" Katrina said, reaching up to touch it.

"You sticking with the ponytail look, huh? You should take it down, though, when you swim or get naked with him. Men like to grab on to something when they're working it."

"Lola, please," she said, choking, her laughter muffled.

"Just trying to school you a little, is all," she said, laughing too, her blonde curls bouncing around her head. "Speaking of which, what does our boy Will like to do? He seems intense. You know, still waters and all?"

"Cut it out. I'm not telling."

"Come on, girl, does it work for you? Hell, it must for you to be considering getting out of your camouflage clothing."

"It's good. I like him. That's why I am going."

"Like, huh? That's good. It's nice to see you smile. You worry me sometimes. All work and no play makes a ticking time bomb."

"I don't think that's quite the way that expression goes, but, yeah, I like him," she said, smiling. She had to admit to herself that she was amazingly happy and looking forward to this trip.

They left early Sunday morning. She and Lola had gone shopping, and she was still in shock at some of the things Lola had picked out. But what the hell, she could let go for a week, couldn't she? So about eight this morning Katrina and her backpack walked the back way to Will's back door. She was thankful for this greenbelt so the whole neighborhood didn't have to watch the daily treks she made to Will's home or he to hers.

She entered the back gate and, en route to his back door, she could see him through his bedroom window, pushing clothes into a bag. Just like a guy, he wasn't putting much thought into what he was going to wear. She stopped and watched him, admiring the muscles moving beneath his shirt. He turned and saw her and flashed her favorite smile, his eyes shining. She smiled back and resumed walking to his back door.

"Hey, I'm almost done," he shouted to her.

"It's okay. Can I do anything to help?" she asked.

"No," he said, walking into the room and touching his lips to hers.

"Most of the things I keep at the condo. I just need clothes. That's all you're taking?" he asked, looking at her backpack.

"Yep. Lola tells me I won't need much, and, as you know already, I'm not much into fashion."

"The 'not needing much' has an appeal," he said, kissing her lips again, lingering a little longer this time. He pulled back and smiled. "Did I tell you I'm really looking forward to this trip?"

"No, you didn't, and so am I."

"Let's go," he said, grabbing her hand and pulling her along to the garage. The jeep sat there ready and waiting for them.

❧

The drive down took about four hours. They stopped to get fishing licenses and to pick up bait, which she wanted no part of. Finally, they stopped at the grocery store, picking up fruit, coffee, and things to eat.

"What, no meat?" she asked at the grocery store.

"That's not much of a confidence builder, Katrina. We'll eat what we catch," he said.

"Okay," she said, "but I'm warning you, I'll shoot you before I eat bugs or snails or anything like that. I'm not a survivor kind of girl. Bugs belong in the garden, not in one's mouth." He laughed. They continued on their drive, eventually pulling into a parking lot near a dock.

"We're here," Will said, getting out of the jeep and beginning to unload their bags.

"Where is here, exactly?" she asked, not seeing anything but docks, boats, and a shop of some kind. He smiled at her question. "We need to take the boat out to get to my place. It's kind of out by itself."

"What does that mean, out by itself?" she asked, looking at him. "Okay, Will, I mean it, there better be no survivor stuff and no chopping me up into little pieces."

"Follow me," he said, walking toward the small building, which turned out to be a combination of small tourist shop, DVD rental place, and bait shop all rolled into one.

"Hey, dude, it's been a while," a big, burly guy said to Will. He was clad in a muscle shirt and shorts that reached below his knees, and had a full red curly beard to match his full head of curly red hair.

"I know. Work's been demanding," Will responded.

"How long you here for?" he asked, walking toward the back of the store and disappearing inside an office, Will at his heels.

"A week," Will answered. A minute later they returned, Will with a key in hand.

"Katrina, meet Bo, the best fisherman in these parts. Next to me, that is."

"Hi, Bo," she said. Bo returned the greeting. Will picked up their things and walked out, Katrina a step behind.

"Bye, Katrina, nice to meet you," Bo called after them.

"You, too," she replied.

She followed Will as they walked out to the dock and stopped near a boat.

"This is us," he said. It was a fairly big boat with what looked like a small cabin in it.

"We are spending a week on a boat?" she asked, growing a little alarmed.

"No, this is a fishing boat only, but it will take us to our final destination."

"Okay, Will, that's it. Before I step on that boat, I need to know where we're going. You said a condo. I assumed it was still in this state, but you're starting to worry me."

"Don't be. I do have a condo not far from here, down the coast a bit. It is easier to access by boat, but we can get there by land. This is much shorter, plus I needed to pick up the boat. Okay?"

"Okay," she said, pacified for the moment. They loaded their gear onto the boat. She helped him, following his instructions as he got them ready to leave, and soon they pulled away from the dock.

Katrina saw his condo as they came around a bend in the water. It sat alone, next to the shore. It was larger than she had expected.

"I purchased the land from G, the same guy who gave the New Year's Eve party," he said, following her eyes. "His family owns the large chunk next to me. He used to own this portion, but he wanted a place not so near his folks, so he sold it to me. He and I used to come down during breaks at school to fish, kayak, or just hang out. I fell in love with the beauty and the solitude of this place. Over time, I started to have it built, using natural and eco-friendly products, of course," he said.

"Of course."

She looked it over, impressed. A large square box in shape, the front part of it appeared to be made of glass, and that portion extended outward from the land onto the water. It was a neat, clean, simple brown structure, blending with the land and water around it. She'd come to think that Will required all his things to mesh with their surroundings; she refused to over analyze whether that posed any complications for her.

"Aren't you worried that a strong wind will shatter all that glass?" she asked.

"It's not glass, but a strong substitute that can withstand winds up to 90 mph," he said. The deck had a dock, which they drove up to and secured the boat.

She helped him empty the boat. Once they were done, she walked over to meet him at the side door, which he'd opened. The condo was nice on the inside, simple in design with not much in the way of furnishing. She knew he favored natural materials and limited pieces of furniture.

"It's really nice," she said, dumping her bag and looking around. They stood in a large room, the one she had seen from the outside, which was surrounded on three sides by windows. A wall stood at her back, with a door in the middle breaking it into two sides. The final wall, behind her, held beautiful cabinets, a small couch, a table, and chairs. She turned to look behind her.

"Where do we sleep?" she asked.

"I've got one small bedroom, bath, and kitchen behind you, through that door," he said, pointing behind her. "I usually sleep in here. I've got a Murphy bed, the one that folds down from the wall, behind one of those cabinets," he said, opening the door to show her a bed.

"I like to sleep admiring the view," he said.

"I could like, it, too," she said.

"Thanks," he said, smiling at her and walking over to pull her into his arms. She went willingly, as always, happy and terrified.

She woke up one morning toward the middle of the week to the comforting sound of rain softly hitting the windows. She lay there, moving her arms above her head, stretching and looking around the room. She loved Will's bed, loved his condo, loved every square inch of his body. She loved him, a first for her.

Will's spot next to her was empty. She turned on her side to look out the large windows. The day was gray from the rain, which was good because she just wanted to lie here with him and do nothing. She'd had a great time so far, and Will was determined to teach her to fish. God, he was so much more active than she'd ever been, he had so much energy. She didn't know if she could keep up with his appetites.

She turned as she heard a noise behind her. Speak of the devil; it was Will walking toward her with a towel in his hand, drying his hair and face. She looked up in question.

"I just checked on the boat to make sure it was secure. It was. Looks like we are in for rain for at least this morning. It's a small storm, supposed to move off by the afternoon," he said, pulling the T-shirt over his head. He unbuttoned, unzipped, and lost his shorts. He had nothing on underneath. He slid back into bed, reaching for her and feeling a T-shirt she'd put on during the night. She'd gotten cold.

"What are we doing with this on?" he asked, smiling, his hand moving down to find the bottom to pull it up and over her head.

He kissed her then, his hands gliding over her body, roaming over her breasts, running down her stomach and back behind her to settle underneath her, his hands cupping her butt as he settled at the junction of her thighs, moving up and back over that part of her that caused her breathing to catch. He loved the way her soft skin felt against his. He loved the contrast of their bodies; his hard, hers soft, his skin color striking against the richness and darkness of hers.

He kissed her, loving the way she became pliable and liquid when he touched her. He spread her legs with his and pushed into her, one arm secured around her waist to hold her in place, the other at her shoulder to lift his body, giving him an angle in which to drive determined, strong, and sure thrusts into her. He watched her respond to him, her eyes closing, small moans coming from her, her hips beginning to push back in the way he'd come to expect and love. She came a moment later.

He stopped and held her, arms moving to wrap themselves under her back and over to grip her shoulder, holding her in place as he continued to kiss her. He started to move within her, quietly and ever so slowly, taking in her sighs of pleasure, giving her a second to recover.

"Ready?" he asked. When she nodded he turned over onto his back, bringing her to sit on him. His hands moved to her hips and he began thrusting into her again, undeterred by anything but his desire to satisfy her. Soon she came again, stronger than before.

"One more time," he whispered, smiling as her eyes closed in pleasure. He started again, his hands now next to her face. He lifted his upper body away from hers he began thrusting again, not stopping until, this time, he came with her. He fell forward to hold her, too wiped out to move.

He looked down at her lying there, her hair in wild abandon against the pillow. Without a doubt he knew he loved her, wanted her with him permanently. He'd yet to say the words, but it would only be a matter of time.

Will watched Katrina clean up after dinner. They'd eaten trout she caught earlier that day. Recalling their time together this week brought a smile to his face. She was too hysterical for words sometimes. The first time they'd gone fishing earlier this week, she had refused to touch anything that moved, so no live bait. The second day she agreed to fish if he would bait her line for her, but she wouldn't look while he did that to the "poor bait". On the third day she tried to bait the hook herself, and on the last two days she'd actually caught some fish. He didn't know who was more surprised, her or the fish.

The best part of teaching her had been training her how to cast. He, of course, had to stand close behind her as it was required to teach her the correct arm movement. He loved how she lined up in front of him, his back to hers. Somewhere she'd become a necessity for him to enjoy his time outside of work. He thought her funny, courageous, and steady.

She had proven to be quite a handful in bed, and he totally loved that. They were scheduled to leave tomorrow and head back home. They had done other things besides fish. They had taken the boat back to the dock and rented some jets skis. He rented two of them, and almost fell over when she walked to him in the smallest bikini he'd seen in a long, long time. She put her vest over it, but not before she'd teased him, laughing hysterically at the reaction on his face. She gave silent thanks to Lola for her very sound clothing advice.

He sat on the couch now, his attention moving between her and the view of the water out back. It was late evening and the sun was starting its descent. He turned as she walked over to sit next to him on the couch. He opened his legs, pulling her to sit in between them, and pulled her back to rest against his chest. His arms surrounded her at the waist.

"So I can add catching fish and cooking it to the list of things you do exceedingly well." He was quiet for a second. The he said, "Have I told you that I had a great time this week with you?"

"No, you haven't, but so have I," she said. "Who knew I would come to enjoy going out on the boat and fishing?"

They were silent for a moment, lost in their thoughts as they watched a blood red sun making its descent.

"Where do you want this to lead?" he asked, broaching a subject he'd been thinking about for a while now.

"What do you mean by 'this'?"

"Us," he said.

"I like us. Is that what you mean?"

"Sort of. I was just wondering if you're happy with us. Would you want more?"

"I like the way we are now. I like being around you a lot."

"Like, huh?" he asked. "What if it's more than that for me?"

She didn't say anything for a moment. Finally she asked, "Is it?"

"Yeah, it is," he said. She turned to him.

"I love you," he said. Her eyes moved away from his, turning to stare out the window to the water, lost in thought.

"What does that mean, you love me?" Not waiting for his response, she continued. "If it means we can stay as we are, I'm okay with that. Is that what 'I love you' means?"

"Yes, it means that, but it also means more for me."

"More as in a long-term commitment?"

"Yes, marriage is a long-term commitment," he said.

She moved her head slightly up and down, eyes tuned out again, as if confirming something within herself as she continued to look out over the water.

"I don't know, Will," she said. "I can't say yes. This fear of being hurt, this need to protect myself from harm, is so deeply ingrained in me," she said, turning to face him, tears glimmering in her eyes. "I can't say yes, at least not now. And are you even sure it's me you want, anyway? I mean, I'm not who you're used to. I'm different enough to be interesting, but are you really sure? I worry about that with you. I am a simple girl, Will, boring, even. You've said it yourself."

"I know who you are, Katrina."

"I don't think I'm up for another loss in my life. Growing up without folks, I'd just about given up hope of anyone wanting me. You don't know what that's like. And if we worked through that baggage," she said, trying to form a smile, "what if something were to happen to you. I love you, too, and—"

"I know what I am asking of you," he said. He pulled her to him. "Hey, it's okay, I'm not asking you to decide anything today. I'm perfectly happy with where we are, and I'm not going anywhere. I understand you, Katrina, better than you think, but at some point in life you have to take a chance on things. On us. Nothing in life is certain. It could all lead to heartache, but it could be perfect for us, the best thing for us."

His hands captured her face, making her look at him, wiping the wetness from her cheeks with his thumbs.

"You're surviving me so far, right?" he said softly, looking at her, giving her a smile. She nodded. "Give me a while longer then, it can work." He pulled her into him for a kiss. She went eagerly, wanting to let him know that she cared for him, loved him, too.

March

The third weekend in March found Katrina at the gardens. Most of the major work had been done. The boulders had been delivered to the garden and were in place over in Will's dry garden. Katrina walked through and cataloged all that had been done so far, comparing it to the design that now lived in her head.

Thanks to the godfathers she'd even managed to come in a little under budget. She was proud of herself again for helping this come to fruition. She loved taking something visible only in her mind, or in this case, Will's mind, and making it visible to others. It was beautiful, and, again, it had been the best decision to have him lead.

She'd left Will tired in bed this morning. Who knew he could get tired, he who worked hard, played hard, and loved hard. Didn't he realize the danger in that? She'd been restless this morning. Will's desire for commitment was making her nervous, and work was starting to creep back into her psyche; she was back to thinking of her business plans, the ones that had fallen off her radar with the arrival of Will into her life.

She hadn't discussed her business plans with him yet. She was already too close to him. His opinion, his presence, had already come to mean so much to her, maybe more than it should. She found herself structuring her life around his. She kept reminding herself that it wasn't a good idea, but did she listen? Of course not; there was nothing but potential hurt coming for her.

She walked over to the edge of the bridge that now spanned the new pond. It was filled with water from the waterfall, which was located toward the front of the gardens. Will had spent a day acting as a drill sergeant to the volunteers in order to get that piece of equipment working. It worked brilliantly now. Of course it did. Will had made it so.

She walked over, stopping in the middle, taking in the fish swimming below. The bridge spanned the widest section of the pond that led one to a small, secluded sitting area designed for contemplation. A stone bench sat there waiting, so she sat to contemplate. It was a beautiful spring day, cool, temperatures in the morning in the high 60s; birds were talking to each other, probably a mother checking on her children or chewing out her mate. Who knew what birds said to each other? Squirrels ran around the garden, playing tag or whatever games squirrels played. She took a deep breath. She had so much to be thankful for, and she refused, for now, to think about her nagging worries.

Will's design had been inspired. The trees had been shaped and trimmed with their new bonsai haircuts. Lighting and garden art remained. She'd located a few items she thought would work including several statues to be partners to Will's small Buddha statue, which was hidden somewhere, tucked away from view until you unexpectedly came upon it. Well, she wasn't going to get anything done sitting here, so up she stood, walking back over the bridge to finish what she had set out to do.

Katrina's clock read 4 a.m. as she lay in bed next to Will. One of his arms lay across her chest and one of his legs was stretched out across hers, holding her in place; this position was a recent phenomenon, as if he suspected she might leave. She turned her head to study him, one of her favorite pastimes; didn't think she would ever grow tired of it. His face was turned to her, and his eyes were closed.

She moved her free arm to trace his face, running her fingers over the almond shape of his eyes and tracing his cheekbones, which gave his face such beauty. Her hand moved to run over and through his hair. She loved this man, unerringly, unfailingly, and fearfully. And he was leaving tomorrow morning for a three-week trip to Singapore.

It didn't look like she was going back to sleep, so she decided to get up. But how to do so without disturbing him? She started with her legs, wiggling them slowly, really slowly, one leg at a time from beneath his. So far so good. She now lay crosswise on the bed, her legs and feet sticking off one side of the bed, her upper torso still trapped. She worked one of her arms free, using it to slowly lift his arm, just a little. She scooted out from under him and then slowly lowered his arm back to its original position. She was now completely free from him, lying there, waiting a second before moving, breathing softly to make sure that she hadn't wakened him.

She scooted over a little closer to the edge of the bed and was about to get up when Will's arm shot out, grabbed her around the waist, and pulled her back to him. She yelped, surprised. She turned to look into his eyes, which were open now and looking intently at her.

This was the intense Will. Most times she encountered the fun and playful Will in bed, but there were times when he was serious, and this was one of them. He just watched her, his eyes never leaving her as he turned his body to lie on his side, pulling her closer to him.

His lips found her neck and he kissed her softly, his right hand moving to run down the side of her body to rest at her hip. He continued to kiss her lightly, moving from her neck to just under her chin, then to her mouth and back to her neck. She lay there, not moving, shutting off any and all thoughts, soaking in the feel of his hands and mouth as they moved over her.

She closed her eyes as his mouth moved back to hers, his tongue seeking entry, which she gave willingly. He kissed her softly. She loved him, love the way he touched her reverently. He ran his hand from her hip to find her core, where it began to work its own brand of magic. He was so good at this.

"Oh, God," she moaned as he moved his head down and began to suckle her breasts.

She knew her breasts were one of his favorite parts of her body; he'd told her enough times and spent major time there. She loved that about him, too—the time, care, and attention to detail that he gave to her body. Between his mouth and his talented hand, she was lost in sensation. He knew what he was doing, and his lips moved to capture her mouth, taking in her moans. He turned onto his back, bringing her to lie over him, gripping her ass and holding her in place as he continued to kiss her while his other hand was so, so busy.

Oh, God, she thought, giving in as her orgasm hit her. She found his lips and put her feelings into her kiss. His busy hands continued their play a few minutes more, and a second orgasm hit her. His hands continued, unrelenting in their play, until a little later she crested on her third. She lay on his body, limp, tingling all over, little electric currents moving through her nerves. *What is my name again*, she wondered as she closed her eyes, suddenly lethargic. He lay still, although she could feel him hard against her belly. He pulled her hips forward along the length of him and she moaned again weakly.

"I don't know if—" He cut her off, kissing her.

"Yes, you can," he whispered against her lips and slid her downward to take him into her body. She felt just perfect surrounding him. He began to slowly move inside her until, finally, his orgasm swept through him. Wow, he thought when he could think again. He was as boneless as she.

"I love you," he whispered into her ear as she drifted off to sleep, still lying on top of him, her head at home just underneath his chin. He would miss her over the next three weeks. She was so important to him; he hoped she knew that. He'd tried to convey that to her as much as he could, as often as he could. He loved so many things about her, even her constant stream of facts. Who knew that could be a turn-on?

He stuffed a pillow under his head and smiled, pleased with the knowledge that he loved her like no other. His head rested on the pillow now and he looked down at her, spread over him. He moved his hands slowly over her body. She was one beautiful girl. He loved her beautiful, smooth dark-brown skin, which was still his favorite feature although he'd come to love her breasts almost equally.

His fingers combed through thick, smooth, black hair, wild around her head. She was his. He hoped she would come to accept that sooner rather than later. He knew she loved him, but he needed her to trust in that love. He wanted her to realize that life could be better, less scary, if you had someone to rely on, that you couldn't guard yourself against the bad things that happened in life. He wanted to be there for her, with her, as they weathered life's storms together.

CHAPTER 15

One week later

Katrina slowed as she drove by Will's home and checked it out, making sure everything was as it should be before proceeding on to her house. One week down, two more to go, she said to herself, mentally checking off the days that Will had been away. Thank God for work and for the gardening competition. There was always something to do, and those things helped her to while away the hours.

This moping around was the downside to loving someone as much as she did him, and it frightened and worried her. If she became this lovesick and sappy with him gone for a week, she didn't want to contemplate not having him in her life.

She opened her door, kicked off her shoes, and walked through the house, down the back steps, and over to Lola's. She reached the back door and knocked.

"It's open. Come on in, Katrina," she heard Lola call out. She entered and found Lola sitting on the couch with the TV on, feet propped up on the coffee table in front of her, toes wiggling, redder than ripe tomatoes too long on the vine, anchored together by that pedicure foot thingy women used when they painted their toenails.

"What are you watching?" Katrina asked, taking a seat next to her.

"Housewives from somewhere," she said absently, her eyes glued to the women sitting around a table arguing about something.

"Why are they so angry?" Katrina asked.

"Who knows, I just turned it on," Lola responded, reaching for the remote and hitting the mute button.

"What's up, girlfriend?" Lola asked.

"Nothing much," Katrina said, watching the ladies move their heads and faces, animated in their exchanges, trying to guess what they were saying by reading their expressions.

"Miss ol' Will, huh?"

"Yep. I'm not going to even pretend. I didn't think I'd miss him this much. It's amazing how quickly you can come to depend on someone, huh?"

"You're preaching to the choir."

"How long have you and Oscar been married?"

"Ten years, give or take one or two," she said, smiling at Katrina, who rolled her eyes but returned her smile.

"When did you know you were serious, that you wanted to spend your life with him?"

"Hell, I knew from the start; it was Oscar I had to convince."

"I should have known," Katrina said, laughing now, putting her feet on the table next to Lola's. "Weren't you afraid?"

"Afraid of what?"

"That it wouldn't work out? That it's too easy, that it's too good to be true?"

"What's too easy or too good to be true? You and Will?"

"Yeah, maybe. He loves me and I love him. He's been great. Surely that can't last. He'll grow tired. He'll want to move on. Even if he doesn't, what if something happens to him? I don't think I could handle either scenario."

"Slow down, Katrina. I think that there is a two-part question lurking in there somewhere, but the answer to both of them is that you don't know and you can't ever know. You have to trust that he will be there for you, based on what he shows you, how he treats you. And you can't control whether something happens to him, just as he can't control whether something happens to you. You have to enjoy each other and not worry about the 'what if'," Lola said.

Katrina stared at the TV again. "I don't know. I'm making a big deal over nothing. Don't mind me," she said, taking the remote from Lola's hand and returning the volume to its earlier setting.

Lola watched her for a second more, choosing to let it go. She knew that this was the longest Katrina had ever been involved with a man. There was hope in that, she thought to herself. She hoped Katrina would give this a chance. Lola wanted to see her happy. She knew Katrina had had more than her share of heartache, but Will had been good for her. She'd been happier and more carefree than Lola had ever seen her.

The time difference made conversing with Will a little difficult. It was his Monday morning to her Sunday night, plus he had to work during the day. He couldn't be expected to sit on the phone all day with her, and that was not even taking into account the expense of that proposition. So she'd confined herself to talking to him twice daily, and sent e-mails often; those were cheap. Texting was too expensive. She'd learned that the hard way.

After leaving Lola's, she made her way home, showered, and went to bed, but was unable to sleep. She had gotten used to Will's hard body next to hers. She turned on the TV, flipping through channels, not really focusing on anything in particular. Her cell rang and she answered, thinking it was Will. It was Colburn.

"Hey, Colburn."

"Katrina, I am at the hospital."

"What are you doing at the hospital? Are you okay?" she asked, sitting up in her bed, her feet immediately going to the floor.

"It's not me; it's Charles. The paramedics said that he may have had a heart attack. He was counting the cash from the register, like he does every night. I came in and found him on the floor. I called the ambulance and they rushed him here."

"Okay, what hospital? I'm on my way. Is he going to be okay?"

"I don't know. They wheeled him in a few minutes ago. Oh, Katrina," he said, his voice breaking. She'd never, ever heard her Colburn sound this way.

"What hospital, Colburn?" she asked again.

"Central, near downtown."

"I know the place; I'll be there in a second," she said, hanging up, already reaching for her clothes. Seconds later she was in her car, backing out and moving down the street.

She was scared again, this episode bringing back all kinds of bad memories as she made her way to the hospital.

"Please, God, not again."

This is what she'd been afraid of with Will, what she knew was coming. The other shoe was always there; as soon as you trusted, put your hopes up, loved someone, it came for you, ready to drop. How many times did she have to witness this before she learned her lesson?

She drove as fast as the speed limit allowed, making her way to the hospital. She knew its location because it was where her parents had been brought after their car crash. She found the emergency room parking lot and, thankfully, a spot. She parked and then ran to the door. She walked up to the window where a nurse or someone in the admissions department sat. Deciding against asking, she followed the sign pointing the way to the emergency room waiting area, which she could see was at the end of the hall.

She approached two glass doors and could see Colburn sitting there. She was surprised by how old he looked. She'd never seen him look old before. She knew the godfathers were in their late sixties, but, up until this point, they'd always looked young to her.

She opened the doors and walked in, going over to stand next to Colburn, who stood up as she made her way to him. He wrapped her in a hug and she hugged him back, tears coming into her eyes.

"How is he?" she asked.

"I don't know. They still have him back in the emergency room. The nurse said someone will come to explain once they figure out what is wrong. Oh, Katrina," he said.

"Hey, Colburn, sit. Let's just wait and see. Uncle C is a tough old guy, like someone else I know," she said, deciding to be the strong one as they had been for her when her parents were here.

Uncle C and Colburn had been partners even before the war. Charles had jumped into the middle of a bar fight that Colburn had gotten into one night in Mississippi. It was a night that had not been conducive to being black. Charles had jumped in and helped two men in uniform, and they were fast friends ever since, growing more so once they'd gotten to know each other. They learned that they were more alike than they were different. Deployments to different platoons during the war had separated them, but they'd survived and had been partners for at least twenty years now. She knew what her Uncle C meant to Colburn. She grabbed his hand and held it while he stared off into space.

"It will be okay," she said, as much to Colburn as to herself. They waited a little over an hour before a doctor entered the room. He looked as young as she in those blue scrubs she always associated with doctors. He was tall and African-American, good-looking and confident.

"James Colburn," he said.

"That's me," Colburn said, walking over to the doctor, Katrina at his side.

"Hello," he said, extending his hand to Colburn, giving them both a quick glance.

"I'm Dr. Charles Gaston, the attending surgical physician for your partner, Charles Abernathy. He is your partner, I understand?"

"Yes," Colburn answered.

"Well, we've run several tests. He has had a heart attack caused by a partial blockage in the left ventricle leading to the heart. Luckily for him, his heart has not sustained any damage. It will, however, require angioplasty."

"Okay," Colburn said.

"Angioplasty is surgery where we open a blood vessel partially blocked by plaque buildup so that blood can flow through it more easily to the heart."

Katrina listened as he continued his explanation, his eyes directed at Colburn. He seemed knowledgeable and confident for one so young, but maybe he was older than he looked. She couldn't tell.

"When will the surgery take place?" Katrina asked.

"Hopefully Monday, but I'll know for sure before I leave. After he's stabilized, he'll be transported to the Coronary Care Unit on the fourth floor, where he'll remain until surgery."

"How long will he need to remain in the hospital?" Katrina asked.

If everything goes well, he should come back to the CCU unit for a few days, then he'll be moved to one of our step-down units, where less monitoring is required. If that goes well, maybe he can leave by the end of the week. But that is if everything works in our favor," he said.

"How dangerous is the surgery?" Katrina asked.

"Surgery is always serious business; this isn't any different. But Mr. Abernathy seems to be in fairly good condition otherwise, so he should be fine."

"Can we see him?" Colburn asked.

"Not right now. We are still running a few minor tests. I'll have the nurse notify you as soon as you can."

"Thank you, doctor," Colburn and Katrina said. He smiled and walked out the door just as quietly as he'd entered. She and Colburn walked back to their chairs and sat to wait. An hour later, they were able to see Charles. Katrina found him lying there with tubes attached to his body. He gave her a smile as she walked over to stand next to him.

"How are you feeling?" she asked, smiling back.

"Fine, now that you're here. How is my favorite goddaughter today?"

"I'm your only goddaughter," she said, squeezing his hand and bending over to kiss his hand. "I'm not going to stay long because I know Colburn really wants to be here giving you a hard time. So you take care and I'll see you after they move you," she said, bending over to kiss him again.

"I love you, Uncle C," she said, looking into his eyes.

"I know. Love you back."

She turned and walked back to the waiting room, where Colburn sat. His eyes lifted up, surprised.

"That was quick."

"I know. Why don't you go back again. I'll sit here until he is ready to go up."

"You sure?" he asked.

"Yep, I'm sure. You go ahead. I know he loves me more, but he's used to seeing you," she said, smiling.

About an hour later, Colburn came out and they both walked to the waiting area on the fourth floor, deciding to stop at a vending machine on the way before making their way to where they would be spending the night. The doctor, looking more tired now, found them there after checking in on C. He would have surgery in the morning.

She was tired. There was nothing nice about sleeping in the waiting room of a hospital. She remembered it from her parents' time here, short as it had been. There were people who spent a good deal of time at the hospital, waiting for their loved ones to improve. They'd known to secure the couches for the night. There was one couch left, and she wanted Colburn to sleep on it; she had to argue a while before he would take it, only to have him give it up to an older woman who arrived later. She knew he wouldn't lie down. He was too strong and old-school to lie down, a throwback to the days when men were men. She pulled two chairs together to form a makeshift bed, leaving Colburn to his chair, and tried to get some sleep. She missed Will.

She didn't really sleep, just dozed sporadically before waking early and getting up, careful to keep her noise to a minimum. She looked over and saw Colburn was still asleep, slouched over in the chair. She went in search of a bathroom and then walked the hospital corridors for a while before heading back. Colburn was still asleep, so she found her chair, which was still vacant, and sat.

Surgical prep for C would begin soon, she guessed; she had to take a deep breath at the thought of losing her godfathers. She loved them both. What would she do if she lost them? She was going to work with them, going to quit her job at the bank and finally take them up on their offer. She wanted as much time as she could get with the people who meant the world to her. And who was she kidding? The thought of doing what she loved every day was great. It held an exciting and extra appeal to her.

And what to do with Will? She loved him as much as she did her godfathers, maybe more, even. What to do about him? Was it better to take what she could and go for broke, as she'd decided to do with the godfathers, or should she let him go completely?

Where the godfathers were concerned, she couldn't go back. They had been with her as long as her parents had. She couldn't, wouldn't, walk away from them. But could she walk away from Will?

Her cell phone rang, interrupting her thoughts. It was Will.

"Hey," she said quietly, standing up and walking out into the hallway.

"Hey," he said.

"What time is it there?"

"It's about nine in the evening," he said, sitting back on the bed in his hotel room. "You sound tired."

"I am. Last night Uncle C had a heart attack caused by a partially blocked artery. I'm at the hospital with Colburn. He is scheduled for surgery later on this morning."

"I'm sorry, Katrina. What did the doctor tell you?"

"He told us that C would be fine in the long term, but it would take a while for him to recover."

"How is Colburn?"

"He's okay. He's asleep now in the waiting room. The sleeping arrangements here leave something to be desired, though," she added, her attempt at levity.

"How are you?"

"I'm okay. Just worried. You know me."

She slid her back down the wall until she was seated on the floor, her legs pulled up to her chest, her knees next to her face. She wrapped an arm around them and lay her head down.

"Hey, you can't know about all the possible things that can happen in life, Steady."

She smiled at the use of his nickname for her. "How are you? How is work?" she asked.

"Work is work. Long days, major meeting on Wednesday. Should be easier around here after that. I miss you," he said.

"I miss you, too. Didn't think I would this much."

"I'm going to take that in the positive way, that you love me more than you'd realized."

She was silent for a while. "I do love you, you're right, but this whole Uncle C thing has me more than a little spooked," she said, pausing and taking a deep breath. "Remember me telling you that I didn't think I could handle it if something happened to us?"

"Yes," he said, sitting back against the headboard of his bed, his feet stretched out before him. His stomach started to churn at the turn in the conversation.

"Well, I've been giving that more thought, and maybe we should slow down, you know, make sure this is what we want."

"This is what we want. I want. Slow down, K, don't panic. We're doing just fine. I'm okay with where we are."

"I don't know that I am," she said, starting to cry, letting go of the pent-up fears caused by C being here. "Coming here again brought back so many memories for me. It's where my parents were taken following the accident, where they died," she said, her voice trailing off a little as she cried again. "I don't think I can handle something more with you. I'm going to quit my job, I'm sure I am, and take the godfathers up on their offer."

"What offer?"

She'd forgotten she hadn't told him about that. "Remember when you found me crying in your backyard?"

"Yes."

"I talked to the godfathers about starting my own business and they told me that they'd planned to leave Abernathy and Co. to me. I could work for them anytime I wanted, give up working at the bank."

Trying not to let the hurt from her keeping something so big from him creep into his voice, he paused for a few seconds. "So are you going to work for them?"

"Yes, especially in light of what has happened to C. He and Colburn need me, and you know how much I love gardening. We could all be happy. I could take care of them both and learn the business, you know, help them."

"What about your life, Katrina? Would that be enough for you?"

"Sure it would. I could take care of them, help them run the business. It would be enough."

"How about you think it over for a while. Give yourself time. Give them time. Don't make any decisions until things settle down. We can talk over your options when I get back."

It was quiet on the telephone for a while. "Katrina, are you there?"

"Yes."

"If you want to work with your godfathers I can certainly understand, but we can still work. It's not an all or nothing deal." Silence greeted that comment. "Katrina, are you still there?"

"Yes, but I better go check on Colburn. People are starting to move around here. I bet they've started prepping C for surgery. I'd better go."

"Will you call me later? Don't worry about waking me. I want to hear about C, okay?"

"Sure," she said.

"I love you, Katrina."

"I know. I love you, too. Get some sleep and don't worry about me," she said, disconnecting.

'Don't worry about me', he thought. Sure, he'd worry; she sounded so sad. He missed her. He wished he could be there with her; maybe he could, he thought, pulling out his laptop. He had that one major meeting on Wednesday. No way he could leave before, not if he wanted to keep his job. But he wanted to be there for her. She scared him. What if he wasn't able to convince her that life with him would work? He could understand her desire to leave her job and work with her godfathers; it was a perfect place for her. He'd also hoped she wouldn't use it as a way to escape life, by shutting herself off from the world—and him.

⚜

Dr. Gaston came to see them after the surgery. He looked tired. They stood and walked over to meet him.

"How did it go?" Colburn asked.

"Great. As smooth as we could have expected. He should make a full recovery."

Katrina felt the relief in Colburn's frame and she put her arm around his waist.

"Thank you," she said.

"How soon will he be able to resume his old life?" Colburn asked. "He was a very active man. We run a local gardening store here."

"I know Abernathy and Co. I love that place. My wife spends way too much money there," Dr. Gaston said with a smile. "It will take some time for him to get back to where he once was. He will have to give up smoking and change his diet," he said.

"Sure thing," Colburn answered, extending his hand to shake the doctor's. "Thank you," he said.

"You're welcome," he said, taking Colburn's hand.

"I've got to look in on some other patients, but if I can, I'll try and stop by his room before I leave," he said, looking at Katrina.

"Sure, thank you."

Dr. Gaston turned and walked out of the room. "That's great news!" Katrina said.

"It is," Colburn said, taking in a huge breath of air.

"Are you hungry? We could get something to eat."

"I'm not sure I should leave. You never know, they may need to talk to me about something else, or Charles may wake up early. You know he has a mind of his own."

"That's fine. I'll go and grab us something."

"Sure. Thanks, Katrina."

It took her about ten minutes to locate the cafeteria. She purchased two cups of coffee and a couple of sandwiches. Colburn was where she'd left him. She took the seat next to him and handed him a coffee cup and a sandwich.

She took a sip, letting go of some of her worry for a few minutes. She smiled at Colburn, who smiled back and added his standard wink. They were more hopeful than they'd been since they'd arrived.

STEADY

April

Charles stayed in the hospital less than a week. Things had progressed better than they'd expected, and he was discharged Thursday morning. Katrina had met Colburn at the hospital early that morning while C signed papers. She followed them home and helped them get settled.

She hadn't been in to work at all this week other than to stop by and talk with her manager. She'd given her notice, and that had felt wonderful, like a weight had been lifted off her shoulders. Those who had loved her—Amber, Lola, the godfathers—had always encouraged her to leave, to work on something that made her feel whole.

When she hadn't been at the hospital, she spent the time at Abernathy & Co. filling in for the godfathers. Although Colburn was back to work, he was visiting C three to four times a day. She was managing the center sooner than she'd expected, and she loved it. Why had she waited this long to do something she so clearly prized? Why hadn't she? Oh, that fear thing again.

She was headed home now for another life-changing meeting. She'd scheduled an appointment with Ms. Morgan, a real estate saleswoman who had come highly recommended. Katrina turned on to her street, unconsciously checking Will's home. She felt awful about him, but it was for the best. No need to drag a goodbye out. She hadn't spoken to him since Monday morning, coward that she was. He had another week in Singapore, so she had time to come up with something other than the "I love you but your love scares the pants off of me" excuse. Katrina pulled into her drive. Ms. Morgan was here early, and Katrina walked over to meet her.

"Hello, Katrina. Nice to put a face to a voice," she said, extending her hand.

"Yes, thank you for responding so quickly," Katrina said, shaking her hand and leading her inside.

"You have a lovely home, and this is a highly sought-after neighborhood. Being contest winners three years in a row makes for low taxes," she said, looking around in the way that only real estate people did, sizing up and calculating.

"Feel free to explore," Katrina said.

She was now walking around Katrina's home, making notes and cataloging the amenities. "I don't have to tell you that you should have no problems selling this home. Are you sure this is what you want to do? You were one of the first to purchase in the new section of the neighborhood, and since then the property value has increased tremendously."

"Yes, I'm sure," she answered, following Mrs. Morgan into the kitchen.

She was pleased with herself for finally taking control of her life, although it warred with the feelings of guilt at not having discussed the godfathers' offer or the decision to sell her home with Will. Not talking to him about it was wrong, she internally argued. True that, she thought, but it was her life and finally she was taking the reins and making changes that should have been made ages ago.

"You have a beautiful garden out back," Ms. Morgan said, interrupting Katrina's internal debate. "It's fantastic. I hope you're ready to move, because this home will not be on the market for long."

"I'm ready," she said. She sure hoped she was.

Finally, he was home. He'd managed to leave Singapore this morning. He'd changed his flight to leave Thursday, thirty hours ago, putting him home Thursday evening, the day after his meeting. He was exhausted; he had worked hard to tie up loose ends to get back to her. He worried most of the ride back because he hadn't heard from her, and he decided he was done with extended business trips.

He was angry and disappointed in Katrina. Beyond their conversation on Monday, he hadn't spoken to her. He knew she was preoccupied, he could understand that, but even so, she could have called at least once. Fuck, she could have just answered his calls. "Busy, C's okay," she responded once to the many text messages he'd sent.

He was angry and afraid as he pulled into his neighborhood. He turned the corner and drove toward his home, taking a moment to look over at Katrina's home, taking in the new sign in her yard, a for-sale sign. It was a sucker punch, and he had to catch his breath. He pulled into his drive, parked, and hopped out of the jeep, long angry strides leading him to her door.

He knocked hard and stood staring at her for a second when the door opened, just taking in the woman he'd grown to love. She was surprised to see him, her eyes wide. He saw love and longing in them, and tried to match those feelings with her selling her home and not returning his calls.

"You're back early," she said quietly.

"It appears so," he said, brushing past her as he walked inside.

He stopped just inside her door and turned to face her, his hands in his pockets, staring at her heatedly.

"What's up, Katrina? You won't answer my calls. There is a for-sale sign in the yard! Weren't you going to even tell me?" he asked, his voice rising in volume. "Don't you think you owe me more than that?"

She watched him struggle with his temper. Hell, she hadn't known he had one. He stood before her looking tired, angry, and hurt. That part she could tell from his eyes. He turned away from her abruptly and sat on her couch. She closed the door and followed him in.

"So that's it, Katrina? I don't even warrant a call? I'm sorry, Will, I'm moving on. This isn't what I want," he said.

"I'm sorry, Will," she said, realizing she had made a huge mistake.

He sat there looking at her, not saying a word, his face set in stone. He stood up, too angry to talk, and left the way he'd entered, closing the door firmly behind him.

She walked over to the door, cracking it a little to watch him walk home. When he disappeared from view, she walked back to her couch and sat down. She hadn't meant for him to find out this way, but really, what had she expected? He didn't deserve to be treated that way.

She started crying again. What was with these tears? She'd cried lately like she'd been assigned rain-replacement duty. What a dufus. The only thing she could say in her defense was that she'd been in turmoil, had been since he'd left two weeks ago. She was scared of her need for him, and Uncle C's condition had amplified her fear.

She'd taken the coward's way out instead of facing him, using her Uncle C as an excuse to not stick it out. *Bad move, Katrina*, her heart said.

Later that evening Will pulled into the driveway of his sister's home. The garage door was down; he hoped they were home. He needed to talk to someone he knew cared about him. He rang the doorbell and waited. Maybe no one was home. He waited a minute longer and it opened. It was Jennifer. Just seeing her made him feel calmer, more in control.

"Hey, Will, you back from overseas, huh?" she asked, stepping away from the door to let him enter. "Your brother-in-law took the kids to their practices today. They just left. I was working out in the yard. Come on back," she said, leading him outside and moving to sit on the sofa.

He sat across from her, his back to the house, and looked out over the yard. Beautiful, he thought. His sister's gardening style was more like Katrina's than his.

"You okay?" she asked.

"Not really. It's been a long two weeks."

"Your trip wasn't productive?"

"No, it was. I cut it short, though. It's Katrina. I returned early for her. One of her godfathers became ill, had a heart attack."

"Is he all right?"

"Yes, better now, and at home."

"And how is Katrina?"

"She's fine," Will said, placing his arms on his thighs and leaning forward, looking out over the yard, restless and angry. "She's selling her home in the neighborhood and is going to work with her godfathers. She quit her job. She's ready to pull back into that shell of hers at the slightest sign of trouble. Tell me that I'm better off without her."

Jennifer was silent, letting him talk, sensing that he needed to.

"Here I was thinking I was going to ask her to marry me. Again. Turned me down once. What am I, stupid?" he said, turning to face her, hurt evident on his face.

She felt bad for him.

"I must not have meant as much to her as I thought."

"I'm sure you do. She's probably going crazy, and this is her way of taking control. You told me she lost her parents, right? Lost her adopted parents, too?"

"Yes."

"I'm sure this is tough for her. You were young when our father died. I was the oldest and knew more than you did. You're the baby boy, remember?"

"As if you'd let me forget," he said, smiling weakly.

"I was scared, too. I know our mother was. Thankfully, we had Grandfather, who was not so old that he couldn't help. He took control and steered us until Mom could get it together. Losing someone you love is painful, and Katrina has gone through that twice. She lived in foster care until she was adopted, and then she lost her parents. It has to be tough for her right now. Just continue to be patient and support her."

"I know. I have been, or I thought I had been, but why, if she believes in me, does she up and make all these changes while I was away?"

"Those changes worry you?"

"Yes, because she's given serious thought to giving up on us. I'm a patient man, more than even I'd realized, but what if she can't overcome her fears? What if I end up without her?"

"Are you willing to quit now?"

"She's not giving me much choice."

"You know, I've watched you climb mountains, ride bikes, surf, ski, anything to test yourself against life. You did those things, but you weren't really afraid. They were small risks for you. You have always been a fearless kid, and now you're a fearless young man. So now life throws you a real curve ball. You've finally, truly found something that you fear losing. It's Katrina. She is your test. Can you keep going, unsure of the outcome, knowing you may be hurt, really hurt?"

Will didn't say anything for a while. He took comfort in his sister's presence, his second mother's wisdom. Here he'd thought he was different from Katrina, less fearful. He had always known that he'd been loved, so he could challenge life and its risks by plunging headlong into each new conquest, one after another, while Katrina stayed close, doing what she considered safe.

Could he, risk this one thing that really mattered to him? Could he quit, cut his potential losses? He knew he would continue on. His heart wouldn't let him stop; not yet, anyway. He blew out a deep breath and turned to look at his sister. She smiled and put her hand on Will's knee, a silent show of support. They sat a while longer next to each other, letting the garden's calm and beauty soothe and refresh their spirits.

Katrina wanted Will back, wanted to risk whatever life had to throw her way with him. She had panicked, plain and simple. Katrina needed Lola.

Lola stood in her backyard watching Syd and one of the Sheppard boys play in her sandbox. Oh, to be four again.

"Hey, girl, what's up? How's the house selling business going?"

"Good, I guess," she said.

"I've got to tell you, you surprised me. I didn't peg you for the type that quit. You stuck around when John would have driven any sane person away, you're always around taking care of those godfathers of yours."

"This conversation is leading to Will, I can tell. And before you get going, I agree with you. It was a dumb move on my part," she said, tears starting to form in her eyes.

"Have you told this to Will?" Lola asked.

"Nope. I don't know where he is or what to do."

"Grovel. It works like magic. He's at home; he just pulled up. But before you go, take this," Lola said holding out her hand, palm up, which was empty.

"What?"

"Take it."

"Take what?" Katrina asked, looking at Lola's empty palm.

"It's your big girl pill. Take it in the name of all the great women in the world who have come before you. Take it and be strong," she said. Katrina grunted but complied, taking the pretend pill from Lola's hand and pretending to swallow it.

"Okay, now step into these," she said, holding her hands out in front of her body.

"Okay, what is that?" she asked, looking skeptically at Lola's hands and the emptiness surrounding them.

"These are your big girl panties. You need to put them on."

Katrina rolled her eyes, but lifted one leg at a time and stepped into Lola's pretend panties. She laughed at Lola, who pretended to yank them up.

"I think your butt is too big," she said, and they both started to laugh.

"Let's go, girl," she said, turning Katrina toward her back gate and pushing her out.

Will sat in his yard, in the misting area, his back against the wall. The door leading into the room was open, affording him a view of his home. The lights were on inside. He just didn't want to be there. He closed his eyes and listened to the chimes, trying to understand Katrina, and better yet, what he needed to do for her.

So far, he'd come up empty. How do you make someone choose you? He knew the answer to that one—you couldn't. She chose fear over him. He thought that she'd come around in time, if he gave her enough room and didn't crowd her. He'd continue with that for a while. He was not ready to quit.

He heard a sound and opened his eyes to see her standing in front of him, her back to him, peering into his home. She stood for a moment looking in, eyes moving from the kitchen and over to his bedroom, before she turned around to leave. She stopped when she saw him and stood there staring for a minute before she walked over.

"What are you doing out here?" she asked.

"Nothing. Trying to relax," he said, watching as she entered and sat down next to him.

"I'm sorry," she said, reaching for his hand.

"For what?" he asked.

"To start with, I'm sorry for not answering your calls and not telling you what was going on with me."

"How are the godfathers?" he asked, taking her hand in his.

"They're fine. Charles was discharged last weekend. Colburn and I got him settled. He is walking; the doctors expect a complete recovery. In a couple of months, he should be back to normal. He has to make some changes in his life. C's going to have to give up smoking, and he finally realizes that. He and Colburn both have to make changes in their lives. I've hired someone to cook healthier meals for them, and someone to clean."

"I thought you were going to do that. Figured that was why you were selling your home and moving away from me."

"I'm sorry," she said again, looking into eyes that were still hurt. "I thought so at first, but maybe it's not such a good idea. I've been thinking about getting a small apartment instead, just to make sure that I work well with the godfathers. Plus they gave me grief about you, so I've been forbidden to move in with them even if I wanted to. They like you more than me, it seems," she said, smiling.

"So you've quit your job."

"Yep. My last day is next week. I gave notice the day after I spoke to you on the phone."

He nodded. "I see. So why are you selling your home still?"

"I've had several offers. You would not believe the profit I'll make. I can use the money as a cushion while I work with the godfathers and start the landscaping part of the business."

"I see," he said, taking a deep breath.

"So now the million dollar question? What happens to us? You could have answered my telephone calls, Katline. I at least deserved that."

"You're right, I panicked, and I'm sorry," she said, looking into his eyes and squeezing his hands. "I thought it would be easier to leave you behind. It seemed like a good idea at the time, when I was consumed with fear. I've got to stop doing that, letting fear dictate my actions. It's hard, though. Sometimes I don't even recognize it as fear, it is so ingrained.

"Anyway, I thought it would be easier to leave you when you were out of the country, but the minute I saw you at my home I realized I'd made a huge mistake. Seeing you again washed all of those fears away," she said, turning her body to face him. "I don't know where this will end, and it's the ending that scares me so much. I don't want to quit yet, but I'm still scared."

"Would you believe I am, too?"

"You? You've never met a risk you didn't like."

He pulled her over to sit on his lap. "You're my big gamble, the one I'm most frightened of. It's risky business loving you, Katrina Jones. But I can't let go or give in, at least not yet. Not when there is still hope. Is there still hope, Katrina?" he asked.

She put her arms around his neck and kissed him, and then pulled away and looked into his eyes.

"There is always hope. I love you," she said.

He kissed her again. "I love you, too."

CHAPTER 16

"Want to take a look at the gardens with me?" Will asked, pulling the hair from around Katrina's head as she tried to wake up the following morning. "We've got one full month. May is a few days away."

"Sure," she said, "I haven't been by since this whole thing with C started. John has taken over. He called to tell me how he walks through the garden reviewing the plans daily. Scary thought, him in charge," she said, sitting up and looking around the room for her shirt. It was on the floor next to the bed. She pulled it over her head, but not before Will kissed one of her breasts. She yelped and he chuckled.

"Let me shower first. Meet me at my house in ten," she said.

She stood, put the rest of her clothes on and walked by Will's mirror, glancing at her hair in fright. She made a face and he laughed.

"See you in ten," he said, pushing her out of the bedroom, down the hall, and out the back door, still grinning.

He gave her fifteen minutes to be safe and drove over to her house. He had barely stopped before she walked out of her house in form-fitting shorts and a T-shirt. It didn't matter what she wore, but he loved her slim body in those. She gave him a kiss as she climbed into the jeep.

"Ready?" she asked, smiling.

He returned the smile, and backed out. They arrived at the gardens within five minutes. They weren't the only ones who wanted to see the gardens. It was crowded. Will parked and they hopped out and walked in. He reached for her hand, which she gave gladly.

It was beautiful here. The last feature, a fence with an oval-shaped opening, would separate the two sides of the garden from each other and create an enclosure for the right side. Tucked behind it was a secret garden. They'd left the larger shrubs in place, and natives were starting to bloom. They had all of May to make the finishing touches. So far, everything was as it should be.

"Well, good morning, you two."

John stood near the entrance, looking down at their entwined hands.

"The gardens are really filling in, and I must say, it's beautiful. I have a really strong feeling about our chances of winning this year, but there is nothing different in that. I feel the same way every year," he said, smiling. "What a great idea to combine Will's design with Katrina's organization and gardening knowledge. Who came up with it, I wonder?" he asked, smiling at them.

"Who knew," Will responded, smiling and winking at Katrina.

"Yeah, who knew," she said, smiling.

"So, Katrina, I saw a for sale sign in your yard, I believe. Is that true?" John asked.

"Yes, it is, I'm moving to an apartment and taking a job with my godfathers over at Abernathy and Co."

"Yes, I heard about Charles. Is he doing well?"

"Yes, he is."

"We will hate to lose you, but perhaps our Will can talk you into staying," he said, giving them an enigmatic smile. "Well, I'll let you two look around. You know you will have the volunteers the last two weekends in May for any finishing touches or extra assistance you may need. They will be here both days."

"Yes, I'll make sure to have things here for them to do," she said.

"Have a nice day," John said, walking away.

They walked over all the gardens, specifically checking the pavilion, the streams, and the pond and waterfalls. All were working nicely. They headed back to the jeep.

She paused a minute, standing next to the passenger door. "You should be proud of your work here," she said.

"That's high praise from you, and I'll take it. Thanks," he said, walking over to kiss her. "It would have gotten done, but I'm sure it would not have been half as entertaining without you. I'm the one who's better for it, right? I now have you and the gardens."

"I won't argue with that," she said, smiling and kissing him back, her hands moving around his back to pull him in close and to hold on tight. She didn't want to let him go ever again.

∞

The second week of May

Katrina pulled on to her street. She was meeting her agent this afternoon to sign the contract officially selling her home to a family moving down from California, two kids and their parents; one of the kids was in college and the other would start in the fall. In essence, she was selling her home to empty nesters. But the idea of their family appealed to her. She'd been giving more thought to family lately as she asked herself what she wanted from life.

The godfathers were good. She loved playing in the dirt, as Lola liked to call her gardening work. No longer at the bank, her days were filled now with all things she loved. Will, the godfathers, and dirt.

She had gone with the godfathers to their attorney and worked through the details of a business arrangement, forcing them to agree on an amount that she would give them. She was using some of the proceeds from the sale of her home, technically buying into the business. She wouldn't hear of it any other way, and they'd reluctantly agreed, stipulating that her additional funding would be used as seed money to start the landscaping arm of the business, which she would manage. Good all around. She'd found an apartment, a small efficiency that she would move into by the end of May if she wanted to.

The buyers of her home had been pre-approved for financing and in a hurry to get to town and into their new home, so she needed to move out quickly. She might not end up needing the apartment; she practically lived at Will's house now. She rationalized that it would be easier to sleep over at Will's since her house needed to be kept clean and neat for showings. She just wanted to be around her patient and loving Will. For the first time, she was giving serious thought to agreeing to make their relationship more permanent.

The name "Steady" suited him much more than her these days. What other way could she describe someone who stuck with her even when she tried to get rid of him, who always loved her and was there for her?

She parked in the garage. Ms. Morgan's car was already parked in front of her home. That was one committed woman. Katrina got out, more than ready to sign the papers that would move her life in another direction, one she was learning to embrace.

A week later Lola and Katrina were packing up her kitchen. She had two weeks to get out. She decided to pack up her home—most of it was going into storage anyway. She had given up on the apartment idea.

"Girl, I can't believe you're leaving me," Lola said. She was supposedly helping her box up her dishes, but instead was using Katrina's blender to make margaritas. Katrina had no idea that packing without margaritas was illegal in most states. Lola had even gone back to her house to retrieve the necessary ingredients.

"I'm not leaving you. I'll just be two doors down. That's still close enough for you to harass me."

"So when are you going to make an honest man of our Will?" Lola asked, giving Katrina a grin as she put ice into the blender.

"Why do you think it's me holding up the process?" she responded.

"Come on, I know you. You sold your house because you're afraid."

"Don't hold back, Lola. Tell me what you really think."

"Come on, Katrina, you can't lie to me. You and I both know you're afraid. Don't get me wrong, I applaud some of the changes you've made. You needed to find a job doing something you enjoyed, so I'm glad you started working at the garden center with our Uncle C and Colburn. Starting the landscaping part was also a good move."

"There is a but in there."

"Yep. You know me, girl, like I know you. Your next move should be to tell our boy Will that you're serious about him. He's a keeper," she said.

"I know, Lola, and I'm working toward that point. I will get there. This is the furthest I've ever been. Just give me time, okay?"

"Okay, but don't take too long, I don't want to have to hurt you," she said, picking up a glass and handing it over to Katrina.

"Girl, I'm good," Lola said after taking a sip of the margarita she'd made for herself.

Katrina took a sip and coughed. "How much alcohol did you put in these?" she asked.

"That's for me to know and you to find out," she said, smacking her lips. "Okay, now I'm ready to get to work. I just needed some go-go juice."

They spent the next couple of hours packing, and the potency of Lola's drinks ensured that both were in a very good mood by the end of the evening.

"Hey," Will called out from the back door, Oscar following behind him. The pair found Lola and Katrina in extremely lively moods, laughing as Katrina was taping up a box. Both turned at the sound of his voice. He looked at the glass sitting next to Katrina and the one in Lola's hand, the blender, the half empty bottle of tequila, and the margarita mix on the counter. He turned to Oscar and grinned.

"Well, if it isn't Will and my lovely husband," Lola said in greeting.

"You ladies are working hard, I can tell," Oscar said.

"Yes, we are," Lola responded. "Can I get you a drink?"

"No, I'm good," Oscar said, walking over to stand next to his wife. "How about we get you home?"

"What? I'm helping Katrina here," she said.

"I can see that," said Oscar, helping Lola stand. She wavered just a little and they all laughed.

"Say goodbye to Will and Katrina," Oscar said.

"Goodbye, Will. I'll see you tomorrow, girl," Lola said to Katrina.

"Thanks for helping me," Katrina said, following Oscar and Lola out the back door. Lola was really leaning into Oscar as he part walked, part carried her home. She stood there watching them until they were out of sight. She closed the door and locked it and walked over to stand in front of Will, who was leaning against the counter, watching her.

"It looks like you and Lola were able to get quite a bit done," Will said, picking up her margarita glass and taking a sip, wincing at its strength. "It's impressive the amount of work you and Lola were able to get done, considering the strength of your drinks." He smiled, sitting the glass back on the counter. Katrina walked over to stand closer to him, pushing her body into his and pulling his shirt over his head. She didn't say a word, just looked at him.

"What?" he asked.

"I love you, you know that, don't you?" she asked, suddenly serious.

"Yes, I know that."

"You're the one who's steady, you know that, too, don't you?" she said, watching him, her hands moving to his face, tracing the sharpness of his cheekbones. "You are always there for me, cutting your trip short, staying with me as I work to push you away. You're steadier than I'll ever be."

"You think so?"

"Know so," she said, taking his hand and walking slowly backwards, towing him along through the living room and into her bedroom, careful of the boxes in her path. She kept walking until her legs hit the bed and she sat down, her hands now moving to the snap of his jeans. She heard his breathing change as she unzipped them. She slowly pushed his jeans down his legs, encouraging him to step from them, taking her hand to rub over him. She heard the hiss of air leave his mouth.

She sat back and smiled, loving the way he looked standing before her in those snug thigh-length briefs. Suddenly she changed her mind and stood up again.

"You lie down," she said, turning him around and pushing him down on the bed.

God, he loved it when she took control, he thought as he fell back to wait. He didn't have to wait long. She lifted her T-shirt and pulled it over her head. She was naked underneath. Continuing with her strip show, she lowered her pants slowly down her legs. When all her clothing was gone, she stood straight before him and jumped. He caught her and laughed, turning her onto her back.

"I love you," he said and kissed her. He pushed her further up on the bed, his leg pushing hers apart as he settled at the juncture of the thighs and rubbed her there. She moaned; she loved it when he did that. He knew her body like his life depended on it.

He moved his mouth to hers, kissing her slowly and softly while his hands found her breasts. He touched them softly, in awe of the way they felt in his hands, and pushed into her slowly. Her hands moved to cup his head, wanting to see his eyes. He looked into hers and whispered, "I love you," and started moving, loving her in the way that only he could. He pushed and she met him, surrendering her fears and love over to him, to his care and protection, telling him that she would love him always.

He heard her ragged breathing and pushed more until she came and he followed. He placed his face into the curve of her neck and savored the scent and sweetness that was Katrina. She turned her face to his and he lifted his head to gaze down into her eyes, kissing her again, laying his head back as he pulled her close to him, secure in the knowledge that they would be all right in the end.

Will woke up the following morning more content than he'd been in a long time. He lay there and watched her sleep until her eyes opened. He smiled, and she leaned in, touching her lips to his.

"To the gardens," she said, looking over at her clock, removing hair from out of her eyes and taking in the time. It was 6 a.m.

"I'm glad you're a morning person, too. It thought to get to the gardens this morning early before the volunteers arrived. Can you believe we have only two weeks left before the judging?" she asked, moving to get out of bed, crawling over him, yelping again as he brushed her nipple with his mouth, an odd habit of his. She laughed but continued her crawl over him and out of the bed.

His eyes followed the bounce of her small butt as she walked away from him and toward his bathroom. He heard the sound of the shower starting up. He sat up, stretching his arms above his head, yawning. Life was good, he thought, as he stood up and went in search of his clothing.

He walked into the bathroom to see her standing under the shower spray.

"Come over when you're done. I'm going home to take a shower," he said, moving his head into the shower and under the spray as he kissed her goodbye. She smiled at that.

"Statistics show that married people have a much greater life expectancy than single, divorced, or separated people," she said, watching his eyes open wide.

He turned the water off and faced her.

"I love it when you talk facts to me. Are you asking me to marry you, Katrina?" he said, giving her a slow smile before moving in and kissing her. The force of it pushed her back against the shower wall.

"Yes," she said, trying to catch her breath.

He moved to stand between her legs, facing her, lifting her right leg with his left hand, positioning her so that she straddled his thigh. Her other leg wrapped around his back. His right hand found her spot, his spot. His fingers parted her, and he worked her into a frenzy as only he could.

"Yes, I'll marry you."

He pulled back from her, bracing her before she fell, and stepped out of the shower. She smiled back at him, ridiculously happy.

She saw him fifteen minutes later walking out of his bathroom door, apparently fresh from the shower, a towel in his hand as she tracked him with her eyes through his bedroom window, her body tingling in remembrance of him. She'd been here before and loved seeing him here now again. She walked into his home, proceeding to his bedroom, and he looked up as she entered.

"That was fast. Give me five and I'll be ready."

He dressed quickly and walked out to his garage, where she was starting to load a few tools into his jeep.

"I'm ready," he said.

They finished loading his jeep and drove over to the gardens. Katrina removed her copy of the garden design and walked away, moving to begin her review, making sure that the garden matched Will's design.

He watched her walk away from him, watched her work. She'd told him the volunteers would be here by nine and that she wanted to have something for them to do. Mostly all that remained needed would be placement of the statues and ornamental art they'd purchased last week. Looking back at his time pre-Katrina and all that had transpired in between then and now, he was happy that he'd started this adventure with her. It was the best risk he'd ever taken.

June

Today was the big day. Judging would take place. Will and Katrina and a boatload of volunteers had worked feverishly the week leading up to the judging day. She, Will, Lola, and Oscar had put in a monster session of packing up her home and moving her out. Home was now with Will. They would be marrying in a few weeks, a small ceremony in the gardens, reception to be held at the godfathers'. They'd be giving her away, a godfather on each arm as she walked down the aisle. She wouldn't have it any other way. They were here, too, talking to their buddies and regular customers.

She hoped her parents were pleased with her progress in the game of life.

The gardening committee—John, Mrs. Washington, Sandy and even Stan—were smiling. They stood a few feet away from Katrina talking to Will, all pleased with how things had turned out. She was proud of him and for him. Who would have thought all those months ago that she would be here, happy, taking chances? The judging committee, if they remained on schedule, would be here by noon. They were the third in the queue to be judged. The winner would be announced that evening. The gardens were to be opened to the public both Saturday and Sunday.

Will's mother and one of his sisters had arrived to support him. She had met them last night when Will picked them up from the airport. She and his sisters were very nice, quiet but welcoming. Jennifer and Dennis were around here somewhere with their kids. Katrina's crew had shown up, too—Amber, Claudia, Darius and his wife; he'd given his girlfriend of old a second chance. Seemed like love was spreading its magic on everyone. What a boatload to be thankful for this beautiful June day. She looked over at Will and smiled, her cup full. Life was good.

The End

ABOUT THE AUTHOR

Ruthie Robinson resides in Austin, Texas with her husband and two teenage children. She holds a bachelor's degree in economics from Clark College and a master's degree in economics from the University of Texas (Go Longhorns!). She worked for more than a decade in the banking industry before turning her love for writing into a second career.

Ruthie enjoys being a mom, gardening, traveling, and reading. *Steady* is her second book. Her debut novel, *Reye's Gold* was published by Genesis Press in November 2009.

2011 Mass Market Titles

January

From This Moment
Sean Young
ISBN-13: 978-1-58571-383-7
ISBN-10: 1-58571-383-X
$6.99

Nihon Nights
Trisha/Monica Haddad
ISBN-13: 978-1-58571-382-0
ISBN-10: 1-58571-382-1
$6.99

February

The Davis Years
Nicole Green
ISBN-13: 978-1-58571-390-5
ISBN-10: 1-58571-390-2
$6.99

Allegro
Adora Bennett
ISBN-13: 978-158571-391-2
ISBN-10: 1-58571-391-0
$6.99

March

Lies in Disguise
Bernice Layton
ISBN-13: 978-1-58571-392-9
ISBN-10: 1-58571-392-9
$6.99

Steady
Ruthie Robinson
ISBN-13: 978-1-58571-393-6
ISBN-10: 1-58571-393-7
$6.99

April

The Right Maneuver
LaShell Stratton-Childers
ISBN-13: 978-1-58571-394-3
ISBN-10: 1-58571-394-5
$6.99

Riding the Corporate Ladder
Keith Walker
ISBN-13: 978-1-58571-395-0
ISBN-10: 1-58571-395-3
$6.99

May

Separate Dreams
Joan Early
ISBN-13: 978-1-58571-434-6
ISBN-10: 1-58571-434-8
$6.99

I Take This Woman
Chamein Canton
ISBN-13: 978-1-58571-435-3
ISBN-10: 1-58571-435-6
$6.99

June

Inside Out
Grayson Cole
ISBN-13: 978-1-58571-437-7
ISBN-10: 1-58571-437-2
$6.99

2011 Mass Market Titles (continued)

July

The Other Side of the
  Mountain
Janice Angelique
ISBN-13: 978-1-58571-442-1
ISBN-10: 1-58571-442-9
$6.99

Holding Her Breath
Nicole Green
ISBN-13: 978-1-58571-439-1
ISBN-10: 1-58571-439-9
$6.99

August

The Sea of Aaron
Kymberly Hunt
ISBN-13: 978-1-58571-440-7
ISBN-10: 1-58571-440-2
$6.99

The Finley Sisters' Oath of
  Romance
Keith Thomas Walker
ISBN-13: 978-1-58571-441-4
ISBN-10: 1-58571-441-0
$6.99

September

Except on Sunday
Regena Bryant
ISBN-13: 978-1-58571-443-8
ISBN-10: 1-58571-443-7
$6.99

Light's Out
Ruthie Robinson
ISBN-13: 978-1-58571-445-2
ISBN-10: 1-58571-445-3
$6.99

October

The Heart Knows
Renee Wynn
ISBN-13: 978-1-58571-444-5
ISBN-10: 1-58571-444-5
$6.99

Best Friends; Better Lovers
Ceyla Bowers
ISBN-13: 978-1-58571-455-1
ISBN-10: 1-58571-455-0
$6.99

November

Caress
Grayson Cole
ISBN-13: 978-1-58571-454-4
ISBN-10: 1-58571-454-2
$6.99

A Love Built to Last
L. S. Childers
ISBN-13: 978-1-58571-448-3
ISBN-10: 1-58571-448-8
$6.99

December

Fractured
Wendy Byrne
ISBN-13: 978-1-58571-449-0
ISBN-10: 1-58571-449-6
$6.99

Everything in Between
Crystal Hubbard
ISBN-13: 978-1-58571-396-7
ISBN-10: 1-58571-396-1
$6.99

Other Genesis Press, Inc. Titles

2 Good	Celya Bowers	$6.99
A Dangerous Deception	J.M. Jeffries	$8.95
A Dangerous Love	J.M. Jeffries	$8.95
A Dangerous Obsession	J.M. Jeffries	$8.95
A Drummer's Beat to Mend	Kei Swanson	$9.95
A Good Dude	Keith Walker	$6.99
A Happy Life	Charlotte Harris	$9.95
A Heart's Awakening	Veronica Parker	$9.95
A Lark on the Wing	Phyliss Hamilton	$9.95
A Love of Her Own	Cheris F. Hodges	$9.95
A Love to Cherish	Beverly Clark	$8.95
A Place Like Home	Alicia Wiggins	$6.99
A Risk of Rain	Dar Tomlinson	$8.95
A Taste of Temptation	Reneé Alexis	$9.95
A Twist of Fate	Beverly Clark	$8.95
A Voice Behind Thunder	Carrie Elizabeth Greene	$6.99
A Will to Love	Angie Daniels	$9.95
Acquisitions	Kimberley White	$8.95
Across	Carol Payne	$12.95
After the Vows	Leslie Esdaile	$10.95
(Summer Anthology)	T.T. Henderson	
	Jacqueline Thomas	
Again, My Love	Kayla Perrin	$10.95
Against the Wind	Gwynne Forster	$8.95
All I Ask	Barbara Keaton	$8.95
All I'll Ever Need	Mildred Riley	$6.99
Always You	Crystal Hubbard	$6.99
Ambrosia	T.T. Henderson	$8.95
An Unfinished Love Affair	Barbara Keaton	$8.95
And Then Came You	Dorothy Elizabeth Love	$8.95
Angel's Paradise	Janice Angelique	$9.95
Another Memory	Pamela Ridley	$6.99
Anything But Love	Celya Bowers	$6.99
At Last	Lisa G. Riley	$8.95
Best Foot Forward	Michele Sudler	$6.99
Best of Friends	Natalie Dunbar	$8.95
Best of Luck Elsewhere	Trisha Haddad	$6.99
Beyond the Rapture	Beverly Clark	$9.95
Blame It on Paradise	Crystal Hubbard	$6.99
Blaze	Barbara Keaton	$9.95

Other Genesis Press, Inc. Titles (continued)

Blindsided	Tammy Williams	$6.99
Bliss, Inc.	Chamein Canton	$6.99
Blood Lust	J.M. Jeffries	$9.95
Blood Seduction	J.M. Jeffries	$9.95
Blue Interlude	Keisha Mennefee	$6.99
Bodyguard	Andrea Jackson	$9.95
Boss of Me	Diana Nyad	$8.95
Bound by Love	Beverly Clark	$8.95
Breeze	Robin Hampton Allen	$10.95
Broken	Dar Tomlinson	$24.95
Burn	Crystal Hubbard	$6.99
By Design	Barbara Keaton	$8.95
Cajun Heat	Charlene Berry	$8.95
Careless Whispers	Rochelle Alers	$8.95
Cats & Other Tales	Marilyn Wagner	$8.95
Caught in a Trap	Andre Michelle	$8.95
Caught Up in the Rapture	Lisa G. Riley	$9.95
Cautious Heart	Cheris F. Hodges	$8.95
Chances	Pamela Leigh Starr	$8.95
Checks and Balances	Elaine Sims	$6.99
Cherish the Flame	Beverly Clark	$8.95
Choices	Tammy Williams	$6.99
Class Reunion	Irma Jenkins/ John Brown	$12.95
Code Name: Diva	J.M. Jeffries	$9.95
Conquering Dr. Wexler's Heart	Kimberley White	$9.95
Corporate Seduction	A.C. Arthur	$9.95
Crossing Paths, Tempting Memories	Dorothy Elizabeth Love	$9.95
Crossing the Line	Bernice Layton	$6.99
Crush	Crystal Hubbard	$9.95
Cypress Whisperings	Phyllis Hamilton	$8.95
Dark Embrace	Crystal Wilson Harris	$8.95
Dark Storm Rising	Chinelu Moore	$10.95
Daughter of the Wind	Joan Xian	$8.95
Dawn's Harbor	Kymberly Hunt	$6.99
Deadly Sacrifice	Jack Kean	$22.95
Designer Passion	Dar Tomlinson Diana Richeaux	$8.95

Other Genesis Press, Inc. Titles (continued)

Do Over	Celya Bowers	$9.95
Dream Keeper	Gail McFarland	$6.99
Dream Runner	Gail McFarland	$6.99
Dreamtective	Liz Swados	$5.95
Ebony Angel	Deatri King-Bey	$9.95
Ebony Butterfly II	Delilah Dawson	$14.95
Echoes of Yesterday	Beverly Clark	$9.95
Eden's Garden	Elizabeth Rose	$8.95
Eve's Prescription	Edwina Martin Arnold	$8.95
Everlastin' Love	Gay G. Gunn	$8.95
Everlasting Moments	Dorothy Elizabeth Love	$8.95
Everything and More	Sinclair Lebeau	$8.95
Everything but Love	Natalie Dunbar	$8.95
Falling	Natalie Dunbar	$9.95
Fate	Pamela Leigh Starr	$8.95
Finding Isabella	A.J. Garrotto	$8.95
Fireflies	Joan Early	$6.99
Fixin' Tyrone	Keith Walker	$6.99
Forbidden Quest	Dar Tomlinson	$10.95
Forever Love	Wanda Y. Thomas	$8.95
Friends in Need	Joan Early	$6.99
From the Ashes	Kathleen Suzanne Jeanne Sumerix	$8.95
Frost on My Window	Angela Weaver	$6.99
Gentle Yearning	Rochelle Alers	$10.95
Glory of Love	Sinclair LeBeau	$10.95
Go Gentle Into That Good Night	Malcom Boyd	$12.95
Goldengroove	Mary Beth Craft	$16.95
Groove, Bang, and Jive	Steve Cannon	$8.99
Hand in Glove	Andrea Jackson	$9.95
Hard to Love	Kimberley White	$9.95
Hart & Soul	Angie Daniels	$8.95
Heart of the Phoenix	A.C. Arthur	$9.95
Heartbeat	Stephanie Bedwell-Grime	$8.95
Hearts Remember	M. Loui Quezada	$8.95
Hidden Memories	Robin Allen	$10.95
Higher Ground	Leah Latimer	$19.95
Hitler, the War, and the Pope	Ronald Rychiak	$26.95
How to Kill Your Husband	Keith Walker	$6.99

Other Genesis Press, Inc. Titles (continued)

How to Write a Romance	Kathryn Falk	$18.95
I Married a Reclining Chair	Lisa M. Fuhs	$8.95
I'll Be Your Shelter	Giselle Carmichael	$8.95
I'll Paint a Sun	A.J. Garrotto	$9.95
Icie	Pamela Leigh Starr	$8.95
If I Were Your Woman	LaConnie Taylor-Jones	$6.99
Illusions	Pamela Leigh Starr	$8.95
Indigo After Dark Vol. I	Nia Dixon/Angelique	$10.95
Indigo After Dark Vol. II	Dolores Bundy/ Cole Riley	$10.95
Indigo After Dark Vol. III	Montana Blue/ Coco Morena	$10.95
Indigo After Dark Vol. IV	Cassandra Colt/	$14.95
Indigo After Dark Vol. V	Delilah Dawson	$14.95
Indiscretions	Donna Hill	$8.95
Intentional Mistakes	Michele Sudler	$9.95
Interlude	Donna Hill	$8.95
Intimate Intentions	Angie Daniels	$8.95
It's in the Rhythm	Sammie Ward	$6.99
It's Not Over Yet	J.J. Michael	$9.95
Jolie's Surrender	Edwina Martin-Arnold	$8.95
Kiss or Keep	Debra Phillips	$8.95
Lace	Giselle Carmichael	$9.95
Lady Preacher	K.T. Richey	$6.99
Last Train to Memphis	Elsa Cook	$12.95
Lasting Valor	Ken Olsen	$24.95
Let Us Prey	Hunter Lundy	$25.95
Let's Get It On	Dyanne Davis	$6.99
Lies Too Long	Pamela Ridley	$13.95
Life Is Never As It Seems	J.J. Michael	$12.95
Lighter Shade of Brown	Vicki Andrews	$8.95
Look Both Ways	Joan Early	$6.99
Looking for Lily	Africa Fine	$6.99
Love Always	Mildred E. Riley	$10.95
Love Doesn't Come Easy	Charlyne Dickerson	$8.95
Love Out of Order	Nicole Green	$6.99
Love Unveiled	Gloria Greene	$10.95
Love's Deception	Charlene Berry	$10.95
Love's Destiny	M. Loui Quezada	$8.95
Love's Secrets	Yolanda McVey	$6.99

Other Genesis Press, Inc. Titles (continued)

Mae's Promise	Melody Walcott	$8.95
Magnolia Sunset	Giselle Carmichael	$8.95
Many Shades of Gray	Dyanne Davis	$6.99
Matters of Life and Death	Lesego Malepe, Ph.D.	$15.95
Meant to Be	Jeanne Sumerix	$8.95
Midnight Clear	Leslie Esdaile	$10.95
(Anthology)	Gwynne Forster	
	Carmen Green	
	Monica Jackson	
Midnight Magic	Gwynne Forster	$8.95
Midnight Peril	Vicki Andrews	$10.95
Misconceptions	Pamela Leigh Starr	$9.95
Mixed Reality	Chamein Canton	$6.99
Moments of Clarity	Michele Cameron	$6.99
Montgomery's Children	Richard Perry	$14.95
Mr. Fix-It	Crystal Hubbard	$6.99
My Buffalo Soldier	Barbara B.K. Reeves	$8.95
Naked Soul	Gwynne Forster	$8.95
Never Say Never	Michele Cameron	$6.99
Next to Last Chance	Louisa Dixon	$24.95
No Apologies	Seressia Glass	$8.95
No Commitment Required	Seressia Glass	$8.95
No Regrets	Mildred E. Riley	$8.95
Not His Type	Chamein Canton	$6.99
Not Quite Right	Tammy Williams	$6.99
Nowhere to Run	Gay G. Gunn	$10.95
O Bed! O Breakfast!	Rob Kuehnle	$14.95
Oak Bluffs	Joan Early	$6.99
Object of His Desire	A.C. Arthur	$8.95
Office Policy	A.C. Arthur	$9.95
Once in a Blue Moon	Dorianne Cole	$9.95
One Day at a Time	Bella McFarland	$8.95
One of These Days	Michele Sudler	$9.95
Outside Chance	Louisa Dixon	$24.95
Passion	T.T. Henderson	$10.95
Passion's Blood	Cherif Fortin	$22.95
Passion's Furies	AlTonya Washington	$6.99
Passion's Journey	Wanda Y. Thomas	$8.95
Past Promises	Jahmel West	$8.95
Path of Fire	T.T. Henderson	$8.95

Other Genesis Press, Inc. Titles (continued)

Path of Thorns	Annetta P. Lee	$9.95
Peace Be Still	Colette Haywood	$12.95
Picture Perfect	Reon Carter	$8.95
Playing for Keeps	Stephanie Salinas	$8.95
Pride & Joi	Gay G. Gunn	$8.95
Promises Made	Bernice Layton	$6.99
Promises of Forever	Celya Bowers	$6.99
Promises to Keep	Alicia Wiggins	$8.95
Quiet Storm	Donna Hill	$10.95
Reckless Surrender	Rochelle Alers	$6.95
Red Polka Dot in a World Full of Plaid	Varian Johnson	$12.95
Red Sky	Renee Alexis	$6.99
Reluctant Captive	Joyce Jackson	$8.95
Rendezvous With Fate	Jeanne Sumerix	$8.95
Revelations	Cheris F. Hodges	$8.95
Reye's Gold	Ruthie Robinson	$6.99
Rivers of the Soul	Leslie Esdaile	$8.95
Rocky Mountain Romance	Kathleen Suzanne	$8.95
Rooms of the Heart	Donna Hill	$8.95
Rough on Rats and Tough on Cats	Chris Parker	$12.95
Save Me	Africa Fine	$6.99
Secret Library Vol. 1	Nina Sheridan	$18.95
Secret Library Vol. 2	Cassandra Colt	$8.95
Secret Thunder	Annetta P. Lee	$9.95
Shades of Brown	Denise Becker	$8.95
Shades of Desire	Monica White	$8.95
Shadows in the Moonlight	Jeanne Sumerix	$8.95
Show Me the Sun	Miriam Shumba	$6.99
Sin	Crystal Rhodes	$8.95
Singing a Song...	Crystal Rhodes	$6.99
Six O'Clock	Katrina Spencer	$6.99
Small Sensations	Crystal V. Rhodes	$6.99
Small Whispers	Annetta P. Lee	$6.99
So Amazing	Sinclair LeBeau	$8.95
Somebody's Someone	Sinclair LeBeau	$8.95
Someone to Love	Alicia Wiggins	$8.95
Song in the Park	Martin Brant	$15.95
Soul Eyes	Wayne L. Wilson	$12.95

Other Genesis Press, Inc. Titles (continued)

Other Genesis Press, Inc. Titles (continued)

Things Forbidden	Maryam Diaab	$6.99
This Life Isn't Perfect Holla	Sandra Foy	$6.99
Three Doors Down	Michele Sudler	$6.99
Three Wishes	Seressia Glass	$8.95
Ties That Bind	Kathleen Suzanne	$8.95
Tiger Woods	Libby Hughes	$5.95
Time Is of the Essence	Angie Daniels	$9.95
Timeless Devotion	Bella McFarland	$9.95
Tomorrow's Promise	Leslie Esdaile	$8.95
Truly Inseparable	Wanda Y. Thomas	$8.95
Two Sides to Every Story	Dyanne Davis	$9.95
Unbeweavable	Katrina Spencer	$6.99
Unbreak My Heart	Dar Tomlinson	$8.95
Unclear and Present Danger	Michele Cameron	$6.99
Uncommon Prayer	Kenneth Swanson	$9.95
Unconditional	A.C. Arthur	$9.95
Unconditional Love	Alicia Wiggins	$8.95
Undying Love	Renee Alexis	$6.99
Until Death Do Us Part	Susan Paul	$8.95
Vows of Passion	Bella McFarland	$9.95
Waiting for Mr. Darcy	Chamein Canton	$6.99
Waiting in the Shadows	Michele Sudler	$6.99
Wayward Dreams	Gail McFarland	$6.99
Wedding Gown	Dyanne Davis	$8.95
What's Under Benjamin's Bed	Sandra Schaffer	$8.95
When a Man Loves a Woman	LaConnie Taylor-Jones	$6.99
When Dreams Float	Dorothy Elizabeth Love	$8.95
When I'm With You	LaConnie Taylor-Jones	$6.99
When Lightning Strikes	Michele Cameron	$6.99
Where I Want to Be	Maryam Diaab	$6.99
Whispers in the Night	Dorothy Elizabeth Love	$8.95
Whispers in the Sand	LaFlorya Gauthier	$10.95
Who's That Lady?	Andrea Jackson	$9.95
Wild Ravens	AlTonya Washington	$9.95
Yesterday Is Gone	Beverly Clark	$10.95
Yesterday's Dreams, Tomorrow's Promises	Reon Laudat	$8.95
Your Precious Love	Sinclair LeBeau	$8.95

Order Form

Mail to: Genesis Press, Inc.
P.O. Box 101
Columbus, MS 39703

Name _____
Address _____
City/State _____ Zip _____
Telephone _____

Ship to (if different from above)
Name _____
Address _____
City/State _____ Zip _____
Telephone _____

Credit Card Information
Credit Card # _____ ☐Visa ☐Mastercard
Expiration Date (mm/yy) _____ ☐AmEx ☐Discover

Qty.	Author	Title	Price	Total

Use this order form, or call 1-888-INDIGO-1	Total for books _____ Shipping and handling: $5 first two books, $1 each additional book _____ Total S & H _____ Total amount enclosed _____ *Mississippi residents add 7% sales tax*